IF I GAINED THE WORLD

Books by

Linda Nichols

FROM BETHANY HOUSE PUBLISHERS

Not a Sparrow Falls
If I Gained the World

If I gained the world

a novel by

LINDA NICHOLS

BETHANY HOUSE
PUBLISHERS
MINNEAPOLIS, MINNESOTA

If I Gained the World
Copyright © 2003
Linda Nichols

Cover design by Ann Gjeldum
Cover photo by Elizabeth Barret/Getty Images, Inc.

Unless otherwise identified, Scripture quotations are from the HOLY BIBLE, NEW INTERNATIONAL VERSION®. Copyright © 1973, 1978, 1984 by International Bible Society. Used by permission of Zondervan Publishing House. All rights reserved.

Scripture quotations identified KJV are from the King James Version of the Bible.

All rights reserved. No part of this publication may be reproduced, stored in a retrieval system, or transmitted in any form or by any means—electronic, mechanical, photocopying, recording, or otherwise—without the prior written permission of the publisher and copyright owners.

Published by Bethany House Publishers
11400 Hampshire Avenue South
Bloomington, Minnesota 55438

Bethany House Publishers is a Division of
Baker Book House Company, Grand Rapids, Michigan.

Printed in the United States of America

ISBN 0-7642-2802-1 (Hard cover)

To Jesus

the Lover of My Soul

Linda Nichols, a graduate of the University of Washington, is a novelist with a unique gift for touching readers' hearts with her stories. *Not a Sparrow Falls*, her best-selling debut novel for the Christian fiction market, was a 2003 Christy Awards finalist in the Contemporary category. Linda and her family make their home in Tacoma, Washington.

www.lindanichols.org

Prologue

2003

IT WAS RAINING when Daniel arrived in Seattle. The bus drove through the slick streets and groaned into the station. Its doors sighed open. He sat waiting until the aisles cleared. No sense standing up as everyone filed out. No sense inviting comment. "You're somebody," they would say, frowning and trying to place him. He'd learned to hate those narrowed eyes, the clearing of recognition that followed. He kept his face down now so no one could examine it. When the last of the other passengers had filed out, he stood and got off the bus.

He took his rucksack from the luggage compartment, went inside the depot, and asked which city bus would take him to the address on the creased, wet envelope he clutched in his hand. The Seattle transit bus came along in a half hour or so, and he rode it up the hill, got off when the driver told him to, and tried to remember the directions the man had given him. He aimed himself the right way and started walking. The rain was pelting down. He walked faster.

A woman came out of a grocery store and merged onto the sidewalk ahead of him. He imagined it was Lenore. He entertained himself with the idea. It was possible, wasn't it? The woman was slim, just like Lenore. She carried an umbrella, so he couldn't see if her hair matched the thick brown rope in his memory. She didn't face him, so he couldn't look for the green-and-gold eyes, the cleft in her chin, the sharp, thin face he remembered. He trudged along behind her, far enough back so that he wouldn't frighten her were she to notice him, close enough to keep her in sight.

The rain poured down incessantly. The woman quickened her step, and so did Daniel. He wished he had brought a jacket, but he had none. He was tired of carrying the heavy rucksack, and for a minute he wondered why he had brought it. Why did he need it? He wasn't staying long. Just a brief in and out. What he had come to do wouldn't take long, but the thought of his mission made him more tired than the heavy load he was carrying.

He followed the woman all the way up the hill, turned left behind her onto Chestnut Street, and by the time he saw the huge old house with the sweeping yard, the graceful porch, saw that the house number on the red mailbox was the same as the one on the crumpled envelope, he knew it really must be Lenore who had led him here.

He stood slack-jawed with amazement. It seemed like a sign, an omen, though he wasn't sure how to interpret it. He opened his mouth to call out to her, but something stopped him. He couldn't. Not just yet. He waited, turning slightly away from her as she opened the gate of the picket fence and stepped through. She closed it behind her and walked toward the house, then swung open the front door—it was unlocked, of course—and went inside. The whole house was lit up, every bulb on, and he felt a smile creep onto his face. She'd always been like that. Wasteful of the good things.

After a minute he saw her appear again in front of the window, just a dark slight shape passing by. He stood there for a long time watching the light spill out into the gathering dusk before he had the courage to open the gate and step inside. Then he stood a little longer, camouflaged behind a huge tree in the yard, watching her pass back and forth. She was setting the table. The rain began pelting down in one of its earnest downpours. She didn't reappear. He was cold to the bone and began to shiver, but still he couldn't bring himself to go to the door.

He went around to the back of the house instead, knowing he might be arrested as a peeping tom, and wouldn't that be a fine reunion? He brushed the thought away, found a spot behind an evergreen shrub that sheltered him from view. The light spilled out from the window here, too, making an arc before him. He was careful to stand back from its borders. She was not five feet away from him, and she seemed so close that were it not for the glass between them, he thought he could have reached out and touched her. He peered intently, looking for traces of the woman he'd known—the angular cheeks, the haunted, hungry eyes.

He saw none of these. This woman had a soft, calm face, and the part of her he could see above the sink looked strong and substantial. Her hair was still thick, hanging down past her shoulders, and while he watched, she stopped her work, twirled the ends together in a makeshift braid, and tossed it behind her. He watched the firm movements of her arms, sure and competent, as she did whatever it was she was doing, working on something below his line of vision. She lifted it up, and he saw what it was. It was a pie. Daniel shook his head in disbelief. A pie? When had Lenore learned to make a pie? She could barely make coffee when he'd seen her last.

He frowned, suddenly seeing the obvious. This was not the same Lenore. This was someone new. This was someone different, and it was that one silly thing—seeing that she had made a pie—that made his hubris clear to him. He had a sudden realization of the years that had passed. Years. Long years, and Lenore had lived them, just as he had. Her years had been full of people he didn't know, experiences he hadn't shared. What had he thought? That she would be where he had left her? Still waiting? That time had somehow rendered her as frozen and unchanged as she'd remained in his mind? What right did he have to come here now, even for this brief errand? Who did he think he was to appear like this? Apologetic. Shredded life in hand.

He looked up again. She was gone, and unaccountably he felt a sense of loss, but then she was back, leaning over the sink, and he saw her face again. He relaxed. She looked happy. Contented. Her cheeks were fuller than they'd been years before and flushed a little, maybe from the heat of the kitchen. She still had the dimple in her chin. Her lips were moving, and he wondered if she was singing or talking to herself. She always used to sing while she worked, he recalled, though the memory was a vague and misty recollection of those years. That life he'd shared with her seemed long ago and far away. He saw himself in the reflection of the window, a tall dark shape against the darker lines of the thick evergreen tree. And it was odd, but he didn't recognize himself any more than he recognized her. He felt the same sensation of looking hard and trying to see something familiar.

She turned and spoke to someone. Smiled. Who was it? Daniel wondered, feeling a flash of jealousy toward whoever had come into the room and lit her face. He tried to imagine himself walking into that room, that it was he who had made her face brighten. A chill wind blew sharply, rustling what was left of the leaves on the trees and tinkling the wind chimes.

A dog barked. The back door of the house next door opened. A man came out, opened the garbage can, and deposited a sack of trash, and that small event made Daniel realize it was time for him to make a decision. He must do one thing or the other. Creep away into the shadows, go back to the bus station, call from there and arrange a meeting. Or go to the door and knock. She disappeared again, and the loss jolted him to a decision. He had to at least hear her voice before he left, to put sound with picture in this last scene. It seemed wrong, somehow, to not remove that thick insulation of silence that had padded the years between them.

He slowly walked back around the house to the front porch. He stood there before the dark red door. He heard his own ragged breath, the steady pelt of the rain, the faint tinkling of the wind chimes, the leaves rustling in the wind. Her umbrella was by his feet, half open, leaning tipsy against a huge pot of pansies. A child's pull toy lay on its side beside a green watering can. A few leaves scuttled across the porch and lodged against it. He stared down at his shoes and breathed hard, as if preparing himself for some great feat of physical endurance or courage. Then quickly, before he could change his mind, Daniel raised his hand and knocked.

One

1988

$\mathcal{E}$VERYONE WONDERED WHY he had chosen her. Lenore thought about that as she peeled the potatoes, a sloppy job she usually rushed through, taking off half the potato along with the skin. She hated peeling potatoes, but Scott had asked for French fries, and Daniel said he would make them from scratch if Lenore would peel the potatoes. She would rather peel an onion than a potato any day of the week. The misery was sharper, but it was over more quickly.

Their own friends didn't wonder, she told herself without conviction, watching the thick brown chunks of skin fly off and stick to the sides of the sink. She should be doing this over the garbage can. She cut her eyes over to see if Daniel was noticing her sloppiness. He was busy prodding the electric can opener with a screwdriver. He looked like Scott when he frowned like that. Lenore went back to the potatoes. It was mostly Daniel's actor friends and the people he worked with at the restaurant who thought they were an odd couple, but what did they know? Still, her stomach twisted as she remembered how their eyebrows would arch up a tiny hair, a millimeter or so, when Daniel made the introductions, smoothly and without hesitation. "This is my son, Scott, and this is Lenore." Letting them draw whatever conclusions they might after a quick look at Daniel, tall and fit and gorgeous, and then at her—thin, pale, too much plain brown hair, a weird chin. Not beautiful. Definitely not beautiful. Then would come the look—a slight squint, a clouding of the eyes with confusion. It was followed, if they were kind, by a swift recovery, an extension of the hand, a rolling on of the social stream, the wake from the slight ripple easily smoothed. But they wondered. And she knew it. It bothered her and made her even more insecure, sent her to the mirror, where she inspected her frail ribs, her flat chest, her too wild hair with something between resignation and despair. It made her feel hollow inside, hungry for something only Daniel was serving.

It was probably just the visit to her mother's this afternoon that had put her over the edge, she told herself, regretting again that she had consented to wear one of her sister's cut-down dresses to the party. The party. Her stomach began twisting at the thought of it even though it was weeks away. Movie stars would be there, agents and producers. Daniel had somehow gotten an invitation, and she had the suspicion that he had been planning on going alone. Had invited her only because she had overheard him discussing it with his agent. But maybe not. Maybe she was just being insecure again. A permanent condition with her, it seemed, and one that the visit with her mother and sister hadn't helped.

"Hey, Lenore, let's do your hair." Her sister had clacked the scissors open and shut.

Lenore's only reply had been to twist the thick rope of hair around her hand.

"Hold still." Her mother had frowned up from the hem, the mouthful of pins making her lips an even thinner line than usual. She seemed exasperated, as if Lenore had failed in some moral responsibility by not filling out the dress.

"I'll fix you right up. Give you a little style." Leslie spoke up again from where she was lolling on her mother's bed. She clacked the scissors once more, then began cutting threads from the chenille spread.

"Knock it off, Leslie!" her mother barked without even looking up.

Leslie grinned, unperturbed. "When's he gonna marry you, Lenore? You know, you ought to have more self-respect."

"Your sister's right," her mother chimed in, looking at her critically. "You want to live with a guy? Fine. You want to have kids? You get married. That's the right way to do things."

As if Mom, who had had three husbands, and Leslie, who would never have any, were authorities on morality.

"Ask him, Lenore," Leslie urged. "I know why you don't," she put in without even waiting, as if the possibility that Lenore might agree to pop the question were miles away from being even remotely conceivable. "You don't want to know. You'd rather not ask than ask and get shut down. I know I'm right." She lifted an eyebrow and smiled, as satisfied as a cat.

Lenore stayed stoically silent, enduring Leslie, telling herself that her sister didn't understand about her and Daniel. Leslie was wrong. Plain wrong. That was all there was to it. She looked at Leslie lolling on the bed and felt a stab of pain, as if she were seeing herself in all her homely glory. She and Leslie looked just alike, except for their hair, of course. Leslie had cut hers short in tousled layers. Lenore inspected her sister: rail thin, straight nose and mouth just like her own, white skin—kitchen appliance white, with not even a hint of flush in the cheeks. And then there was the jutting chin with the huge dimple or cleft or whatever it was, the family curse that was visited on all the Vines.

She remembered her mother inspecting Scott in the hospital just after his birth. "He doesn't look like a Vine," she'd said doubtfully.

"Ma, you might be a little confused about who the father is, but the mother is a pretty sure thing," Leslie had smarted off.

But her mother was right. Scott didn't look like a Vine. She could see him in the living room, watching cartoons, even at four a small copy of his father. The same dark hair, though Scott's was cut in a bowl shape. The same brown eyes and golden skin. He looked like beautiful Daniel.

Lenore looked at Daniel again now, sidelong, and he was still deep in concentration, poking the little gears of the can opener with the point of the screwdriver. She felt a stab of pain and wished he were not so beautiful. She wished that Daniel, the real Daniel, could have been packed up inside some other wrapping, a nice package, but only nice enough. Now, as she peeled the last potato—surely six would be enough with only the three of them—she wondered again why he had chosen her and if he would move on.

Love is blind, she told herself, and beauty is in the eye of the one who sees. She washed the grimy potatoes and set them on a paper towel beside the sink, unearthed the pan—from the bottom of the stack, of course—poured a good amount of oil into it, and turned the burner on high.

"You put everything on high," Daniel said, not looking up. "Then you go off and forget about it."

"You're watching," she reminded him and began slicing the potatoes.

There was no reason to worry, she reassured herself. As she sliced, she began to hum, determinedly, to keep her mind from her fears. She picked one of the hymns Mrs. Larsen had played. Mrs. Larsen, the odd little babysitter her mother had employed the summer they'd lived in Hood River, Oregon. She'd been the organist and soloist at the Lutheran church, so every day after school as Lenore and Leslie had eaten cookies and drunk milk and watched cartoons, they'd listened to Mrs. Larsen's reedy voice warbling out hymns to the windy accompaniment of the Hammond organ she kept in the corner of her living room. Leslie had hated it, but not Lenore. Rather than being a distraction, the music had comforted her somehow. She'd liked listening to those songs, even though she hadn't understood them. She still didn't, really. But they had grounded her, made her feel that something somewhere was solid and immovable, even if nothing in her world was. Mrs. Larsen's world was a good world, a solid, heavy world, where things stayed where you put them. Mrs. Larsen didn't wake up every morning and wonder if today would be the day Mr. Larsen would leave, and once again she felt a familiar twist of insecurity over that unanswered question.

Maybe Daniel would feel differently about marriage now. Her pulse sped up just from coming near the subject in her mind. They had discussed it, of course, especially when she'd found out she was pregnant. But she had been the one who had objected then. "I don't want you to marry me because I'm pregnant," she had said, hoping he would say he loved her and would insist it had nothing to do with her pregnancy. He hadn't. He'd just nodded and left the subject. And later when it came up again, he had joked about it. "If it's not broken, don't fix it," he had quipped, then kissed her. But that had been at least a year ago. Things changed, didn't they?

She watched him as he worked, as she waited for the oil to heat. His skin had a healthy glow, and he had that smudged, dark-around-the-edges look that made Lenore think of the Middle East. But he was from middle-eastern Kentucky, and even though he had the looks of the movie star he wanted to become, that wasn't what she loved about him. In fact, after having lived with him for six years, the thing that made her break out of her little bubble of control, that made her wager everything—now, right in the middle of getting supper—was the wrinkles around his eyes. She certainly wasn't planning on changing their lives while she peeled potatoes and Daniel worked on the can opener. But those tiny lines reminded her of marriage and old age and grandchildren, and hope sang out to her. She had a sudden rush of memories of their life together, as if it were played on fast-forward for her audience of one. She saw him putting the Big Wheel together last Christmas Eve, the two of them afterward, sitting on the couch sipping mulled cider. She thought of Scott's face on that Christmas morning when he'd found the toys they'd scrimped and saved to buy. She thought of all the Christmas Eves and Christmas mornings and of Daniel's kindness to her on the other days. She remembered how he had brought her tea and crackers before she got out of bed when she was sick and pregnant with Scott, and even now the way he cared about little things like fixing the can opener. She hesitated, teetering between fear and longing.

"Come on, Dad," Scott called from the living room. "Come play cars and trucks."

"I'll be there in a minute, buddy," Daniel said, and that was when the scale tipped.

She dried her hands on the towel, never taking her eyes off those little wrinkles, those little Y-shaped lines, those tiny forks in the road, those little signs of imperfection, reminders that they were alike, really, under the skin. She went to him. She moved the can opener and wound her arms around his waist.

"What?" He gave a half smile. She could feel the ropy muscles of his back. He pulled her close and rubbed the top of her head with his chin. It was bristly. He laced his fingers together and rested his hands in the small of her back, and she laid her head on his chest.

"What?" he asked her again. She could feel his voice vibrating under her ear.

"I love you, Daniel. I love you so much."

"I know you do." He sounded a little surprised. "I love you, too."

"Daniel, will you marry me?"

Silence.

His body tensed. She stayed perfectly still, though, somehow hoping his words would make things right. But no words came. She knew then what his answer would be, and she knew she had taken everything, everything, and in one foolish gesture she had wagered it and lost.

He finally spoke, too kind to let that silence go on any longer. He gave her a little squeeze, a small chuckle. "Do I have to give an answer right now?"

"No," Lenore said too quickly and disentangled herself from him. She returned to the potatoes, but she couldn't see them anymore, and everything, the walls around her and the walls inside her head, had gone slick and white and blank.

Scott came in and leaned on Daniel's leg. "Come play with me, Dad."

"I'm coming, buddy." Daniel's voice was smooth. "You go pick out some cars for me."

Scott scuffed away in his gorilla slippers. Daniel came behind her and put his arms around her waist. She could feel his rough cheek next to hers. "You caught me by surprise," he said in a whisper. "That's all."

She nodded and laid her arm across his, reached back and stroked his face with the other hand, but it seemed as if only their two bodies were here and that something precious had already flown away and left them.

Daniel finally went off to play with Scott, came back and fried the potatoes Lenore had washed and peeled and sliced. She overcooked the hamburgers. They were hard, crisp little pellets, islands in the middle of a huge sea of bun.

"I burned the burgers," Lenore said and felt the full sponge inside her getting ready to squeeze itself dry.

"It's no big deal," Daniel said quickly and took a big bite, eyeing her, flashing her an encouraging smile. Scott didn't seem to notice anything. They finished supper and watched television, then put Scott to bed. All the normal things of a normal day. Daniel stepped around her carefully for the rest of the evening, as if feeling his way on ice after a thaw.

When it was time for bed, Lenore went into the bathroom to change clothes, unwilling to be near him, to let him see her. She suddenly felt ashamed. What was she doing here, after all? Living here, giving herself to this man who wasn't who she'd thought he was. She pulled off her jeans and hung them on the hook on the bathroom door. They were still hanging in the shape of her body—half a body—the seat gently rounded, knees slightly bent, as if poised for flight. She put on her nightgown, barely able to take in the fact that the arms and legs she moved belonged to her.

She went inside the bedroom. Daniel was sitting on the bed, and when she saw him, the wound inside her got wider, as if its edges were being pulled apart. She began to cry. He looked helpless, and yet he wouldn't say the words that would make the edges come together and start to heal.

She sat down on the bed beside him and covered her face with her hands. It would be so simple, really, for him just to say, "Of course I want to marry you. You're the mother of my child, aren't you? You're the one I've lived with all these years, aren't you? You're the one I come home to every night, who knows what kind of socks I like and that I sleep on my back and that I like grilled cheese sandwiches and tomato soup when I'm sick. Of course I'll marry you." And even if he couldn't say that he loved her in quite that open-souled, end-of-the-world way she had always loved him, just to say he loved her would be enough. Maybe it wouldn't have been enough an hour ago, but it would be now. Anything to put a stitch into that gaping wound. *Say it,* she willed. *Say "Of course I'll marry you."*

But he didn't say it. "Don't go," his only words.

She got up, went into the bathroom, and stayed there until there was no more creaking and adjusting on the bed, until there was no more sound at all. She came out, then stood in the dim room for a moment, taking in his still face, his closed eyes. His mouth was slightly open, his chest rising and falling with the lightness of his life. So easy, in and out, but such a vapor. So precious. So easily lost.

Two

$\mathcal{D}$ANIEL WOKE BUT KEPT his eyes squeezed tightly shut. It didn't help. Reality still found its way in along with the bold light from the lone window. He wished that he would come fully awake and realize it had been a dream. He had been wishing that for the last week. That he would rise, giddy with relief, go out to the kitchen, and find them doing some simple thing, hold them both close, grateful to feel their warmth, to see their faces. He opened his eyes all the way. The bedroom looked dim and gloomy, and dust motes floated in shafts of light on either side of the curtains. He lay there for a moment, then sat up and checked the clock. It was nearly nine, and he had an eleven o'clock audition. A car commercial. His eye fell on the smooth bedspread and untouched pillow beside him. Lenore had slept on the couch again, as she had every night since that day.

"Let me," he'd offered, but she'd shaken her head in that stubborn way she had, and he had let her go.

He couldn't hear anything now, no voices or feet from the other rooms. He tried to think of where they might be, and he felt a surge of panic, suddenly afraid that they had left him. He sat up and rubbed his face, and the familiar feeling of bewilderment and dread settled into his gut. Mostly bewilderment. Somehow he hadn't counted the cost, hadn't realized that the things he'd wanted, those possibilities he was protecting, would come at such a steep price. And even now, as he agonized over whether to pay it or not, the transaction went forward.

He pulled on his sweats, opened the bedroom door, and walked through the quiet apartment. He was reassured to find the remains of their presence—Scottie's rumpled bed, his clothes still in the closet, toys still strewn around the floor, a wet towel tossed onto the hamper, two empty cereal bowls atop last night's dinner plates.

Daniel made coffee, and when it had finished dripping, he took a few sips, but it was mixing unpleasantly with the acid that was gradually rising from his stomach up to his throat.

He sat down at the table and looked at the bits of Lenore scattered around the kitchen: a disheveled stack of cookbooks, a plastic Ronald McDonald watch Scott had given her for her birthday last year, a few empty cups, a bad watercolor of a Russian River vineyard done by her sister, an insurance calendar turned to next month. Once again he wondered how things had come to this end and why he didn't take the simple, obvious step to fix them.

There was no one else. There had never been anyone else in the years they'd been together. Years. He shook his head at the thought of that. All his other relationships, and he supposed there had been quite a few, had died a natural death at some point. But at the time when his and Lenore's probably would have ended, that point at which the two of them would have looked at each other and realized the time had come to marry or go their own ways, Lenore had been pregnant, and leaving hadn't seemed the particularly gallant thing to do.

And he loved their life together. He loved her. She didn't bore him the way some of the other women he had been with bored him, all the riches of their gene pool deposited into their outermost millimeter of skin. She was chipper and bright, and he had enjoyed talking to her when they were both going to school at UCLA and working at the same restaurant. She was interesting. He loved her straight little back as she worked in the kitchen, the way her thin face lit up when he came through the door, the way she played with Scott and read to him. There was something sensuous about her, too, even taking into consideration all her sharp corners and plain vistas. She was kind, funny, clever, warm, and generous. So one thing had led to another, one day had faded into the next, and then she was pregnant.

That had been a bad day. He still recalled the panic he'd felt when she'd told him, the desire to run as far as he could in the opposite direction. He hadn't, of course. His uncle's relentless morality had rubbed off on him at least that much—enough to know that a man took care of his responsibilities. In fact, the one time in their relationship he had promised Lenore faithfulness and devotion was around the time Scott was born.

"We're in this together," he would say. "I'm not going to leave you." Perhaps he was trying to convince himself as well as her. Of course she had believed him. She was so simple and childlike in some ways, and she loved him so completely. His mere presence seemed to satisfy her, as if there was nothing more she could ever want or need besides him. He liked that feeling, the knowledge that he could create that kind of bliss. It was like a hit of a drug.

Then Scott was born. He still remembered the awe he had felt to see his son emerge, and the most surprising thing of all to Daniel was how much he loved being a father, the surge of protection and love he had felt for this small thing, this unknown person. He used to rise in the night, sliding out from under the covers carefully so as not to wake Lenore, then go and watch the baby sleep. He had looked so unprotected, his fist balled, his little mouth making sucking motions in his sleep. It was shocking, in a pleasant sort of way, how much he loved his child.

But lately he had been feeling a sort of bewilderment when he thought of the coming years. He couldn't picture himself a father to Scott the schoolchild, in the world and trying to make sense of it, or to Scott the teenager, trying to find his own way. He felt empty when he thought about that, and a strumming panic had taken to playing background to those thoughts. How would he learn the task? The fathering he'd gotten had been patched together. Everyone had done the best they could, but Daniel still felt the void. As long as his son was an appendage, a shadow trailing after him, easy to entertain and undiscerning in his love, Daniel felt confident. But actually teaching him how to be a man? Well, that was something else, wasn't it? Lenore seemed to be concerned, as well. She had brought the subject up in a roundabout way, talking vaguely about guidance and values. He knew what she'd meant, though he hadn't let on at the time.

Thinking of Lenore brought him back to his problem. He shook his head and reviewed the facts again. He loved her. He loved Scott. Why, then, couldn't he take the next logical step and marry her? It wasn't as if the thought had never occurred to him or the subject had never been discussed. He had even bought a ring a while ago, a cheap little fragment of a diamond that had been sitting in his dresser drawer for months.

He got up and drifted into the living room, moved a pile of Legos from the couch cushion, and sat down. He took another sip of the coffee. Rose up and went to the window. The car was gone, ruling out his guess that they had walked to the park or the grocery store. He went into the bathroom, closed the door, and started the shower. Lenore's robe swung from the hook on the back of the door. He gathered up a handful of the material and smelled it. The scent of her shampoo lingered around the collar. He saw himself in the mirror, and the gesture reminded him of some phony stage trick, a way to show the audience what a tender, compassionate guy his character was. He dropped the robe, and his face looked back at him from the mirror, scornful. He stared back.

For as long as he could remember, no one had gotten much further in their perusal of him than his face. He acknowledged the fact, but it didn't move him. It wasn't as if he were the only handsome man in his family. They were all variations on the same theme. Best-looking men in Harlan County, everyone said, but in Kroger, Kentucky, that would get you all the women you wanted and a job at the mine. The one skill he'd had that had lifted him above that, had shown him the way out, had been his fastball. He had applied for scholarships, hoping, even praying, that some school would pick him up.

"Stay close to home until you get things figured out a little more. Go to Eastern Kentucky," his uncle had urged, but Daniel had been hot to leave.

It wasn't that he didn't appreciate what his aunt and uncle had done for him. He'd have been a ward of the state if they hadn't taken him in. He remembered the chaos of life with his mother. From the time of his father's death when Daniel was five, she'd been in and out of rehab, leaving Daniel with his aunt and uncle for months and years at a time. Finally, when he began high school, they'd all decided it would be better if he just stayed. By the time he'd graduated, his mother had succeeded in drinking herself to death, and it had seemed to him as if the entire state of Kentucky was a tight, stifling box. UCLA had seemed about right. When he'd driven into L.A. and seen that low spatter of lights, he had felt something in him open up. He'd expanded his lungs, filled them with the metallic taste of exhaust and heat, and felt he could breathe. And if he hadn't torn his rotator cuff, he might even be playing professional ball somewhere. Minor league, probably, but that would have been good enough. But things had gone another way.

He'd drifted for a quarter or two after his surgery. Tried majoring in business, which had been a mistake. It had bored him stiff. He remembered his advisor shaking his head at his transcript, then looking at him ruefully.

"Let's face it. You don't seem to have any desire for management, and you look like you were born to be in the movies," he'd said, his voice almost regretful. "Why don't you change your major to drama?" And Daniel had done so with a sense of inevitability. Why not? Why not cash in your stock at the only place it was worth something? Spend your voucher at the company store, so to speak?

It suited him. The first time he'd stepped onto a stage he felt as though he'd come home. "Here," they would say, "this is who you are, at least for a few hours. This is how you're supposed to act." He accepted the fact that his looks defined him as the price of admission to the world he wanted to reside in. A permanent, if regrettable, fact of his existence. His looks seemed to be the only gift he'd been given. He might as well get the most mileage possible from them.

He stared, viewing the arrangement of his features as a curiosity. His dark hair would, if he was lucky, go gray around the temples first. Dark brown eyes. Dark complexion. Strong jaw. Good smile. Good teeth. He had the raw material, but like any lump of coal knew, that wasn't always enough.

But he had a shot. He'd been getting lots of auditions lately, and his parts had been improving in quality. His resume was almost to the point that he didn't need to constantly embellish it. He'd done a slew of commercials and had had roles in three sitcoms so far. He'd been the handyman in *Fine and Dandy.* Too bad it had gotten canceled after one season. Then he'd been the dance instructor's boyfriend in *Swing Dancing.* He'd had a bit part in *Laurel Canyon,* a cop show that, unfortunately, had been canceled after two episodes. But his chance would come. If he was patient. He knew in some way he couldn't explain that he had what they wanted. It was in their faces. In their slightly heightened attention when he read for a part. He knew. It would only be a matter of time before he hooked up with the right agent and landed the right part. He ignored the odds, refused to acknowledge the fact that the possibility of becoming a star was about as likely as one falling from the sky and landing on a lanai. He had a sense that his career was about to take off, had a feeling of momentum, of a forward movement that at any moment might become flight.

He turned his face away from his reflection, stripped off his clothes, and stepped into the shower. He heard the apartment door slam shut and felt a rush of relief. She was back.

He let his breath out, felt his chest loosen, and he realized that even now it wasn't too late. He could marry her. He could. It would be easier than this. Easier than watching everything vital leak out through her eyes. Easier than feeling his own gut twist with pain at the thought of losing them. He watched the water spatter onto the tile walls and could almost see her image as she had looked later that night. After she'd asked the question he couldn't answer. Her brown hair had been thick and wild, her skin even paler than normal. She'd been wearing the pink cotton gown, threadbare from too many washings. He could see her grief-filled eyes, and he felt another lurch of urgency. He could probably fix it. It wouldn't take much. Any acceptably phrased proposal, any clumsy explanation would be welcome to them both, would relieve the unbearable tension of two parts of a whole being ripped apart. He could almost feel the tear of flesh and smell the blood.

He stepped out of the shower and dried himself, used his towel to rub a clear spot on the steamy mirror, squirted out a handful of shaving foam and patted it over his face, then carefully followed its curves and lines with the razor, watching his features emerge. He finished, rubbed the specks that remained onto the washcloth, and tossed it in the hamper. He felt angry at himself for hurting her. She was so sad, and the love she had for him was like a sharp knife turning over and around inside her.

He wrapped himself in a towel and opened the bathroom door, letting out a cloud of steam. His heart felt divided, just exactly as if there were a thick stone wall running down the center of it. And whenever he thought about Lenore, he careened into that barrier. There was only one way to keep her and Scott. Take it down, surrender all he was to her. He wondered if he had the kind of courage it would take to risk everything on one person. To toss all of himself onto her and promise to hold on no matter what came. He felt a kind of panic when he considered it, a fear that seemed greater than his sorrow at losing them.

He dressed, putting on his laundry-starched shirt, tucking it into his pants, then tied his tie, combed his hair, and splashed on some cologne. He clipped his watch onto his wrist and put his wallet in the breast pocket of his jacket.

He had forgotten to brush his teeth. He went back into the bathroom. He could hear *Sesame Street* coming from the living room now and the clattering of dishes in the kitchen. He could still make things right, he realized, and that saying made sense to him now, that expression that had come to mean marrying the woman you lived with. Making things right. That's exactly what it was. It was restoring a tipped balance, replacing something valuable that had been stolen.

He thought about it hard as he brushed and spit, carefully shielding his tie and jacket, then rinsed with mouthwash and checked his face for froth. He wiped his mouth with the towel again and looked himself in his red eyes. He took the bottle of Visine from the medicine chest and dropped a little into each eye. They'd come this far, and there was Scott. It seemed almost evil to allow this thing, such a little thing when held up to the good things they had, to come between them. This little fear. This protective shielding of possibilities.

In fact, he had opened his mouth the other night to say the words. He was just preparing to say, "Let's get married, then," to hurtle down off the cliff without thinking of how he would land, when she'd become angry, and he was suddenly overwhelmed with the knowledge that it had become more complicated. He would have to soothe her first, and that would take more than just the few words he could eke out, and it had been easier to stay where he was and let her move away from him. And now it would be even harder to move close to her. Days had passed, and that first anger had hardened into something even more formidable.

He sighed at his reflection, then went into the living room.

"Dad!" Scott ran across the room and flung himself at Daniel's knees.

"Hey, buddy."

The clattering in the kitchen stopped.

"Dad, come watch *Sesame Street* with me."

"I can't, buddy, I've got to go to work."

"Can I talk to you for a minute, Daniel?" It was Lenore, standing in the doorway, speaking to him in a deadly white voice. Daniel nodded and followed her into the kitchen. For days they had both been calm, controlled, behaving like adults, which disturbed him, gave him a sinking feeling of hopelessness that a dish flying by his ear would have relieved. He was shocked when he came into the room and saw that there was a stack of boxes by the sink and Lenore was packing things into them—pots and pans, dishes, glasses, and bowls.

Daniel didn't say anything. For the life of him, he couldn't think of what to say.

She faced him, her face and eyes anything but calm. "Scott and I are leaving," she said in that tight voice.

He stared at her blankly for a minute. "Let *me* leave," he finally said. "This is Scott's home. I'll find another place."

Lenore's eyes filled up. She picked up a plate and began wadding newspaper around it. "No. I mean we're really leaving. We're leaving town."

Daniel felt as if someone had punched him in the gut or hit him in the elbow. He felt that moment of numb, breathless shock before the pain begins.

"No." More plea than refusal.

She lifted her head toward him and tilted it, just a fraction, as some people do when they're trying to catch a distant sound, listening for something. Her face softened a shade.

"Please don't take him away," he begged.

A brief flash of pain shot across her eyes. He watched as she drew it back in. When she spoke her voice was weary. "Daniel, L.A.'s a lousy place for kids unless you're rich. The schools are terrible. The neighborhoods aren't safe. And besides, I just can't stay here." Her hurt seeped out through her eyes, in the dragging lines of her face. "I don't want to hurt either of you, but I can't stay." She sniffed and wiped her wet cheek with the palm of her hand, leaving a dark streak of newsprint on her face.

He reached out and brushed it before he thought. She stiffened and turned away. He withdrew his hand and cleared his throat. "Where will you go?" he asked after a moment. Perhaps it would be somewhere relatively close. He could drive up on Friday, pick up Scott, and return him Monday morning.

"I don't know," she said without turning around. "I'm thinking the Northwest. Oregon or Washington," she said, and his little bubble of hope shattered.

I don't want you to go. The words waited on the edge of his tongue. But how could he speak them? He had no right to object to any plans she made.

She set the plate in the box. Her hands were trembling. She raised her face. It was drawn with sorrow, her white skin as pale as death, her hair a wild crown around the torn green eyes.

He could call a halt right this moment. He could say, *No, I won't let you go. I love you,* and then he'd make the promise. But it would take a rooting out, a painful surgery, and a dying of that little part of him he'd nurtured and kept secret through the years. That little desire, so like a seed, waiting only for the proper conditions to germinate and take root.

He breathed in a pull of air and blew it out in a sort of passive despair. "When will you leave?" he asked.

Three

"I T'S YOURS. TAKE IT." Lenore tried not to sound petulant. They both looked at the chair, and Lenore felt her tears beginning to leak out again, so she went into the bathroom. She stayed awhile, crying and blotting her eyes. It was her normal state now, liquid. She felt formless and chaotic, a choppy sea of grief and misery. She finally blew her nose and splashed her face with water. When she came back the chair was gone, and Daniel was standing where it had been.

"You keep the car," he told her in exchange. It had been his car when they'd met, and he was the one who kept it running, whether by mechanical skill or magic, Lenore wasn't sure. She looked out the window and could see the old Datsun parked at the curb. The borrowed truck was parked beside it, and there was the leather wing chair she'd bought him for their first Christmas, regal amidst the boxes stacked in the back.

"What will you do for transportation?" she asked.

He shrugged. "I'll manage. You take it."

She nodded and sniffed.

Daniel cleared his throat, then looked up and met her eyes.

"I'd like to have Scott come for Thanksgiving," he said. "It's a month and a half away. That'll give him time to get settled."

Lenore was shivering even though the sun was shining outside. That well of tears threatened to overflow again. She didn't answer.

"Could he come?" Daniel pressed.

"No." She shook her head. Pressed her lips together.

Daniel didn't say anything, but his jaw tightened. He bent and picked up the rucksack he'd packed with the last of his things, then drew up and gave her a look that started angry and ended tender.

It undid her. Again. It was like that. One minute she would be stiff and hard with anger and, yes, even hatred, and the next minute a remembrance of an expression of his or a kindness shown would cause her to blame it all on herself and wonder why, even now, she couldn't just take it back and let them go on as they had been. Daniel turned and started toward the living room to tell Scott good-bye.

"Wait," she said.

He stopped and looked back at her, his face still gentle. She began to cry again. She had cried so much in the past weeks that she wasn't even ashamed any longer.

"He can come at Thanksgiving." She wiped her tears away with the sleeve of her sweatshirt.

"Thank you." He paused, as if he were about to say something else, but all he did was repeat it again. "Thank you."

He hesitated, then walked back toward her and stopped just inches away, his face very close to hers. "I guess this is good-bye." He looked past her eyes, a little to the left, then shifted back. His own eyes were dark and full of pain. He took his hands from the pocket of his jacket, held her gently by the shoulders, leaned down, and brushed his lips against her cheek. He hadn't shaved again this morning. His face felt scratchy and rough.

She leaned her head against his shoulder for just a moment, and it reminded her of the way she'd rested against him in labor. She straightened up and stood back. She felt broken, shattered, the rubble of their life jagged and sharp inside her.

He said good-bye to Scott then, and if she had thought her own good-bye was the worst pain she would feel, she had been wrong. She watched their two sad faces side by side, earnestly talking, then kissing, saw Daniel rise stiffly and pick up the rucksack and head for the truck. Scott cried out and went after him, running in that bobbing way of his. He was such a little boy. She hadn't noticed before how small he looked, how vulnerable to evil people, evil things. Why, even a stiff wind could knock him down. He caught up to Daniel, and Daniel, bless him, turned back, put down his bag, and held Scott. He rocked him in his arms, and she wondered again, as she saw Scott's small hands on the back of Daniel's neck, if he would stay. But he just brought Scott back inside the apartment to the couch and held him again, comforted his tears, coughed back some of his own, told Scott how much he loved him, and promised a day they would be together again.

"Go get the calendar," Daniel told Scott, and Lenore handed him the insurance company calendar with the pictures of Big Sur and the Hollywood sign and the giant redwoods. Daniel turned ahead to November and circled a day. "There," he said. "On this day, you'll see me again."

She finally held Scott so Daniel could leave. Scott wrenched away from her, and she was afraid he would run after Daniel again, but he seemed to know better. Instead, he ran to the window.

"Daddy!" he cried out, but Daniel didn't hear, or if he heard he kept walking. He got into the truck, started the engine, and drove away. Lenore wanted to go into her room and climb under the covers, to close her eyes and make believe she wasn't here, that this hadn't happened, to go back to some time she could bear. She stood behind Scott instead and was there to receive him when he turned away from the window and buried his face in her legs.

She stopped at her sister's to say good-bye but could barely wait to leave. Leslie's unflattering analysis of Daniel's psyche and off-the-cuff career guidance for Lenore were unbearable. Her visit with her mother was even more brief. There was a new man on the scene, and besides, they were leaving themselves. The new boyfriend was a professional gambler, so they were headed for the casinos, packing up and moving to Las Vegas.

Lenore said good-bye and drove away, leaving L.A. in her rearview mirror, the drone of the road a welcome respite for her mind. She hated Los Angeles. Even the pretty suburbs were flat and featureless. The city itself was slums, haze, and freeways. The only good thing about L.A. had been Daniel.

She stopped in Yreka for the night, then again in Portland, Oregon. She didn't like it there. She couldn't say exactly why. It felt lonely and a little menacing. She made a stop at Powell's Bookstore. She wasn't sure what she'd expected, but when she got there, it was like Grand Central Station. She couldn't find anything she wanted, and there were too many books, really, so they just wandered around. She paid for the picture book Scott had chosen and left. They bought some burgers and brought them back to the motel. The room was cheap but dank and greasy and smelled of old cigarettes, and she found hair in the shower pan.

They ate. Scott ate, actually. She put him to bed, then just sat there for the longest time, the television a flickering blue light, a murmur of voices. The light cast long, gloomy shadows. She held a map under the lamp and tried once again to decipher the knot of freeways winding through and around downtown Portland. She wasn't sure which one to take on her way out tomorrow. She set it down. Her hands were shaking again, and she tried to hold them steady as she opened her purse and counted her money for the tenth time. There wasn't any more than there had been before, and she wondered again what she had been thinking.

Why had she done this? Taken her son and set out on this skittish, dangerous voyage?

A commercial for a television show came on. A woman, bold and flamboyant, proclaimed that Jesus could heal you everywhere you hurt. Lenore's eyes flooded, and she wished with all her heart that it were true. The woman disappeared, and someone else came on talking about auto glass repair. She turned it off.

She wished there really was someone watching, someone wise and kind who would help the traveler, would guide the lost. She wanted to contact Him. To put in her request for guidance, for help. She moistened her lips and her heart beat fast. If He had existed, she had never known Him. Did He speak to strangers? She lowered her head. She wondered how she should address Him, and she was afraid that whatever language she used would come out false and stilted, heavily accented in flesh, and therefore unacceptable.

"Oh, God," she prayed, whispering so as not to wake Scott. "We're . . ." She'd started to say they were lost, but they weren't. She knew where they were. At the Flamingo Hotel just off Interstate 5.

There were noises outside, footsteps by her door. A shadow passed in front of the window. She tensed and held her breath, her eyes flickering to the flimsy chain across the door. The shadow moved on.

She exhaled, closed her eyes, and saw herself as from above, as from a great distance, a minuscule speck in an anonymous motel room in Portland, in Oregon, in the United States, in the world, in this one of a multitude of solar systems He must keep track of. She shook her head, feeling audacious and unimportant. She tried to remember how Mrs. Larsen had prayed. *Heavenly Father,* she had said. Lenore shook her head. She could claim no relationship. "Oh, God," she began hesitantly, "are you there?"

There was no answer. Just the soft sound of Scott's breath and her own ragged whisper. She moistened her lips and continued on, speaking into the cold darkness.

"I'm sorry for all the wrong I've done." She felt as if that wasn't enough. As if she really should ask forgiveness for who she was instead of simply for what she'd done or forgotten to do. She didn't know how to do that. She took another deep breath and hurtled toward the only thing she knew to ask, the only prayer she could think of.

"Oh, God," she begged, and as fervently as she'd ever wanted anything in her life she wanted someone to be listening. "Would you watch over us?"

And even as the words came from her lips, the picture she had seen in her mind as she began to pray started to change. Instead of widely focused and diffused, it beamed in tightly, drawing down on her in that dark, dirty motel room in a closely focused gaze.

"Lead us, God. Please. To someplace we'll be safe?" She finished up tentatively, a request made out of desperation rather than confidence.

She sat there a moment longer. Nothing happened. No sign. No voice. She finally got up, brushed her teeth, and put on her gown. But somehow, as she settled in next to Scott and lay there willing sleep to come, she had the feeling that Someone, somewhere, had heard her.

———

In the morning she headed back up Interstate 5. She entered Washington, passed by Chehalis and Centralia because she didn't think she could find work in what looked like farming communities. She passed by Olympia because it was the state capital and she had a sudden vision of herself sitting at a metal desk, punching numbers into a calculator, and coming out with the wrong answer time after time. She blew past Tacoma because all she could see from the freeway were factories, Federal Way because the name reminded her of prisons, and the next thing she knew, she was in Seattle.

She took the middle of the six exits because it wasn't the one that led toward the tall buildings, and when she found herself in a yellow-tiled tunnel, she felt claustrophobic and wondered if she should have gone on to Canada. But then she emerged and saw a little lake and the jutting masts of sailboats, and she followed the road around it. Actually, she had no choice, since she was in the right lane and the right lane had to turn right onto Westlake, and then she was on Nickerson Street, then it peeled off onto Bertona, and she was climbing up Third Avenue West. Suddenly she didn't seem to be in the city at all but in a quiet little maze of streets on a hilltop full of old houses under trees so big and gnarled that their roots buckled the sidewalks. It had stopped raining. The late afternoon sunlight was making dappled shadows on the pretty green lawns. Everything was graceful and old and beautiful.

"Where are we, Mom?" Scott crawled over the backseat and landed beside her on the passenger side with a thump.

"We're somewhere in Seattle," she told him and wondered if fate had led her here or if she was only lost. "Buckle your seat belt."

"I'm hungry," he said, and she reached inside the snack bag and brought out the cheese and crackers. Scott opened a package and began to eat. She continued to drive, looking at the graceful old houses, but gradually the neighborhood became stores and shops, gas stations and parking lots, and then they had blended back into downtown Seattle. She looked ahead to the bottom of the very steep hill they were now descending and saw Dick's Drive-In. She had a vision of thick hamburgers and greasy fries. It sounded good. She turned in, parked the car, got out, stretched her legs, and looked around her. Seattle looked as good a place as any to land. She bought a *Seattle Times* with the last of her change, and with Scott bouncing ahead of her, she locked the car and went inside the restaurant.

It was odd, really. One minute she felt as though she didn't have the energy to do anything, even put one foot in front of the other, felt as if she would dissolve from the sheer quantity of tears she had shed. And then there were other moments when she operated as if programmed, going about the daily business of life, buying papers and hamburgers, looking for jobs and apartments, her sad little bundle of emotions wrapped too tightly to squeak and packed firmly away. Like now.

They finished their hamburgers, and Scott wanted to go outside and walk around, so they did. There was a Best Western motel close by, which cost more money than Lenore had intended to pay, but she had a feeling it would be all right. She rented the room and stayed up long after Scott was asleep, circling apartments and jobs in the classifieds.

The next three days were a blur of repetition. She would look at the want ads, locate the address on the city map she'd bought, painstakingly find the apartment for rent, look at it, then repeat the process. In the end she took the first apartment she'd looked at, though not until she'd looked at ten or twenty others. It wasn't what she wanted, but the truth was, it was less depressing than the others, and it came furnished. In fact, it looked a lot like the Best Western motel. Lots of iron poles and concrete. The tree-lined sidewalk-buckled streets seemed a world away, even though they were just on the other side of Queen Anne Hill, which she realized after a day of driving around. They were on the north side. She was on the south side. The poor side.

The apartment itself was two furnished rooms and a bath, the kitchen a corridor between the living room and bedroom. It didn't take long to unpack the car, and after she settled Scott she sat down at the cheap Formica table to count her money again. That's when things began to come unglued. It was funny how it worked. She held it together. She came unglued. She held it together. She came unglued. Usually she was able to wait until Scott was asleep or occupied before falling apart. And she had learned to do it quietly.

She put her head down on the table, felt it cool under her cheek, and wondered which would be better, to think or not to think. She had no job, and even though Daniel had given her all the money, she had only $320 left after she'd paid the deposit on the apartment and the first month's rent. That wouldn't last long. She had to see about finding Scott day care or a school, and she had to look for a job, she hadn't really felt well since she'd eaten that greasy hamburger days ago.

Lenore held her pale hand in front of her, rotated her wrist, looked at the pink palm with its faint lines, then turned it. It looked familiar but seemed as though it belonged to someone else. She looked down at her denim legs and felt the same way. Disconnected. They were someone else's legs.

There. She felt better. If it wasn't her body, then she could be here for a while. If it wasn't her life, she could stand it. She was just taking care of it for a bit, making a few decisions until the owner could come back. She heard herself give a little laugh and wondered if she was going insane.

She couldn't go insane. She didn't even have a telephone number for Daniel, and there was no one to take care of Scott if she went insane right now. She could go insane later. Maybe tomorrow.

She sighed, looked down, and it was her hand again. The same hand she'd carried around all of her twenty-four years. The fingernails were chewed into the quick, and there was the scar from the wart she'd had frozen off her pinky finger. There was the ring her father had given her on her eleventh birthday, and there was the knuckle she'd broken playing baseball. It was her hand, all right. She sighed and turned back to the want ads.

Four

IT HAD BEEN A WEEK since they had moved into their apartment, and Lenore felt as if she were sleeping in a canoe that was moving down a river of slow taffy aimed for a waterfall. The effort of rowing upstream was unendurable. She knew she ought to try. She knew so many oughts as she lay in the dark bedroom and listened to Scott watch cartoons or play Nintendo, Daniel's parting gift. Much too extravagant, she had crabbed before they'd left, but she was glad of it now.

She couldn't get out of bed. She didn't know what was wrong with her, whether she was sick in her body or in her mind, but it ground down to the same fact. She couldn't get out of bed. The thought of getting up led to too many other thoughts that were like mountains of glass, too slick and steep to climb, so she just lay there, sleeping, listening to the electronic music of the game. She got up from time to time and made them some food, went to the convenience store to get more, but then she would feel so sleepy she would find herself dozing again on the couch or find herself somehow back in bed.

She wanted to call Daniel, to tell him to come and get her. To come and find her, since she couldn't even tell him where she was beyond an address. Where was she? Why had she come here? What had possessed her to give up her sweet home? Sometimes it would strike her funny, and she would begin to laugh, but softly and under the covers so as not to frighten Scott. But she frightened herself.

She began to wish earnestly that Daniel would come and find her, and sometimes she would wish it so intensely that she could almost feel the warmth of his body just inches from her. Sometimes she would hear him knocking on the door, and with a reasonableness she thought was insanity, she felt if she listened closely, she could hear his voice.

She was hearing it now. She listened carefully and then came fully awake. She looked at the clock by the bed. It was three o'clock, and from the slice of daylight coming from the living area she deduced it was three o'clock in the afternoon. Of course. Now she remembered the morning. She had fixed breakfast for Scott, Cheerios and toast, and had cut up an orange, which he hadn't eaten. She hadn't eaten, either. The thought of the yellow orange, with its sour taste and bold color, had made her nauseated, so she'd gone back to lie down for just a minute while Scott watched cartoons, and now it was three o'clock, and she heard voices.

She pulled on her robe and went out into the daylight, squinty eyed. It was the television. A somber-voiced announcer told her she could get money for her personal injury case by calling the law offices of Howard G. Reynolds. Scott sat on the floor, Cheerios beside him as well as the empty milk carton. He cast a glance at her, as serious as the man on the television.

"I'm hungry," he said, his voice plaintive. "The milk's all gone."

She nodded and surveyed the small living room. It was trashed. Old newspapers, takeout food containers, dirty dishes, and clothes were strewn about. She felt a piercing pain that she had left Scott to fend for himself. "I'll get dressed," she said. "We'll go get a burger." The thought nauseated her, but Scott jumped up and went to find his shoes. He was a mess, too, she realized, watching him go. He was wearing a torn pajama top and sweatpants. No socks. She went back into the bedroom and put on some clothes. She brushed her teeth and splashed a little water on her face. She had no energy to attempt dealing with her hair. Scott had found his jacket and had his shoes on and was waiting by the door. She gathered up her purse and keys, locked the apartment, and squinted again when she stepped outside, even though it was gray and a misty fog hung low.

She went to the car, unlocked Scott's side, then got in herself. She put the key in the ignition and turned it. *Click, click, click.* She rested her head on the steering wheel. She tried it again but knew it would do no good. The battery was dead. She sat there awhile, fighting tears. While a part of her mind asked her if she had finally lost it—over a car battery?—another part was prostrate, crying out that it was just too much. If it hadn't been for the milk, she would have gone back inside to bed. Scott watched, quiet and tense beside her, equal parts worry and hope.

She moistened her lips and took a deep breath. What were her options? She could take a bus. She immediately rejected that thought. The complexity of figuring out which one to take, where to get off, and how to get back again was overwhelming. She looked around the apartment complex. It was mostly deserted. She remembered the manager, a kind-looking man whose last words to her had been, "Call me if you need anything.

I'm here and happy to help." With a sigh she got out of the car, took Scott by the hand, and headed for his apartment. When she found it, she stood on his doorstep for a moment, taking in the potted tomato plants, a few red orbs still hanging onto the vines, the huge window box full of geraniums and pansies, the lawn chair under the window, and she had a strange feeling. She felt as if this one small act, the decision to knock on this door this afternoon, was somehow important, one of those hinges of life that determines everything that follows. She raised her hand and knocked.

Before Lenore had even finished explaining her problem, Joe Caputo was nodding and reaching for his coat. She felt almost weak with gratitude, and for the first time in weeks she felt like smiling. He was a funny-looking little man, no more than five feet tall, shiny bald with a huge mustache. He smiled at her and followed her out to the parking lot, unlocked his trunk, and took out his jumper cables. To no avail.

"Maybe it can be recharged," he said.

Lenore nodded and crossed her arms. Seattle was cold. It was only October, but she felt a damp chill seep inside her body, inside her bones. She was too tired to think what to do next. She sat down on the concrete curb. Mr. Caputo stood watching her, then took a handkerchief from his pocket, wiped the oil from his hands, and sat down beside her.

Scott was playing a few feet away, trying to coax a fat black cat from behind a rhododendron bush. Lenore wondered, almost idly, what Mr. Caputo would say.

"You know, I've got some friends coming for dinner."

Not what she'd expected, and she felt a surge of embarrassment that she'd been so selfish, that she hadn't asked about his plans before dragging him out to the parking lot. "I'm sorry," she apologized. "Don't let me keep you."

He shook his head. "No, what I meant was, why don't you join us?"

Scott had abandoned the cat. He came back toward the two of them and seemed interested in how she would answer.

She shook her head, the thought of social interaction overwhelming her. She glanced at Scott. His eyes were bright, obviously hoping she would say yes.

Mr. Caputo spoke again before she could answer. "I have plenty of food, and I think you would really hit it off with my friends. They're wonderful people, and if you don't mind my saying so, it looks like the two of you could use a little encouragement right about now." He smiled apologetically. He was so sweet and sincere, and the bald dome of his head shone, giving it a halo effect. "How about it?" he pressed. "Let me feed you, and afterward I'll take your battery to get recharged. I know a good service station just over the hill."

"Can we, Mom?" Scott begged.

Lenore hesitated, but she knew she would say yes. What other choice did she have? She realized that one of the things that was keeping her sleeping in that bed was terror. Sheer terror. At being alone under the crushing burden of finding a job and taking care of Scott without Daniel. She felt as if she didn't even speak the same language as the people around her. She nodded at Mr. Caputo and swallowed down her tears.

"Good." He patted her hand, and she found the gesture oddly touching. "You can come over to my place and help me finish things up."

She was suddenly aware of her unkempt state, of Scott's neglect. "Let me just freshen up a little."

He nodded, his eyes almost disappearing when he smiled. "You know where I live."

She called to Scott. They went inside, and she did the best she could to clean them up. She took a quick shower, dressed, combed her hair, and put on a little lipstick. She found Scott some clean clothes and combed and wet down his hair. It had been sticking up for days now from where he had slept on it and made it bumpy, and she saw that it was dirty, as well.

"We need to make sure you get a bath tonight," she said, and she saw Scott's eyes clear with relief.

They went back to Mr. Caputo's apartment. Scott already seemed cheered. He was chattering as they waited for their host to come to the door, telling her about the movie he'd watched on television about a dog that had been chased by a wolf. Lenore smelled the spicy scent of Mr. Caputo's tomatoes and remembered how much she had hoped for a place with room to plant a garden. She had always wanted a garden, but another year had passed without one.

Mr. Caputo came to the door, greeted them warmly, invited them inside, and took their jackets. Lenore looked around her as he hung them in the closet. The walls were covered with framed photographs—old and new, black and white as well as color. The furniture was old and mismatched. A Navajo blanket was draped over the couch. Two huge shelves were filled with books, and a fat Siamese cat was draped lazily across the recliner. On the table beside it was a Japanese-English dictionary, two remote controls, a steno pad, a half-filled cup of coffee in which the cream had settled into a ring, two Waterman fountain pens, and a black leather Bible with what looked like a telephone bill stuck inside as a bookmark. Lenore could smell spices and tomatoes.

"I'm so glad you're here." Mr. Caputo beamed. "My friends should be here any minute. They come about once a month, and I make them my polenta and chicken."

Lenore didn't ask what polenta and chicken was. She didn't ask any questions at all. She just nodded.

Mr. Caputo saw to Scott first. He covered the coffee table with newspapers, then went to the hall closet and brought out a box with scissors, paste, paper, a hole punch, markers, brass fasteners, and an armful of *National Geographic* magazines.

"I thought you might like to make a book, Scott. You can choose between animals and your favorite places."

"That's nice of you," Lenore murmured.

Mr. Caputo shrugged. "I keep that stuff for my grandkids."

"Do they live around here?"

"Vancouver, British Columbia. I don't get to see them enough," he said, but smiled. "Come join me in the kitchen," he invited.

Lenore followed. She chopped vegetables and added them to the salad, things she never would have thought to put in a salad, and watched Mr. Caputo stir up the thick cornmeal dish that would accompany the chicken and tomato sauce he had made. She watched him grease a pan and deftly squeeze off rolls from a mound of dough he said had just completed its rising.

She helped him set the table. She realized she was hungry. The first time she'd felt hungry in days. He didn't ask her any questions, though she had thought he might. Instead, he gave her little jobs to do, and by the time the door buzzer rang, the table was set, the coffee was brewing, and the rolls were turning a golden brown in the oven.

Lenore felt as though she had been on a solitary island and had been plucked from it and set back down into the current of life. And she felt a stab of gratitude to the fat little man, the neighbor she had just met.

She followed Mr. Caputo into the living room, actually interested in who the other guests would be, the first time she'd been interested in anything in weeks. In the doorway stood three people. A pretty, middle-aged woman with freckles and chin-length ginger hair sprinkled with gray, a man in his thirties, medium sized, wire-rimmed glasses, brown hair combed back from his plain, earnest face, and a younger woman, probably his wife. She was beautiful. Short, full, golden hair, blue eyes, and a mouthful of perfect teeth. They all beamed at her, as if she were an unexpected treasure strewn across their path.

"Come in, come in," Mr. Caputo said. He waved them inside, took jackets, and made introductions. Lenore put names with faces. The middle-aged woman with the freckles was Edie Hamilton. The couple was Matt and Jenny Reynolds. They all said they were happy to meet her and Scott.

Mr. Caputo started telling Matt about Lenore's battery. Jenny Reynolds knelt beside Scott, obviously interested in what he was doing.

"She's a teacher," Edie Hamilton said, smiling at Lenore, warm without being overwhelming. She greeted Scott, too. Already the floor around him was covered with scraps. Mr. Caputo didn't seem to mind.

After a few moments of chitchat they went right to the supper table and ate. Lenore was grateful for the number of people. The conversation flowed pleasantly around her. She gave brief snips of information about herself. She was new to the area. Had just met Mr. Caputo. She learned that Matt was the pastor of Mr. Caputo's church and that Edie worked there, too. She didn't ask what kind of church or where. She didn't really care, was just happy to be in out of the rain, so to speak. Scott ate voraciously, even though he didn't usually like spicy food. But this was good, and the atmosphere felt safe and warmed her right to her bones.

"So, Lenore," Edie said, leaning forward on her forearms, "what made you choose Seattle?"

She gave them a sketchy explanation. No real reason. Moved from California. Looking for a job. She was vague when Edie asked what kind of work she did.

"The last job I had was as a physical therapy aide in a nursing home," she said and was relieved when the conversation switched to the topic of the Seattle job market. When they were finished eating, Scott went back to his cutting, and Mr. Caputo filled their coffee cups with thick, steaming coffee and served huge slabs of Dutch apple pie to each of them.

"Were you from Los Angeles originally?" Edie asked, apparently still looking for the thread that would draw Lenore into the conversation.

Lenore shook her head, thinking of a polite way to put it. "My mother was a wanderer," she said. "We moved around a lot when I was growing up. I wouldn't have stayed in L.A. except that I met Scott's father, and we . . ." She stalled, not able to finish that sentence. Her voice broke. Her eyes went wide with embarrassment. She blinked furiously, tightening her throat until it ached.

Edie had an expression of pain on her own face now. Matt and Jenny's faces became concentrated concern, and Mr. Caputo leaned forward and patted her hand.

That was what undid her, that hand pat. She felt her face crumple, and the cry rose up from her tightened throat. She grabbed the napkin and pressed it against her face. She rocked in silent sobs, the only sound the intake of breath between them and the soft whisper of Edie Hamilton's voice murmuring words Lenore couldn't understand.

It spent itself after a few minutes. Mr. Caputo pressed a tissue into her hand, and she blew her nose, sparing the linen napkin. She mopped her face, then looked up. Their faces were still focused on her, and she could almost feel their warmth. And then she heard herself telling them the whole story, beginning with that moment in the cozy apartment in Los Angeles in front of the sink scrubbing potatoes. She could feel the polenta and chicken and the apple pie starting to churn inside her.

Edie Hamilton covered Lenore's hand with her own when she had finished. "Let us pray for you," she said, and something in the calm gentleness of her tone made Lenore's stomach stop its viselike twisting, but if Edie had suggested that Lenore open wide and let her extract a molar, Lenore couldn't have been more surprised at the suggestion. Praying wasn't something anyone had ever done for her. She nodded dumbly, though, and still shuddering sobs, she bowed her head. She wondered if she should cross herself or kneel.

"Lord Jesus," Edie said in a calm voice, "we know you're here."

"Yes, Lord," Mr. Caputo murmured.

"That's right, Jesus." Matt's voice rang out loudly in the little room. Lenore was a little taken aback. It had never entered her mind that the Lord was here instead of up in His heavenly realms somewhere, and ordinarily it might have worried her a little. Today it didn't, though. It was a comforting thought, that Jesus might be right there in the empty chair beside Joe Caputo.

"You promised to be near the brokenhearted, Lord," Jenny said, as if reminding the Almighty, "that you would heal the crushed in spirit."

They went on like that for quite a while, each one saying things, their voices weaving in and out in a quiet tapestry. She felt something in her chest. It had felt tight and painful, but it started to loosen now. She felt as if a great pressure had been lifted.

"Let your peace descend, Father," Matt finished.

There was silence for a minute. Lenore opened her eyes. She was calm. Her tears were gone. And her stomach was settling. No one spoke for a few minutes. Mr. Caputo got up and refilled everyone's coffee cup. Lenore took a sip. It was hot and strong, and although it tasted bitter, it comforted and warmed her.

Edie spoke after a while of sitting in silence. "It would give us great joy if we could help you. May we?"

Lenore looked around the table, and every head was nodding, waiting for her to answer.

It would give them great joy. Lenore shook her head a little, more in amazement than refusal. She had never met people who talked like that. "I don't know how you could help. I don't know if anyone can help."

"Well, now, that's the enemy right there," Matt said, not condemning but triumphant, as if he had nailed a difficult diagnosis. "Despair is never from God. He's the God of all hope." .

Lenore blinked, taking that in. She had never heard anyone talk about God in that way, so sure of His attitudes. As if they had just spoken to Him on the telephone before leaving home.

"I can think of some places to start," Edie said, smiling. "If you're willing."

Lenore nodded. Really, what did she have to lose? She needed help, she realized.

Jenny spoke up. Her voice was soft and melodious, a pretty counterpart to her husband's bold baritone. "Lenore, it's like you've taken a fall. You've landed on the pavement, and you keep bouncing up and landing hard again. You need people in your life, and so does Scott. I think God has put us here. We're your safety net."

Lenore wasn't sure about the physics or the consistency of the metaphor, but the safety net sounded wonderful. And suddenly the prayer she'd prayed that night in the motel room came back to her. She had asked for help. She had asked God to lead her somewhere they'd be safe. It was odd that Jenny would choose that exact word. She blinked back a fresh flood of tears, this time of gratitude, nodded, and took a few deep breaths. She concentrated on Edie's soft hand patting her own. When she looked up, Mr. Caputo's eyes were squeezed shut in a smile, and a small slice of sunlight had emerged from the last of the day's gray fog and was beaming onto his dining room table.

One thing can lead to another. Lenore was beginning to see that just as one bad thing can lead to another and another until you are so sad and lonely that you can't get out of bed, one good thing could lead to another and then another.

After supper Mr. Caputo and Matt took the battery out of Lenore's car and headed for the gas station. Edie and Jenny volunteered to drive Lenore to the grocery store for milk and went back to her apartment with her so Lenore could get her purse. Scott brought home the book he'd made, a jagged conglomeration of animal heads and foreign vistas glued in bumpy furrows onto lined notebook paper.

"It's my jungle book," he said proudly and propped it in the living room window.

Lenore gathered up her purse and tried to surreptitiously count her money. Her stomach lurched as she saw there were only two hundreds and a few twenties. If she had to buy a new battery, that would deplete her cash significantly. She wondered how many groceries she could afford.

"We're paying today," Edie said firmly when she saw. "Put that away."

"We have money set aside for just this purpose," Jenny confirmed, nodding her pretty head, her eyes shining as if it was a great privilege to buy Lenore's groceries.

Lenore chewed her lip, not sure if she should feel alarmed. Her parents hadn't held much with organized religion. *"Whatever you do,"* her father had been fond of saying before he left, *"don't ever fall into the hands of the church."*

And here she was, having done exactly that, it seemed. But what were her other options? She thought of the days she'd spent lying in bed. She looked toward the bedroom and could see the unmade bed, with blankets and sheets bunched into a rumpled mountain range. She felt weariness at climbing the vast hill rising before her called her future. "I need help," she admitted.

Edie nodded, her face solemn.

"Let's go," Scott said, breaking the tension.

They went. The four of them climbed into Edie's car. They drove to the Safeway by Seattle Center. Edie took a cart, put in her first selection, a bouquet of red and orange chrysanthemums and daisies. Scott and Jenny wandered off to look for a coloring book. Edie led the way to the bakery, then to the meat department, and to the produce area. The pile of groceries in the cart grew. They finally finished. Edie paid with a check, and they loaded up the groceries and drove back to the apartment. Mr. Caputo and Matt were connecting the battery wires as they drove in, and by the time they were all preparing to leave, Lenore's car was running, her cupboards and refrigerator were full, a bouquet of flowers sat in the middle of the little Formica table, and she had an appointment at the church for nine-thirty in the morning.

"We'll see about helping you find a job if you like," said Edie. "And we run a preschool and a kindergarten. If you want, Scott could try it out."

"I probably can't afford it," Lenore said bluntly.

"We have scholarships," Jenny put in.

"I can't take your charity."

"Why not?" Edie shot back, just as bluntly. "You need it, don't you?"

Lenore was trying to think of what to say and coming up blank. "I just wish there was some way I could thank you."

"Oh . . ." Edie nodded, the certainty in her eyes tempered only by her smile. "Your turn will come to say thank you," she promised. "Don't doubt that for a minute."

Five

$\mathcal{D}$ANIEL STOWED THE CHAIR in Lou's garage. Lou, the gaffer he'd met on the set of *Laurel Canyon,* who always seemed to have a favor ready for a hundred or two. Daniel had carefully placed the burgundy leather wing chair behind a pair of water skis and a rusted metal chaise lounge, gently covered it with a sheet, and watched the past play itself for him like a bittersweet movie.

Lenore had bought the chair for him the first year they were together. She had spent way too much, especially considering they were going to have a baby in a few months, but that was just the way she was. He had come out on Christmas morning, and there it was, regal in the small apartment. It had looked completely out of place amidst their cast-off furniture and concrete block bookshelves, but he had loved it. He remembered her joy as she watched his face. Her eyes had lit with happiness, and she'd clapped a hand over her mouth like a child. That's what he had remembered that day in Lou's garage. A week and a half ago. He had told himself his feelings would pass.

They hadn't.

He'd woken up again this morning feeling out of sync and scattered. He had managed to muddle through the day, but even now, sitting in Lou's dim living room sipping a lukewarm beer, he felt confused, as if some key he needed to make his way through life, some vital piece of information, had gone away with her. *Be a man,* part of him lashed out. *Accept all the consequences of your decision.*

Get her back, another part cried with pressing urgency. And it was that part that continued to knock at his heart like an unexpected guest who had shown up on his doorstep and refused to leave.

He could go and get her. He could. He had enough money to take the United shuttle to Seattle. And he had her address on the corner of the envelope she'd sent. Inside had been a brief, terse note giving their new address and phone number. He kept it in his wallet, took it out and looked at it once in a while, that small act reassuring him that she hadn't dropped off the face of the earth. She was there, at 303 Highland Drive. Apartment 120. He could go and get her.

He could climb aboard that plane, then take a bus or a cab, and within a week they could be back here with him. She would come. If he went now. But he had the sense that time was important, that with every hour that passed, every day, the odds became greater that the three of them would fly apart like objects on different orbits, that the pull of their universes would gradually take them far away from each other. But it still wasn't too late. If he acted now.

He rose from the table and went to the telephone, called information and then the airline. There was a flight leaving at midnight that would arrive in Seattle at 2:38 A.M. There were plenty of seats available. He could show up on her doorstep in time for breakfast, claim them both, and bring them home. And he would marry her to prevent any chance of this happening again. He felt an aching loss, a soreness, almost literal, around his heart. He sat back down, his decision taking shape. He would go tonight. After the party.

The party. His pulse sped up just thinking about it. Lou had gotten him the invitation months ago. Lou, his one true friend, sixty if he was a day, a dried leather string of a man who smoked Camel filters nonstop and had a strange habit of not moving his upper lip when he talked. He also had a way of showing up when Daniel needed help. An odd, wrinkled, dried-out guardian angel. A week and a half ago he had run into Daniel at the Spout and Toad. The day Lenore and Scott had left, in fact, as Daniel was finishing his third shot of whiskey. Lou had squinted his watery blue eyes Daniel's way, looked him over top to bottom, and called him a train wreck but came to Daniel's aid again, offering his couch and a corner of his garage for a mere two hundred a month.

Daniel had taken him up on the offer. Of course, he didn't have the two hundred *now*, having given most of his money to Lenore. But Lou was understanding, and Daniel told him he had a check in the mail. He had stowed his few boxes and, of course, the chair, and had moved into Lou's duplex on Tarzana and Virburnum. It was a musty, dusty place, too hot, with the smell of broccoli and stale smoke always hanging in the air.

The party was one of those big opening night bashes. A dog of a picture—something about giant spiders—but the guy who was catering was a buddy of Lou's, and the buddy was owed a favor by the guy who was working the door, so out of the goodness of Lou's heart and three hundred dollars, Daniel was in.

He got up now, poured out the rest of the beer, then spent an hour in the steamy bathroom getting ready. He put on the rented tux, careful to avoid even thinking of Lenore and Scott. He borrowed Lou's car, finally found the place, a huge glass-fronted house in the Hollywood Hills, and was waved in by the big dude working the door after telling him his name and mentioning Lou's. He stood at the doorway listening to the glasses clink, the bobbing waves of conversation, and the synthesized music.

He had pinned all his hopes on this evening. He remembered with a burst of shame that he hadn't really wanted Lenore to come with him, though he'd invited her all the same. He had wanted to be free to mingle and work the crowd. Well, he had his wish, he realized bitterly. He blinked and forced his mind in another direction.

He prepared himself mentally, telling himself who he was, what he wanted, and reviewing how to go about getting it. He talked to himself, stepped into the character of the man he needed to be just now, then threw back his shoulders and strolled in.

"Sylvia Wiley, this is Daniel Monroe." Belinda made the introduction to her agent, and Daniel turned on the full wattage of his smile. Sylvia gave him a once-over, interested. He could always tell.

"Daniel was my costar in *Fine and Dandy*," Belinda said, and Daniel owed her one. He'd had a bit part in the sitcom, but Belinda had liked him. It was a stroke of luck that he'd found her here. He kept his face interested and engaged while Belinda continued chatting with Sylvia. They covered Sylvia's last vacation and Belinda's current project, but he noticed Sylvia's eyes kept darting back to him. He flashed her a smile, and sure enough, after a few minutes the conversation wound around his way again.

"What else have you been in?" Sylvia asked, turning toward him. "I know your face."

He rattled off the sitcoms, the cop show. He calculated, then decided it was time to make his move. "As a matter of fact, I'm glad we got a chance to meet. I'd been thinking of giving you a call. I'm actually looking for new representation."

He hoped she didn't ask who was currently representing him. He'd never actually seen his agent. He operated out of his home, an apartment in the valley. "So what do you say, Sylvia?" he continued smoothly. "Think we'd make a good team?" He knew Sylvia Wiley was the new kid on the block at Creative Talent. She'd be looking to fill her stable, and this could be his ticket out of the small-time roles into something bigger and meatier.

Belinda was watching, amused.

Sylvia narrowed her eyes and gave Daniel a penetrating look.

"What do you say?" he repeated. He caught her gaze and held it, let the corner of his mouth hint at a smile, let it slowly spread. He sent her warmth through his eyes and could almost feel her moving closer to him. She must have felt it, too. She gave her head a shake, broke eye contact, and gave him a wise look.

"Save it." She reached into her bag and pulled out a business card. "Give me a call." She lifted a hand to Belinda, gave Daniel one more ironic look, then turned and strolled off.

"Well done," Belinda said with a quirk of her eyebrow and a slight nod. She signaled the waiter for another drink.

Daniel said nothing. He relaxed the smile and pocketed the card.

"There's Doug Levine," Belinda said, nodding at a short, balding man at the bar.

Daniel knew who Doug Levine was. A casting director. A good one. An important one.

"Want to meet him?"

Daniel nodded, the thought barely registering that it was time for him to go if he was going to catch the midnight flight to Seattle. He would have barely enough time to leave the party, change out of the tux, and catch a cab to the airport.

"Come on, then," Belinda invited. She took his hand and started across the room. He followed her. It was no big deal, he told the part of him that objected. He could catch a flight tomorrow.

Six

LENORE'S ALARM WOKE HER at seven-thirty. It took her a moment to remember, and when she did, the events of the night before seemed too good to be true. She felt for her emotions, sticking a toe into their waters. Sorrow still dragged at her heart, but she felt a little more alert, without the flat hopelessness she'd grown accustomed to. Her stomach felt better, too. So far, so good. She sat up, looked around the small bedroom almost as if she were seeing it for the first time. There was nothing much here. One small window. A dresser. A bureau.

She remembered she had someplace to go today, and the thought was a spot of brightness. She had something to do. She looked toward her son. Scott slept deeply beside her. His face was sweet and so like Daniel's, it gave her a stab of pain. His long dark eyelashes lay on his cheek, his mouth gently open.

She slid quietly from the bed, used the bathroom, washed her face, inspected it in the mirror. It stared back at her hollow-eyed, her skin almost transparent. She tugged the brush through her hair and twisted it onto the top of her head, blinking her eyes at her reflection. She felt like someone else without Daniel. She was so used to seeing herself through his eyes that she barely recognized the face that stared back. She inspected it, for once without the usual loathing. It was a face. Plain, but not ugly. It would do. She turned off the light and passed quietly through the dim bedroom and into the small corridor that was the kitchen.

The table was cluttered, stacked with dishes that needed to be put away. She found a saucepan and filled it with water, put it on the ancient stove, and turned on the burner. The faucet was dripping. She turned the handle as far as it would go, but a slight trickle of water still dripped down. It needed a new washer. She would have to buy one, and she realized she had no idea where the closest hardware store was. She had done no exploration at all, none of the usual things a person does when they move to a new neighborhood.

She walked into the living room, which looked considerably better since her little spurt of domesticity last night. It had started with her looking for the alarm clock; then one thing had led to another. She had had to dig through a few boxes and in the process had unearthed some of Scott's toys and put them out.

"Hey, I forgot about these!" he'd said, his eyes lighting up. Lenore didn't see how a handful of G.I. Joes and a tank could brighten someone's day to that extent, but it had given her a sharp joy to see how happy Scott was.

She had gone ahead and unpacked the rest of the box. There were more toys, bringing more cries of delight, and some bath towels, which she folded and put on the back of the toilet. Then she'd had to find a dress for herself, so she'd ended up putting away two boxes of her clothing. She'd finally found the dresses, but they were wrinkled, so she had to find the iron, and by the time she had found everything she needed for her appointment, she'd also unpacked six or seven boxes, which were now stacked neatly by the door, ready to be taken to the Dumpster. When she'd finished her labors, she'd slept deeply and with no disturbing dreams, not the half in, half out restless tumbling she'd been doing lately.

She looked around her now, surveying the apartment's cheerless furniture. There was a brown tweed couch and a chair, Danish modern end and coffee tables, two enormous brown lamps. The artwork consisted of three small prints of elves and mushrooms. The television was still sitting on an overturned box. She walked past it and opened the curtains.

It was gray outside and misting a light rain. She didn't mind, actually. It was soothing, gentle on her nerves. She looked across the parking lot and concrete courtyard to the doorways beyond them. Some of the people had flowers on their porches—some just a pot or two, while others had an entire garden arranged by their doors. Lenore squinted but couldn't tell what kind of flowers they were. She just saw blurs of red and gold, a few patches of green. The few scrubby trees around the apartment complex were losing their leaves. A door opened in the apartment across the courtyard. A woman stepped out in a housecoat, bent to retrieve a newspaper, and went back inside. Lenore heard a low whisper. Her water was boiling.

She went back into the kitchen, made herself a cup of tea, opened the new sack of sugar Edie had bought her. The events of the evening before still surprised her. She was involved with church people. In fact, she was going to a church today. Mind-boggling. Not that she was particularly opposed to the idea, just that it had never entered her mind. Her experience in life had taught her to expect condemnation and judgment from religious people, certainly not the warmth and kindness she'd experienced last night. She'd been living in sin, after all, and yet no one had even brought that up. When did something like that ever happen in real life? She smiled. That's what Daniel had always said to Scott when they saw him on television in one of his commercials or programs. *"That's make-believe,"* he would say. *"That would never happen in real life. Real life is us—here—me and you and Mom. This is real life."*

Had it been? she wondered now. Had that life with Daniel been the real life? Who was to say? Now that she had some distance, she wondered. Which had been the real life, and which had been the make-believe? She sat down on the couch and stared at the blank television screen.

"Can I have Cheerios for breakfast?" Scott stood in the kitchen, and she could tell by his face that he was testing the waters, just as she had done.

She turned, putting a smile on her face. A deliberate decision, just as she would put on her dress and shoes in a few minutes. "Sure," she answered. "Before or after bath?"

Another expression of relief. "Before," he said.

She got up and found the cereal, set him up at the kitchen table. It looked pretty good. She had a bowl herself.

"How about going swimming in a tropical sea?" she asked when he had finished.

He brightened. Lenore went to the bathroom, ran the tub full of water, and squirted in some blue and green food coloring and a liberal squeeze of dishwashing detergent. He climbed in. She washed his hair and rinsed it. She left him to play while she made the bed. A moment of normalcy, and for just a moment she could almost imagine nothing had happened. She sat down on the bed, lay down for just a moment. She imagined that Daniel would come into the room. His voice would call out her name, and she would answer, and they would be as they had been.

"I'm done." A smaller voice. She sat up. Scott had come out of the bathroom. He'd put back on his pajamas. Inside out. He was watching her again.

"Are you a prune?" she asked him.

He came close and held out his wrinkled fingers.

"Let's read a book," she suggested, and her voice sounded chirpy and false, but he didn't seem to notice. "I think I remember which box they're in." She unsealed it, grabbed the top four or five books, and took the extra blanket from the foot of the bed. They went into the living room, and Scott curled up beside her. They read *Mike Mulligan and His Steam Shovel, Horton Hatches the Egg, One Morning in Maine,* and *Blueberries for Sal.*

"We'd better quit now, Scott, or we'll be late," she finally said. She set the last book aside and went into the bedroom, gathering up the clothes she'd found for him to wear.

"Am I going to stay at the school, Mom?" he asked as she helped him pull off his pajama top and put on his T-shirt.

"Do you want to?"

"I don't know."

Lenore looked at his face, so sweet and trusting, and felt a fresh wave of grief. This was just as hard for him as it had been for her, and she'd been leaving him to deal with everything alone. She made herself a promise that she would not do that again. She would find her way, she vowed. She would step carefully around the dangerous crevasses, the mined fields. She would find a safe path. She had to.

"Well," she said, helping him on with his pants, "why don't we decide together after we see what it's like?" She smiled at him and dug the shoes with the Velcro closures out of the closet. They didn't have time for Scott to tie his own shoes today, and he wouldn't let her help him anymore.

"I want to wear the others."

She sighed as he slid off the bed and went to the closet to get them. She usually made him obey, but this seemed so unimportant, and what little energy she had should be spent on bigger things. "I guess you can tie them in the car," she said.

She followed the map Edie had drawn for her, driving through downtown Seattle, then up James Street to the top of the hill, and turning right. There it was, a big red brick building, set back from the street. The sign on the building said *Greater Grace Tabernacle*. The neighborhood was old and a little shabby. There were a few men loitering on the corners, but the grounds of the church were immaculate and nicely landscaped. Several evergreen trees shaded an ivy-covered rock on which were carved the words *Proclaiming Truth. Extending Hope.*

Lenore pushed open the double doors and stood still for a moment in the high-ceilinged lobby. The carpet was old but clean, the walls freshly painted. She held Scott's hand and just looked around for a moment. Hallways led off on either side, and ahead of her were the double doors of the actual room in which they held their services, she supposed. To her left was a glass-walled office. A woman was talking on the telephone. She raised a hand in greeting and waved her in furiously. Lenore went in.

"I gotta go, Francine. I got somebody here. Yeah. Okay." The woman hung up the phone and turned to Lenore. She had a kind, honest face and iron gray hair. "How are you?" she asked, beaming at her and Scott in turn.

Lenore smiled. "I'm here to see Edie Hamilton."

"You go right through those doors," the woman directed, pointing toward the double doors of the sanctuary. "Then go through the first doorway on your left." Lenore thanked her and followed her directions.

They passed the kitchen. Two women were busy doing something at the sink. They went past what looked like a food and clothing bank, staffed by a happy-looking, round-faced man. She opened the doors and entered the sanctuary. It was a huge room, very much like a theatre. The altar was adorned with a banner that stretched from one wall to the other: *The Christ of Calvary Still Changes Lives.*

Lenore stared at it for a moment until Scott tugged at her hand, then she turned and found the first doorway on the left. Edie was standing up in the middle of her office digging through a box, a frustrated look on her face, and it didn't take much to understand why. It was a small room. Very small. And cluttered. Filled with beautiful furniture and decorations, all in shades of pink and peach and lavender and cream, as well as stacks of paper and boxes and bags of who knew what. The place was a mess.

Lenore smiled.

When Edie looked up, the frustrated look on her face was replaced by a huge smile of her own. She stopped her rummaging through the box—of clothes, Lenore noted, seeing the leg of a pair of jeans hanging loose.

"Here you are!" Edie said as she came toward them, and Lenore felt relieved. Somehow she had worried that this morning Edie would have changed her mind, would have realized sometime during the night that Lenore and Scott were too big of a project. Too needy and requiring more than she cared to give.

Edie stopped in front of Lenore, and Lenore thought she was going to hug her, but instead she took one of Lenore's hands in both of hers and squeezed it, her face beaming with joy. "I was praying you'd be able to make it," she said, looking Lenore straight in the eye. "And, Scott," she said, leaning down toward him, "you're right on time to visit our school. Would you like to go and see what they're doing this morning?"

Scott shrugged.

"I think the puppies are coming today."

He perked up.

"Once a week the lady from the Humane Society brings kittens and puppies for the children to pet."

"I guess I'll go," Scott allowed.

Edie walked them to the rooms used by the preschool. The children were busy doing some kind of art project. They came to a stop in front of a black woman, large but not fat, with streaks of pure white through her black hair. She wore an apron that had handprints and names all over it.

"Grandma Eileen, this is Scott and his mom, Lenore," Edie said. "They're visiting us today, and Scott is deciding if he wants to stay."

Lenore looked at Scott's face. He was standing a shade behind her, but he was looking around, interested in spite of his uncertainty.

"Well, we're just so glad to have you, Scott," Grandma Eileen said warmly. "You know, we're having some special visitors to our class a little later."

"The puppies?" Scott asked.

Grandma Eileen put a hand on her hip and looked at him in mock amazement. "Now, how did you know that?"

He smiled and shrugged his shoulders.

"Yes. The puppies will be here after snack. And what we're doing right now is making pictures to hang on our wall," Grandma Eileen explained carefully. "We are taking these leaves and dipping them in the paint and pressing them down on the paper, like Jeremy is doing here." Grandma Eileen put her hands on the shoulders of a little boy. He looked up briefly at Scott, then went back to his project.

Scott was taking off his jacket, and Lenore took it from him. He didn't glance up at her.

"Where's the paper?" Scott asked Grandma Eileen.

"I can put a piece for you right here next to Katie," Grandma Eileen said in her careful enunciation.

"It looks like we're not needed here," Edie said, smiling.

"I guess not." Lenore felt relief, like someone had unbuckled a belt that was too tight.

"I'll check with you before I leave, Scott," Lenore said to him.

He looked up briefly, a leaf half in and half out of red paint, making dripping rivers across the newspaper on the table. "Bye," he said.

They went back to Edie's office.

"So," Edie indicated the loveseat in her office and sat down on the chair beside it, "that went well. Now let's see about you."

Lenore nodded and sat up straight. This felt like a job interview. She wondered if she should try to make a good impression.

"Want a cup of coffee?" asked Edie.

"I'd love one," said Lenore and realized her stomach felt much better than it had in days. Edie went to get the coffee, and Lenore looked around her office. It was a beautiful old room. The ceilings were high, the walls plaster, the floors a scarred, dark wood. Edie's furniture was old, as well. There was an antique teacher's desk in the corner of the room, an overstuffed chair in the other corner beside a low oak table. All were completely covered with files and papers. There were all kinds of things on the walls, as well—two big corkboards full of newspaper clippings, scraps of paper, and cartoons. The picture was what drew her attention, though. It was an old-fashioned lithograph in a curved-front frame. A woman, obviously in distress, knelt clinging to a cross as the waves tore and broke upon her. The cross was embedded in a massive rock in the middle of the sea, and in fact, that was the name of the picture. The Solid Rock. Lenore stared at it, feeling a kinship with the battered woman. That's just how she felt, she realized, as if she were that woman there on the rocks, but with nothing to hold on to except the cold, slippery boulders themselves. Each time the waves hit, she wondered if she would lose her grip and be swept away or dashed to her death against the cruel coastline.

She turned her attention toward the wall of books. It was too far away for her to read the titles. The table beside her had on it a pad of paper, a woven basket full of pens and pencils—at least forty or fifty of them—a quilting magazine, a paperweight made from seashells stuck in plaster of paris, and two books: *Strong's Exhaustive Concordance* and *Vine's Complete Expository Dictionary of Old and New Testament words.*

"Well, here I am."

Edie's voice brought her back to attention. She came steaming back into the room, a small tray in her hands. She was moving so quickly the coffee was slopping over the edge. Lenore was beginning to realize that Edie never did anything slowly. Haste seemed to be her way of life.

"I had to wait for it to finish dripping," she apologized. "I keep telling Matt we should spring for one of the pots you can rob in midstream, but he says we don't need it, that I should learn patience."

Edie set the tray on top of the magazine. There were two big mugs of coffee and an assortment of little packets of sugar and a paper container of half-and-half. "I noticed you took cream and sugar," Edie said.

"I'm impressed. I didn't even notice if you drank coffee last night."

"You had your mind on other things."

They doctored their coffee, and Lenore took a sip. It was good. Hot and strong. She looked up to see that Edie was looking at her curiously.

"What?"

"I was just trying to imagine how I would feel if I were in your place."

Lenore raised her eyebrows. She had never known church people to be empathetic. Mostly they had seemed to want to get her to do something, be something, or believe something. None had been curious, at least about her.

Lenore thought about what answers she could give. Confused, lost, terrified would be accurate. She said nothing, just gazed back into Edie's kind eyes.

"Would you mind if I prayed?" Edie asked.

Lenore shook her head, a little more used to the idea since last night. In fact, she'd been expecting it. She was beginning to see that these people didn't make a move without consulting their Heavenly Chairman of the Board. Edie prayed a short prayer, asking God to help her help Lenore. When she'd said amen, Lenore opened her eyes again. She sat awkwardly for a minute, wondering what Edie would do to help her find a job. Give her a battery of tests? Ask her probing questions?

"I made a phone call this morning," Edie said, her face alight. "I'm so excited. I just had a feeling. No, I take that back. It was the Lord. He put it on my mind. Anyway, Erik Ashland is a doctor and a member of our church, and he'd mentioned to me last week that he's looking for some help in his office. Told me to keep an eye out, and I agreed but really didn't think any more about it. But then I met you!" She beamed, as if the implications were obvious.

"I've never done anything medical," Lenore murmured. It was slightly overwhelming to think about learning a new job, especially one as involved as working in a medical office must be.

"I thought you worked in a nursing home."

"Oh. Yes, I did. But that isn't really the same thing."

Edie shrugged. "Well, nobody's born knowing how to do things, are they?" She smiled confidently.

Lenore thought for a moment, then shook her head. "No. I guess not."

"Just come with me and meet him," Edie urged. "After that the two of you can decide what feels right."

That sounded reasonable enough, and she did need a job.

Edie stood up and Lenore followed her outside. She peeked in the door of the preschool as they passed. Scott was sitting in a circle with the other children listening to a story. Lenore caught a few words. Something about Jesus and a storm. His face was rapt, eyes huge.

They stepped outside. It was still overcast, and the mist felt cool and kind on her face. Lenore wondered if it always rained in Seattle, but actually she didn't mind. It was refreshing after the relentless heat and sunshine of Los Angeles. Thinking of Los Angeles made her think of Daniel. She felt a twist of sorrow and forced her thoughts in another direction.

They chatted and walked for two blocks through the small shopping district of the neighborhood Lenore learned was called First Hill, the oldest in Seattle. It had been lovely once. The streets were lined with huge maple trees, now turning beautiful shades of gold and orange and red, but there were small signs of decay. A broken bottle here, graffiti there.

"Here we are," Edie said as they approached a low and long brick building. It looked as if it had been built in the forties. The sign read *Erik Ashland, M.D.* and *Wesley Bannister, M.D. Pediatrics and Family Practice,* respectively. They walked up the small stoop and pushed open the door, which jingled when they entered. The waiting room was full of people: an elderly man, a woman with a toddler and a baby, a pregnant woman, and another woman with what looked to be about six-year-old twins.

"Hi, Sophie," Edie greeted the receptionist. "This is Lenore. Erik told me to bring her by."

Sophie was tall and willowy, beautiful, with white-blond hair. She smiled, showing dimples. Lenore was suddenly aware of her own unruly hair, her plain dress and face.

"I'll tell him you're here," Sophie said. She came back after a minute and motioned for Lenore and Edie to follow her. They waited for five minutes or so until Dr. Ashland emerged from an exam room. He looked to be about thirty-five years old. He was medium height with a serious, rough-hewn face, blond hair beginning to recede, gray eyes, a mustache. He wore khaki pants, a white lab coat, and clogs. Lenore stared. She had never seen a man wear clogs before. Edie made the introductions, then retired to the waiting room.

Lenore followed him into his office, another cluttered room full of files and books. She sat down awkwardly in the chair he offered, and it was a pathetic job interview if that's what it was. He asked her what kind of work she'd done before and she told him. Waitress. Nursing home aide. He nodded. It was impossible to read his face. She should embellish, she supposed. Daniel was always saying she needed to learn to put her best foot forward. Translation: lie or exaggerate her abilities.

"I can type," she volunteered, moistening her lips and clearing her throat.

Dr. Ashland looked doubtful, and she felt her spirits sink. She hadn't even realized she'd wanted the job until now, until she felt the despair clasp hold of her throat.

"Maybe I wasn't clear with Edie," he said. "This job isn't front office. It's for back office assistant."

Lenore stared at him blankly. "I have no idea what that means," she admitted.

He blinked; then his face relaxed into a smile. The first one she'd seen. "You'd be assisting me," he said, "with patients."

"Oh." Her voice sounded as low as her spirits. "I don't know how to do that."

He said nothing. After a minute she looked up. He was clicking his pen open and shut, obviously in thought. "I suppose Connie could train you—Dr. Bannister's assistant," he finally said. "I guess you could learn as you go along."

Lenore wasn't sure what to say. Was he offering her the job? Suddenly she fervently hoped so. She was unemployed and had a child to support. "I want the job," she said and tried to keep the desperation from her voice.

Dr. Ashland seemed to be considering. He nodded and gave her a slight smile. His eyes were kind, and she felt a flicker of hope. "I've never gone wrong with Edie's recommendations before," he finally said. "We could give it a three-week trial. You don't faint or get sick at the sight of blood, do you?"

"No," she said, shaking her head vehemently.

He gave her one last look, and she thought she understood what she saw there. Compassion mixed with the tiniest bit of dread, as if he knew what his kindness to her would cost him. Delays, inefficiency, more work. But it was also as if he knew the decision had been inevitable from the moment she had walked through the door and cast her shadow across his path. As if she were wounded, lying by the roadside, and he, ever the kind Samaritan, would do what was right. She realized she was holding her breath.

He gave her one last appraising look, then a brisk nod. "We start at nine," he said, standing up. "Stick around, and I'll have Connie show you the ropes."

Scott gave rave reports of the preschool and Grandma Eileen. The puppies had been a great hit. Now they were fulfilling his homework assignment, finding fir cones for tomorrow's craft activity. They had to walk a little way from the apartment before they located some kind of needle tree. The ground beneath it was covered with cones.

"What are you making?" Lenore asked.

"It's a secret," he said, shaking his head firmly as he bent down to pick up the cones. "Let's get some extras," he suggested. "Grandma Eileen said we should bring some to share if we can. In case somebody doesn't have what they need."

Lenore stared at her son, her eyes ridiculously filling with tears. "I think that's a very good idea." She bent over and brushed them away, then worked beside him, filling the small bag they'd brought. It came clear to her then as they walked the blocks home through the gathering fog, as she scuffled through the leaves and smelled the peaty smell of earth and the salty smell of Puget Sound, that everything had changed. In just one day. From knocking on just one door. Yesterday she had been lying in the bed, too sad to move, and here she was—employed, her dark apartment feeling more like a home, cupboards full, son happy and loved. She saw again how one thing could lead to another and how much could depend on just one person's actions.

The trees were rich, mellow daubs of color but soft behind the diffusion lens of fog. The air felt moist and cool, the sky a perfect soft gray, cedars and tall firs dark smudges against the mountains in the distance.

She walked along thinking, and suddenly in this cool place so far removed from endless freeways, screaming cars, hot metal and glass, littered pavement and brokenness, things seemed possible. She felt as if a life was being offered to her, held out in the same hand that had misted this evening, had set those mountains in place, had carved the channel for the bay beneath her.

She looked around her at the bluff, at the sailboats, at the Space Needle and the tall buildings of Seattle, at the ferry chugging slowly across the water. She walked with her son down the steep hill, and for the first time she dared to think that maybe, just maybe, things would be all right.

Seven

$\mathcal{S}$OMEHOW DANIEL NEVER got around to taking the plane to Seattle. He called Sylvia on Monday morning instead of driving to the airport as he had planned.

"Come to my office," she invited. Daniel agreed, of course, and borrowed Lou's car. It was a dented brown Volvo with no rearview mirror and two bumper stickers: *Jesus Protect Me From Your Followers* and *The Last Time We Mixed Politics and Religion People Got Burned at the Stake*. The heater was permanently on, so Daniel rolled down the windows and hoped he didn't sweat. He drove through town, barely noticing the garbage, the smells, the sharp sunlight glancing off the chrome of the cars in front of him. He changed freeways by the civic center, looked out toward the bald, scorched hills, past the stunted trees and the tufts of dead brush. A few homes perched on the rocky cliffs, sharp, unwelcoming, like fortresses. He got off on Santa Monica Boulevard, drove through Hollywood, which was choked with tourists, as usual, and then he was in a different world. The traffic, dust, and dirt were left behind, and everything opened up. There were wide boulevards, eucalyptus and palms, clean, sharp skyscrapers, fountains, and pristine streets lined with designer boutiques and exclusive restaurants. Creative Talent Agency occupied a long, low building. Daniel found a place to hide the car a few blocks away. He slipped on his jacket as he went through the wide revolving doors.

Sylvia checked her makeup in the small mirror she kept in her desk drawer. It was fine. She closed the drawer, then one last time read over the contract she'd prepared. Standard agency agreement. Standard provisions. She looked up and stared at the wall. She hoped she wasn't making a mistake with Daniel Monroe. She knew how it was. One mistake, all right. Two, people started to wonder. Three, and you had the stench, the smell of failure, and around here that was enough to make them stop returning your phone calls. She felt a twist of dread when she thought about that possibility.

She rose up and went to the window. Wilshire was busy, the traffic a steady, sluggish throb, mostly of tourists hoping to catch a glimpse of someone important. The irony was that they had no idea who was important. The people who wielded the power were mostly invisible. Their faces weren't the ones on the billboards. She had a slight contempt for those whose were. They seemed tainted somehow. She wished it were possible to do her work without them. They were greedy, hungry children, all clamoring for the same breast.

She heard voices from the lobby. She sighed, dropped the shade, and turned toward the door. It opened, and her assistant poked his head in.

"Daniel Monroe is here."

She nodded and went to meet him. "Daniel," she said, putting warmth into her voice she didn't feel. "Welcome. Come in."

He came in. Sat down. More pleasantness. He was handsome. And he had the aura, too. She wanted to shake her head. What was it they had? Magnetism, she supposed, but she imagined it as something more crass. The power of an enormous, starved, vacuumlike ego, able to suck everyone into its vortex. Well, if he could project it onto the screen, that's what was important. She hoped it was strong enough to suck dollars from wallets.

She watched him sign the contract. His hands were strong, tanned. They moved without hesitation. He put the pen down and looked up at her, his dark eyes looking like melted chocolate. He sent her one of his smiles, the slow-building kind that seemed to give off heat. She began to worry less about having made a mistake. "Here's the name of the casting director. He's expecting you in the morning," she said.

"Thank you, Sylvia." His voice was mellow, deep, and rich.

She tilted her head in acknowledgment, allowed her hand to be clasped in his warm grip, then watched him walk away. The suit, an Armani, probably rented, looked as if it had been made for him. Would he make it? She gave a mental shrug, closed the door, and went back to work. They'd know soon enough.

———————

Three weeks later Daniel was out of Lou's duplex and living in an apartment in Santa Monica. He gazed at himself now in the rearview mirror of his leased car and tried on the new persona.

Sylvia had scheduled him for the audition the first week, a real plum, one of the leads in an established television series, *Court of Law*. He had gotten the part. He still couldn't believe it.

He'd sent some money to Lenore and Scott, and it wasn't that he had forgotten them or stopped missing them. But to tell the truth, his years with them were becoming a sort of alternate reality, time spent in a parallel universe, but it could be that the science fiction movie role he was reading for had colored his thinking. He still thought about Lenore, though, every day. Usually at night as he lay on the bed, the only furniture he had in the new apartment besides the wing chair. He felt bad when her face shimmered up in his mind. Then he lost the giddy excitement and felt empty, full of dread. He would lie there listening to the traffic on the boulevard droning like the rushing of a river. He would tell himself to get a grip, would remind himself of his good fortune, and finally the hollow feeling would pass. He was always relieved when morning came, though. He got up then and resumed his life.

His new life. It was as if he were two different people. The one who had spent all those years with Lenore and Scott—and Daniel Monroe. His image had begun salting Los Angeles on billboard advertisements for *Court of Law*. Yesterday he had seen his face go by on a bus. What an odd feeling. He'd been in the background, to the left of the main star, but still, there he was, a serious face pointed toward the judge's bench, pulling out from the transit stop in front of the Zippy Mart on Sunset Boulevard. He had felt it take hold of him then, and it reminded him of catching a wave and riding its crest. He felt as if he were caught up in something bigger than himself, something that would make him solid and firm and real.

He felt a strange sensation when he saw his image up there with the famous ones. It was odd, and it was interesting. Deflating, or too heady to take in. There were two possibilities, as far as he could see. Either he had somehow changed from being ordinary and had become extraordinary, or there was really nothing very unique or special about them, despite what he'd always thought. They were just the same as he was. He wasn't sure which was true. In fact, he wasn't very sure about much at all.

Take right now, for instance. Who was he, really? Was he Daniel Monroe, costar of the hit series *Court of Law*, driving a leased BMW on his way to have lunch with Renee Lapin, his costar? Or was he Scott's father? Lenore's—whatever? His aunt and uncle's prodigal? Someone who couldn't hold together the most elemental relationships of life?

Whatever the answer, right now, at this very moment, he didn't feel regretful or empty or lost. He felt extraordinary. He decided to keep his attention focused on this second in time.

He arrived at the restaurant a few minutes late, let the valet park the car, went inside, and saw her. There she was. Renee Lapin. Waiting. For him. She was on her second glass of chardonnay by the time he slid into the chair across from her.

"You're late." She looked interested rather than angry.

Renee Lapin, he told himself. *I'm having lunch with Renee Lapin.* Maybe not a megastar, but not junior varsity, either. People knew who she was. "Sorry." He flashed her the smile. "I got tied up with some contract negotiations."

She gave him an ironic glance. "I'll bet."

Daniel smiled at her. He had always wondered if they would be a disappointment close up, these women he saw on the big screen, wondered if their faces were retouched, the jiggle in their step edited out with airbrushes or something. But here she was, firm bodied, russet hair, bronze skin, perfect features, wide-set blue eyes, long, long legs stretched out under the table. She was gorgeous. She picked up the wine glass, curled her perfectly manicured fingernails around the stem, and took another sip of her wine.

"So how's it going?" she asked.

"Good." He nodded. "How's it going with you?"

"Fine," she said. She finally smiled then, showing perfect white teeth. He leaned forward in pleasure, but there, just at the gum line, he could see the faint line where the cap ended before the flesh of her gum began. He leaned back, wishing he hadn't seen. He felt disappointed, as if someone had told him there was no Santa.

"Are you ready to order?" she asked.

"Anytime you are." He forgot about the caps, concentrated on the happy thoughts again. The ones that had carried him on a cloud all morning. He was having lunch with Renee Lapin. He looked around at the other diners in the restaurant as Renee signaled the waiter. A few darted glances their way.

"I'll have a shrimp salad with raspberry vinaigrette on the side and bring me another one of these." She tapped the edge of her glass.

Daniel ordered something. He didn't really care what he ate. He looked around again and was gratified when he recognized a few people. It wouldn't be long, he told himself, before they recognized him, too. He felt a rush and a certainty that it wasn't just wishful thinking this time. Sylvia had said so. "You're something special," she'd told him when he'd signed the contract for the series, her voice genuine and true. "You're going to be a Hollywood brand name." He wasn't exactly sure what that meant, but he liked the sound of it.

"So," Renee said, "how's it going?"

Daniel looked back at her, somewhat startled by the sound of her voice. Hadn't she just asked him that?

"Fine." He nodded and beamed her another smile. "Just fine."

Eight

BY THE TIME THE DATE Daniel had circled on the calendar came, Scott had corresponded with his father twice by mail and Lenore had called Daniel to arrange Scott's visit, her stomach churning when she'd heard his voice. They'd kept their negotiations short, and she'd managed somehow to let Scott climb onto the United shuttle to L.A. with Daniel's firm promise that he would be there in person to meet him. They'd called her from the terminal at LAX to assure her the delivery had been completed, and Scott had stayed a week with his father. Though Lenore had expected he would be unhappy when he had to return home, Scott had been fine. Happy to be here, actually. It probably helped that he was anxious to see his new best friend, Derek. He'd gotten up and dressed himself for school the next day and had taken the armload of souvenirs he'd brought back with him for show-and-tell.

"That's Daniel?" Edie had asked when she'd seen the snapshot of Scott and Daniel tacked on the bulletin board for show-and-tell.

Lenore nodded and wondered if she was comparing the dark, brooding face with her brown hair and milk white skin. But Edie had just looked at the picture and then looked at Scott and then said, "I've seen him before."

Lenore had explained about Daniel's television shows and commercials. She had waited for questions, or at least the look she knew so well, but it had never come. The conversation switched gears, and they hadn't discussed Daniel again.

Lenore looked out at the apartment parking lot now, anxious to put Daniel out of her mind. There was no sign of Carlene yet, but then again, one thing she'd learned about her new friend was that she operated on a different clock than the rest of the world. In fact, she was different in most every way. Lenore had never met a religious person like Carlene before. She was an odd combination with her single-minded devotion and unwavering faith, her big hair, flashy clothes, and gaudy makeup. Carlene talked about Jesus with an easy familiarity, but there was nothing shy or retiring about her. And the thing that surprised Lenore most of all was that she liked Carlene so much. She smiled, just thinking of a few of the escapades she'd related.

"I once made a fan belt out of a rope," Carlene had boasted the first day Lenore had met her, when she had delivered Scott to Carlene for his after-school care with much trepidation and doubt. In fact, if it hadn't been for Grandma Eileen's recommendation, she would have turned around and gone back home. "She's a character," Scott's teacher said, "but she loves the Lord and she loves children. That's her little boy, Derek, right there." She'd pointed to a freckle-faced little boy with a broad smile.

Edie had echoed Grandma Eileen's recommendation. "She's got a good heart," she said. "You can trust her."

And Lenore had found that to be true. Whenever she showed up, even unexpectedly, the boys were happy, entertained, and well cared for. And she never had to wonder what Carlene was thinking. But Lenore didn't mind her bluntness. In fact, she found it refreshing to be around people who meant what they said.

"So you're working for Doc Ashland, huh?" Carlene had asked that first day.

Lenore nodded.

Carlene made a face and shook her head. "No. I could never do that," she said firmly, quick and definite in her rejection, as if Lenore had suggested she should.

Lenore just smiled, beginning to see that Carlene was a find if for nothing more than entertainment value.

"But you gotta do what you gotta do, that's what I say," Carlene had continued, then detailed exactly how she had tied the rope-turned-fan belt, trimmed the knot with fingernail clippers, and driven twenty miles to the nearest gas station. "If you know how something's supposed to work, you can fix it, right?" she'd asked, twisting her face into one of those goofy expressions she always wore.

Lenore didn't know. But she was learning. She had learned a lot from Carlene already in just a few weeks. After Lenore had gotten used to her wild outside, she'd begun to glimpse the good heart beneath the tough-girl exterior. She realized again how lucky she was that things had worked out the way they had. She realized how unlikely their friendship was but how grateful she was for it.

"It'll be great," Carlene had enthused when Lenore had first approached her about after-school care. "Derek's in the same class, so it's no trouble at all. I clean the church while he's doing school, and I can take Scott home with us when they're done."

Lenore watched Scott now, sitting on the curb in front of the apartment, anxiously waiting for his friend. Derek was six months older than Scott, making him an instant hero. The boys never seemed to get tired of each other's company. And Scott loved his new baby-sitter. She was free and easy, pulling the boys in when she needed to, but giving them room to play. Literally.

"I take them to the park every day and let 'em run around. Saves wear and tear on the furniture," Carlene told Lenore. And the four of them had already gotten together once for a movie—a matinee of *Oliver and Company*—and they'd had so much fun they planned today's trip. "I'll show you around my favorite shopping place," Carlene had volunteered. Lenore glanced out the window again, hoping for a glimpse of Carlene's red station wagon. She checked her watch. Carlene was only ten minutes late. It could be a while. She took off her coat and picked up the material Dr. Ashland had given her, the catalog and time schedule for North Seattle Community College.

"They have a nursing program," he'd said with a pointed look. "And if you want you can transfer to the university and get your bachelor of science in another year and a half. You should look into it. You have a natural ability."

Lenore had flushed under his praise. She was enjoying her job. Dr. Ashland said he liked her calmness with the patients, the way she seemed to know who needed firmness and who needed tenderness. But the thing that Lenore liked best about it was the feeling of finally being adequate. When hurt and sick children came to Dr. Ashland, he could fix them up. And she could help. Even if it was just recording their height and weight, taking their temperature, and passing on his instructions. She went home each day tired but gratified, knowing she had struggled hard but had done something worthwhile. She looked down at the catalog again, trepidation stirring in her gut. This, though, was something different. She wasn't sure she had what it took to go back to school. Just making the arrangements seemed overwhelming.

"You can schedule work around your classes," Dr. Ashland volunteered. "Eventually it will help me as well as you. You'll be able to do more around the office. Besides, you don't want to support your son forever on your wages as a medical assistant."

She supposed not. But, actually, cash flow hadn't been as much of a problem lately. Daniel had sent a letter to Scott last week and included a short note to her, along with a check for more money than Lenore had seen in a year. The thought had flitted across her mind that he had done something illegal until she'd read the explanation. *Got a good part. Will send more. Love, Daniel.*

Love, Daniel. Her jaw had tightened. Adrenaline had surged, for her grief had hardened into something more formidable of late. She had deposited the check, tossed the note in the garbage, and shoved down the turmoil of emotions. She would sort through them. Another time.

A flash of red from the parking lot diverted her attention. Carlene was here. Lenore locked the apartment door behind her, and by the time she'd gotten to the car, Scott was already in the backseat. Carlene extinguished her cigarette and fanned the air inside the car. "I thought we'd hit the St. Vincent thrift store at Lake Union. We ought to be able to find some good stuff there."

"Sounds fine," Lenore agreed, buckling her seat belt and suppressing a smile. Carlene hadn't thought much of the Danish modern furniture that had come with Lenore's apartment.

"Can she get rid of this stuff?" Carlene had asked Mr. Caputo.

"Sure," he'd answered with his ever-present smile, apparently not offended. "I'll just put it in the storage unit."

"I don't have money to buy furniture," Lenore had protested, and she'd been telling the truth at the time. It had been before the check from Daniel had come.

"You can afford anything where I shop," Carlene had assured her.

Lenore wondered briefly what Daniel would say if he knew she was going shopping at a thrift store. But then again, he probably wouldn't mind as long as no one else knew where the things had come from. That was what Daniel was concerned about. Looking good. On the outside. She was clenching her jaw again. She purposely relaxed it and turned her attention to Carlene.

"So they've got good furniture at this place?" she asked.

Carlene nodded. "Better than what you've got. Having all that junk around would depress anybody."

"I'm not depressed," Lenore retorted and thought maybe it was even becoming true, but Carlene wasn't listening. She was reaching into her purse and leaning over the back of the seat, handing each boy a candy cane and snaking wildly from side to side, barely staying inside her lane. Lenore readied herself to make a grab for the wheel, but Carlene straightened herself up in the seat, and the car stopped swerving.

"What?" she asked, giving Lenore an indignant look.

"Nothing." Lenore suppressed a smile and took the candy cane Carlene handed her.

Candy canes. She shook her head. It was hard to believe it was almost

Christmas. Scott would be leaving to spend a few days with Daniel the day after. The thought brought a pang, a twist of sorrow. *Why?* she wondered. It wasn't that she resented her son the time with his father. In fact, it was the opposite. *Take me, too,* she wanted to cry, but another equally strong voice shouted hateful things, things that a child who was hurt and angry would say. She shook her head again and thrust the bitter thoughts away. Her thoughts were an angry stew—confusing, contradictory, and tumultuous. There was only one thing she was sure of—she had no desire to celebrate the holiday. She supposed she would have to make the effort, though, for Scott's sake.

Carlene drove into the parking lot of the huge thrift store. They parked the car and went inside, and it didn't take Lenore long to realize that Carlene was right. There were treasures here if you didn't mind the fact that someone had owned them before you. She found a mahogany coffee table and matching end tables, only slightly scuffed, and two beautiful old white porcelain lamps that Carlene said would be fine with new shades.

"I can rewire them if they don't work," she said, "and for two-fifty apiece you can't go too far wrong. Look here," she'd continued, holding up a set of white ceramic mugs that at one time had had a Santa face painted on them. She scrubbed at one with her fingernail. Her chipped red polish looked as spotty as the Santa's piebald cheeks. "You can scrub it off, and then it's just a white mug in the shape of Santa. Cute, huh?"

"Very," Lenore agreed. Carlene nodded smartly and put all six of them in Lenore's cart along with an artificial evergreen wreath for the front door. "You need some cheer," she said. "If you don't have enough money, I'll pay."

"I've got money," Lenore said, her heart expanding at Carlene's clumsy kindness. "I have to have a real tree, though. It wouldn't be Christmas without a real tree." Where had that come from? Just seconds ago she'd decided she wasn't celebrating.

"Oh, totally," Carlene agreed, her smile a little smug. "Decorations are over there behind housewares."

Lenore followed Carlene's directions and looked through the ornaments, interested in spite of herself. She found three boxes of tree decorations, some of them classics, small glazed glass balls from the fifties, and before they left she'd also found a pair of black pants and a red sweater for Scott to take with him to his father's. If he needed anything fancier than that, Daniel could buy it, she thought bitterly. She shook her head, amazed at how quickly she had settled into this poisonous state, this venom toward him. Hostility shimmered around her like heat.

"You made a haul," Carlene enthused, taking Lenore's mind off Daniel again. "And in a month you'll never know the difference than if you'd bought it new."

Lenore nodded. She would clean everything off with Lysol and wash and dry the clothes, and when she was finished, it would be just like Carlene said. No one would tell the difference. The clothes would be sweet smelling with fabric softener, the furniture waxed and shining, the lamp bright, and the Christmas decorations merry.

Carlene took one last drag of her cigarette, then ground it under her heel before getting into the car.

"You shouldn't smoke," Lenore scolded her.

"Oh, I know." Carlene looked stricken with remorse. "But I always do it outside or I go in the bathroom and open the window. I'm quitting again on Monday."

They stopped at the Bi-Lo Grocery on the way back to Carlene's house, bought the makings for pizza and fudge, bought a six-pack of pop, and rented two videos for the kids: *How the Grinch Stole Christmas* and *Frosty the Snowman*. They talked and laughed and made dinner while the kids watched their movies. Afterward the boys went off to Derek's room to play, and she and Carlene sipped coffee, ate fudge, and talked, the television a muted buzz in the background.

"We'd better go," Lenore finally said around ten o'clock. Carlene went to get her keys and tell the boys to come.

As Lenore was gathering up the plates and cups, the television news went to a commercial, and Lenore heard a voice, a familiar voice, only what it was saying didn't make sense. "Your honor," Daniel said, "I object."

Lenore turned and stared at the screen, her mouth a small O, trying to make sense of what she was seeing. There he was, as beautiful as ever, in a sleek, dark suit. Suddenly it was clear to her where all the money had come from, why Daniel had so confidently asserted that there would be more.

Carlene came back into the room just then, Scott and Derek behind her.

"Hey, that's my dad!" Scott shouted. "That's my dad!"

Carlene looked from Scott to the screen, to Lenore to the screen, then back to Lenore.

Lenore nodded.

"That's the guy you just left?" Carlene clarified, her finger pointing to the television.

Lenore nodded as the announcer showed the last clip, of Daniel arguing with another character. Daniel in a clinch with the beautiful female lead. She waited for Carlene to laugh, to say no way, to simply disbelieve her. She did none of those things. She stood staring at the television until the commercial ended, then turned toward Lenore.

"Oh," she said, and Lenore saw understanding light her eyes.

Christmas came and went. Without great joy. Without great sorrow. Lenore had to work the day before and after, for which she was supremely grateful. On Christmas morning Scott opened his presents. After Mr. Caputo returned from church, they joined him and Edie for a turkey dinner.

"Oh, you're a doll," Mr. Caputo said when he opened Lenore's gift to him—a pen and pencil set. Scott's gifts were more personal. He'd given Mr. Caputo and Edie each a reindeer ornament he had made at school. Their bodies were clothespins, their antlers pipe cleaners.

"I love it," Mr. Caputo announced and then gave Lenore and Scott their gifts. Scott tore into his immediately. It was an art kit complete with paints, colored pencils, markers, and paper. Lenore opened hers slowly, wondering what it could be.

"You asked for some of my recipes," he said shyly.

She took off the last of the paper. It was a wooden box, and when she lifted the lid, she saw it was full of recipe cards for the meals Mr. Caputo was famous for. There in the front was Polenta and Chicken. Unaccountably her eyes blurred. She threw her arms around him and enfolded him in a hug. He gave her a pat on the shoulder.

"I never learned how to cook." She sniffed back her emotion.

"Nobody's born knowing how," Mr. Caputo said, and Lenore thought it was odd that he'd used the same phrase Edie had when she'd proposed the job for Dr. Ashland. "I can teach you."

Edie's gift had been a gentle hint: a leather assignment book. "I hope you can use it," she said, gently campaigning for the decision Lenore was closer and closer to reaching. "You'd make a terrific nurse," she encouraged.

Scott was delighted with the new G.I. Joe tank Edie had given him, and Edie seemed equally pleased with the gift they'd given her—a tiny silver filigree frame Lenore had found at an antique store by the church. It had cost more than she'd intended to pay, but it had looked like something Edie would love.

The day passed more quickly than she'd expected. She went to bed when Scott did, using the excuse that she had to rise early in the morning to take him to the airport. She knew she did not want to sit in the tiny, empty living room looking at the Christmas tree and thinking about where she'd been a year ago.

She took Scott to the airport the next morning, went to work, then came home, phoned Leslie, wished her a merry Christmas, and got her mother's new number. She left a Christmas greeting on her answering machine, then made Christmas disappear back into the storage unit until next year. Scott came back after the scheduled three days, another check tucked into his suitcase. And Lenore found an immediate use for the money. It would compensate for her reduced hours at work and pay for her tuition and books. She had decided to go back to school. In fact, the decision was actually helping her frame of mind. Terror was a fine distraction from sadness and anger.

By the time the first day of winter quarter arrived, her abject fear had toned itself down to a mixture of excitement and anxiety. Excitement was winning—by a hair. She drove to the campus, parked her car in the student parking area, and got out. The canvas tote containing her brand-new books and sack lunch felt heavy. By following the map they'd given her at orientation, she found without too much trouble the building that would house most of her classes. She was early and joined the crowd of people milling in the hall outside the lecture room.

"Hi." It was a woman with short brown hair, barely five feet tall. "Looks like we're the mature students," she said.

Lenore was surprised. The woman looked about forty, Lenore guessed. But Lenore didn't feel old. She wasn't old, she told herself. She was only twenty-four.

"I guess so," she agreed and followed the woman into the room.

They sat down at their desks, odd, tiered things in a new lecture hall that held about a hundred students.

She got out her notebook, wrote *January 5, 1989, Anatomy and Physiology,* hesitated, then put her pencil down and looked around her. The room was starting to fill up. A boy wearing a T-shirt with the name of a band she'd never heard of sat down in front of her. A young girl with a mass of brown curls tucked into a baseball cap took the seat next to him.

As the instructor entered the room, the lights dimmed, and an animated cell appeared on the screen at the front of the room. More students trickled in, and the light from the open door cut across the image each time it opened and closed.

"Anatomy and physiology are nothing but the sciences of chemistry and physics as applied to the human body," the instructor said. And school began.

The next morning she rose while it was still dark, made coffee, then brought out her books and sat at the kitchen table that she and Carlene had found on another outing, this time to the Goodwill store. It was oak. A little dinged, but solid, real, and genuine.

Lenore opened her anatomy and physiology book and started studying cell biology. How hard could it be? she'd comforted herself. Well, she was finding out. It had been a long time since high school, and the instructor hadn't been kidding about the chemistry and physics. There was a lot more to this than memorizing the names of the little parts of the cell. He wanted them to know the chemical composition of the cell membranes, the electrical charges on the ions that passed through them, and a lot of other things they hadn't covered in high-school science class. Lenore was glad she was retaking general chemistry. After the first few pages it had became obvious she needed a review.

She turned the pages and scribbled notes on the pad beside her, trying to make sense of concentration gradients and ionic and covalent bondings, why they would form and why they would break and how they affected things getting in and out of the cell and how that would make someone sick and what could be done about it. She felt a moment of panic. She would never understand this. *You're too old,* the voice inside her head was accusing. *Why are you even thinking of attempting something like this? You're not fit to be anything but a waitress, and even that's a stretch.* The voice sounded like a cross between her mother's and Leslie's.

She shook her head, looked at the wall, and breathed. In . . . out . . . in . . . out. Slowly, as she had done during her labor with Scott. It would be all right. She could do this. This wasn't too hard.

"One thing at a time. All things in succession." She repeated the advice Edie had given her but obviously didn't follow if the hurricane in her office was any indication. Lenore smiled; just the thought of Edie brought a little calm. She went back to her books, and before she knew it, the hours had passed and it was time to wake up Scott.

Nine

THE MAKEUP TECHNICIAN deftly feathered the side of Daniel's cheek with a brush.

"Just a little more on this side," Daniel suggested, stifling a yawn. He was sleepy. He'd gotten up at five for the fifth morning in a row after staying up until one o'clock memorizing his lines and cues. He wanted a cup of coffee, but his hair still had to be styled.

"Okay. You're done." The tech motioned, and Daniel slid over a chair without removing the drape that covered his clothes.

"Think I could get a cup of coffee?" he ventured to ask.

"Esme, fetch Daniel a cup of coffee, will you?" the hair stylist called over his shoulder.

Daniel didn't hear an answer and wondered if there was anyone there at all. He didn't know if he was being paranoid or perceptive. More and more he was beginning to feel as if he was being managed.

He rubbed his eyes, careful not to smudge the makeup, and almost expected to see Scott playing with his trucks in the corner, the bored intern he'd paid to baby-sit during his son's brief Christmas visit looking sleepy and out of sorts in the chair beside him. But Scott wasn't here. He'd gone back home almost three months ago.

"Here." A girl, maybe twenty, wearing blue jeans, a huge sweater that draped off her shoulder, and a ponytial emerging from the side of her head, set a Styrofoam cup on the counter. The sides of the cup were brown with coffee that had sloshed and dried. Daniel tried not to wonder why a fresh cup of coffee would have stains. He picked it up, careful not to lean out from under the stylist too much, and sipped it gratefully. It was barely warm.

"Tip your head," he said.

Daniel was trying to remember his name. Harold or Howard. Something like that. He tipped his head.

Harold Howard combed and fluffed, snipped, repeated the process. Daniel thought about Scott.

The two visits had been wrenching jolts. The first one, especially. It had reminded Daniel of when he'd been sixteen and learning to drive. He'd accidentally shifted into first while going sixty-five on the freeway. Looking at Scott's small figure as he came off the airplane holding the hand of the flight attendant, Daniel had felt that same jolting to a stop, all progress impeded. Scott had looked awed, excited, a little frightened, joy and relief on his face when he'd located Daniel.

"Daddy," he had cried out, and hearing that name had made Daniel's heart thump. Daniel had covered the ground between them in a few strides, bent down, and picked up his son.

"Oh, buddy, I've missed you," he'd said and closed his eyes, feeling that skinny little body, those bumpy little ribs, that silky hair and cheek next to his, and it seemed as if they had never been separated at all. In fact, he had looked behind Scott, halfway expecting to see Lenore coming through the doorway next, but there had been no slight, angular figure with a crown of wild hair and a blazing smile, just the flight attendant shifting her weight from one foot to the other, waiting to be dismissed. Not that he had ever really imagined she might come. When they had spoken on the phone, her voice had been too businesslike, too brief and clipped, yanking him out of his daydream of reunion.

Once they'd left the airport, once they'd driven through the clogged freeways to the apartment in Santa Monica, everything had become different between him and Scott, as well. For there was no Lenore oiling the machinery of his fathering, and he realized immediately how much she had done. She had taken care of the mechanics—the food, the bed, the clothes, the necessities—leaving him to play. With no Lenore he had had to do it all, and it had been awkward and uncomfortable. Even the basics had been difficult to arrange. Daniel had paid a gofer from the studio to buy a bed and put it together, but neither one of them had thought of sheets, so Scott had made do with blankets and pillow on the bare mattress. Daniel hadn't bought a television yet. They'd eaten most of their meals out. It had been a patched-together time, an imitation of home, and Scott seemed to feel it, even though he hadn't complained.

Christmas had been more of the same. Daniel had taken some time off. The studio had shot around him for two days. Daniel had taken Scott to the mall and let him pick out some toys, but it seemed pointless to wrap them and present them as gifts. Besides, there wasn't any tree. Again, no time. They had gone to Denny's and had pancakes for breakfast, then to

Knott's Berry Farm, then gone home and played with Scott's toys. By the end of the three days, at one of the early begun, never-ending days of shooting, Scott had looked up from the expensive toys with a blank face and asked when he was going home.

He would do better next time, Daniel promised himself, though when the next time would be was sketchy. Maybe Scott's spring break. Maybe summer vacation. He yawned again and continued his ruminations. It was a season for reunions. For in addition to Scott's visit, Daniel had finally heard from the folks back home. Not the congratulatory call he'd been half expecting. Instead, his uncle's somber voice had greeted him from the answering machine last week after he'd returned home at midnight from a long day of taping.

"Your grandmother died," he'd said, his voice heavy, thick with the accent Daniel had worked so hard to rid himself of. "Funeral's Tuesday. I don't suppose you'll be able to make it." A slight pause, then, "I saw your show on television." Daniel cringed and wondered which episode he'd seen. It didn't matter. There was something in every one that his uncle would find offensive. "I can't believe this is really happening to you, Danny." His tone saying the rest. "Anyway. Your aunt Dorothy made copies of Grandma's pictures and fixed up a little photograph album for each of you boys. We'll send it on." A weary sigh. Then a click. No good-bye.

"There." Howard Harold pulled off the drape, and Daniel stood up, his bones grateful for the stretch.

"They're waiting for you in wardrobe," he said.

By the time Daniel finished in wardrobe, breakfast was no longer being served. But one of the servers, a young girl who could have been the twin of Esme, filled a plate for him and stuck it in the microwave. The eggs were too hot and the bacon rubbery and barely warm, but Daniel was grateful all the same. He supposed he could ask for an earlier pickup tomorrow. He took a sweet roll from the box on the table and refilled his coffee, not even worrying about the grimy cup, and waited for his first scene.

He was lucky to be here, he reminded himself. This part was a plum. He realized it only too well. Jack Forester, the guy who had played the district attorney, had opted out this season to see if he could make it in films, and Daniel had gotten the part of his replacement, the brash young lawyer.

A low, lustrous voice came from the cluster of chairs behind him, and he turned. It was Renee. He turned toward her, and she smiled and said something in a lower voice to the woman she was talking to. They were talking about him. He could tell. Daniel's attention wandered to the other

female star, currently the object of the director's angst. Her boyfriend had
brought their baby to the set again. Apparently it was a thorn in the director's side that she was holding up shooting while she breast-fed.

"It's in the contract, Todd," she called out breezily and used her little
finger to break the baby's suction on her breast so she could switch sides.

Daniel grinned and found himself remembering Lenore and Scott. He
had loved the way Scott would look after he had nursed, head lolling to
one side, stomach distended, a lazy look of contentment on his face, bluish
white milk dribbling down his cheek. He felt a sharp pang.

He finished his coffee with one long swallow and pitched the cup
away. He checked his watch and counted how many hours until lunch.

The promised family photograph album was waiting for Daniel when
he arrived home. It was late—nearly one in the morning, and he was tired.
But he made himself a drink and sat down in the chair. He tore off the
brown wrapper, opened the bumpy black cover, and stared. The first picture, an old black-and-white snapshot, presented itself to him like a scene
from a film. He drew close and examined it. It featured a long table
covered with several overlapping tablecloths set, oddly enough, with plates
and glassware, silver, and cloth napkins. Odd because it was outside, a table
in the wilderness, so to speak, with a birch forest the backdrop, the mottled
silver Vs of the tree trunks rising up behind them. His five aunts, the wives
of his father's brothers, lined the right side of the table. Renata, the
German war bride, looking plump and timid. Betty, pretty, dark-haired,
flashing eyes, and white teeth. Susie, plain and sour-looking, the same as
he'd always remembered her. Dorothy, blond and dimpled. Wanda Jean,
looking tired already, one of the perpetual babies at her breast. His own
mother was on the other side of the table. Face smiling, dark hair waving
softly back from her face. His father, thin, wearing his navy whites, stood
behind her, his hands on her shoulders. There were children clumped
around. He recognized a few of his cousins. What had they been celebrating? he wondered, with the mounds of fried chicken, the white cake
high on the raised plate, the jugs of iced tea, the mounds of potato salad.
A birthday? An engagement? He looked again at the smile on his mother's
face. He turned the heavy cardboard page.

Another black-and-white photo with scalloped edges, of him this time,
a fat-cheeked baby on his grandmother's lap. A cornfield the backdrop.
She sat in a ladder-backed chair. Another odd setting. As if someone had
dragged the chair far away from the house, plunked it down on the freshly
plowed earth, and invited her to sit to have her picture taken. He leaned
forward to examine her. She was tall, he remembered that, and had a plain,

oblong face. Very ordinary. Homely, in fact, though he had never thought of her that way. She wore wire-rimmed spectacles, and the photographer had caught her with her eyes closed, which gave her a peculiar sense of humility, of modesty. As if she were protesting her worthiness to be caught on film. Daniel's own infant face gazed at hers adoringly. One of her hands was over his bare foot, protective, affectionate. He stared at that for a long minute before he turned the page, and suddenly he felt a sense of loss at her death. Eleanor Houston Monroe. Who had she been? He didn't know. He didn't suppose he ever would.

He tried hard to remember her and came up with a few memories patched from the sporadic visits his mother had arranged after his father's death. He remembered she had a feather bed, and he had loved to sleep at her house. He had liked feeling it mold to his body, then waking in the morning and feeling the dent where he had lain. He would rise early and find her already in the kitchen frying eggs, the bacon draining, the grits on the back burner, the supper's pies already lined up like soldiers on the sideboard. He remembered her sitting at her oak table, reading her Bible, a large black leather affair, its cover cracked with age and probably tears, he realized when he thought of his father's escapades. She had had a kind manner, a loud, cackling laugh, and an equally loud voice. She had meted swift justice and at times had had a ruthlessness he'd admired. He remembered her wringing the neck of a chicken with quick, passionless dispatch, scalding it, and plucking out the feathers as he watched, fascinated.

He had gone with her to church a time or two and been frightened by the intensity of her faith, with the pain it seemed to cause her. *"Ask Jesus into your heart,"* she had urged him. He had repeated the prayer because it seemed to ease her distress. She had smiled, satisfied, as if some deep, eternal business had been transacted. He had been nine at the time. He thought again of that whispered prayer, at its obvious lack of effect. He wished he had something traumatic to which he could attribute his inoculation to faith.

He flipped through the rest of the album. There were a few photos of the coal camp, the place his grandmother had made her home before the labor unions demanded a living wage, before the bulldozers had carved tidy little housing developments out of the hills and hollows. He flipped past his mother and father sitting on the porch steps, his father's '57 Chevrolet, another one of him with a cousin, a flighty girl of ten at the time, wearing a fluffy peasant blouse, a mean squint in her eye. Pages and pages more.

He stopped again at the last one. His grandfather and grandmother in this picture, and it must have been taken just before his grandfather's death.

The old man was in pajamas yet was still regal in his straight-backed rocker, his hands folded on his lap. His wife sat beside him, equally gaunt and imperial, her white hair a crown. Behind them a bed, a crooked picture, a curtained closet, a calendar. Daniel turned the last page. The family cemetery. A small square of ground fenced with iron and climbing ivy. The neatly marked marble headstones all bore his name: Monroe.

He closed the book, feeling as unsettled as if someone had told him that all these years he'd gotten his own name wrong. He stared, not sure what to make of it. As he was confused, he resorted to his usual method of organization. He sent money. A generous check toward the headstone, a graveside wreath the size of a sports car.

Ten

"I DON'T WANT to watch *Mr. Rogers.*" Scott had that tone again. "I want to watch *Ninja Turtles.*" He looked at her, wary, and changed the channel without breaking his stare.

Lenore turned away without commenting and made a note that she shouldn't start fights that she wasn't prepared to win. She had been carefully consistent in disciplining Scott, who seemed to be going through a stage of testing limits. But this time she knew she was wrong. Her rule was arbitrary and only recently enforced. *Ninja Turtles* had been forbidden because it played on the same channel that ran *Court of Law. It's 7 A.M.*, she told herself, *and during cartoon hour they would be advertising action figures and breakfast cereal, not prime-time adult dramas.* She was getting paranoid in her zeal to avoid seeing Daniel's face.

Something had changed in the months since she'd left him. At first she felt as if she'd been turned liquid inside and poured out into great pools of misery. Now she was learning that hurt coagulates into a sort of stiff self-control, and that, in turn, hardens into cold anger. It felt like a piece of metal—lead, perhaps—that she carried around with her between her breasts. It took up more room than she had available and made her stomach feel constricted and her heart flattened, each beat jarring as though it were pressing against something hard.

The first few weeks after her flight she had rerun that last little scene with Daniel in the kitchen, regretting the hasty words she had said. But those thoughts had been replaced. Now she kept remembering what *he* hadn't said. He hadn't said he'd marry her. How could a man do that? she had wondered times beyond counting. How could a man say over and over again that he loved a woman and yet let her go, along with the child they had together? She cast back in her mind and went over every bit of their life together, the parts she cherished and the memories she tolerated, and all were reinterpreted in this last insight, this last key to understanding Daniel. He had never really loved her. She saw that now. How could she ever have thought differently? She looked at herself each morning and evening and despised herself. She had seen the pictures. Of the woman Daniel had chosen after her.

A picture of them had been on the cover of one of the tabloids last week. She'd been standing in the line at the Safeway, and there they'd been. Daniel and Renee Lapin, or whatever her name was. The hot gossip was that Renee was married, so it was actually more about her, Daniel just being the pretty face, the boy toy marriage wrecker. Still, every week there was more of him and in places she'd formerly considered safe. He was like some monster with tentacles that reached all the way up the interstate, surprising her when she least expected it—when she sat down to eat breakfast, when she watched a movie with Carlene, when she waited in line to buy a gallon of milk.

The series Daniel starred in had already been a success, and Daniel, of course, was an instant hit. They seemed to feature him in every clip, smartly dressed and darkly handsome. She couldn't avoid him, so she took to turning the television off. She'd even tried to extend her zealous avoidance to Scott, but obviously that wasn't working too well.

She had bought a tabloid last week, surreptitiously, as if she were buying pornography. She'd read it and reread it, studied the picture, looking closely, examining the corners of his eyes, the set of his mouth. Looking for some little hint of unhappiness that would bring her sharp joy and then piercing pain. She had wept, then taken it out to the Dumpster. She did not love him, she reminded herself hotly. She would never love him again.

She finished packing Scott's lunch now and then went into the bedroom. There, on the dresser, was a framed photograph of Scott and his father at Knott's Berry Farm, taken at Christmas. Lenore clenched her jaw, angry at yet another intrusion. She turned it sideways, just enough so she didn't have to see it. She heard a slight noise. She turned, and Scott was watching her, his face blank, hurt swimming in his eyes.

She finished with work a little early, and instead of heading straight to Carlene's to pick up Scott, she turned toward the church. It was cold and sunny now, but a clump of dark clouds obscured the sun from time to time. It had been one of those unpredictable March days that blazed sunshine and pelted rain by turns. She passed the shuffling crowd waiting for the bus, one of the old electric streetcars. Its arms followed the cables strung above the streets. How nice, she thought, to have your route planned. To know that there were no more choices. No decisions to make. No surprises but no mistakes, either. This far you may go. No farther.

She drove up the hill, past Harborview Hospital. The News 7 van was parked across the street, satellite dish high. The reporter was standing in front of it, talking into a microphone. They always came here and stood outside the hospital for their newscast when there was a particularly gruesome accident, a car wreck, a fire. This was where they brought people when they were the most crushed and wounded, the sickest, the worst off. If they couldn't help you here, no one could.

A few vagrants sat shapelessly, hopelessly, on the concrete stoop out front. Patients in various bizarre outfits propped broken limbs and sat in wheelchairs outside the emergency room, smoking. It seemed odd to see them. Wounded people. Broken people. Lingering around the entrance. Not staying inside where there was healing and help. She drove past them, felt their eyes on her, turned the corner, and parked beside the church.

She went inside to Edie's office. The light was on and the door open. It was in its usual state of elegant chaos.

"Hi," Lenore said.

Edie looked up from her computer, her face breaking into a smile. "Hey, you. Come in."

Lenore went in and sat down in front of her desk.

They chatted, but after a moment, Edie narrowed her eyes. "My finely honed powers of perception tell me something is on your mind. Care to spill?"

Lenore didn't smile. In fact, when she opened her mouth, the poisonous words spilled out like acid. More words than she'd intended to say. More than she'd known were inside her.

Edie cocked an eyebrow. "Maybe you should elaborate," she said wryly. " 'I hate him so much I wish he'd die isn't exactly the kind of detail I was hoping for."

Lenore told her the details, every ugly thought and feeling. She told about Renee Lapin, her beautiful hair, her fine, thin features, her tall, elegant body, her beautiful lips and golden skin. Edie listened quietly, then nodded. She reached across the table and took both of Lenore's hands in both of hers. Her eyes were calm but serious. "Bitterness will eat you alive," she said. "You have to deal with it."

Lenore stared at her bleakly. Bitterness seemed like such a hard word. So settled. Like it wasn't going anywhere and would never change. For a moment she felt fear replace the hard anger. She didn't want to feel like this forever. She couldn't imagine feeling this way forever. "I'm afraid it will grow and grow until I can't love anyone," she said.

"It will," Edie confirmed, and Lenore felt another chill. "It's already started taking root."

"But what am I supposed to do?" Lenore asked, her tears stinging again.

"Nothing," Edie said, and Lenore looked up at her, surprised. "There's nothing *you* can do. But *He* can."

Lenore wanted to scream. She didn't need to ask who Edie meant. *He* was the subject of every conversation. They talked about *Him* as if He were sitting across the table from them right now. *He told me this,* they would say. *He showed me that.* She'd been coming to church with them for weeks now, and none of it made any sense to her. Scott, on the other hand, had come home last week and made an announcement.

"I asked Jesus to come into my heart," he'd said. Great. Now *He* had moved into the apartment.

"Oh," she'd answered, having quickly considered and discarded several other options. "That's nice" seemed too trivial. "Why?" too rude. She'd finally settled on "Tell me about it."

He had, brown eyes firm in his decision. "Grandma Eileen said our hearts have bad things in them, but if we ask Jesus to come in, He cleans everything up." He said it matter-of-factly, as if the fact were common knowledge. "You could ask Him, too, if you want."

She remembered that now. "You could ask Him, too, if you want."

"You know what I'm going to tell you," Edie said, almost reading her mind.

Lenore nodded. They had had several conversations on this subject. No matter what question she asked—How do I make a wise decision? What do I do when Scott asks about his father? How can I feel better? And now what do I do with this anger? No matter what the question, the answer seemed to be Jesus. Asking Him in, as if He were a wealthy guest who might take over the house payments.

"I'd have to forgive Daniel, then, wouldn't I?" she asked.

Edie nodded slowly. "But He would help you. And really—would you rather keep going on like this?"

Lenore didn't answer.

"It's entirely up to you," Edie said. "He's a gentleman. He doesn't break down the door."

Lenore sat still and could hear the clock ticking on the bookshelf behind her.

"But the consequences of whatever decision you make will belong to you, as well."

"What do you mean?" That sounded frightening. Permanent and ir-revocable.

"You get whatever you choose," Edie said, "in this life and the next. Healing and forgiveness or bitterness and alienation from everything good. It's up to you."

Lenore opened her mouth and felt her face grow red. "But Daniel's the one—"

"I know. I know!" Edie held up her hand. "And before you start, no, it's not fair that he hurt you like this and he gets to go free. None of it is fair. But the command to forgive is because God wants *you* to be free, not because Daniel deserves it. But it's still your choice. You can cut your losses now and forgive, or you can keep on paying and hoping that some-day you can pass the charges on to him. But believe me," she said, and her face twisted into some private regret of her own, "it's never as sweet as it seems."

Both of them were quiet for a few minutes. Lenore could hear her breath coming in ragged bursts. She was feeling something inside. The cold lead turning molten and burning her again. "How can I forgive?" she asked Edie, her voice plaintive, like a protest.

"You start thinking about Jesus," Edie said, and Lenore glanced toward the other picture she had on her wall. Jesus as a healthy, fit man, face glowing, rowing a boat across a lake, a large group of people waiting for Him on the other side. "You think about what He gave up to be able to make you His child. What He did for you when you didn't deserve it. Then maybe what Daniel has done won't seem unforgivable."

Lenore sat there for a few minutes longer. She was afraid she might cry, so she stayed silent until she felt she had herself under control. She thanked Edie, took the Bible she offered, and left.

It was almost like it was a conspiracy. She'd gotten no more than a few steps into the hall before she heard her name being called. She turned. It was Matt, standing in the doorway of his office.

"Hi," he said, his earnest face looking happy to see her. "I was just telling Jenny this morning that we needed to call you and Scott and check on you."

"Thank you." She didn't know what else to say.

"Have you got a minute?"

She sighed and nodded. Matt went into his office and reappeared wearing a jacket. "I was just heading next door to meet Jenny. It's our night out. Care to join us for a cup of coffee before you head home?"

Another religious chat was the last thing she wanted. She checked her watch. "I need to get Scott," she said.

Matt smiled and shrugged. "Fifteen minutes, tops. Carlene won't mind, will she?"

"Probably not," Lenore said and forced her face into a smile.

Matt led the way to a small coffee shop on the next block. *Spiro's,* the sign said. Jenny was waiting inside and waved at them from her table by the radiator.

"I was just thinking about you," Jenny said, beaming. Looking happy to see her.

"Sorry to crash your date," Lenore apologized.

"I twisted her arm," Matt said, leaning down to give Jenny a kiss.

The three of them chatted about nothing. The waitress came. Matt ordered coffees and baklava. He insisted on paying, peeling the bills from the thin bundle he pulled from his pocket. Lenore felt a sudden humility and shame at her churlish attitude.

They talked awhile longer. About Scott, about Dr. Ashland, about nursing school, about Jenny and Matt's kids. The waitress delivered the coffee and food. They sipped and stirred and nibbled the sweet nutty pastries.

"How are you doing?" Matt finally asked. His eyes were kind, revealing no ulterior motive. He had none. And neither did Edie, Lenore realized. She, after all, had been the one who'd come asking for advice.

"I'm fine," she said, determined not to spoil their evening with a recitation of her personal woes.

"Really?" Jenny asked.

"Pretty much," Lenore said. "I am struggling with a decision," she admitted, keeping her statement as vague as possible. "That's what I came to talk to Edie about."

Jenny nodded and waited for her to go on. Matt didn't press her for any information, either. He added a dollop of cream to his coffee.

She nibbled at her baklava. It was very good. The nutty flavor rolled around her tongue; the honey stuck to her fingers. She washed the sweetness down with a sip of coffee. It was hot and strong, just the way she liked it. "Did you ever have something that you thought you were supposed to do, but you didn't understand, and you didn't want to do it?" she asked.

Jenny nodded.

"Sure," Matt said.

"What was it?" she asked boldly. Maybe he'd tell her it was none of her business.

"Coming here to this church," he answered just as bluntly.

She frowned. Not the answer she'd been expecting. He finished the baklava with one more bite, wiped his fingers on the napkin, then took another drink of his coffee. She waited for him to go on. He didn't.

"Well, what happened?" she finally prodded.

He shrugged. "I've never been to seminary," he said, "or even to Bible school." His blue eyes were straightforward. "I went to college at the University of Washington and lived in a Christian men's house. My mentor was a retired missionary who was into church planting." He gave a wry smile. "You can probably fill in the blanks."

Lenore shook her head. "I'd love to hear the details."

Matt smiled. "They had a church here on First Hill, an old congregation, a dying star. Multiracial. Greater Grace Tabernacle. At first he just asked if we could fill in for four weeks. I could preach." He nodded toward his wife. "Jenny could sing. I told him I wasn't qualified. 'Ask God,' he said. 'If He calls you, what other qualifications do you need?' I asked God. We prayed about it for two solid weeks, and at the end Jenny and I both had the same feeling. We were supposed to say yes. Well, we showed up on the first Sunday, and I have to say, the place was on life support. The first week I preached, we had a grand total of thirty in attendance and about half of them came late. Jenny and I did the service, went home, and marked one week off our calendar. The month dragged on, and at the end of it my friend called to say the pastor had decided he wasn't coming back from his sabbatical. The church sent a delegation to ask us to stay." Matt grinned. "I still remember what I did. I went home, went into my little closet office, fell down on my knees, and said, 'No. No. I won't do it. Absolutely not.' " Matt grinned. "Don't ever say that to God. It's like waving a red flag in front of a bull."

Lenore smiled, took another sip of her coffee.

"We said we'd give it a few months. We found out there was a small group at the church led by Eileen Wilson—Grandma Eileen," he clarified, "who'd been praying that God would raise the church up to be a beacon. We began praying with them. There were about seven of us. Things didn't get much better at first. The only new people we got were homeless folks who wandered in from time to time and drifted out halfway through the service. About half of what was left of the congregation didn't like my preaching and left. It looked like we would lose the building because we couldn't make the mortgage payments. Finally I realized I didn't have the answers. I was discouraged, exhausted, completely frustrated by the spiritual apathy of most of the people I was supposed to be leading. Things came to a head one Sunday morning. I just quit preaching in the middle of the sermon. I went to the altar and invited everyone else to join me. I knew I needed to be broken before God until He spoke or the last person left. We prayed the rest of that Sunday morning. Picked up where we left off on Sunday night. Continued Wednesday. Sunday morning again. Every service we knelt at the altar. Jenny played. We sang and fell on our faces before God. And something happened. In me as well as in the people. I quit trying to find the solution, the answer to our problem. It was right there in front of me. The cross of Calvary. After three weeks of seeking the Lord's face by falling on our own faces, there were fifteen people left. At some point we felt the Lord telling us to lift our heads. We drew our chairs in a circle and covenanted with Him."

Lenore realized she was leaning forward, intent on Matt's story.

"He had very clearly impressed on each of us individually through the Scriptures, through the voice of the Spirit, what He wanted. 'Lift me up,' He said, 'and I will draw people to myself. Seek my face; humble yourselves. Lift me up, and I'll take care of everything else.' We promised to make praise and prayer the cornerstone of our church. And God has blessed us."

Lenore thought of the three bulging services, the spill of bright-faced people, the eager workers. The joyful singing. She didn't know what to say.

"The Christ of Calvary still changes lives," Jenny said quietly.

Lenore met their eyes for a moment. She felt something stirring inside her. It troubled her. She looked away. No one said anything for a few long minutes. After a while she cleared her throat. "I'd better go."

Matt stood up, smiling. "We should, too. We want to catch the early show so we can get home before the baby-sitter puts the kids to bed."

"Thank you for the coffee," Lenore said.

"Our pleasure." The three of them put on their coats and made their way out. He held the door open for her and Jenny, then the two of them waved good-bye. Lenore watched them cross the street, hand in hand, and merge into the crowd of people.

She picked up Scott, fixed his dinner, played with him, read to him, put him to bed. But she kept thinking of the last words Jenny had spoken: *"The Christ of Calvary still changes lives."* She knew, in some way she couldn't explain, that those words were true, and she felt herself poised on the edge of another decision on which the rest of her life might hinge. That night after Scott was in bed, she took out the Bible Edie had given her, an old one of her own. She opened it at random. She flipped open the page and her eye landed on one verse, underlined and highlighted in yellow.

Unless a kernel of wheat falls to the ground and dies, it remains only a single seed. But if it dies, it produces many seeds.

Wasn't that what she had wanted? To have her meager life count for something? Suddenly she had the image of a huge, productive garden. Rows of peas and beans and tomatoes, corn, and vines shading plump, round, dusky globes of grapes. Fruit. Lovely, beautiful, nourishing fruit. That's what she wanted. That's what she had always wanted, she just hadn't known it.

The man who loves his life will lose it, while the man who hates his life in this world will keep it for eternal life.

Edie had written a quotation in the margin: *"He is no fool who gives what he cannot keep to gain what he cannot lose."*

Lenore stared at the page in front of her. The words stabbed her with their truth, for that's exactly what she'd been doing for as long as she could remember. Trying to keep. Trying to keep her life together as her mother and sister strove to unravel it. To keep Daniel, to keep their life together, and now she was trying to keep him away. The exhaustion and utter weariness of it tore down to her bones. She couldn't think why God would want her. She shut the book and went to bed but lay there for a long time not sleeping.

It was one week later, exactly, that she became the new Lenore. She was sitting at the kitchen table, Scott asleep in the bedroom behind her. The small apartment was quiet, the only sound the slight buzzing from the stove clock. She was reading the Bible again, and it was the oddest thing. She opened it up at random again and just began reading, since she had no idea how to go about it, and right there on the page before her was the simple phrase: *Here I am! I stand at the door and knock,* and she realized that's exactly what she'd been feeling, been hearing, for the last weeks and months. It was just as if He had been patiently but persistently knocking. Not pounding down the door in an angry frenzy, but not timid little taps, either. They were good strong raps, but only every so often. And she knew, as well, and the thought sent a chill down her back and arms, that, ever the gentleman, He would not continue to knock forever. He knew she was here. Eventually He would assume she had made her choice. She had a feeling of panic then, shame at her stubbornness and pride, and an irrational urge to go to the apartment door and fling it open, and if she had found Him there on the plastic welcome mat, a part of her would not have been surprised. Instead, she squinted her eyes shut, bowed her head, and clasped her hands together tightly.

"Please, come in," she whispered urgently. "Come in. You can have me. Do anything you want. I give up."

What a rush of relief accompanied those words, what clean winds blew in with Him. What sweet fresh air. What a deep, flowing river of peace began to surge from between her breasts. She could have laughed or sung. Instead she wept, silent tears coursing down her face. She didn't need to read the next words to know that something had transpired. Something had taken place and been transacted. Something had been handed over, and something had been received. Her eyes fell on them anyway. She ate them up, treasured them, received them into the deepest place of her bruised and tattered heart. *If anyone hears my voice and opens the door, I will come in and eat with him, and he with me.*

She wiped her eyes and had a vision of the first day at Mr. Caputo's, when she had shown up at his door, lonely and bedraggled and frightened. She remembered that table, loaded with delicious food, lined with kind faces and tender hearts. There had been an empty chair, she remembered, and now she could almost believe He had been there. Sitting, waiting patiently for the right moment.

She bowed her head and wept bitterly, as suddenly the choices she had made with her life seemed shabby and unworthy of His presence. She told Him so, and as she did, peace seemed to find the hidden corners and twists of her heart. She didn't know how long she stayed there. She would turn pages and read, then stop and talk to Him, feel His answers, and see them in the words before her. When she finally felt finished, it was nearly two o'clock. She wasn't as exhausted as she might have expected. She felt fierce and, for the first time in her life, solid and immovable. She lay down and slept, the leather book on the pillow beside her, her hand over her heart.

———

She began to see that Edie was right. She felt as if her pain had cut a deep channel inside her, but now instead of the molten lead, little trickles of joy were starting to flow through it.

It began the next night when she wrote the letter.

Dear Daniel, it began. *I've been angry at you, but I'm not anymore. I pray God will bless you in every way.* She tried not to imagine him reading it or to guess what his reaction would be. She just sent it, along with one of Scott's school pictures, feeling as if she were casting seed into the wind. It wasn't her job to make them root. It hurt, but it was a clean, healing hurt. She felt as if her bitterness and gall had been drained away and now the healing could begin.

Little by little she could feel her edges, torn and ragged from having been ripped apart from Daniel, begin to heal. She prayed, and in her simple-mindedness she could almost imagine Jesus speaking back to her. She prayed for Daniel, and soon she actually began wishing him well, wanting blessing and peace for him, and in a strange way she desired him less. Now that someone else had moved into her heart.

She read the letters this Someone had written to her—surging, passionate declarations of love. *Fear not,* He said, *for I have redeemed you; I have summoned you by name; you are mine. . . . You are precious and honored in my sight.* She gazed at herself in the mirror, and it seemed that even her face had changed. It was softer. It shone. He thought she was beautiful, and that fact seemed to make it true.

She whispered her love back to Him, and every night before she went to her studying, she spent a little time writing things down. Things she didn't want to forget, and she promised herself that she would try to always remember how it had felt to be alone, to have no friends, not even a single face that was familiar and kind. She wrote down how she had felt when she had been rescued by Mr. Caputo and Edie Hamilton, for that was how she thought of it now. Because it was only now that she could see what they'd really done for her. She'd been rescued. Their hands had reached down and pulled her up when she was sinking into the sucking mud that had become her life.

She told them about her decision to give her life to Jesus. She went to the Bible study at church on Wednesday night, and they cried and hugged her.

"You've met life's truest friend," Mr. Caputo said, his eyes shining with tears.

She tried to thank them again, but Edie said not to worry and repeated what she'd said that first night—that if she knew the Lord and His ways, Lenore's turn would come to say thank you, and Lenore began to think about how that might work out. And she made a vow then that she would never let someone go away hungry when she had food on her table, or be homeless or alone or friendless when she had a bed or room on the floor and a sleeping bag. And she felt a thrum of excitement, a whisper of anticipation. Now she felt that she, as well as Daniel, was on the cusp of great change.

She was sure of it when Daniel's birthday came in May. She took out the card she had bought for him, and she wrote another note. Simple, clean, but wishing him well. She included another picture of Scott, this one a snapshot Grandma Eileen had taken of him. He was sitting in the front of the class with a crown on his head. All the other children had told him what they liked about him, and Lenore included a copy of the paper Grandma Eileen had sent home with their compliments written down. She put it in the envelope inside the package from Scott. She shed a few tears then. Not for herself this time. For Daniel. For how much he was missing. Did he regret his choice? she wondered and wept again, but then she felt better after she had done it. Sad, but with a warm comfort inside.

It was the next day that the commercial came on, and that was when she was sure God had healed her bitter heart. She was folding laundry and there was Daniel again, and without even thinking she shouted for Scott to come. He was in the bedroom playing a game with the kids from the apartment next door.

"Scott, come here—quick," she hollered, and all of them came running. She pointed to the TV screen. "Look!" she said, just in time to see Daniel do battle with a Kung Fu master and send him careening off the hood of a parked car.

Scott looked at the screen, then at her, eyes shining. He turned to the other boys. "That's my dad," he said, his face reverent.

"Cool," said the other kids in turn. "That is so cool."

And Lenore felt nothing but deep, warm peace.

Eleven

IT WAS A LONG, BORING DAY, and Daniel kept dozing off as he waited. He wasn't sleeping well these days. He took a drink of his seltzer water in an effort to rouse himself, squeezed the lime over it, then licked the tangy oil from his fingers. This time he was waiting for lighting to be adjusted so he could go onto the set of *Court of Law* and film the final argument scene. He rubbed his eyes. They felt gritty and burned. He could catch a nap, but the couch was too small, and he'd probably be shaken awake just as he dozed off and have to shoot the scene groggy. He thought about turning on the television mounted in the corner of the RV, but it seemed like too much trouble. He stared at the wall instead. It was textured and covered with something that looked like homemade paper and was a nubby beige like the loveseat in the corner. He checked his watch and stretched, tried to let his mind blank out so he could pass a little faster through the interminable waiting that had become his life.

At least he got a little more respect from the crew now and his own RV dressing room. But his schedule was boring and harried at the same time. They would film the new episodes of *Court of Law* in a marathon three-month session, then dribble them out over the year. After that he would go to Hong Kong to shoot his new action movie with a Kung Fu master. American detective teams up with Chinese policeman. A little strange, but who could tell? The martial arts were big. If this movie became a success and his next movie—a drama—hit a chord, this could be his launch.

He felt a little shudder, like a draft on his neck, when he thought of the other possibility—that they would tank and take his almost-career with it. Even the thought of that felt like a death, or at least a terminal diagnosis.

It was okay, he told himself. It would take more than one bomb to ruin his career now. Even more than two. He was on his way.

And he was happy, he reminded himself. He'd seen himself in the tabloids last week. The third party in Renee Lapin's love triangle. Her megastar husband was in the foreground, but who cared? It was all just hype anyway. Renee and Charles were separated, with paper work on the way. But being in the *Globe* and the *National Enquirer* was a rite of passage for him, a sign he'd passed some kind of milestone. His agent had even told him he had a few dozen fan clubs, and she'd given him a list of them. "The Official Court of Law Fan Club," one boasted. Then there were the others: "Jennifer's Daniel Monroe Adoration Group," "Kelly's Daniel Monroe-athon." And so on. They noticed him now, the fans, when he went into a restaurant, when he walked along the street.

Sylvia called him every so often, whenever his name was mentioned somewhere. "Be sure to check out *Variety* today, page twelve." Or "I'm sending you *Entertainment* magazine. You're in the 'Hot Deals' column." And *People* magazine had called Sylvia and said they wanted him for the cover. It would be a montage of him plus six or seven other actors with the headline "Stars on the Rise." He'd gone for the shoot and later he'd looked at the proofs of the page. There he was, in his black Armani suit with cigar in hand, arrayed in a square with the other actors. How odd it would be come spring to see his own face—small though it was—staring back at him as he waited in line at the grocery store. And how odd it already had become to not be able to go to the grocery store without stares and clumsy approaches by strangers. Last week a photographer had trailed him down the street like a clicking ghost. He watched it all as if it were happening to someone else.

"You're becoming that Hollywood brand name I told you about," Sylvia teased him.

The tightness inside had eased. Eased but not disappeared. And oddly enough now, as he waited for his call and thought about it all, he remembered an aunt of his. *"That woman is mentally unbalanced,"* his mother would say whenever her name came up in conversation. *"No sooner does she wean one baby than she starts on another. She should have litters instead of children."*

Daniel had wondered from time to time, in an absent sort of way, what kind of compulsion made his aunt want to fill up that cradle every year, but now he felt a different version of it himself. His wasn't a compulsion to reproduce anything but success, but he wanted to do it again. And again.

He had always thought that his first big success would prove something to him, and to *them*, whoever *they* were. But even though he'd achieved success on the television show, he felt it really had proved nothing. Then they had moved his character more into the spotlight. It wasn't enough. Now he wanted to do films. With every success he felt the need to surpass it and to succeed more quickly and decisively the next time. *Do it again; do it again!* the cheering squad in his ear kept whispering. *Bigger. Better.*

He took another sip of the seltzer and heard a scuffling outside his door. He gave a sigh and checked his watch again. It couldn't be much longer now.

Why did he need to do it again? he wondered, returning to his line of thought. He was already a household word—even the question to an answer on *Jeopardy*. Just last week he'd been watching television, sitting here as a matter of fact, and the category "Shared Surnames" had come up. The answer was, "This star of a prime-time courtroom drama shares the same name as the fifth president." And the science teacher from Cincinnati had gotten it right. "Who is Daniel Monroe?"

Who is Daniel Monroe? The answer seemed farther away and more elusive than he had ever thought possible. His memories—of sweet joy when he held Scottie for the first time or of lurching pain when he held him and said good-bye the day he left—had receded into a dim past. They were harder and harder to recall on command. Instead, they came to him when he didn't expect them. When he didn't want them.

Who is Daniel Monroe? He was beginning to put that nagging question out of his mind in a number of ways. He wasn't an alcoholic, but once or twice a week he got quietly slammed, sitting in the chair, drinking whatever he had. He supposed he should get out more. He was alone a lot, except for Renee. Maybe if he got out, he would start to feel better.

He heard the scuffle get closer, and someone knocked on the dressing room door and opened it at the same time. No one ever waited for him to invite them in. It was odd to be so lonely and have so little aloneness. He took one last sip of his seltzer and nodded at the woman in the doorway.

"We're ready for you now, Daniel." It was the young assistant, the one who had a crush on him. She gave him a brilliant smile.

"Be right there," he said and walked out, pulling on his jacket as he went.

———

Daniel let himself into the apartment, set the package and letters down on the floor beside his chair. He went to the window and pulled open the drapes. The traffic was clotting the promenade and boulevard even though it was after midnight. The lights of Santa Monica glared at him, dull and hazy. He had decided he didn't like Santa Monica. It had the feeling of just missing to him. Of being just outside the borders of the place where

. . . where what? He wasn't sure. But whatever it was he craved, it wasn't here.

And this place, this apartment that had seemed so luxurious to him just months ago—what had he been thinking? What had been wrong with his eyes? How could he not have seen that it was on the last decent block, right on the edge of the poor section? He vaguely remembered Lou's couch, the duplex on Tarzana and Viburnum. He supposed that's why this small one-bedroom had seemed such a step up. Not anymore, though. Now he just felt a flicker of shame when the driver from the studio picked him up, aware of the trail of bums drifting over from Venice Beach, of the cheap concrete-block houses just a half mile away. He had decided last week to look for someplace a little more upscale. Maybe in the Hollywood Hills. He wasn't rich yet, but there must be a few places he could afford in better neighborhoods. He would call someone. Tomorrow.

He checked his watch. It was late, and he had a six-thirty pickup in the morning. He ought to go to bed, he realized. He poured himself a glass of Scotch instead and sat down in the wing chair to look at his mail. After all, today was his birthday.

His aunt and uncle had remembered, of course. There was a small thin box, and as expected, it yielded a tie. He opened the card, dreading it. Also as expected, there were Bible verses. One on the front next to the man fly-fishing and another inside, written in his aunt's uneven hand under the pleasantly banal sentiment, *May God Bless You on Your Birthday.*

He read the front again. *You open your hand and satisfy the desires of every living thing.* He opened the card again and read the other. *I have come that you might have life, and might have it abundantly.* She had added a short note, hoping all was well with him. The usual reference to Scott and Lenore was painfully absent.

"Oh, Danny, I'm so sorry," she had murmured when he'd told her they'd left. "She is such a precious, sweet girl. It was just the *situation* we objected to." He had said he understood, had given her Lenore's new address and phone number, and had ended the conversation before it shifted to him.

He dropped the envelope at his feet and opened the next one—heavy white stock with Creative Talent's logo on the return. From Sylvia. How sweet. A note jotted on her embossed stationery. He added it to the pile and sorted through the other envelopes. Two bills. A few ads. Finally there was just the package. It sat there at his feet like a bomb in a shoebox. The voice started whispering to him again. Daniel had first heard it the day he'd received the letter from Lenore.

What have you done? it had asked him. Not excited or angry. More deliberate, as if the asker already knew the answer but wanted him to see it.

He hadn't answered that question, in fact, had stifled the feeling that accompanied it—the churning, sick suspicion that he had made a terrible, horrible mistake. He still remembered how he had felt as he'd opened that first letter from her. Actually, he didn't have to remember, for he felt that way again right now. His heart was thumping from anticipation or dread, he didn't know which.

Dear Daniel, she had written. *I've been angry at you, but I'm not anymore. I pray God will bless you in every way.*

He had sat there for long minutes just looking at the letter. There wasn't much more. She had signed it *Love, Lenore.* She had included a picture of Scott. And suddenly it had come clear to him what he had done, the bargain he had made. It was as if someone, just for a moment, had flashed on a light, and even now he could still remember the sick, thudding regret he had felt as it had shone.

Fortunately, it hadn't lasted long. After a moment or two his common sense had asserted itself again. He became habituated to the words in the letter, to Scott's bright face smiling up from the small square of glossy paper. The glaring pain had dimmed. He had decided to put the picture in his wallet. The letter in his bureau drawer. They were both still in their places, hidden carefully away.

But now here was another uninvited guest, this box wrapped in brown paper. He sighed and pulled off a strip of tape. The paper fell off. It was, indeed, a shoebox. Not a name brand. Something he'd never heard of, and it had to have been Scott's shoes that had come inside it. Black and white, size five, Spiderman with light action heels. So Scott had Spiderman shoes that lit up when he walked.

He lifted the lid. His hand shook slightly. He took another sip of Scotch, brushed away a layer of tissue, and lifted out a cellophane-wrapped package. Fudge, with nuts. His favorite. He blinked. Sniffed. Took out the next item. Something balled up, fuzzy. A pair of socks. Lime green. He smiled. No doubt Scott had picked those out himself. On the bottom something was wrapped in more thick layers of tissue. He extracted it. A piece of plaster of paris with his son's handprints pressed into it. He stared at it for a long time, as if it were a hieroglyph that might yield some piece of wisdom if he could read its meaning.

Finally he opened the card. It was simple. Nothing overly sentimental. A photograph, a nice one actually, of a vineyard. He remembered the Russian River painting Lenore's sister had given her one Christmas and smiled. Lenore had always had a thing about grapes, had always said she wanted to plant them, had been fascinated by the way the dusky globes of fruit hid beneath the wide, scalloped leaves. He stared in disbelief. More Bible verses. *I am the vine* was lettered across the bottom of the card in calligraphic script, *you are the branches. If a man remains in me and I in him, he will bear much fruit; apart from me you can do nothing.*

He gave a little frown. He had never known Lenore to be religious, and this was the second time she had said something about God or religion in as many letters. He wondered if she had gone off the deep end. He read the phrases again and realized something about the sentiment unsettled him. And it was certainly an odd thing to tell someone on his birthday. Was it a small jab? He opened it up. Blank inside. She had written *Happy Birthday, Daniel* in her own hand. *We are well. Hope all is good with you.* And again, *Love, Lenore.* Scott had signed his own name in wide, sticklike letters. There was another picture of Scott. A snapshot of him at school. Daniel stared at the picture for a minute. His son with a crown on his head. He looked down at the paper, at all the nice things the other kids had said about him. He felt a strange sense of looking at himself. Could feel their approval soaking in and filling something up inside him. He shook his head and brushed the thought away, and before he had a chance to feel anything else, he quickly stashed everything in his drawer. He couldn't sleep, though, even after he had closed the curtains and gone to bed. He just lay there, eyes open, staring at the blank, dark room and hearing the swish of the traffic going by outside.

Twelve

1992

THEY HAD MERGED INTO a seamless team. All day long they worked in tandem. Dr. Ashland didn't need to tell her what to do any longer. Lenore knew, without having him say a word, what he would need and when he would need it. And he knew her, as well. Knew when she was in over her head, when patients were stacked in the waiting room, when phone messages were stacked on her desk. He would come and sort through them, also without saying a word, taking half with him. Often she would see him in his office, long after everyone else had left, writing in charts, phoning patients. She had felt guilty that she only worked half time and had often urged him to find someone else to take her place. He had steadfastly refused. He had been her biggest supporter as she had worked her way through nursing school. Two years at the community college for her RN certification, then another year and a half to earn the degree. And he had been there last week when she had gone through graduation ceremonies at the university, had clapped and cheered wildly along with Edie, Mr. Caputo, Matt and Jenny, Carlene and Derek, and a little contingent of church members when she received her diploma—a bachelor of science in nursing.

She smiled, savoring the joy. She realized with a surge of gratitude that she never would have made it without Dr. Ashland. She had grown to respect him greatly over the years. Had it been years? Almost four, she counted, as she waited for him to finish writing the prescription for the newborn with an ear infection. She felt her usual stir of compassion for him. He seemed so driven. And so lonely.

There had been a Mrs. Ashland, she knew. She had found that out soon after she had begun working for him. She had been in his office looking for a chart in the pile on his desk and had seen the framed picture on the credenza. An attractive woman. Small, with short dark hair. The two of them had their arms around each other's waists. Both were wearing shorts and hiking boots, standing on a lookout. He had come in behind her, and she'd felt as guilty as if she'd been rifling through his desk drawers instead of just looking at a picture in plain view.

"My wife, Michelle. She died," he had said shortly. "Last year."

She had turned and stared at him. His face was stark, his gray eyes full of pain.

"A drunk driver." Nothing more. But what more was there to say?

"I'm so sorry," she had answered quietly.

He had nodded, and for a moment his eyes had stared past her to a place she couldn't see.

His telephone had rung, and the moment was broken. She had watched him draw his pain back into that deep place where he kept it, and by the time his hand had reached for the receiver, his face was controlled, back to its usual pleasant expression.

In time she had learned more about him. He lived in a modest house in North Seattle. He had no children. Not even a dog or a cat. His life was defined by his work. And church, of course. He was on several committees and the board of elders. Truth be told, at first Lenore had been a little afraid of him. In awe. But he had thawed over the last three years, and she thought she knew what had happened. The grief had receded, allowing the real Erik to reemerge. It had happened to both of them, she supposed.

"Here you go," he said, handing her the chart and the prescription. He flashed her a smile, then hesitated. "Wait a minute."

She waited as he took the billing sheet, crossed out the standard charge for an office visit, and wrote in half the regular amount. "Husband's out of work," he explained briefly and handed it back.

She nodded and felt almost reverent as she carried it back inside and handed it to the grateful patient. Oh, how she knew that feeling of helpless dismay as the waves broke on your small island. She hoped she never forgot.

She saw the last patients out, then went back to the nurses' station to work her way through the telephone messages on her desk, steadfastly ignoring the warm June afternoon beckoning her from the window. She checked her watch and was relieved to find it was only five. She would be out of here in time. Edie had been positively mysterious about their errand. If she weren't so busy, she might be more curious. She put the matter out of her mind again and picked up the telephone to call the mother of the baby with the rash.

It was five-thirty by the time she left the office and nearly six by the time she picked up Scott, went through the McDonald's drive-through, and arrived back at the apartment. It was a dazzling day, and she consoled herself that there was still plenty of it left to enjoy. Every now and then Seattle seemed to apologize for its sullen weather by blazing out gloriously. This was one of those days. The air was balmy, the sky crystal clear. Mount Rainier loomed to the southeast.

Scott went outside to play. She changed her clothes and went outside herself, onto the stoop to enjoy the sunshine while she waited for Edie, taking the study guide with her out of habit. She sat on the concrete step and flipped through a few pages, but her heart was definitely not in the task. She had thought she was finished with studying, and she would be as soon as she passed the state nursing board exams. She looked down at the study guide with weariness. It would be over soon, she consoled herself, and focused her attention on the paragraph she'd been perusing. Diabetic ketoacidosis, symptoms and treatments. Scott and his friends began a game of kickball. She set the book down and surveyed the porch of her apartment, now crowded with her garden—three huge pots filled with an assortment of pansies, marigolds, petunias, and geraniums. She stretched her legs out across the flowered welcome mat.

Inside, the apartment had finally become home. She had long ago relinquished the bedroom to Scott. She and Carlene had found shelves at Goodwill that now covered one whole wall for his toys and books, and she'd bought an inexpensive set of bunk beds so he could have friends spend the night. She slept on the couch, staying up late each night, reading either her nursing texts or the Bible Edie had given her, still her favorite, though she'd purchased several more. She had no idea when it had happened, but at some point, when she hadn't been paying attention and without even trying, she had become happy.

It hurt to think of Daniel, of course, but the pain had lessened with time. In fact, she had bought Scott a scrapbook and some rubber cement and had helped him find and paste in clippings about his dad—at least the ones that were fit for his son to read.

Perhaps the explanation was that her heart had been given to another—to this stranger she had met. Her initial surrender to Him had grown into a fierce, protective love. She smiled now as she thought of it. At the thought that He needed her protection. She shook her head, knowing that wasn't it at all. It was her own love for Him she jealously guarded, and she was ruthless in dispatching anything that came in the way of it. Her prayers were passionate, hot, and all consuming. She held nothing back. She was His, and the knowledge filled her with a hot joy, a surging peace wilder than any thrashing river. She was His. What more did she need?

She often read the story in the Bible of the woman who poured out the costly perfume and anointed Jesus' feet. She prayed, imagining herself there, salving on the precious ointment, washing the callused feet with her tears, drying them with her hair. She vowed away her life, recklessly, joyfully, and whispered her deepest desire to Him each night, for His ears alone. "Do whatever you have to do to keep me close," she told Him. "Take me to be with you, but don't leave me here without you."

She prayed this way because she knew herself. She knew the weakness of her will, the unfaithfulness of her heart. "Hold me close," she whispered and pictured the painting in Edie's office, the woman on the rock, the waves crashing around her, her slender arms clasping, clinging to the cross, and she knew that He would never let go of her. It was her own fickle grasp she distrusted. "Save me from myself," she told Him, authorizing in advance whatever He needed to do. Better to go into His presence with His name on her lips and in her heart than to live here without Him, to go back to that futility, that emptiness, that longing for who knew what. She would not go back. She vowed it; she prayed it.

"Don't let me outlive my love for you," she whispered, and she felt He took that devotion and sealed it tight. She smiled, thinking how some would think her crazy, unbalanced, to take comfort in the thought of death. But to her, it wasn't like that. Not an end, not a casket lid closing on hopes and dreams and life. It was a step. That was all. A foot extended from this dry, dusty place, coming down on fresh, living soil. Her heart would find its true home there.

Edie drove up. Lenore waved a greeting, then went inside quickly and put the study guide on her desk, which occupied a corner of the living room. She eyed the bookshelf beside it, lined with nursing textbooks. One more hurdle and they could be packed away. She felt a sense of release and anticipation, marred only by her slight sense of letdown that she wouldn't be going to work at a hospital. And it wasn't that Dr. Ashland hadn't practically invited her to quit. She gave her head a small shake. Erik had given her a chance when she'd had no other options. She wouldn't desert him now that she could actually be of some use to him. He had offered her a raise in his usual no-nonsense way. She had thanked him and taken it, though money still wasn't much of a problem. Daniel had been as good as his word about sending more, and her savings account was getting quite healthy. In fact, she'd been thinking about moving, postponing the decision until after school was finished. Well, she realized, that time was here. She stashed the matter with the book, locked the apartment door, and climbed inside the car. Scott had come from across the courtyard where he'd been playing with his friends and was already in and buckled into his seat belt.

"Okay, so what's the big mystery?" Lenore asked, climbing in and buckling her own seat belt.

Edie shook her head, still tight-lipped. "I've got something for you to see," she repeated, the only information she'd dispensed on today's errand. Lenore didn't mind. She liked surprises.

They drove down James Street to First Avenue, then turned north onto Queen Anne Avenue, and as they climbed the hill, the neighborhood began to look familiar. When they passed Dick's Drive-In, Lenore was sure of it. This was the serene neighborhood she'd wandered through her first day in Seattle. The land of the big old houses, the huge trees, and buckled sidewalks. They wove through the quiet, shaded streets, and finally Edie parked the car before a beautiful old home, its wide green lawn surrounded by a picket fence. The door was dark red. A wide porch spanned the entire front of the house. The yard was shaded with trees—maples and firs and cedars. It was a grand old house, square and settled far back from the street, stately and calm. Lenore followed Edie out of the car, stood on the spacious porch, and waited, almost holding her breath, while Edie fiddled with the key. She had a sense of anticipation, of portent. Even Scott was oddly quiet. The only sound was the tinkling of faraway wind chimes.

Edie turned the key, swung open the door with a mellow creak, and motioned them in. The entrance hall had dark oak hardwood floors under faded Oriental carpets. The same was true in the living room and dining room. A soft, diffused glow of sunlight filtered in through ivory lace curtains. The one or two exposed windows shimmered with old, wavy glass. Lenore felt a sense of familiarity. As if she'd been here before.

"Most of the furniture went to the family, but Mrs. Hosford, the owner, left some of it."

Lenore nodded, a tingly excitement building as she waited for Edie to unfold the story. She followed her into the dining room. It was huge, and the owner had left an oak dining table of gigantic proportions. It would seat at least fifteen. There was a built-in china hutch, a lovely chandelier out of what looked like pewter with tiny acorns adorning it. Even with the size of the table there was plenty of room to walk around. The floors were hardwood and covered with another old Persian carpet.

"The kitchen is sort of old-fashioned," Edie said, sounding apologetic. "But it could be updated." Lenore followed her in and looked around, smiling in delight. There were old-fashioned enameled units for the sink and cupboards, and in the corner was a massive black Monarch wood cookstove.

"There's an electric range, too," Edie said. "This carpet would probably have to go," she added, indicating the yellow shag.

Lenore grinned. It looked warm and cozy to her. "I love it the way it is. I wouldn't touch a thing." She could hear Scott's feet echoing on the stairs. Edie led the way and they continued their tour.

The living room was huge and empty. The study had three walls of built-in bookshelves, still full of books, and the wall facing the street was all windows. The second floor had five bedrooms, and two more gabled ones were on the third floor. There were three bathrooms. The basement had been finished into two rough bedrooms, a laundry area, and a storage room.

The back yard was huge. Outside the back door there was a brick patio, a pergola covered with grapevines, and a garden with a fountain and a gazing ball. Everything was choked by weeds, and the grapevines had gone wild, covering everything in their enthusiasm, but it was beautiful. Lenore sat down on the step beside a huge purple bush. A butterfly bobbed over it, and as she watched, a fat, fuzzy bee joined it. She swept her eyes across the neglected yard. It had been beautiful once. It could be beautiful again.

Edie sat down beside her. "Tiffy Hosford was a heroin addict. She died when she was nineteen," she said, holding out a yellowed newspaper clipping. Lenore gave her a questioning look but took it and examined it when more information didn't seem to be forthcoming. It was an obituary. Tiffany Marie Hosford. She glanced at the date on the corner. Five years prior. Born, died, survived by, visitation at. Nothing distinctive. She looked up at Edie, questioning.

"She died of an overdose, but that's not the point." Edie handed her another obituary. Patricia Anne Hosford. Born in 1925. Again the obituary was brief. She had died last week. No cause of death. No family listed.

"Tiffy showed up at the food bank at the church. We tried to help her. Got her cleaned up a time or two, but she'd always go right back to the streets. After Tiffy died, we got a nice note from her grandmother"— she held up Patricia Hosford's funeral notice—"thanking us for everything we'd done. Matt and I phoned her to see if there was anything we could do for her. She thanked us and said no. She was a believer, but a very . . . oh . . . reserved woman. We both felt that was the end of it. We wished we could have done more, but that was that."

"Okay." Lenore nodded again. She felt like one of those bobbing dogs people kept in the back of their car windows.

"The executor of Mrs. Hosford's estate called Matt last week. She left her house to the church."

Lenore could feel her eyes growing wide. "This house?"

Edie nodded.

"Wow." She couldn't think of what else to say. It was lovely. A beautiful gesture, and she had a glimpse at what it must have meant to the woman to know that someone had been kind to her granddaughter. She blinked, remembering her own hopelessness and the kind hands that had rescued her. She didn't have a house to give them, but suddenly she wished she had.

"Anyway, I wanted you to see it. Now, if you don't mind, we have one more stop to make."

"Sure," Lenore said. She felt a pull of regret as she left the wide, kindly halls, as they pulled the door shut and locked it, as they walked to the car. She stared at the gracious old house, its rambling big bones, its worn beauty. Soon there would probably be a *For Sale* sign on the lawn, and though the church could always use the money—this would fetch a lot—she hated to see it fall into the hands of strangers. Somehow she felt a connection to this house. To this place. They drove away from Chestnut Street, back down the hill, back to the gritty real world. She gave a sigh. It had been a lovely little trip. But it was time to get back to reality.

———————

They faced her, a warm, beaming group around the long table. Lenore would have felt afraid under other circumstances, but today she was too puzzled to be intimidated. Edie's stop at the church had turned into a meeting with the pastor and the elder board. If they hadn't all looked so happy, she would worry she was being called to task. Erik was there, a small smile playing on his lips.

"Well, you've seen the house," Matt said without preamble.

Lenore nodded, caution and excitement competing inside her.

"Mrs. Hosford's will specified that the house was ours, to do with as we pleased. But she had a desire for its use," Matt continued. He picked up a piece of paper and read from it.

"I have wished for this house that I've loved so well to be a blessing, to be used for God's kingdom rather than to benefit just one family or a few individuals. It is also my desire that it be a home again. I suppose these two are mutually exclusive wishes. I shall leave it to you to sort things out as you see fit."

"We've been praying since we got the news," Matt continued, "and we feel the Lord leading us in the same ways she was led. We feel the house is to be set apart for kingdom business. And we feel it is to be a home. We also feel that the Lord has given us some additional direction. Your name and face kept coming to each of us when we brought the matter to the Lord in prayer."

Lenore looked around the table. The five men smiled again and nodded.

"I don't understand," she admitted. Her heart was thumping out agreement, though. Whatever it was they had in mind, she knew she wanted it. Without question. She was on the edge, ready to leap. *Slow down,* she cautioned herself.

"We also felt the Lord directed us to a portion of Scripture," Matt continued. He opened his Bible and began reading aloud. " 'A father to the fatherless, a defender of widows, is God in his holy dwelling. God sets the lonely in families, he leads forth the prisoners with singing; but the rebellious live in a sun-scorched land.' " He set down the book.

Lenore absorbed the words, and they landed in her heart with sure, sweet certainty. She didn't fully understand them, but she knew she would.

"So after much prayer we feel that the Lord wants to use that house to bless people without families," Matt continued. "That He wants it to be a home where people can live and be family to one another."

"Who would they be?" Lenore asked. "How would it work?"

Matt shrugged. "The *who* will be whoever the Lord sends. As to how, I guess that will work out as we go along."

She sat thinking about what he'd said and about the part he hadn't yet clarified. *"Your name and face kept coming to each of us,"* he had said. She wanted it so badly she was afraid to come near the thought. She opened her hand under the table. *Whatever you want,* she told Him in the silence of her mind. *That's what I want.*

"Would you and Scott like to be the first residents?" Matt asked quietly, and her joy lit into flame like a starved fire when the door is thrown open.

"Yes!" she cried out. "Oh yes!" From the time she'd seen the old house, she'd known it was to be her home. The thought of filling it up with other people gave her joy. "Could Mr. Caputo come, too?" she blurted out.

"I *knew* you were the one to head it! I told the board today!" Edie was almost jumping up and down in the seat beside her.

"That's exactly what we were thinking," Matt confirmed with a smile. "You and Joe would be the charter members, the first occupants."

"Who else?" Lenore asked, thinking of all those empty bedrooms.

Matt shrugged. One by one the elders shook their heads. Edie turned toward her and smiled. "They'll come along when the time is right," she predicted. "Just keep a candle in the window for them."

Thirteen

LENORE GATHERED UP the last of her cleaning supplies and loaded them into the car. One more day and things should be finished. The church had already thrown a massive work party last weekend. They had painted the inside of the house, cleaned out the gutters, mown the tall grass, and trimmed the shrubs. Today was the finish work, as Carlene called it. She checked her watch, called for Scott, and climbed into the car. They were going to be late. Sure enough, Carlene was waiting for them when they arrived at the doughnut shop, the designated meeting place.

"Sorry," Lenore apologized with a smile.

"No problemo," Carlene answered. She ground out her cigarette and dropped the butt into the trash. She was fastidious about her smoking etiquette in an attempt to atone for the habit. "I got doughnuts," she said, holding out a bag. "And coffee. One for Joe, too."

Lenore thanked her. Mr. Caputo was already at the house, working on the yard. He had vowed she would have her garden this year, even though they'd be getting a late start.

"I'll follow you in my car," Carlene said. "I'll take the boys."

Lenore nodded, waved, and drove slowly so Carlene could follow. It wasn't far. She drove onto the street—her street—and felt the joy again as she saw the house that would soon be her home.

Mr. Caputo came around from the backyard and helped them carry in their cleaning equipment, then went back to the garden. He was happy with his progress. "By the time we're moved in, I'll have the weeds gone and the ground tilled." Lenore had already checked some books out of the library and had plans for a vegetable garden and flower beds. She was looking forward to seeing them restored to their former glory. Scott and Derek ran outside to join Mr. Caputo. She could see he had cleared a spot along the back fence for his tomatoes. It was a good place, according to Mr. Caputo. "They'll get direct sunlight, and the stone wall will keep them warm," he'd explained.

She went inside, looked around for a moment, then went to work tearing out shelf paper and wiping out cabinets. She could hear Carlene's none too dainty footsteps as she looked over the house. She came back from her tour, pronouncing her opinion as if delivering a verdict.

"This is okay," she said. "It's big enough for Sherman's army, but I like it."

"I'm sure it will fill up. Why don't you move in with us?" Lenore asked again. Carlene had been the first person she'd approached after Mr. Caputo, exercising her newly minted authority to invite anyone as she felt led.

Carlene had thanked her but still declined to move into the house with them.

"It's not my style," she'd said. "Besides, they wouldn't let me smoke."

"You could smoke outside," Lenore had argued.

"Uh-uh," Carlene shook her head. "No thanks."

Now Carlene reached into her tote bag and pulled out a pair of rubber gloves. "I just got my nails done," she explained. She went to work on the stove, and before Lenore had finished one cupboard, Carlene was already finished scrubbing the top and had the burners dismantled. She was spraying Easy-Off on the inside of the oven and talking at the same time, turning her face away to avoid the fumes. "You know, I bet there's hardwood under this carpet." She eyed the yellow shag carpet with barely disguised contempt. "Want to rip it up?"

Lenore didn't trust the gleam in Carlene's eye. Besides, that was another day's project. "Not today," she said, taking the firm tone she had discovered was the only thing that tempered Carlene's enthusiasm.

"Whatever," said Carlene, shaking her head as if some people were beyond her understanding and going back to work on the oven.

They worked steadily, stopping to order pizza at lunchtime. By the end of the day they had polished and washed and cleaned, vacuumed and shampooed, dug and swept and watered. The gardens were bare brown earth, ready for seeds or plants, the three tomato plants lined up staunch and solid in their new home. Lenore stood quietly watching the last beams of sun shimmer through the old leaded-glass windows, watching the lace curtains flutter and float against them with the breeze. It was beautiful. And it was her home.

The housewarming party was the following week. There were about twenty people gathered for cake and coffee and blessing.

"This is for you," Edie said, and Lenore wondered what was in the large package wrapped in brown paper. She tore off the wrapping, then stood shaking her head, not able to believe it. It was the lithograph. The woman clinging to the cross.

"Oh, Edie."

"Don't say you can't take it. It's supposed to be here. I just know," she added, anticipating Lenore's question.

Lenore blinked. She had always loved that picture. "I'll hang it right here in the living room so that everyone who comes through the door will see it."

Carlene was not to be outdone. She'd made a welcome sign in her painting class. It was beautiful, Victorian in style, with vines and rosebuds and calligraphic letters. *He has set the lonely in families,* it said.

"Edie suggested the words," she explained. Lenore didn't fight her tears this time. She hung it in the hallway so it would be the first thing she saw when she came through the door.

Carlene seemed pleased.

Matt called them together and blessed the house. "Use it for your purposes, God. Make it a beacon of light, and draw those here whom you call. The ones on whom you decide to pour out your awesome love."

"Amen," Lenore said, and she wondered who the people would be. Where they would come from and when. She imagined a man, bending his head against the sharp wind, making his way here. Or perhaps a woman, holding her child against a frightening, lonely world, and she remembered herself in that motel room, hearing the noises through the filter of darkness, praying in her inchoate way for someone, somewhere to have mercy on her. To lead her someplace safe. She wept then, the tears streaming down in quiet, hot rivers. She wiped them away. "Amen," she repeated. "Amen."

By the end of summer they had settled into a sweet, peaceful routine. Lenore continued to work for Erik Ashland. Carlene still watched Scott during the day. Mr. Caputo protested, but Lenore didn't want to wear him out. Scott was eight now and, especially when he had a friend or two over, could create a lot of energy. By the time Lenore and Scott got home in the afternoon, Mr. Caputo was putting the finishing touches on dinner. They ate together, Lenore and Scott did the supper dishes, and then they all sat together and read or watched TV or went for a walk or just sat in the garden—the normal little things that families do.

She tended the garden. Mr. Caputo taught her what he knew, and they learned the rest together. The huge square in the sunny south corner was the vegetable plot, with neat rows of corn, pole beans, peas, lettuce, cabbage, cucumbers, zucchini, squash, and carrots. Mr. Caputo was the tomato man. The plants lined up against the fence, green and healthy and covered with plump red orbs.

Lenore had cleaned out the borders around the house and planted hydrangea, snowball bushes, tree mallow, and rose of Sharon. On one side of the front porch she set a wisteria vine and on the other side a honeysuckle. She discovered the potting shed, an old, musty building at the edge of the yard, full of old shovels and trowels and broken pots with a fine haze of dust over everything and the sweet smell of earth hanging rich and heavy in the air.

She worked. She planted and dug and felt the rich soil in her hands and the warm sun on her head. She watered, spraying the hose up in a wide arc, watching the water fan into a brilliant prism of color as it hit the light.

She received the results of her state board exams. She was officially a registered nurse, and apparently Erik Ashland received notice, as well. That very day he called her into his office after work.

"You're underutilized here," he said. "I think you should at least give the hospital a try. You owe it to yourself." His face was set, though his eyes were regretful, and she felt something she didn't care to analyze. "You can always come back if you don't like it," he promised. "You know how I feel about you."

Lenore squirmed and her face flushed. "I'll put in a few applications," she agreed, her excitement competing with a sense of loss.

But she took his advice, even though she felt no need to apply at more than one place. She knew exactly where she wanted to work. She made a beeline back to First Hill. She passed by the sidewalk crowded with broken people and went to the Human Resources Department of Harborview Hospital. She was hired and assigned to the night shift.

She became a nocturnal creature, going to bed when others were getting up, spending the after-school hours with Scott and Mr. Caputo before heading to work when they went to bed. She knew she couldn't last indefinitely. Nor did she want it to. Still, there was a certain feel to the hospital at night that she liked. It was a little world that never slept. There was a sense of pulse, the feeling that whether she was there or not, it went on, people coming to work and going home, meals being made, laundry being done, messes being made and cleaned, people being arranged and rearranged, ministered to and cared for. She missed the familiar warmth of Erik's office, the sweetness of his small patients, but she felt as if she had come home here, too. That she had landed in a place where she belonged. The fall passed into a rainy winter. An opening came up on day shift, beginning the first of January. The month of new beginnings. She applied and was accepted.

She liked going to work in the morning, driving the half-dark streets, sometimes shiny with rain, nursing her commuter cup of the thick, rich coffee Mr. Caputo made her every morning along with hot cereal.

"It's true what they say," he would admonish, nodding his bald head up and down as he watched her eat. "It'll stick to your ribs, and as hard as you work, you'll need the energy."

She parked her car in the employee lot now and took the elevator to her wing, the seventh floor medical surgical ward. Her shoes squeaked along the corridor, just as she had imagined they would when she had dreamed of being a nurse.

"Morning." It was Erlene, one of the night crew, looking tired and out of sorts.

"How was your night?"

"Busy," she said through pursed lips, her head bent over a chart. "Three new admits from ER."

Lenore left Erlene alone and went into the staff room, hung up her coat, and found her locker. It was ten minutes until time for report, so she passed the time scanning the employee bulletin board for new notices. There was one announcing a staff in-service next Friday. Another advertised a house for rent, and she felt another surge of gratefulness for her home.

It was really beginning to feel like home. She had arranged Scott's things the way he wanted them and then had gone to work on her own room. She'd found a chenille bedspread at the rummage sale of the retirement home on Carlene's side of the hill.

"There's great stuff there," Carlene had said, and they had met early to get the best picks. Lenore thought again about Carlene's boundless energy, her ability to turn ordinary things into treasures.

She'd found a curved-front dresser at the Goodwill and refinished it, another one of last summer's projects, but her prize and glory was the quilt. Edie had made it for her and given it as a Christmas gift. It was the Log Cabin pattern in russet, mahogany, gold, and scarlet.

"The colors that go with your hair," Edie had said, smiling, and it had surprised Lenore. She had never thought of anything beautiful going with a feature of hers.

The quilt did look beautiful folded on the bottom of her bed, though. The red fir floors were in decent shape, and she'd found a few woven rugs to throw over them. She had a radio and some pictures she had collected over the years and a big overstuffed chair in the corner, where she could read and listen to music for a few minutes before she went to bed.

She refilled her coffee cup now and went to the nurses' station. The night crew was ready to give report. She spent the next half hour organizing by priority the jobs she had to do and the patients she needed to care for. She went and spoke to each one, checked on how they were faring, making a plan for each one to receive whatever tests, medications, or treatments had been scheduled.

She had two new admits on her shift. One was an appendectomy and the other an exploratory laparotomy that had revealed a large metastasized cancer throughout her abdomen. She took special care with Cass Hendrickson. She had everything ready when they wheeled her back from recovery.

"Family's in the waiting room," the orderly said. "I told them you'd call when they could come in."

Lenore nodded. Mrs. Hendrickson was sleeping heavily, still drugged from her surgery. Lenore checked her drains and IVs, checked the orders her doctor had given, and made sure her pain medication was on board. There was no reason for her to suffer now. There would be enough of that later.

Mrs. Hendrickson was a large woman, forty-five years old according to the chart, but Lenore knew she would soon shrink and curl inward as the cancer and the pain grew. She felt a sense of frustration and a surge of anger. She hated it when there was nothing she could do. She gave Cass's IV one more look to make sure it was dripping and not infiltrating. She smoothed the covers over her and fetched the family so that a familiar face would be present when Cass came out of her groggy state. At least Lenore could do that.

She liked it when she could help, when she could watch the bunched brows relax, the tight face clear. And she liked seeing the fear and anger of the families ease when things were explained to them. She had even gotten the chance to pray with a few. In just the few weeks she'd been here, the other nurses had called her to talk to patients when they were uncooperative or scared, and in every case, by the time she'd spent a few minutes rubbing their arms or just talking to them, depending on what it seemed they would like, they had settled down. It gave her a good feeling that she was valuable and could be used. She felt as if she had become a different person from that frightened woman who had arrived here in Seattle over four years ago, that one who couldn't bring herself to get out of bed.

One day eased into the next, one month into another. Lenore had been at the hospital one year, and Scott was in fourth grade, and their little family had been together for over a year when Mrs. Callahan and Angie came to live with them.

Fourteen

LENORE CHECKED THE chocolate cake she was baking. Today was her day off, and she had planned on getting some cleaning done, raking the leaves that were piling up in the backyard, and catching up on her laundry, but it was already ten o'clock, and she hadn't started anything yet. She had just sat at the table and drunk a second and then a third cup of coffee and read a novel. It felt like such a luxury to just sit and do nothing, to give no medication, change no beds, check on no one. Scott was at school, Mr. Caputo was in his own room, and Mrs. Callahan and Angie had gone for a walk to the shops at the top of the hill. She closed her eyes in silent prayer for a moment. Adding the two new members to the household had not been the seamless addition she had imagined.

Mrs. Callahan was about sixty-five, Lenore guessed. She had gotten used to seeing women that age with youthful haircuts, wearing tennis shoes and stylish clothes. Mrs. Callahan was from Knoxville, Tennessee, and was old-school sixties. She wore dresses and Hush Puppies, and her hair was a mass of tightly permed silver curls. Lenore had liked her right away.

"She came up here to help raise her granddaughter," Edie had explained, predelivery. "But then the daughter took off, and Mrs. Callahan is stuck here. She already gave up her apartment back in Knoxville, and she doesn't have money to go home. She plans on moving back eventually, but I don't know." Edie had made a doubtful face. "She's on a fixed income. It'll be a while."

"Bring her on," Lenore had invited, and Mrs. Callahan had soon arrived with Angie in tow. Angie was eight years old, the child of Mrs. Callahan's youngest daughter.

"That kid's a brat," Scott said after their first introduction, during which Angie had broken apart the Lego castle he'd been working on because he wouldn't let her open and close the drawbridge.

"She needs some discipline," Mr. Caputo had agreed.

Lenore explained that Angie had had little attention and that grandparents weren't always as good at saying no as parents, but Scott had just looked at her darkly. He didn't seem to buy her softened explanation. And it hadn't taken Lenore long to see that something would have to be done to address Angie's behavior. She had a way of demanding everything, from a drink of water to one of the cookies that were just coming out of the oven, in a tone that made Lenore want to say no just for the pleasure of it. She had too many toys, which she scattered over every square foot of the house, and poor old Mrs. Callahan stooped her arthritic back over twice a day and picked them up.

"I could find Angie and have her do that," Lenore had suggested just this morning.

"Oh, it's easier just to do it myself."

"No doubt," Lenore had muttered under her breath. The entire household had been treated to one of Angie's tantrums the night before when bedtime had come before she was ready to sleep.

"*No!*" she had shrieked. "I'm *not sleepy*. It's *not* bedtime."

So she had stayed up until eleven, when she had finally fallen asleep on the couch. Lenore had finally roused her enough to walk her up to her bed, a small cot in the corner of Mrs. Callahan's room.

"She can have her own room," Lenore had offered.

"She has nightmares," Mrs. Callahan said, and Lenore could see tiny purple shadows under her eyes.

Lenore tried to be tolerant. Who knew what kind of neglect the child had suffered before her grandmother had taken custody of her? Mrs. Callahan didn't like to talk about it, but Edie said the daughter would take off for days at a time, leaving a loaf of bread and a jar of peanut butter and the television blaring as company for the little girl.

She checked the cake. It was still raw in the middle and wobbled as she pushed it back to the center of the rack and closed the oven door, which screeched "like a long-tailed cat in a roomful of rocking chairs," Mrs. Callahan had quipped last night. Lenore smiled again when she thought of her. She was bright and funny and had a very good heart. Lenore felt a stab of pity for her at having such a hard lot with her granddaughter. Not to mention her daughter, whom no one had heard from in months.

"She's done this before, apparently," Edie said. "She takes off, usually with a guy, and then comes back six months later, wanting Angie again. I think the courts are involved this time, though. Mrs. Callahan is asking for custody."

Lenore shook her head now and wondered what kind of life Angie had had—what neglect had led to her spoiled self-indulgence. She shook Ajax into the sink and scrubbed the yellowed porcelain until it gleamed white, then stood staring out the window but hardly seeing the bare branches of the late autumn trees and the well-stocked woodpile.

It was odd how the mind took care of itself. When it was stretched or hurt, it tried to compensate. Lenore had seen herself do it. When she'd been feeling at her worst because of Daniel, she'd taken to her bed in an effort to protect herself. She thought it was probably bound up in the genetic code, tied tight within the pieces of human beings to not want to suffer and to take care of themselves. And that was all right. That could even be a good thing, she supposed. Until it got out of hand.

The front door slammed, hard enough to make Lenore worry about her cake falling, and she heard Angie and Mrs. Callahan talking, actually mostly Angie, who was complaining in a loud voice about something. Lenore sighed and dried her hands.

After two long weeks of tantrums, sass, and raveled nerves, matters finally came to a head one night at suppertime. Angie didn't like the meatloaf Lenore had made for their dinner.

"This stuff is gross." She made a sickened face, crossed her arms, and leaned back in her chair, obviously finished.

"Well, is that any way to talk?" Mrs. Callahan shook her head and gave her teeth a little click.

"I want some Lucky Charms." Angie spoke airily, as if to a servant. Mrs. Callahan rose up to fetch them, Lenore presumed. She got up and followed her into the kitchen.

"Mrs. Callahan," Lenore began.

Mrs. Callahan looked guilty, but she was already reaching for the box of Lucky Charms she'd bought at the grocery that morning and getting down a bowl.

"It's not my place to tell you how to raise your granddaughter," she prefaced.

"Well, she's had little raising, I can tell you that." Mrs. Callahan shook her head. "That's the problem, I'd say."

"Well, I agree, but isn't it better to get a late start than none at all?" Lenore smiled and tried to keep her tone positive.

Mrs. Callahan stood with the cereal poised in midair, hesitation and dread on her face. "I suppose you're right, but it's so much easier to just let her have what she wants."

"Maybe in the short term," Lenore reasoned. "There may be a few miserable days, but if we stand firm, we'll all be happier, including Angie."

"I suppose you're right." Mrs. Callahan clutched the box of Lucky Charms like a life preserver. "I just feel like I don't have the energy." Mrs. Callahan shook her head. Not a curl budged.

"It's unpleasant at first," Lenore conceded. "It got pretty loud for a while when Scott went through that." She remembered Daniel urging her to give Scott what he wanted. She had stood firm. The only thing she had needed to strengthen her resolve was to think of how her younger sister had turned out after being given everything she wanted whenever the whim struck her.

"Scott used to be that way?"

"Every kid is that way," Lenore said. "You just have to help them get over it."

"I don't have the energy," Mrs. Callahan repeated. "But I can see it's what needs to be done." She looked at Lenore, her face imploring.

"I could try if you like," Lenore offered, feeling like the maiden about to be thrown into the volcano.

Mrs. Callahan's face cleared into lines of relief. "I'd appreciate that." She handed Lenore the box of Lucky Charms. Lenore put it back in the cupboard. The high cupboard. The two of them walked back into the dining room.

"I'm sorry, Angie," Lenore said, her tone reasonable, her face pleasant. "There will be no Lucky Charms until you've finished your supper. Then, if you're still hungry, you can have a bowl for dessert instead of pie."

Angie paid her no more attention than if she'd been a fly buzzing around the window. She addressed her comment to Mrs. Callahan, acting as if Lenore hadn't even spoken. "Granny, I want my Lucky Charms."

Granny didn't answer. She got up and helped Mr. Caputo, who was serving the cherry pie.

"Granny!" Angie demanded again, and Mrs. Callahan finally faced her granddaughter.

"It's like Miss Lenore said," she confirmed, her voice just the tiniest bit tentative. "No Lucky Charms unless you eat your supper."

Angie stared for a moment; then her face crumpled up, and she began weeping—deep, heartbreaking sobs. Mrs. Callahan looked at Lenore pleadingly, but Lenore just shook her head.

"Your food will be waiting for you if you get hungry," she said to the back of Angie's head. She had to raise her voice to be heard over the girl's wails. Mr. Caputo and Scott and Mrs. Callahan decided to take their pie into the study.

"Angie," Lenore continued, reaching over to stroke her head and getting her hand smacked out of the way for her trouble, "you can help Mr. Caputo make dinner tomorrow. And when it's Granny's and your turn to cook, you can pick whatever you want for supper." *And also see how much work it is to cook and clean up,* she thought. Angie turned angry then, her sobs becoming more shrieks than laments. Lenore could hear conversation from the study and the sounds of *Wheel of Fortune.*

She began to clear the table and do the dishes, keeping an eye on Angie, who had decided to vent her anger by tearing apart a book Mrs. Callahan had bought her the week before. She tore it, kicked it, and threw it in a demolished pile onto the Oriental rug in the hallway, then sat down beside it and started sobbing again. Lenore tried to approach her twice, but each time she did, Angie threw off her hand and continued sobbing. Lenore finally left her alone, putting away all the food, including Angie's uneaten supper, which she covered with Saran wrap.

By the time Lenore finished scraping the plates and loading the dishwasher, Angie had fallen asleep on the hallway floor. Lenore swept the kitchen floor and wiped down the countertops, brushed the crumbs from the tablecloth, and blew out the candles; then she fetched Mr. Caputo, who carried Angie upstairs and put her on the cot, grumbling all the while about belts and woodsheds.

She was a pretty little girl, Lenore thought as she pulled the covers over her. She had long, dark hair and brown eyes. Lenore thought of Daniel and wondered if this is what a daughter of theirs would have looked like. She tiptoed out and left the bedroom door open and the light burning in the hall.

The next morning Angie ate the bowl of oatmeal that was put before her without comment, much to everyone's relief. She took the sack lunch Mr. Caputo packed for her and headed off to school. When she came home, she was a little more cheerful, ate some cheese and crackers, and then helped Mr. Caputo fix eggplant parmesan. She looked doubtful when it came to eating it, though, but everyone, including Mr. Caputo, was anxious to give her a little leeway.

"Eggplant parmesan isn't for everyone," he nodded, his cheeks red and round as he smiled. "Here, have another piece of bread and some fruit salad."

The night after that, Angie helped Mrs. Callahan make chicken and dumplings. She cleaned her plate and gave Lenore a brilliant smile as she had a bowl of Lucky Charms for dessert.

Fifteen

Scott lay in bed thinking about the fact that he was supposed to be going to his dad's for Christmas and he didn't want to go. It wasn't that he would get homesick or miss his mom or anything. He was in fourth grade now and big enough to not get homesick. That would be a baby thing to be. He swallowed hard and blinked. It would be okay. He could go.

He tried not to think about what they would be doing at home. About what he would miss. He would miss playing with Derek while Mom and Aunt Carlene made Christmas cookies. He had gotten to help decorate the tree, but he would miss hanging up his stocking on Christmas Eve, and Mr. Caputo usually took them Christmas shopping at the dollar store, and he would miss that, and he would miss going to Uncle Matt and Aunt Jenny's this year for Christmas Eve breakfast. He would miss hearing Angie play *Away in a Manger* on the piano at the Christmas program, but that was a good thing. She made a lot of mistakes.

They didn't go to church on Christmas at Dad's house. "I'm not a churchgoing man," Dad had said when Scott had asked him. At Dad's, Christmas wasn't really that much different from any other day. Last year Dad had had to work on Christmas Eve, so Scott had gone to Disneyland. With Donelle. Donelle worked for Dad. He had a gun and a walkie-talkie and a phone in his car. Afterward they'd gone shopping at the toy store, and Scott got to pick out everything he wanted. Then they'd gone out to dinner, but the place didn't have turkey and dressing like they had at home, only steaks. Dad said he didn't have to work this year. He would take Scott out to Disneyland and dinner himself, and he was going to buy him a Super Nintendo for a present. Scott wasn't as excited as he had thought he'd be.

Maybe Esperanza would let him come to her house for Christmas. Scott brightened a little. She was Dad's maid, but she had taken Scott home with her once, and he had stayed the whole day. Her grandkids had come over, and they'd gone to the park and to the swimming pool and then played kickball in the street, and Esperanza had made them pizza. But then he'd had to go back to Dad's.

Dad's house was kind of cool, though. It was kind of like a castle. It even had a fancy fence all around the huge yard, and Dad had shown him how to make the gate open by pushing a button inside the house. He liked the Jacuzzi and the pool and the pool house and Dad's convertible. But he didn't like going to the studio with Dad. All he did was sit and wait, and the baby-sitter Dad hired didn't talk to him. She just listened to tapes on her headphones. He didn't want to go. But he would. Dad would be sad if he didn't. But it felt lonely there or something. Even when Dad was home.

Scott lay still and listened. The house was quiet, and then he heard a door open and close and feet on the stairs. He knew it was Mr. Caputo. Lots of times Scott woke up in the night and heard him going down the stairs to have a cup of hot chocolate, and sometimes Scott would go down, too. Sometimes he didn't, though, like tonight. Sometimes he liked to just lie here and listen to the creaks and groans the house made. They didn't scare him. They reminded him of the way Mrs. Callahan and Mr. Caputo groaned when they sat down. Mrs. Callahan said the house was just getting comfortable.

Taking a load off, like Mr. Caputo said.

"It's the tree roots coming under the house," Mom had told him last summer. "One of these mornings we'll wake up and be up in the limbs—a tree house."

He wanted a tree house. Really bad. But Mr. Caputo said he didn't know how to build things, and Mom said she didn't, either, and for sure Mrs. Callahan didn't.

He had asked Dad to come to Seattle and build a tree house, but Dad said he probably couldn't do that, and he had looked so sad that Scott hadn't asked him why not. Then Dad had asked a lot of questions, like how was it living in the big house with all the people and what kind of stuff did they do and did Mom have a boyfriend. Scott said he didn't know about a boyfriend, but he liked it fine living with Mr. Caputo and Mrs. Callahan and Angie. Sometimes they got tired of each other, and Angie could be a pain, but when he wanted to be alone, he could just go in his room and close the door. Mom did that sometimes. She'd go in her room and hang out the Do Not Disturb sign Aunt Carlene had made for her in her painting class, and when she came out, she wasn't in a bad mood anymore.

"I don't know how you can live like that—crawling all over each other," Aunt Carlene had said when she gave Mom the sign. But it wasn't bad. At least there was almost always somebody to talk to when he wanted to. If Mr. Caputo was in his room with the door closed, Mrs. Callahan or Mom was probably in the kitchen making popcorn or watching TV in the den. And there was always Angie.

"Does your mom have a boyfriend?" Dad had asked him again the last time he'd called.

Scott had said he didn't know. He didn't like it when Dad asked him questions. Mom never asked him questions when he came back from Dad's, except "Did you have a nice time?" and stuff like that. But Dad thought it was weird that they all lived in the same house and none of them were related. It wasn't weird, though. It was good.

He liked coming home from school and watching *Duck Tales* with Mrs. Callahan and Angie. Then he'd go to the kitchen and eat popcorn or cookies and do his homework while whoever was cooking made dinner. When Mom got home from work, they ate. After supper he and Angie cleaned up the dishes, and then he could watch TV for a while or play a game or something. Then Mom helped him make his lunch for the next day and he took a shower and then Mom came in his room and they prayed and he went to sleep. They always prayed for everyone in the house and for Aunt Edie and Uncle Matt and Aunt Jenny and for Dad, and sometimes when Mom had to work or go somewhere, Mr. Caputo prayed with him.

On Saturdays they usually went somewhere—to the library or to Baskin-Robbins, or they went grocery shopping and to McDonald's. On Sundays they went to church.

He turned over on his bed and tried to get comfortable again. Five more days until it was time to leave. This week was the last week of school before Christmas vacation. He was supposed to go to Dad's on Friday. He wondered again if he should tell Mom he didn't want to go. He thought about how sad Dad would feel, and then he felt sad himself. Really sad. He blinked and sniffed. He would go. Scott lay in the dark and listened to another pop and creak and heard Mr. Caputo come back up the stairs. He heard Mr. Caputo open and close his bedroom door, and then everything was quiet.

Sixteen

IT WAS CHRISTMAS EVE, and Scott sat at his dad's kitchen table staring at the tuna sandwich and bag of potato chips. He felt sad. It had been okay until Dad had left. Serena had gone somewhere, too, but he didn't really care that she had gone. In fact, he was sort of happy about that. He didn't think Dad's girlfriend liked him much. But after Dad left, Mom had called, and that's when he'd started feeling sad. Now Esperanza was leaving, and only Donelle was here, and nobody knew when Dad was coming back. Donelle's music was thumping from the other room. *Boom-bumpa-boom-bumpa-boom-bumpa-boom.* Scott blinked his eyes hard and watched Esperanza pick up her purse and coat. She turned toward him and gave him a big smile.

"Okay, Scottie," she said. "You have good Christmas. Donelle is here if you need something before your father get home." She opened the door, and Scott didn't mean to, but the words just came out of his mouth.

"Please, can I go with you?" he begged.

Esperanza stopped. She closed the door and turned back toward him. She was frowning a little bit. He'd tried not to whine. Grown-ups didn't like it when you whined.

She came over to where he was sitting at the kitchen table and sat down beside him. She put her hand on his head and sort of rubbed his hair. "Your father be very disappointed, you don't stay on Christmas," she said. He liked the way she talked, and her eyes looked like Mom's but not the same color. Esperanza's were brown, and Mom's were—he couldn't remember what color they were, but they didn't look the same. But they were looking *at* him the same. He was trying hard not to cry. Esperanza put her arm on his shoulders and gave him a pat.

Then he couldn't help it anymore. He put his head down on the table so Esperanza wouldn't see his face. He could feel her arms around him. They were soft and pillowy. He let her hug him, and after a minute he stopped crying. Esperanza picked up the napkin she had put beside his glass of milk and tuna sandwich and wiped off his face.

"Nose," she said, handing it to him.

He blew his nose. Esperanza held out her hand for the napkin. He gave it to her. She threw it away, then came back to the table and sat down again.

"You wish to be home," she said.

He nodded. He started thinking about what everybody would be doing on Christmas Eve. Wrapping presents. Putting them under the tree. Going to church.

Esperanza nodded, too. "Is hard sometimes when parents go different ways."

Scott's throat started to hurt again, and he didn't really know all the reasons he was sad. Just the biggest one. "I miss my mom," he said.

Esperanza's face was soft. "I know."

He felt like he might start crying again. He knew Esperanza wasn't going to let him go home with her. He guessed he had known it all along, but he wanted to tell somebody how bad he was feeling. And he couldn't tell Dad.

"You know," Esperanza said, looking off in the distance, "my sons all grown up."

Scott sniffed and wiped his nose on his sleeve. He took a drink of his chocolate milk. Esperanza always made him chocolate milk.

"Years and years since they little boys like you." She smiled at him. He smiled back at her. He guessed he was feeling better. A little bit.

"You eat the sandwich while we talk," she said. She put her purse down on the floor.

He picked up the sandwich and took a bite. It was pretty good. He had some potato chips, too.

"They grow up. Get jobs. Always busy. I miss them." Now it was Esperanza who looked sad. "With just me and the husband? Something not right." She shook her head.

Scott tried to think of what he could say to make her feel better, but just then Esperanza smiled again. She had pretty white teeth.

"But every year at Christmas they all come, and I feel good. I feel happy." She covered her heart with her hand. "When they come, I feel like everything all right. The way is supposed to be. You know?"

He nodded.

She smiled again and tapped him gently on the chest. "And that's the way your father feel when you come. His heart fill up till the next time he see you."

Scott finished half of his sandwich and started on the other half.

"Sometimes is hard for you. You miss mother. Other family. But think about this. You go home in two days." She held up two fingers. "Just two days, and you're back where you want to be. And you take something with you."

Scott thought about the games and the toys, but Esperanza tapped him on the chest again.

"You take happiness deep inside that you brought joy to father."

Scott thought about that while he finished his milk.

Esperanza smiled and looked over toward the living room where all his presents were stacked under the Christmas tree with the fake snow and pink ornaments that Serena had bought. Somebody had brought it, with all the decorations on it already, to the house in a big truck. He had never seen that happen before.

"The toys?" Esperanza said with a wave of her hand. "They break. You lose. Whatever." She shrugged. "But this?" She pointed toward his heart. "This you get to keep."

He didn't know what to say about all that. But he felt better.

"You finish sandwich." Esperanza got up, but instead of leaving she took off her coat and hung it on the hook again and put back on her apron. "I stay until father come home. We make something good." She smiled at him again, then started humming and pulling things out of the cupboard. "We make churros."

Scott finished his sandwich and started swinging his feet, bumping them against the table legs. He didn't know what churros were, but he felt happy Esperanza was staying until his dad came home, and he felt warm in his chest, on that place she had touched right over his heart.

———

Dad came home with a turkey. Serena came in right after Dad did, and she saw it and got really mad. Scott didn't know why, but she got even madder when Esperanza put on her coat and said good-bye.

"Where are you going?" she asked Esperanza, really mean and loud. "And what's with this? It's almost seven o'clock, and the kitchen's bare." She waved her hand around the kitchen. "I thought we went over the menu for tonight."

Esperanza stood up really straight, and Scott could tell she was mad. "Mr. Monroe say he take care of dinner. He tell me go home at noon. I stay a little later with Scott." She gave Scott a quick smile.

Dad came in with the rest of the groceries and put them on the counter. "Wait, Esperanza," he said and reached inside his pocket. "I'm glad I caught you before you left. This is for you." He handed Esperanza an envelope and gave her a kiss on the cheek. "Thank you for everything, and merry Christmas."

"You're welcome," Esperanza said and gave Scott one last smile before she turned around and left. Serena got even madder then. Scott was starting to feel bad again.

"Well, this is just great," Serena said, waving around at the kitchen. She looked at the turkey Dad had set on the counter. "I hope you don't expect me to cook that."

"I'm going to cook it," Dad said. "This is our dinner."

"It's seven o'clock, Daniel. Turkeys take hours to cook. Are we eating at two in the morning?"

"Tomorrow," Dad said. "I thought we'd eat out tonight."

Serena got a little less mad then. "Fine. I'll call El Gaucho."

Then Dad said they weren't going to El Gaucho, and Scott got up and left the table. He went into the living room and watched TV for a while, and he could hear Dad and Serena still fighting. Actually, it was Serena he heard. Donelle turned the TV up, but after a while he said, "Good-bye, kid, have a happy Christmas," and left. When the noise died down, Scott got up and peeked into the kitchen. Serena was talking quieter now, but she still looked real mad, and Dad was drinking some of his special drink that Scott couldn't have.

"Look," Dad finally said, and now he sounded kind of mad. He didn't get that way very often, but when he did, Scott knew not to argue anymore. "Scott's hungry," he said. "You can come or you can stay here, but we're going to go get some dinner."

"Don't expect me to be here when you get back," Serena said. Dad didn't say anything.

"Let's go, buddy," Dad called out, but then Serena started yelling at him again.

Scott tried to remember what Esperanza said—that he was filling up Dad's heart with joy, but it didn't feel like that anymore. It didn't feel like that at all.

Serena wasn't happy. And when Serena wasn't happy, no one was happy. Daniel supposed she would get over it. She always did.

"El Gaucho is no place for kids," Daniel had protested, "especially on Christmas Eve." It would have been torture to take Scott to that exclusive restaurant. The Coach House was perfect. There was something for everyone here. Scott could have his turkey and pumpkin pie, and he could have his scotch and soda. He sipped one now—his second—listened to the rain pelt the window, and watched his son finish his dinner. He checked his watch. Past ten o'clock and the place was empty. Everybody else in the world was at home having visions of sugarplums or hanging up their stockings or doing whatever normal people did on Christmas Eve. He could barely remember. The turkey he'd brought home had been a vain attempt to replicate that feeling he so dimly recalled. Instead, it had only set Serena off.

It had been one of their monumental fights. Not a fight, exactly, he corrected himself. A fight implied two people interacting. When Serena went into one of her tempers, there was no reasoning with her. He listened and watched. She ranted. And she had done a fine job of that, as always. The husky voice he had so admired became a shrill rasp. Her fine skin had been flushed pink. Her lips red and in full pout, a striking contrast to her glossy black hair. She'd looked beautiful, Daniel had noted with detachment. Now he had a sudden disturbing vision of Medusa with a writhing headful of snakes instead of hair.

He had tried to make Christmas materialize out of an ordinary day the way Lenore always had. He had tried as he had bought out the toy store and would continue trying tomorrow as he cooked the turkey and unwrapped the store-bought pumpkin pie and lit a fire in the gas fireplace. But he had no illusions that he would succeed. And he had failed to factor Serena into his calculations. Which had been a mistake. Serena's idea of domestic comfort was having the cook make dinner at home instead of eating out.

Still, there were some things Serena did well, Daniel admitted. She could sell whatever her image was plastered on. She could draw a crowd at the box office. Her mantel was full of award statuettes. And she could blister hide when she went on one of her furies. She had covered a lot of ground in this one, beginning with his lack of consideration for her work schedule, proceeding on to his general ineptness, and ending with the accusation that he was spoiling his son. Daniel squirmed uncomfortably as he thought of that last part. Of all the things she had said, that one actually had the ring of truth.

Scott didn't look spoiled, Daniel reassured himself as he glanced toward his son. He didn't act spoiled. But he acted bored. Bored with the house, the pool, the home theater, the game room, and the mountain of toys Daniel had bought for him since his arrival last week. He was jaded to them, indifferent. And sad. Last night he had plaintively asked Daniel when he was going home.

"The day after Christmas," Daniel had told him with some relief, for which he felt a tremendous amount of guilt. What had happened? he wondered with the same feeling of helpless inevitability. And what could he do to stop it? He ruminated for a moment, signaled the waitress, and ordered another drink. His third. His last, he promised himself.

The waitress brought it. The manager went through with the vacuum cleaner, taking not so surreptitious glances at his watch. Daniel ignored him.

"Does that turkey taste as good as it looks?" Daniel asked Scott, forcing a cheerfulness into his voice he didn't feel.

"Sure," Scott answered in the flat voice Daniel had grown accustomed to. "I guess so."

Al Younger inspected himself in the steamy mirror. His eyes were bloodshot. He took the eye drops from the medicine chest and squirted a few in each eye. He had had yesterday off and had spent it the way he spent most of his free time—sitting on his stool at Handy's. He had closed the place down last night and slept most of the day away today. He buttoned the top button of his uniform shirt, adjusted his tie, checked his badge, strapped on his gun. His stomach was burning again. He took a handful of Rolaids, ran a comb through what was left of his hair, and just for a moment, as he was turning to leave the bathroom, he got a glimpse of himself in the mirror and thought he'd seen his father. He looked back, intent. Yes, it could be. The same watery blue eyes. The same close-cropped crew cut, slowly fading from blond to white. The same weathered, careworn face. His father's had been aged from years of farming in the hot sun, his own from hard times, mostly self-inflicted.

He turned off the lights in the small apartment and went to switch off the television. Somebody was blathering about religion. They ought to take all that junk off the air. It was noise pollution. A commercial came on. A bunch of kids sitting on Santa's lap, and Al noted absently that it was Christmas Eve. Realized it without the hollow sadness it would have brought once. Without the reminders of the girls when they'd been little and sweet and not brittle like their mother.

He hadn't seen the girls in years and could barely remember when he'd lived with them, and it was little wonder. He'd always been gone. Always working. That, in fact, was the very reason his wife had given— along with his fondness for the bottle—for leaving him. Nearly twenty years ago. Up and left. Took the girls and, just like on one of those cheesy TV dramas his mother used to watch, left a note leaning against the coffeepot. *Dear Al.* And so on.

He shrugged into his jacket. It was raining and a little cool, but he would have worn it anyway to cover up his uniform. He locked his apartment, got into his beat-up Dodge. He refused to bring home a cruiser.

Didn't want the neighbors knowing he was a cop. Didn't want them show-ing up on his doorstep whining when the husband backhanded them or one of the kids didn't come home on time. He had a job to do and he did it, and after he put in his time, he wanted to be left alone. He wasn't a hero. Never had been. Never would be. In fact, he knew, with a cer-tainty that he couldn't explain, and had never told a soul, that the only thing separating him from those he arrested was a thin, tenuous line. A boundary that he walked carefully and never crossed. He had come close a few times but never put his foot over. And it was odd, but in his mind that knowledge led to a sort of pride. Whatever else he may or may not have done, he had never stepped across the line. Therefore he despised, with a quiet hatred that was nevertheless intense, all those who did.

He lit a cigarette and drove to the station, hating again that he'd been reassigned from Rampart Division to Hollywood. Downtown Hollywood was all right, but he hated Beverly Hills. Hated responding to their silly burglaries, their domestic disputes. The same stuff went on there as in the slums, only it was hidden better. Covered up and dressed up with layers of money. He sighed, parked the car, went inside, signed in, and sat through roll call; then he and his partner took their cruiser out. They'd barely started the engine when the call came. Al listened while his partner took down the address, then he turned the cruiser around and headed for Beverly Boulevard. His partner was shaking his head. Al cursed a steady stream as he drove. He hated calls like this. Hated them with a passion. Some pond scum of a movie star had run over a kid.

Seventeen

IMAGES ASSAULTED DANIEL'S eyes and brain. The scene around him was surreal and fevered, full of disconnected pieces with no relationship to any coherent whole. His brain struggled to put meaning to them. The flashing blue of the police car, the red of the medic unit. The static fizz of their radios, the wet splash and slow drone of the traffic veering around them, the cones, the flares. The cars moved slowly so the drivers could peer out and look at him, could point and exclaim. The rain poured down in sheets. Scott was crying. The other boy was white, crumpled, looking small inside his too-big coat and pants as he lay on the wet, dark street. Too still. Daniel felt as if the blood had drained from him, as well. He was lifeless, numb. He tried his best to follow the orders of the angry police officers. He touched his nose, blew into the mouthpiece. He was put into the back of the cruiser none too gently. Handcuffed. Scott began to wail louder.

"Please," Daniel said to one officer, the tall one with the blond-white crew cut, "take care of my boy."

A tightening of the jaw. "He'll be taken care of," his only answer.

It was the other boy they were concerned with. The older one, who lay so still as the paramedics surrounded him. The one Daniel hadn't seen.

He had been trying to pacify Scott, leaning over to say something, to pat him on the knee. "Hey, buddy," he had said, "what do you think are in all those packages under the tree?"

He didn't know.

"Do you think we should open them tonight or tomorrow?"

He didn't care, and then Daniel had seen the kid in the crosswalk. Out of nowhere he had appeared, and now Daniel understood that trite phrase, the one on every television show and movie, the one spoken in real life by those who, like him, had glanced away at just the wrong moment. The boy had come out of nowhere, their first introduction the youngster's shocked face as he had locked eyes with Daniel, as he had realized Daniel was not going to stop.

He had slammed on the brakes, of course. There were skid marks to prove it. He had stopped the car, barked at Scott to stay, then run to the place the boy had landed, fifteen feet or so ahead, thrown by the impact. He had covered him with his coat and called for help. He had prayed as he'd knelt over the youth, willing him to breathe, praying incoherent prayers that it wasn't too late.

He sat in the back of the cruiser now, head in his hands, listening to Scott wail.

"Please, could I call my wife?" he begged, and as soon as the words were out, he realized he had meant Lenore.

———————

It was Mrs. Callahan who, unexpectedly, proved to be a source of strength after the 2 A.M. telephone call. Mr. Caputo slept through the ringing, but Mrs. Callahan tapped on Lenore's bedroom door just as Lenore was hanging up from the brief call.

"Is everything all right?" Mrs. Callahan asked, opening the door a fraction, poking in a head covered with pink foam rollers.

Lenore shook her head. She was shaken and panicked. After Daniel's first sentence, her brain, so efficient in others' emergencies, seemed to shut down completely. "It was Daniel," she said. "There's been an accident."

Mrs. Callahan came in and crossed the room. "What exactly did he say?" she asked, sitting down beside Lenore and taking her hand into her own soft, veined one.

"Just that." Lenore's voice trembled with panic and emotion.

"Was either Scott or Daniel hurt?" Mrs. Callahan asked quickly.

Lenore shook her head. "No. But another boy was. A child. Daniel hit a child, and he's under arrest. For drunk driving."

"Dear Jesus," Mrs. Callahan said, and it took a glazed moment for Lenore to realize she was praying, not exclaiming. She bowed her own head, thankful someone had the presence of mind to take what was the only thinkable course of action.

"Give us calm, Lord. Give us your peace," Mrs. Callahan murmured. "Your Word says you've not given a spirit of fear, but of power, of love, and of a sound mind." There was a long pause, and Lenore could feel her breathing return to normal. The reminder that she wasn't in charge, didn't have to be in charge, asserted itself. She began praying when Mrs. Callahan paused.

"And, Jesus," Lenore prayed, "take care of the injured child. You're the great physician. Bring your healing power on him. And be with Scott and Daniel. Protect Scott from any dangers, Lord. Comfort his heart. Send someone to help him," she begged, struck with the obvious solution. "You must have someone there you could send, Lord. Draw them to my boy."

They began talking again without saying amen, leaving the line open.

"I need to call someone and find out what they'll do with Scott." Lenore voiced her most pressing concern.

"Does Daniel live with anyone?" Mrs. Callahan asked.

"I don't know," Lenore admitted. Daniel's domestic arrangements were definitely too complex a subject for her present state of mind.

"If there's no one available to take him, they'll most likely put him in a receiving home," Mrs. Callahan said, and Lenore realized she had probably had more dealings than she cared to with the foster care system. Lenore dialed information and asked for the number of the LAPD. And she needed to call the airlines to see when the next flight left for L.A. She felt a panicky urgency to get there quickly, to rescue her son.

"Maybe you could call Daniel's house to see if anyone there knows anything more."

An obvious step and Lenore wondered why she hadn't thought of it. She wrote down the number the operator gave her for the police, then called Daniel's home, but it appeared to be a wasted effort. She got the answering machine. She left a message and called the LAPD number then. Wrong precinct. Three transfers. While she was on hold, she pulled on her jeans and sweatshirt, the same clothes she'd been wearing when she'd finished baking her cinnamon rolls at midnight. It seemed so irrelevant now, and she was struck again by how quickly a life could change course. Finally she reached the Hollywood division. She spoke to the desk sergeant, the watch commander, and finally, after being put on hold once more, she was given the victim-witness coordinator. Fitting, she supposed, since Scott was the victim of his father's irresponsibility. A hot anger began to replace the numb shock. She couldn't be distracted by it now. She handed it over to Him and pressed on.

"I'm coming to get my son," she told the woman, a no-nonsense type. "Where will he be?"

"Probably in a receiving home," the woman said. "I'll find out and call you back."

"There's no time," Lenore shot back. "I'm coming now."

"Come to the station," the woman said. "I'll have some answers for you by the time you get here."

Lenore had a sudden vision of Scott lost in the bowels of the California foster care system and felt a sudden irrational fear that she wouldn't be able to find him, wouldn't be able to get him back.

"Transfer me back to the station," Lenore said, just as briskly as the woman, her brain coming out of its numb state. "I want to talk to whoever has my son."

———————

Al couldn't say exactly why he had stayed with the boy, taking sick time for the rest of his shift so he could save the kid from going to the home. It hadn't been the urgent pleas from the mother. He was immune to those. He turned his collar up and passed by hysterical females without a second glance. Too many crying hissy fits when his girls were growing up. Always a crisis, though he supposed this situation would qualify even in his book. It was a bum deal when your ex had the kid and he got himself tossed for DUI. Al felt his jaw clench as he thought of the broken boy in the emergency room and all because he happened to get in the way of some movie star's Porsche. Give him twenty minutes alone in the room with Daniel Monroe, and he could straighten him out on a point or two. Orient him to his place in the universe. In the real world.

Al glanced down at the boy who was sitting in the orange plastic chair beside his. Not the boy's fault. But even so, Al still didn't know exactly why he had volunteered to stay here at the station with the kid until his mother could get here from Seattle. He checked his watch. It was nearly eight in the morning. She'd said she was catching the six-thirty flight. He could be here awhile yet, and he wondered again why he had decided to play the Good Samaritan, brushing off the victim-witness woman's patter with the brusque retort that he couldn't release the kid until the paper work was done.

"I'm leaving in twenty minutes," the social worker had said. "If he's not ready by then, you get to baby-sit."

"You do what you have to do," he'd said without looking up from his typewriter. So here he sat on Christmas Day, watching the rest of his shift beat a hasty retreat while he shuffled papers, pretending to be busy. He didn't know *why* he had done it, but he knew *when* he had known he would, though he hadn't admitted it then even to himself. It had been right at the very beginning, when the kid had been standing on the side of the street bawling, watching the paramedics work on the other kid. He didn't know why, but he had gone over to him, knelt down, and grasped his shoulder. "Hey now," he had said, and because he couldn't think of anything else to say after that, he had stopped. Telling him to get a grip wouldn't do. Not with the boy in such obvious distress. "Be a man" wouldn't do, either, though he remembered his own father shoving those words at him like a rag in the mouth every time he shed a tear or even looked as if he might. "Hey now," he'd repeated, adding a pat on the

IF I GAINED THE WORLD

back this time, and the boy had stopped crying. Not immediately, of course. It had taken a minute or two, but he'd slacked off and finally stopped, creeping closer to Al as he wiped his face on the sleeve of his jacket.

"You want to come sit in my cruiser?" Al had asked.

The kid had nodded.

They'd sat, the boy's shuddering breaths the only sound for a little while.

"Nobody's going to hurt your dad," he'd told the kid, and the relieved look in his eyes told him he'd hit the bull's-eye. "And the boy's probably gonna be fine. They'll take him to the hospital and fix him up. You'll see."

"It was an accident," the kid said.

"Yeah." No need to say more.

"I want to call my mom."

"We'll let you do that when we get back to the station. In just a little bit."

The kid had sat there, sort of rocking back and forth, but at least he'd stopped crying.

"I'm Al," he'd said for lack of anything better. "What's your name?"

So that's when they'd become acquainted, he and Scott Monroe. He'd brought the kid back to the station, let him ride in the back of the cruiser with his dad, and even uncuffed the dad so as not to freak the kid out. He didn't need one more hysterical person on his hands tonight. He heard the two of them back there talking. When they got to the station, Al's partner took Daniel Monroe off to fingerprint and booking, and Al let the kid call his mother. The kid had handed the phone to Al after a minute or two, and that hadn't been a pleasant deal. Not by a long shot. And if that had been all there was to it, he probably would have just let the victim-witness lady, obnoxious cow that she was, take the kid off to some receiving home. But what the kid said to his mother just before he hung up the phone sealed it. Made him realize he had no intention of letting them take the little boy off to some sketchy place if he had any say in the matter.

"Don't worry about me, Mom," the kid had said. "I'll be okay. I'm with Al." And he'd looked at Al with some look on his face that Al hadn't seen before. At least not for years and years. Al puzzled for a minute now, looking up from his paper work, trying to name it, and when it came to him, it was accompanied by a rush of some strong emotion. It was trust. That's exactly what it was. He looked up from his typing. The kid was examining Al's badge, drinking a can of pop, kicking his legs gently against the orange plastic chair. He looked up and gave Al a smile, actually sort of a squint that scrunched up his whole face. Al gave a nod and bared his teeth, the closest he came to smiling. The kid trusted him, and that was hard to walk away from, though he had been known to do it before.

The mother wasn't what Al expected at all, and neither was his re-action to her. First of all, her looks didn't go with the pretty boy in lockup. She was soap-and-water fresh, with creamy skin, big green eyes, and red-dish brown hair. Lots of it. She was wearing jeans and a sweatshirt, and it was the strangest thing, but Al swore he could see a floury handprint on the seat. She looked like she'd been in the middle of fixing Christmas dinner when the phone call had come and hadn't even bothered to put on her coat.

"Mom," the kid had cried out and split off running. Actually, both of them had been running. The little mom took off from the watch commander's desk, and the look on her face when she wrapped her arms around her boy, when she closed her eyes and started moving her lips in what Al suspected was a prayer, made him glad he'd done the right thing. And here was another thing he liked about her. She didn't collapse into tears. In fact, her eyes were bright but fierce, as if she'd come all this way to find her boy, and heaven help anybody who got between the two of them.

"Are you Al?" she asked, and for a minute he felt nervous. As if he'd done something to cross her and now she was going to set him right.

"I'm Al," he affirmed, putting a little extra starch in his voice to make up for being off balance.

She grabbed his hand then, held it in something a little more than a handshake, and her eyes got a little brighter. "How can I thank you?"

"It was nothing." He shook his head. A reflex. Automatic.

"It was not nothing. You gave up your Christmas."

"No problem." He shifted his feet uncomfortably and took back his hand.

"I can never thank you enough," she said, and he was glad when the kid spoke up and changed the subject.

"Dad's in jail," Scott said, and now that Mama was here, he looked like he might cry again.

She didn't say something stupid, Al was glad to see, just shook her head and held the boy a little tighter.

"Can I see him?" she asked, and then Al shook his head. "He's still being processed. He'll be arraigned tomorrow morning, and he'll probably post bail. You can see him then."

"No," she said, and the look on her face was odd. It was sort of a sad firmness. "No. I'm taking my son home."

As he would have done. Let Daniel Monroe work things out for himself. High time.

"We'll have Dad send your things," she told Scott, and the kid didn't seem to care. He seemed as anxious to leave L.A. behind as his mother was, and Al couldn't say that he blamed either of them. He would leave himself if he had anyplace else to go.

"I'll drive you back to the airport," he offered, and the words stunned him as much as if they'd been spoken by someone else. He certainly hadn't planned on saying them, but something about the starchy way she'd lifted her chin, the set of those thin shoulders, made him want to make sure she got home safely. He'd rest better once he'd seen her off.

"Thank you so much," she said, and then she smiled. She had the prettiest smile. She was a pretty girl and much too real for a faceplate like Daniel Monroe. He wondered what had ever possessed her to get hooked up with him in the first place.

"Let's go, then," he said, short on ceremony. They made the drive to the airport quickly. No one was traveling today. Everyone was already parked where they wanted to be. He wondered, idly, what she had had to pay for a ticket, walking up to the ticket counter with no advance notice. She didn't look as if she cared much. He parked the car and walked them in, helped them find the right ticket counter, waited while they booked the next flight out, even went to a fast-food counter and bought everyone a hamburger to eat while they waited, as it was lunchtime now. The prices were ridiculous, but this was Christmas dinner, after all. She got happier the closer the time came for them to leave, and so did Scott. He talked. He laughed. It was like a weight had been lifted from his shoulders. No doubt the questions would come back again. The sadness. Probably tonight when the boy got ready to go to bed. But for right now things were good. Things were cool. Al found himself actually enjoying their company. "So what do you do in Seattle?" he asked in a brief foray into conversation.

"I'm a nurse at Harborview Hospital."

Well, that figured. He could tell she had a good heart just by looking at her.

"Have you ever been to the Northwest?" she asked.

He shook his head. "I've got a sister there, though."

"Where?"

"Edmonds."

"Oh, that's not far at all. Just a little north of us."

"Mmm." He couldn't think of any other questions to ask that

wouldn't lead to minefields, so he just kept quiet. She talked some, but it wasn't the buzzy, chatty kind of talk that drove him crazy. She asked for his address, and he gave it. Reluctantly, though he couldn't say why. It wasn't as if she was likely to show up on his doorstep. She gave him hers, though he didn't ask for it. They talked some more. When it was time for them to head for their gate, he was actually sorry to see her go.

"Thank you again," she said, clasping his hand once more and giving it a squeeze.

"Thanks, Al," Scott said. He reached across, and before Al knew it, the boy's thin arms were around his waist. Al accepted the hug and gave him an awkward pat on the back in return.

"No problem," he said again, and he watched them leave. The kid was okay now, walking by his mom's side. She had her arm around his shoulders, and every few minutes she would give him another squeeze. Al watched her back as she went through security, the glistening waves of hair, the flour-dusted jeans, and he felt a sudden sense of loss. He knew he would never see them again, and for just a second, he wished it weren't so.

Eighteen

LENORE WALKED A CAREFUL PATH for the next six months, praying she would not make a misstep. She spoke the truth plainly but in love. "Daddy's in jail," she said, "but he's not a bad person. It was an accident, but he broke the law."

"He shouldn't have been drinking alcohol and driving." Scott would repeat Lenore's explanation like a catechism.

"No, he shouldn't have. He broke the rules, and now he's taking his punishment. But he loves you, and he cares about the boy he hurt."

A slight understatement, and once again Lenore had the irreverent thought that the encounter with Daniel Monroe's Porsche might be the luckiest thing that had ever happened to the fifteen-year-old boy. Lenore didn't know what Daniel had finally paid, but whatever it was, neither the boy nor his family would ever worry about money again. It had cost the boy a broken femur and a concussion, but he could definitely quit his dishwashing job at the ritzy restaurant in Beverly Hills. He could probably buy it if he wanted to, knowing Daniel's generosity and his guilty conscience.

Daniel had called once and written once a week. The first letter to her had been one of apology. Lenore had prayed long and hard before answering back.

"How can I not tell him what's happened to me?" she asked Edie. "How can I not invite him to the party?"

"Of course you must," Edie had urged. "You've got the light. Shine!"

So she had written back, telling Daniel in as plain a fashion as she could how she had come to Christ. Or rather, how He had found her. And she invited him to join her.

"It's fumbling and awkward," she'd said to Edie.

"It's powerful and true," Edie pronounced.

She'd sent it. Daniel had answered back after a week or so. Thanking her for her concern. Happy for her faith, but—how had he put it?—he was not there himself. He had written to Scott after that. Lenore had read one of the letters. The first one. It was poignant. *I'm sorry,* Daniel had written. *I'm sorry I hurt that boy, and I'm sorry I hurt you.* Scott read them, answered them after a fashion, but the letters he waited for each week weren't the ones from his father. They were the ones from Al Younger.

It was an odd juxtaposition really, and Lenore might have laughed if it had been funny. A letter from Daddy the jailbird. A letter from the arresting officer. Al's letters were just as terse as he was in person, but each time he would include something: a giveaway badge, a baseball cap with the LAPD logo, a bumper sticker, a DARE key ring. Scott hoarded the treasures, and once again Lenore thought it ironic. His father was a movie star with posters, magazines, and fan clubs, and he expressed his love by opening his wallet. But it was the desperado policeman who seemed more like a father to the little boy.

"I'm going to be a policeman," Scott would say now. "Like Al." He wanted Al to come and visit and asked Lenore for permission.

"Of course," she answered but without any belief at all that it would ever come about. Al didn't seem like a man who sought adventure. Perhaps after thirty years or so of cruising the streets of Los Angeles, just arriving home safely each evening was adventure enough.

For nearly six months the letters from Al came like clockwork each week, which is why she became worried when, without explanation, they stopped.

———

Al retired the first of June. He didn't tell the boy. He wasn't sure why, exactly, though in his more honest moments he thought it might have to do with the way the boy's eyes had shone when he had looked at the badge, the way he'd hung on Al's words, looked up to him when he'd given him that unexpected hug good-bye. His admiration poured out even though the letters. *I want to be a policeman just like you,* he'd said. Al the policeman was who the boy loved. Not Al the do-nothing drunk. He continued to answer Scott's letters for a while, but soon he couldn't keep up the pretence of being the hero the boy thought him to be.

He couldn't say exactly why he had finally taken his retirement after dreading it and putting it off for so long. He thought maybe he'd just gotten tired. Tired of all the emergencies. Tired of the tears. Tired of the blood and hatred, and tired of the noise and the flashing lights. He wanted peace. He wanted quiet. He wanted to be left alone.

Which was strange because he spent all his free time at Handy's, his rear parked on the barstool beside three other old-man-loser drunks like himself. When he wasn't there, he felt empty and cold. Like he was missing things. After he went to Handy's, exchanged grunts with the regulars and bartenders, and downed a few drinks, it started to ease off. He supposed the word for his feeling was loneliness, though he'd never admitted it to himself till now.

That summer was miserable. The heat rose up and shimmered. The traffic was bad. The air stank. There was noise—boom boxes, car stereos, televisions—everywhere, and that swirly graffiti that looked like Arabic was scrawled all over the buildings, the sidewalks, the trash cans, and Dumpsters. He hated it here. He'd leave if he had anywhere else to go.

His life became a dull routine. He drank at Handy's, he came home, slept a little, woke up, made himself coffee, and drank that until Handy's opened again. It was in July that it started to tell on him. He didn't know what was wrong with him, but he was afraid it was something bad. His clothes were loose sacks that hung from his rack of shoulders and his thin hips. His skin looked bad. He felt bad through and through.

The first time he passed out was at the bottom of the stairwell of his apartment. He didn't go to the doctor, just cleaned himself up, though he thought he might have cracked a rib. The second was a bloody mess. He fell and cut his forehead on the curb, and some do-gooder called 9-1-1. He ended up in the county hospital where a serious young Indian doctor with a British accent lectured him. "If you don't change your lifestyle, you're going to die," he said. "You have diabetes. You will be on insulin for the rest of your life. If you drink, not only are you doing further damage to your liver, but your body will not be able to cope with the alcohol."

The third time, he came to with broken ribs and a concussion. He dried out. Had the DT's. When he was sober, he decided he was more afraid of death than of life without the booze. But he knew he couldn't kick the habit himself, so he did the only thing he could think of to do. He called his sister.

She arrived in California and announced her intention to take him home with her. Marie was none too happy to have him on her hands, he could tell, but she was bound to do her Christian duty. He shuffled along behind her, watched her dispatch his meager household with her usual no-nonsense way. She supervised, hawklike, as he learned to check his sugar and take his shots. She herded him onto the airplane with the steamer trunk and two suitcases that now held all his earthly belongings. She checked him into the Seattle Rescue Mission's inpatient alcohol recovery program, a twenty-eight-day stint designed to teach him how to stay sober.

Then his sister's daughter had another baby, and he didn't see her much. She called now and then, but that was it. He didn't blame her. Why should she care? She'd already done more for him than he'd ever done for her.

He was in Seattle now. Down on Pike Street by the public market where the winos and bums hung out, slept on the sidewalk, or passed out. He was one of them, and he was almost glad to be here where he could look at them every day and see what he'd become. He wondered if that was part of the Mission's plan, or if they had just put their business where the customers were. They offered Jesus and a hot meal every day to anyone who wandered in. Those in the program had a more demanding schedule. They went to classes, were twelve-stepped to death, cleaned the place, cooked the meals, and worked the program. Al did his share, worked the twelve steps, and he was serious about it. He was as serious about this as he had been before about staying on the right side of the line. That was it, he realized. He had just moved the line. Before it had been set at the very edge, his only task to keep from doing anything that would land him in jail. Violence against his own body allowed. Now he'd moved it further. He couldn't drink. He mustn't smoke. He had to eat three squares a day, check his sugar, take his shots. Sometimes it seemed ridiculous. Why was he going to all this trouble? There wasn't a soul on this earth who cared if he lived or died, but even as he thought it, he remembered the boy and felt a stab of guilt. He hadn't written the boy in weeks. The boy would be worried. Well, he would see to that. He would go and visit him before . . . before what? He didn't know. He counted the days until the program was finished, not knowing what he was counting toward. But interestingly enough, he did care. He wanted to stay sober. It became his new goal. Beyond that he had no ambitions and certainly no plans.

———

The director of the mission was a young man, thin, with hair that looked as if it had been cut with a buzz saw. He wore wire-rimmed glasses and clothes that looked like they'd come from the thrift shop downstairs. His name was Jason, and Al had been drinking for thirty years before he was born.

Al sat down in the chair and tried not to glare at him. Something about him put Al off, made him feel uncomfortable. He supposed it was because he was religious. This whole place was religious, but nobody had seemed offended when he'd politely declined. They could keep their Jesus. He would take sobriety, but he wouldn't end up a fanatic. He had his dignity, after all.

The thought of that brought a smile as he remembered himself lying at the bottom of the dirty stairwell of his apartment building, passed out cold. Jason must have thought the smile was for him.

"You're about to graduate, Al."

Al nodded. No need to elaborate on the obvious. Tomorrow he would be finished with the program, and there were others waiting for his bed. He would go . . . somewhere.

"Where will you go?" Jason asked, his mind following the same track.

Al lifted his shoulders in a slight shrug.

Jason waited for him to answer. Another one of their quirks around here.

"Don't know," Al finally said.

"What will you do?"

"Don't know."

Jason gave him a stare that Al had to respect. "Not good," Jason shot back.

"I know."

There was a long silent pause.

"Do you want help?"

Another stare.

Al gritted his teeth and clenched his jaw. He shrugged again.

Jason waited.

"Sure," he finally said. They were big on helping around here but also big on making you ask for it. It went against Al's grain.

Jason nodded, apparently satisfied with the one syllable. He flipped open the address book on his desk. "I may know someone," he said and punched in some numbers. Al felt a grudging respect for the kid. He had himself together. You had to give him that, Jesus or no.

"Matt," Jason said as the other person came on the line, "this is Jason Thomas at the rescue mission. Good. Yeah. How about you?" Slight pause. Smile. "Yeah, I know." Another pause, then on to business. "Hey, do you folks still have the house? The one on Chestnut? Uh-huh. Yeah. I have a client here who may be in need of a place to stay until he gets his feet back under him. No. No trouble. He's a retired police officer. Absolutely." He wrote something down. "Thanks, Matt. I'd appreciate that." He hung up the phone and scribbled some more, then looked up at Al. Jason's glasses had slipped down. He shoved them back up absentmindedly.

"Local church runs a house. You might be able to stay there for a while. It's up to this woman. You'll need to go by and meet her. Here's her name and phone number."

Al took the paper. He read it, then looked back up at Jason. Bland stare. Al squinted, then looked back down at the name and address. It had to be a trick. Rigged somehow. He read it again. A third time. *Lenore*

Vine. 33. Chestnut Street. There couldn't be more than one Lenore Vine in Seattle, and that address was where he'd been sending letters to Scott. His mouth got dry, and his palms started to sweat. It was freaky, that's what it was. What were the odds? He laughed, but he didn't really feel amused. He felt odd, freaked out. A little scared.

Nineteen

LENORE STARED AT THE kitchen wall and listened to Matt on the other end of the telephone as he described their prospective housemate.

"He'll be a tough nut to crack," Matt said, "but without a place to go, he'll probably end up back on the streets. He's not a believer. Far from it. I spoke to Jason again this afternoon, and he said the man's hostile to the whole idea. It's up to you," he finished, "and don't feel guilty for saying no."

She called a meeting, of course, and fortunately Mr. Caputo and Mrs. Callahan were both at home. The three of them gathered around the dining room table, Mr. Caputo looking concerned, his round face sober.

In the background Lenore could hear Scott and Angie, who, if not fast friends, at least tolerated each other. They were playing Hungry Hungry Hippos, some kind of game of Angie's. Lenore could hear the marbles clacking against each other all the way from the living room.

"He'll be discharged this afternoon," Lenore informed them. "He has diabetes as well as an alcohol problem. If he goes back to the streets, he'll probably die, and there are no halfway houses that will take him with his medical problems." She felt grieved as she recounted the man's sad history and strangely fascinated with the chain of events that could take a productive human from a normal life to the streets in a period of months. She'd found a common denominator. Most always it involved some kind of substance abuse, and this time was no exception.

They prayed together for a while, and as they began, Lenore knew that it was no accident that Mrs. Callahan had joined them. It seemed right, somehow, as if hers was the missing voice they'd needed to hear.

"Lord, you said the Spirit searches all things," she said in her southern drawl, "even the deep things of God, and that we've received your Spirit.

Tell us now what you want us to do, Lord. We're all here listening. Just speak in that still, small voice, and we'll do it," she said, her voice firm with faith.

Mr. Caputo and Lenore murmured their agreement.

"Lord, you know everything," Lenore began. "If you've sent us this man, would you confirm it in our hearts?"

There was silence for a few minutes. Then Mr. Caputo prayed, "Father, you said that whatever we do for the least of these brothers of yours, we do for you." As he said the words, Lenore began to remember. She remembered lying on the bed, so sick and tired and terrified. She remembered dragging herself out. She remembered the *click, click, click* of the dead car battery. She remembered knocking on the door of Mr. Caputo's apartment and the delicious smells rolling out to meet her. She remembered Edie and Jenny taking her to the grocery store and everything that followed after that. All the small steps that had led her here to this warm, sweet home and family had begun with one person saying yes. She felt an urgency then, as if the opportunity might take wings and fly away, as if things hinged on this one decision, things she couldn't even imagine now. She opened her eyes. The others were looking at her.

"Yes," Lenore said quickly.

"He should come," Mr. Caputo affirmed.

"Thank you, Jesus," Mrs. Callahan said, her voice firm and settled.

He looked familiar, and for the barest fraction of a second Lenore tried to place him. She opened the door and smiled, searching her memory, but it was Scott, descending the stairs with a whoop, who identified the gaunt stranger in the doorway.

"Al!" he shouted loudly. "I knew it! I prayed you'd come!"

Lenore looked from her son to Al Younger. Yes, it was him. She could see that now. He was thinner. Much thinner. His color wasn't good, but his eyes were the same searing blue, and his jaw still clenched in that way she remembered. It was odd. It was fantastic. Too much of a coincidence to be believed, and yet it was exactly the way God worked. She had seen it happen again and again. He wove lives together and apart, bringing one home, taking one away, working His tapestry, creating His picture from the raw mistakes and false starts of their lives.

"Why didn't you write me?" Scott demanded, his joy at seeing Al tempered by his hurt feelings.

"I've been sick," Al said. A truthful enough statement. Lenore ushered him in and left the wooden door open. It was warm and sunny, a beautiful late September day.

Scott's face sobered. "Are you okay now?"

"I think so. Maybe. I dunno. I'm not a policeman anymore," Al said in a rush, as if it was important to him, somehow, to get that truth on the table.

Scott blinked, taking that in. Lenore wondered herself if it would matter to Scott. If his hero worship had been tied to Al's occupation or to Al himself. "Want to see my guinea pig?" Scott asked.

"Sure," Al answered, looking relieved. He trudged upstairs after Scott, and after fifteen minutes or so they came back downstairs. Lenore had coffee made. She set the table with two mugs, cream, and sugar.

"Scott, Al and I need to talk now," she said when they found her in the kitchen. "You can come back down in a little while."

Scott groused but went out. Lenore shut the kitchen door and poured them each a cup of coffee. They sipped quietly for a moment. She smiled and shook her head.

"What?" he asked.

"I was just thinking how strange it is that we should be brought together again like this."

"You're telling me." Al's eyes were a little too wide.

"Although it shouldn't surprise me," she said.

He stared at her, unblinking. Not asking why. "I'm a drunk," he said flatly. "All that good-guy policeman stuff—it's a load of crap. I'm a raging alcoholic." He spoke quietly. He was pale and washed-out but still lean, all muscles and sinew, ropy and tense. He clenched his square jaw, and behind his clear blue eyes she could see nothing.

"Were," she corrected.

"Huh?" He looked confused.

"You *were* a raging alcoholic. That was then," she said quietly. "This is now. The Christ of Calvary can still change lives."

He stared at her for a moment longer, gave his head a little shake, then spoke. "I have been a policeman, mostly in south central L.A., for the last thirty years." His voice was passionless and flat. "I have seen every possible perversion and deviation known to man. There isn't any way to sin that I haven't documented and observed or done myself. That's what I know about. I don't know anything about your Christ."

She nodded and suspected that was precisely what had eaten up his soul. For that's what it seemed like. Something had crept in while Al Younger was carrying on his daily business of eating and drinking and arresting and sleeping and getting up to do it all again, and it had eaten away at his soul, one nibble at a time.

Al took another sip of his coffee and spoke again, finishing the emotionless rundown of his life. "Wife left," he said. "Twenty years ago. Kids long grown. Got a sister here and the two daughters in Oregon, but they don't want nothing to do with me." He took another sip of coffee and changed the subject. "So what is it you got here? A rooming house?"

"Not exactly," Lenore said.

"It's not some kind of hippie deal, is it? 'Cause I'd rather stay at the Y than get hooked up with something like that."

Lenore smiled. She almost laughed. Here was Al Younger, desperately in need of help and looking critically at the hand that reached out to pluck him from the cliff. "Nothing hippie," she answered mildly. "We all just want to be here, Al. We've come to feel like family to one another. That's all."

"But you're all religious?"

No need to quibble over terminology at this point. She knew what he meant. She nodded.

"Do you go to the same church or something?"

"Two of us do, but church attendance isn't a requirement. You're welcome just as you are."

"You sure about that?" He looked doubtful.

"We'd love to have you, but only if you want to be here." She felt that it might be important for him to say so.

He thought about that for a few minutes, then gave a brief nod. "So . . . do I have to pass a test or anything?"

She shook her head, then posed a question of her own. "Do you want to live here with us?"

He gazed at her warily, as if he were trying to sniff out a scheme. "I guess I'll give it a try if all of you are game."

"We're game." She smiled into Al Younger's eyes, but they were guarded, and he didn't smile back. He took another sip of his coffee, and neither of them spoke. The only sound was the ticking of the kitchen clock.

Twenty

A L HAD BEEN WITH THEM nearly three months when his birthday arrived two days before Christmas.

"I'm sixty-six," he said, and Lenore thought he looked at least ten years older than that. She looked at his eyes, so world-weary and full of pain. Who was he? she wondered. She was beginning to find out. To see glimpses of the man God had created him to be.

She thought of where Scott had spent the day. In the tree house Al had built for him. She smiled. Today had been her and Carlene's annual cookie bake. Carlene brought recipes and makings for four kinds of cookies, and so did Lenore. Then they doubled the recipes and split them all when they were finished.

"It's very efficient," Carlene had told her when she had first gotten the idea years ago. "Both of us get all our baking done in one day."

Lenore had agreed, though it usually took the person whose kitchen they used a full day just to clean up. It had been her turn this year, and when they were finished, the counters were littered with dirty measuring cups and waxed paper, and there was flour everywhere, along with huge bags of the chocolate chips and nuts and flour and sugar she'd bought at the discount grocery store. But they had cookies galore, and Scott and Derek had spent the day in the tree house with cookies and a thermos of cocoa, snug and warm. Al had built it so tight, they could probably live out there in comfort.

He and Scott had begun making plans soon after Al moved in. They had made numerous trips to the hardware store, spent several days poring over plans. Finally they had spent all the money in the freezer bag on materials for the tree house. Everyone who lived in the house had to vote on using the money, of course, because it was what was left over after the food was bought, but no one begrudged it. The only stipulation was that Angie must be allowed up there, too. But today she had had a friend over, as well, and the two little girls had spent the day upstairs playing Barbies.

Al had shown Scott how to measure and cut, and Lenore had been moved to see them working together. The roof was shingled, the walls were insulated and covered with Sheetrock, and there was carpet on the floor. Al was an artist with wood and nails.

She thought about these things as she set the table. She had taken special care today, ironing the Christmas tablecloth, putting new candles in the holders, turning the best side of the crimson poinsettia centerpiece toward Al's place. She used the good china—the Johnson Brothers' Christmas dishes Mrs. Hosford had left with the house—and had put the special red birthday plate where Al usually sat, arranging his cards and gifts around it.

It was her turn to cook, and as usual the fare was just plain food, hot and savory, nourishing, and plenty of it. Tonight there was stew, already bubbling in a huge pot on the back burner, blueberry muffins, some canned peaches from last summer, and a low-sugar chocolate peppermint birthday cake that Al said he was sure he could eat. Lenore made him promise to test his sugar afterward, and he agreed.

She could smell the chocolate already, filling up the house like a sweet, comforting friend. It was a wonder she wasn't as big as a 747, as much as she loved the smells and tastes of food. She looked down at her solid middle, her filled-out legs, the small mound of stomach. She had gained a little weight. Well, maybe more than a little, but what difference did it make? Plain and thin or plain and plump. It didn't matter, did it?

It was probably Mr. Caputo's fault. When it was his turn to cook, he would make polenta and chicken, or tortellini, or calzones, his famous bread, or rolls that filled the kitchen with their yeasty perfume. And Mrs. Callahan didn't help. When it was her turn, they had southern food—fried chicken or fish and coleslaw, pinto beans and corn bread, or roast beef with new potatoes and green beans, string beans she called them, and always something decadent and delicious for dessert. In the three months since he'd come, Al usually ordered Domino's pizza or took them out to a restaurant when it was his turn to cook. Everyone agreed it was best if he took charge of cleanup, which he did cheerfully and well.

She went into the kitchen and stirred the stew, checked her cake and muffins. Everything was progressing nicely. She sat down at the table and looked around her, satisfied. It was a motley, warm, mismatched, inviting mess. And always changing. She kept adding little things she found at the Goodwill or at St. Vincent de Paul. She'd found a green-and-white enamel breadbox, an old washboard, a milk bucket that she'd filled with dried flowers. The rest of the house had filled up, too. The living room and small den were furnished with overstuffed couches and chairs, homemade pillows, quilts and afghans, bright, colorful pictures, green twining plants, rows of books, shelves of games, and baskets of toys. All mismatched, worn, and above all, comforting and comfortable.

They would sit together most evenings, except for Al, who would be down in the basement doing his woodworking, but even he came up when it was time for his cop shows. She and Mr. Caputo usually read or planned next year's garden from the seed and farm-supply catalogs that came to the house. Mrs. Callahan always had a needlework project going. Angie and Scott did their homework or played. They were like a colony, Lenore mused. A commune. She grinned at the unlikelihood of this motley collection of people under that title. But parts of the stereotype fit. They grew most of their own vegetables, and they used the wood cookstove for heat when the power went out, which, though not often, still gave Lenore a good feeling. It was the same feeling she got just from living here with all of them. Secure and grounded. As if she had a place where she belonged.

She looked around her now at the kitchen, still her favorite room. The heart of the home, as Mrs. Callahan said. Its most dominant feature, of course, was the yellow shag carpet. It clashed miserably with the Christmas decorations the kids had hung around. Lenore smiled again.

"Why don't you rip that stuff up?" Carlene continually harped. "I bet there's hardwood under there."

"There probably is," Lenore agreed, steadfastly refusing to touch it. She liked the kitchen the way it was. It had an easy, homey feel to it.

The oak table, broad, solid, and scarred, was the one she had found at the Goodwill when she had first come here. The sink was an old enameled unit, chipped in a few places but still beautiful, positioned under the window. She could look out over the back yard and beyond it, across the bay to Bainbridge Island on a clear day, or on a foggy one, to the graceful fir and vine maple just outside in the yard. The windowsill underneath it was cluttered, as usual: Mr. Caputo's tiny pots of herbs, a clay bowl Scott had made in school, Mrs. Callahan's Christmas cactus, which was covered with violently pink blossoms, a coffee cup—oh, that's where she'd left it—a small note card she'd put there herself with a Bible verse written out: *I will never leave thee, nor forsake thee.*

Beside the stove was a huge oak cupboard, covering half the wall. A potted ivy plant spilled down, its cheery little leaves curled around rows of canned goods: green beans, pears, peaches, pickles, applesauce, and Mr. Caputo's tomatoes. Above it, along the ceiling, from corner to corner, was a string from which dangled dried herbs, bunches of lavender, garlic, roses, and a clump of dried orange Japanese lantern blossoms, as well as a home-made Santa head that Angie had created from red and white and black construction paper and cotton balls.

Lenore's eyes flicked toward the calendar by the table, having made the full circuit around the room now. Its squares were covered with scribbles in a rainbow of ink. Today, December 23, *Al's birthday* was written in Mrs. Callahan's neat hand and black pen. Each week's cooking schedule had been lettered in red in Mr. Caputo's block printing. Christmas day was a mass of jottings in different colors of who was coming and who would bring what.

Scott would not be going to Daniel's this year. He hadn't wanted to go. Had made it very clear. He was ten years old now. Old enough to have an opinion about things, and after last year's fiasco, who could blame him? Still, this would be Daniel's first Christmas without seeing his son at all. She felt a heaviness for him, almost physical, and she wondered what he was feeling right now, this very minute.

She had made Scott call him. Scott had shrugged and said okay, obviously not excited, but Lenore had visions of Daniel sitting alone, deserted by friends and family. It seemed the least they could do. She had dialed the number for Scott and felt a strange mixture of relief and disappointment when she reached his machine. There was a woman's voice on the recorded message, and it said in smooth tones, "Hi, you've reached Daniel and Serena. We're not in right now, but leave a message." In a tone that said Who knows? Maybe we'll even get back to you. She wondered who Serena was. She wondered who Serena was to Daniel.

Daniel had phoned back barely an hour later, but Lenore had been in her room putting away laundry. Scott had answered the telephone. They had had a brief conversation, and after it ended she felt empty, bereft. And relieved. Crazy, as usual.

The truth of it struck her again. Their lives would always intersect as long as there was Scott. For better or worse, she thought, not missing the irony of using that particular phrase, her life and Daniel's would always be intertwined. She thought of the wisteria and the honeysuckle she'd planted by the front porch. They had become tangled together, and even though the honeysuckle stayed green most of the mild winter and the wisteria died off, it was impossible to clip one without ruining the other. She thought she and Daniel were probably like that.

She wondered if she would ever see him again. She had lived apart from him now as long as they had lived together. Did that erase things? Even them out like positive and negative numbers?

She began absently tracing the swirls in the oak tabletop. She wondered what he would look like up close, without the lights and makeup. She wondered if there was any of the Daniel left that she had loved. She closed her eyes and could still see his smoky eyes and hear the tone in his voice, cajoling and sweet, that he always used with Scott. "No." She said it aloud. She shook her head firmly, then stood up. Self-pity and this kind of muddy introspection were luxuries she didn't have time for today. She took a deep breath and finished getting supper.

Lenore served the low-sugar cake and ice cream to Scott's and Angie's glum expressions and polite murmurs of thanks from the adults. Al thanked her, then ate silently. He seemed discomfited at the special place, the pile of presents and cards. He had looked at her warily, as if she had laid some trap for him. They had eaten and talked around him, chattering, laughing. Now that it was time for him to open his gifts, she wondered what he would do.

"This stuff is nasty," Scott said, taking a bite of the cake and earning a frown from Lenore.

"Here, open mine first," Angie demanded in her usual imperious manner. She thrust a rolled-up piece of paper at him. Al glanced at her suspiciously and slid off the ribbon, unfurled the roll. It was a huge Santa with all kinds of toys coming out of his pack. A recurrent theme in her recent artwork, Lenore noticed.

"I made it," Angie said, then seemed to wait for the praise she was confident would come.

"He's got no neck," Scott said.

"He does, too," Angie defended.

"I like it," Al said briefly, glaring at Angie as if she'd wrestled more from him than he'd been willing to give.

Angie smiled, beneficent, gratified.

"It's stupid," Scott muttered.

"Y'all hush," said Mrs. Callahan and handed Al the gloves she'd gotten him. "For when you go out to chop wood," she explained.

He nodded. "Thank you kindly." His voice low and gruff.

Next he opened the gift Lenore and Scott had gotten him—a flannel shirt.

Mr. Caputo's present was a woodworking tool.

Al opened his gifts silently, inspecting each one, then setting it beside his plate with a terse word of thanks each time. His mouth was a tight, grim line, and Lenore wondered if they had made a mistake. If they should have let the day pass quietly. Her doubts were laid to rest when they were finished. The silence lengthened for a moment or two. Al stared past the stack of gifts to the wall beyond, and his pale blue eyes grew a little more watery. He cleared his throat roughly.

"That's the best birthday I ever had," he said. "I mean it." He spoke gruffly, as if they might challenge the truth of it. Before any of them could speak, he rose, put on his new gloves, and went out to fill the woodbox.

They didn't talk about him when he left the room. Angie and Scott ran off to play. Mr. Caputo caught Lenore's eye and gave her one of his blinding smiles. Mrs. Callahan began clearing the table, singing "What a Friend We Have in Jesus" softly under her breath.

Twenty-one

$\mathcal{S}$ERENA HAD STUCK BY HIM. Daniel supposed the least he could do was marry her. It certainly seemed to be what she wanted, though for the life of him, he couldn't figure out why. It was almost as if the accident—he felt ashamed of the term, it was too sterile, somehow, too sanitized for what he had done—had brought out her sense of drama. It was as if it had thrust her out of her ordinary, fault-finding mindset toward him into the supercharged, heightened reality of the movies she made. Now Daniel was the downtrodden prisoner, the misunderstood, chemically dependent loner, the alienated star. She was the woman who understood him, the true love who would save him from the gutter.

She stuck fast the entire time he had served his sentence. The rest of his friends had ditched him, had run for the hills at the first stink of trouble. But Serena had seen her chance to shine, and she had taken it. She'd stayed around during the three months it took them to bring him to trial, then made weekly, well-publicized trips to the L.A. County Jail, camera shutters whirring and clicking around her. She had staunchly proclaimed his innocence to the paparazzi, never mind that pesky guilty plea. It had been an accident, nothing more, she maintained. He hadn't been impaired in the least, intoxicated only in the letter of the law. In person she exhibited the same solicitous concern. Somehow she really believed she was rising to the occasion, standing by him in his hour of trial, which would have been well and good if he hadn't known clearly, without hesitation or the slightest glimmer of doubt, that he was exactly where he deserved to be. He deserved all they meted out and more.

He served his time quietly, without fanfare, and as with most things the reality was nowhere near as awful as the thought of what it all *meant*. In fact, the reality wasn't much different from life on the set. He was told when to get up, when to go to bed. He shuffled from one activity to another, and the jail food wasn't much worse than the studio commissary. He felt the same boredom, the familiar lack of purpose, received the same bored, jaded looks from those in his immediate vicinity, for no cameraman or gaffer was impressed with the star any more than a plumber was en-amored with his pipe wrench. There were no fans here. No one in jail cared a whit that he was Daniel Monroe. Certainly not his cell mates—a twenty-year-old wife beater, an innocent-looking drug dealer, and a young man who'd robbed a convenience store. Not the guards, who gave him looks of barely disguised contempt.

He tried to occupy himself. He read books from the library. He watched television, seeing the occasional blurb about his own misadven-tures with the law. In short, he tried to do anything to keep from thinking. And for the most part, he was successful.

Lenore's letter gave him a bad turn. He hadn't been expecting it. He knew she'd had some kind of religious experience, but what she described was disturbingly similar to the same drill he'd grown up with. He felt disturbed and off balance. It had been easy to dismiss when his aunt and uncle were urging him on in that direction. Somehow having Lenore give voice to the same things unsettled him, though he wasn't sure why.

He was released in September after serving six months and, after a bare three nights at home, was shipped off to rehab in the Arizona desert. It was his agent's idea, which he submitted to, hardly being in a position to argue. It was scorching and dry. In every way. But again, much like jail. Much like his ordinary life. Someone else was telling him what to do, how to think, what to be sorry for, how to change. He complied. He came back home after two months, in late November, and that's when Serena told him her plans. There would be a Christmas wedding. She showed him the press release. He read it. His own words served up to him. All he had to do was say them, I've served my time. I'm on the straight and narrow. I'm settling down. Her love kept me going.

Whatever. It didn't seem to matter anymore.

He wanted to visit the boy he had hit. His lawyer said no, to send a note if he must but stay away. They didn't need any more headaches. He had gone to the hospital right after it happened, of course. That had been painful, that apology to the family. To the boy. They had received it with silent stares. He had given them a cash settlement, which of course proved nothing, took care of nothing. Didn't even salve his conscience. After he'd returned from rehab he'd driven to the boy's house—actually, had his driver take him since his license was still suspended. He'd waited outside until he saw the boy come out, call to the neighbor, get in his car—a new

Mustang—and drive away. He started feeling a little better then and quit having the dreams.

It had been Serena's idea to get married on Christmas Eve. He would have said no if Scott had been coming, but there would be no Christmas visit. He was reasonably sure there would be no more visits at all by his son, though the subject had been carefully skirted in all their correspondence. Their letters had become more and more empty, mostly air and flat words, there being too much emotion to fit on a page. He needed to see Scott. To talk to him. To hold him. He would fly to Seattle. Soon. Just as soon as things settled down, he told himself, without thinking very hard about what that meant exactly. After the wedding.

Serena had quickly put the event together. Not that you could tell. For all the glitz and glitter, it might have been months, even years, in the making.

She was in high spirits tonight about something besides the nuptials: the release—tomorrow, as a matter of fact—of her latest film, *Sugar Daddy*. It was about the daughter of a sharecropper who becomes the richest madam in New Orleans. Or something like that. Daniel wasn't sure of the details. He'd been out of circulation, after all.

And now here it was, his wedding day. The guests were assembling, the scattered friends wooed back by Serena's determined efforts. She was mingling pre-ceremony. The wedding would be performed by some friend of hers who was licensed in the Church of Scientology to marry and bury. She was vivacious and charming tonight in a red silk gown, much like the one she wore in the crowning scene of her film. Daniel wondered why a woman would want to dress like a madam for her wedding, but he certainly wasn't going to say anything like that to Serena.

The room was filling up. It was decorated exquisitely with red and silver froufrou of some expensive kind, and the jazz band was starting to play. The buffet table was decorated with ice carvings of snowflakes, each different with exquisite detail, already starting to melt. They were serving lobster. For two hundred. He wondered, in an abstract sort of way, what the bill would be. Not that he cared much. Serena had plenty of money and so did he, in spite of what he'd paid out for the accident. And he had just signed a contract to do an action flick about a Vietnam vet who goes berserk, apparently his own substance abuse and scrape with the law lending a bit of realism to the casting. Once assured he would show up on time and stick it through, they'd offered the part. He would do it, though he wasn't excited. He sloshed the ginger ale around in his fluted champagne glass.

He could see Serena across the room greeting people, flashing her ring, and Daniel had a sudden stab of something he couldn't name. He was going to marry Serena. In moments. The irony wasn't lost on him. He didn't love Serena. So why was he going to marry her when he had so steadfastly refused to commit to the mother of his child? Ah, that was it, wasn't it. This marriage had a feeling of impermanence. Serena was demanding marriage. He was just as sure she would eventually demand divorce. She caught his eye and waved, and he waved back and smiled.

He thought about Lenore. He wondered what she was wearing tonight, Christmas Eve. Nothing clinging and no cleavage. He would bet on that. He smiled at the thought and was suddenly pierced with a loneliness so deep that he would have set down his glass and left if he'd had anywhere else to go.

"Daniel!" Serena was waving at him and motioning him over. The photographer she'd hired snapped a picture of him, pensive and alone. Uh-oh. He would pay for that. He heaved a great sigh that seemed to come from the bottom of his feet.

"Daniel, come *over* here!"

He gave her a little nod and finished off his drink with one long draw, then wishing he had something real to drink, something to just take the edge off, he started across the room. Serena couldn't touch Lenore, he thought fiercely, and as he walked toward her, he argued as hotly as if someone were standing right in front of him comparing the two women. Serena couldn't touch her, he repeated again to himself. Not a hair on her head, he thought, leaning over to give Serena a kiss on the cheek and sliding alongside her.

Twenty-two

THE HOLIDAY ITSELF reminded Lenore of a fireworks display, one beautiful surge of events after another, all coming too fast to properly appreciate, a lively stomp of color and laughter and food and torn paper. It ended Christmas night. They scattered, each to their own spots, leaving behind the devastated living room and the sweet strains of Mr. Caputo's new Christmas music. This particular melody was haunting and lovely, something she didn't recognize. Lenore looked around her, then down at her watch. She should go to bed. Instead, she sat down on the sofa, set her tea on the end table, then watched the dying fire glow and pulse and fall in spraying sparks through the grate. It had been another good Christmas.

They'd opened their gifts to one another on Christmas Eve this year. They alternated, since some of them were used to opening on Christmas Eve and some on Christmas morning. This year was Christmas Eve. They'd had supper, then opened their presents in front of Al's crackling fire.

Lenore couldn't bear to get Angie another toy that would just end up on the floor, so she had gotten her a book instead. *Mrs. Piggle-Wiggle*. She and Scott had walked to the bookstore on Queen Anne Hill and bought it along with a copy of *Cabins in the Laurel* for Mrs. Callahan and *A Guide to Bird Behavior* for Mr. Caputo.

"What kind of book can we get Al, Mom?" Scott had asked, and Lenore was stymied.

"Maybe Al's not a book kind of guy," she'd said, but then Scott had found a book of woodworking plans, and they had settled on that.

After opening their presents, those who wanted to had gone to the candlelight service at the church. They'd left Mr. Caputo at home this year, though. He'd had a cold, and Al, who didn't believe in organized religion, stayed home. Mrs. Callahan usually went to the Baptist church in the Greenlake neighborhood, but this year she went with Lenore and Scott. Angie, surprisingly, sat quietly through the whole thing.

On Christmas morning there had been rain rather than snow, but they'd had a good time anyway. Mr. Caputo was feeling better so he made everyone blueberry pancakes for breakfast, and the adults had sat around drinking coffee and watching Scott and Angie play with their presents. Scott had gotten some woodworking tools from Al, and Lenore had bought him an erector set with part of the money Daniel had sent. The rest she had deposited into his bank account, which was becoming substantial, due to what she felt was Daniel's overindulgence. Angie had gotten an Easy-Bake oven, so she'd mixed up a chocolate cake and put it under the light bulb.

"Does that thing really bake?" Mr. Caputo had asked doubtfully, grunting to bend and peer into it.

"Sure it does," Angie protested indignantly.

More company had come for dinner. Edie and her nephew, a sailor stationed on a ship in Bremerton, and one of his friends, Carlene and Derek and Carlene's new boyfriend, Robbie. Matt and Jenny and their children had stopped by for dessert. They all had a noisy, cluttered, happy time. It had been a lovely day.

She laid her head back. Even her bones seemed to relax, their weariness giving way to the soft couch. She sipped her tea and felt it warm her.

When she had lived with Daniel, they had had a Christmas ritual. They would stay up late on Christmas Eve putting Scott's presents together and stuffing his stocking, but on Christmas Day, after the presents were opened and dinner was over and Scott was tucked into bed, they would meet in their living room. The room would still be littered with the detritus of Christmas—paper and whatever new toys Scott had gotten, their presents to each other half in and out of their boxes, tissue paper flung open, wrapping nearby. They would sip something warm, put on their favorite Christmas music, and just sit on the couch, close together, looking at the lights on the tree. Then they would relive the day.

"Did you see Scott's face when he saw that tricycle?" Daniel would ask.

"And he liked the good-smelling markers," Lenore would say, fitting her head in the notch between Daniel's chin and shoulder. "I hope he doesn't put them in his mouth." They would sit like that, listening to the music, sharing those common little intimacies, and eventually one or both of them would fall asleep.

She started feeling sad. She got up, picked up a piece of wrapping paper that had missed her first cleanup, and added it to the fire. It blazed briefly. She leaned behind the tree, a noble fir that was very dry by now, since it had been up since the first of December, and retrieved a card and another piece of wadded paper. She added them to the fire, too, shoving them underneath the last, dying log with the poker.

She put on the tape Mr. Caputo had given her and went back to her spot on the couch. The saxophone played *White Christmas* in high, clear tones that seemed like bubbles of sound that would break at the slightest movement or breath. The melody sounded lonely, like something floating on the wind. She sighed and gave up the battle of trying to keep the sadness at bay. What was it about Christmas that caused such a mix of beauty and pain? Maybe it was the very meaning of the holiday. The baby born to die. Maybe there was no separating the joy from the sorrow. Perhaps it was a mistake to even try.

She let herself remember. Scott's first Christmas came to mind. She had gotten Daniel a new pair of sweats. That was all he wore around the house, those scrubby old sweats and an old T-shirt, whichever one he could scrounge up. He'd gotten her a pair of woolen slippers that year because her feet were always cold. Green ones. She still had them up in her closet somewhere. They were worn through, but she couldn't bring herself to throw them away. She and Daniel had gotten Scott books that year. He had always loved books. That year it had been *Goodnight Moon* and *Pat the Bunny,* the one that had different textures for different things—sandpaper for Daddy's cheek, soft fur for the bunny. She smiled and sat there on the couch, her eyes pointed at the last of the yellow orange coals slipping through the grate but focused beyond them. The last song she remembered was "I'll Be Home for Christmas," in the same haunting clear bubbles of sound, and then she drifted to sleep.

———

The next morning Lenore got up and was having a quick cup of coffee before she left for work. Al was tending the fire he'd made in the cookstove. Lenore thought she would take just a minute to look at the headlines. She briefly scanned the front page, the local news, the entertainment section, and then suddenly there he was. She stared, trying to make sense of the picture. He looked the same as she remembered, except for the tuxedo, of course. He was standing beside a woman, fiercely and darkly beautiful, wearing a clinging red dress split up to the hip. Lenore read the caption, then read it again, not able to take it in.

"That's Serena," Scott said matter-of-factly, coming up behind her, looking over her shoulder.

"You know her?" Lenore heard her voice as if it belonged to someone else, sounding high and bewildered. Al turned around, a frown on his face.

"Sure I know her. She's a dork."

Lenore continued to stare at the picture. She heard Scott scuff up the stairs, and still she sat there looking at the picture.

"Is everything okay?" Al sat down across the table from her. He looked concerned, she noted in a sort of clinical way. Her mind was suddenly that same blank, glazed surface it had been when she had asked Daniel to marry her and he had waited so long to answer. And now he had married *her*. This Serena. Serena LeMasurier, the column said.

"What's she got that I haven't got?" she asked Al. Then she laughed, her voice still sounding high and wild.

"Huh?" Al frowned darkly.

"Her. Right there." Lenore slapped the paper down in front of Al, came around behind him, and poked her finger at the picture over his shoulder. She laughed again, a little hysterically. "What's she got that I haven't got?" She felt the tears begin to run down her cheeks, and she picked up the paper, crumpled it up, and threw it onto the floor.

She could see Al fighting to control his own emotions. He looked at the crumpled paper as if he'd like to do it violence. He came toward her, took hold of her elbows, and steered her back down into the chair. "Wait a minute," he said to her, his voice sounding angry. "Wait just a minute," he repeated. Lenore held her breath to keep from crying. She reached for a napkin.

"What's this?" Mr. Caputo came down in his robe, his fringe of hair bent sideways, his face in a frown. "What's this?" He looked at Al as if he were responsible for the state of affairs.

"Take a look." Al pointed down to the floor where the paper had landed, then hovered over her again, awkwardly protective.

Mr. Caputo picked up the paper, smoothed it out, and held it at arm's length. "I haven't got my glasses on. What's it say?"

"Scumbag got married."

Mr. Caputo's face went from confusion to comprehension to grief. "Oh, honey." He came beside her and put his arm around her. "Oh, honey," he repeated.

Al cursed softly under his breath.

"Oh, honey," Mr. Caputo repeated again, and patted her back.

She cried awhile longer, then went to the sink and washed her face. She stood at the kitchen window and dried her face with a paper towel. She could hear Mr. Caputo clucking like a worried hen. Al was muttering darkly about things Daniel needed done to him. She focused on the small orchard she had planted. The apple trees needed to be pruned. Why hadn't she seen that before now? And now was the time. In the cold of winter. She would have taken her saw and gone out there now if she hadn't needed to get to work. She turned, cleared her throat, and told them all good-bye, taking note of their worried faces as she assured them she was fine.

She drove through the crisp, cold December morning, watching the sun gradually come up behind the jagged roof line of the east side, its rosy glow lighting the apartment buildings, the telephone lines, the roof of Harborview Hospital, the radio antennas of the helipad. She parked her car in the employee lot. She had forgotten her lunch. Well, no matter. She didn't need to eat. In fact, the mere thought of food sent her stomach roiling, and for a second it reminded her of the way she'd felt before. When Daniel had—never mind.

She was severe with herself, stiff and cold. *You will not,* she threatened herself, and she remembered a time when she was a child. Her mother had left her and her sister at a new day care. Leslie had gone off and played, but she had begun to cry. The baby-sitter, a fierce, threatening hulk of a woman, had fixed her razor eyes on Lenore. *"You. Will. Not,"* she had vowed. Lenore had stared into those black piggy marbles and had immediately seen that that danger far outweighed melancholy. She had kept herself frozen but tearless, making up stories, pretending that she was hiding from soldiers and the slightest sound would give her away. She felt that way now, as if she might turn and see Hulga fixing her with the black stare. *You. Will. Not.*

She went through the day. Her patients were sick. She had no time to think. A blessing, but of course her thoughts were frozen toward Him, too. She had nothing to say. Nothing to ask. She was icy and fine. On the way home she turned the radio on to the all-news station. She parked the car in front of the house and for once came in without her usual moment of thanksgiving. There was a message from Edie. She left it beside the telephone. Mr. Caputo and Al tiptoed around her as if she might fall into fragments. Mrs. Callahan said nothing but gave her deeply sympathetic looks. She went upstairs and changed into sweats and her jacket.

"I'm going for a walk," she announced. "Don't wait dinner for me."

"Whoa there." Al was out of his chair. "It's dark outside."

"I'll be fine." She turned and left before he could argue.

She was seven blocks away before she realized he was following her, a tall, lean shadow, a tattered guardian angel in a worn woolen coat.

Al never said anything but continued to growl whenever Daniel's name came up in conversation. Mr. Caputo came into her room the second day after Daniel's wedding and tried to talk to her.

"I'm fine," she assured him. He left doubtful but left all the same. Lenore felt a strange mixture of relief and regret.

Lenore kept getting up and going to work and coming home, and it was all like eating sand, and it didn't help when Carlene decided to take her out to lunch again. Under the guise of a shopping trip, as Carlene had a good job at the airport now, cleaning the jets in between flights, and had graduated from thrift stores to antique shops. They went to a few in Wallingford, and Carlene suggested they stop at the Blue Moon and have a burger.

"Sure," Lenore agreed and regretted it as soon as they went inside and sat down, as soon as Carlene opened her mouth.

"It's time for us to talk"—Carlene gave her a hard stare over the rim of her coffee mug—"about your love life."

Lenore didn't even have the energy to banter, to parry and thrust, this time. She just gave her the flat look that best captured how she felt. "There's nothing to talk about."

"No." Carlene held up her hand. Her fingernails were almost purple today, Lenore noticed. "You are going to listen to me. Now he's married. Edie told me so."

Lenore sipped her Coke and looked out the small square of window onto the patch of gray sky.

"It's time for you to move on."

Lenore said nothing, just examined the roots of Carlene's hair. They were brown. The rest of her hair was blond. It was the style, she had told Lenore last week. What an odd thing, she thought. To try on purpose to look slovenly and unkempt. Carlene was pretty, she realized, looking at her friend's upturned nose, her sprinkling of freckles, her long-lashed blue eyes and heart-shaped face. But Carlene seemed to take her looks for granted. She wondered what it felt like to be beautiful. She couldn't imagine.

Carlene was still talking. "I happen to know Erik Ashland's had it bad for you for years!" She shook her head in irritation. "But both of you are so absolutely pathetic, it could be years longer before anything happens." She shook her head, then waved a hand in front of Lenore's face and snapped her fingers. "Hey!" she snapped. "I'm talking to you."

"I hear you," Lenore said. It was not a new piece of information. She had known herself, besides which, Edie had initiated a similar conversation a few weeks ago, though with considerably more finesse than bull-in-the-china-shop Carlene.

"I've noticed Erik Ashland trying to approach you," Edie had said, "but whenever he makes the slightest move, you seem to bolt in the opposite direction. It seems as if that whole area is like an injury you guard. I love you," she had finished, covering Lenore's hand with her own. "I want you to have all God has for you."

Lenore thought of Erik now. She could call him up in her memory, could see him carefully reading the charts before he went through the doors of the exam rooms, could see the crease between his eyebrows as he thought. He knew most of his patients by name. He called worried parents personally, and when they brought their child in too often or for minor concerns, he never brushed them off but listened and considered, always seeming aware that he was a fallible human being.

She still saw him, though not as much as she had when she'd worked beside him every day. He greeted her at church and even came over every week or so, ostensibly to see Mr. Caputo, who might or might not be at home, to return a book or to leave one. Erik usually ended up having coffee with her. She knew he came to see her, regardless of what pretext he gave, but it seemed to suit both of them to preserve the fantasy that he was just dropping in. Just happening to be in the neighborhood. She could call up his face with very little effort. Could see the blond hair going silver around the temples, the craggy face, the cool gray eyes focused in the distance.

One of the books he had brought to Mr. Caputo had been *Don Quixote,* and that seemed right to her. Erik wasn't silly and ineffective like the befuddled old man who tilted at windmills, but he seemed to have the same single-minded, heroic determination. He was a hero, she realized. Every day he got up and faced situations that everyone else would have gone great distances to avoid. Children too sick to heal, sad and troubled teenagers, too many patients and too little time. And his own personal grief. She supposed that was what kept him at a distance. She wondered what her own reason was. Her irritation at Carlene dissipated.

"You keep brushing the poor guy off," Carlene was saying. "And it can't be an easy thing for him to approach you to begin with."

"I don't brush him off." And it was true. He was just as cautious as she was. They were two porcupines, she realized, circling each other, debating courses of action. The second half of Carlene's statement registered. "What do you mean it can't be easy for him to approach me?"

"I *mean,* if guys know your history they might be a little intimidated to ask you out. After all, how can they compete with *him?*"

Lenore thought about that. She thought of Daniel, only not the way she'd always pictured him in the past. Not tall and easy and loose in his jeans and sweatshirt, on the floor, propped on his elbow and playing a game with Scott. Or lying on the couch or standing at the sink or in any number of easy, familiar poses. Instead, she saw him standing straight, head slightly tilted, looking down at his darkly beautiful, sparkling bride in her crimson wedding dress.

"There's no one to compete with," she said in a tight, flat voice. "Our relationship—or whatever you call it—was just a fluke. Nothing that was ever meant to be." She tried to put herself into that picture, to imagine it was she standing at his right hand, lovely in a sparkling red dress, that it was she to whom he tipped his face, with whom he posed for the camera. But the image seemed like some strange freak of nature, as organic as a virus, as good and right as a mutation, a grotesque mistake.

Carlene gave a huge sigh and shook her head. She let the subject drop, but Lenore knew it wasn't over. And she knew it was no coincidence that Erik Ashland called the next day and invited her out for New Year's Eve.

Twenty-three

LENORE ALLOWED EDIE to come over and dress her, wind her hair up on top of her head, brush her cheeks and lips with red, fasten antique garnet earrings to her ears and a matching necklace around her throat. She wore a dark red dress with black velvet trim. Erik had looked surprised and pleased when he had seen her.

She felt frivolous, silly, a little embarrassed, as if she had made too much of a casual invitation. But perhaps not. He was dressed nicely in a gray suit and silk shirt. He took her to an elegant French restaurant. She felt acutely self-conscious whenever his arm brushed hers or touched her back. She decided dating was an unnatural ritual, a torturous gauntlet. She would much rather ease gracefully from friendship to love without all this.

Their conversation stopped and started like a car running out of gas, both of them a little off balance at this new thing they were doing.

"What do you like to do when you're not working, Erik?" she asked, the question coming out in a rush.

His eyes had a strange quality. He could look at her, smile, and still seem somehow distant. "I like to read," he said.

"What are you reading now?" she persevered.

"Augustine. *City of God.*"

Well, that was interesting, wasn't it? She nodded, intrigued, and waited for him to go on.

"There's a part in there," he said, "about God separating the darkness from the light. Augustine thinks that's when Satan was cast out of heaven. That's when hell was created. All in between two verses in the first chapter of Genesis."

Lenore pondered that.

"You know, God didn't call the darkness good," Erik said quietly, his face growing still. "He called everything else good. But not the darkness."

She watched him without speaking. He was unaware of her, off in his own mind or memories. He came to after a second and flashed her a smile.

They talked of work until supper was over, both of them seeming grateful to retreat onto familiar, if not exciting, ground.

After supper they walked along the waterfront. Lenore was glad she'd borrowed Edie's warm, black wool coat. At least it wasn't raining, she thought. It was a clear, crisp night. She could see the stars over Bainbridge Island, could see the brightly lit ferry chugging across the bay. She thought briefly of Daniel, not sure why. Were he and his new bride honeymooning? She forced her mind along other lines. She looked up at Erik. He was staring off, as she had been, and suddenly she felt ashamed of herself. This must be difficult for him, too, and she had been thinking only of herself. She felt a surge of warmth toward him. He wasn't a stranger, after all. This was the man who had helped her, had given her her first job. She knew him. She did. They began walking again. She took his arm, feeling daring, as if she were stepping onto a rope bridge across a great chasm. He didn't react except to give her a brief smile, to press her hand with his own. They began to walk back down the pier. He shortened his long stride to match hers.

They left soon for the second destination of the evening—a little night spot in Pioneer Square. The band was good, Lenore decided, though she knew nothing about jazz.

At midnight, when all the other couples were cheering and kissing, Erik leaned across and brushed his lips across hers. Her face pulsed with some strong emotion. Was it fear? She didn't know. Now she wished she had kept her hands in her pockets when they'd been taking their walk, and she had another bad moment when the evening was over, when Erik pulled his old Volvo up in front of her house. Even though she knew Erik shared her moral code, she didn't know if he expected to be invited in. He parked the car, opened her door for her, walked her up to the porch. She wasn't sure what to do then. Everything seemed very confusing and awkward again. The only thing she was sure of was what she wanted—to go inside, peel off the dress, take a hot bath, and put on her flannel nightgown.

She thought about kissing Erik Ashland—really kissing him, not the brush on the lips they'd exchanged earlier, but twining her arms around his neck. She tried to imagine feeling his rough chin under her palm the way Daniel's used to feel. She couldn't do it. Fortunately, she was spared any further awkwardness. Before either one of them had a chance to do or say anything, the front door flew open, and Scott and Derek burst onto the porch, each with a handful of firecrackers.

"What do you think you're doing?" Lenore cried, and the ensuing discussion broke any romantic mood that might have existed. She confiscated the firecrackers. They settled for sparklers, which she would supervise. Erik lit them with the kitchen matches, then the two of them sat in the swing, gently rocking, watching the children play here in the dead of night on this cold, dark New Year's morning. They sat without speaking and watched the boys dance and leap, making wide, swooping arcs and swirling scribbles, watched the bright lines of gold streak across the darkness, then fade as the sparks sputtered and died. She closed her eyes, and even after they were finished, she could still see, not just remember, the bright lines of glittering fire.

———

She heard from Erik twice over the next few weeks. He came over to dinner once. They had plans to take in a movie another time, but Scott came down with strep throat, and she had to cancel. She wasn't very disappointed.

The days came and went, but something wasn't right. She had a vague notion that she should do something about the situation, but she was at a loss to know what. The image came to mind of herself on her knees. She had been praying all along, of course, but they were short, terse prayers, tight-lipped exchanges as one might give the husband who had deeply hurt her and refused to apologize. She went to church. She listened attentively to the sermons, but her heart was as cold and dreary as the rainy Seattle winter.

Edie tried to talk to her, taking her out for lunch. "You're not yourself," she said, her kind face concerned. "I know this thing with Daniel has upset you."

"That's all long ago, Daniel and me. I don't even want to talk about it," Lenore had said, sounding more curt than she'd intended.

"That's fine. That's probably best, anyway," Edie had said in a surprising agreement. "What is there to say, after all?" She had taken a sip of her water and squeezed the lemon into it. "What's done is done. He's married now."

Lenore felt a lurch at that and then a spurt of anger. It was done? That was it? She was formulating her reply, but Edie went on.

"What I was going to say is maybe you should do something different. Something daring. Change your life."

The suggestion took Lenore by surprise. It was out of the blue, certainly not the kind of suggestion she would expect from sensible Edie. "What do you mean?"

"I don't know," Edie said, shaking her head. "Pray about it."

She did and came to the conclusion that Edie was right. That was her problem, she decided with a burst of relief. She was bored. Bored with doing the same thing every day. It was a week later that she stopped by the Trauma Intensive Care Unit at Harborview, the destination of the broken people brought by helicopter, by medic unit. The ones no one else could help. Her friend Anita had transferred from the surgical floor a few months before. Lenore talked to her a little, but really it was walking through the unit that got her blood racing.

She applied for an opening and was hired, then quickly began the three-month training session. It was exhausting. Three days a week in the classroom, the other two on the unit.

It seemed to help what ailed her, though. When there was a constant state of emergency, she didn't have to think about anything but the patient before her. They were so hurt. So desperately sick. One came and then another, a constant succession. The nurses rotated, switching patients every few days so they didn't get attached, so they didn't weep to come in and find a bed empty.

It must have been what she needed, this distraction from her own pain. She began to feel better. She began to pray again, to really pray, coming back to God with shame for her anger. She felt Him welcome her back and knew there was nothing she could do to make Him love her less or more. She continued to see Erik. More chaste dates, both of them toeing carefully that line between friendship and love, which once crossed could ensnare so easily. When summer came, she felt better still. Her friends and family seemed relieved to see her working in the garden, planting rows of potatoes and carrots and onions, cauliflower, beets, and broccoli, sunflowers, cabbage, zucchini. And by fall, when she brought in the sweet, crisp harvest, Daniel was divorced.

Twenty-four

I'M GOING HOME NOW, Mr. Monroe, if there's nothing else."

Esperanza was the same, Daniel reassured himself. Esperanza, his housekeeper, and Sylvia, his agent, were constants. But everyone else was new. His life, he realized, was like a play that completely changed cast every few years, or like the round robin interviews he endured every time he released a new film. A table full of eight or ten reporters every half hour or so. New faces, same questions. One batch, a minute of peace, then the next batch took their places. And his life was just like that. It had been full of Serena and her bunch, and now it had changed again. Serena had left. Her entourage had gone with her, along with most of their friends. Now he was back to what he'd had when they'd met. The constants—his agent and his housekeeper. And the hangers-on. He could hear them having one of their incessant arguments, their loud rap music blaring in the background.

"That's fine, Esperanza," he answered the housekeeper. "I'll see you tomorrow." He watched her leave through the back door and had the sudden urge to follow her. To ask if he could go to her house, eat whatever she was having for dinner. Meat loaf or tacos or spaghetti. He didn't care.

"I told you it was Vic Damone!" He could hear Donelle arguing with his cousin from the other room along with the throb of the music. Daniel walked past the living room and could see them with a few of their friends sprawled across his furniture. He thought about telling them to leave, but it didn't seem worth the effort. He went upstairs to shower and try to sleep.

What was it, he wondered, about the very poor and the very rich that always seemed to involve having an army of friends lying around with nothing to do? He remembered when he and Lenore had lived in the apartment on Verdera Street. The neighbors next door had lived on welfare. He knew this because of the tantrums they threw whenever the checks were late. There had been a woman with bleached blond hair. He still remembered her name—Bobbie Garrison. She had lived there with her daughter, a queen-sized woman who wore petite-sized jeans. Bobbie had kept a spiral notebook, and every time she talked on the telephone, she would write down the substance of the conversation. He and Lenore had stopped in one evening to return a piece of mail delivered to the wrong address.

"Jim called," Bobbie had said to her daughter. "He wants to go to the Outrigger tonight." Daniel had looked down at the notebook on Bobbie's lap. She had written down almost the same words. Jim called, 2:30, wants to go to the Outrigger tonight. And then after a few minutes she'd repeat herself, aiming her comment to anyone who would listen. "Like I said. Jim called and he wants to go to the Outrigger tonight." It was enough to drive a person crazy.

Any time of the day or night there had always been at least one friend, sometimes five, hanging around their apartment, parking in Daniel's parking place. In the summertime they'd be out on the patio, their cigarettes glowing in the dark, drinking beer and arguing about whose turn it was to get more, yelling now and then at the kids who were up too late, still playing in the parking lot.

It was like that now. Only *he* was Bobbie Garrison, living in the same boring sameness, the same deadly banality. And always a bunch of people hanging around his place, people he barely knew, helping themselves to things from his refrigerator, watching his TV, drinking his booze.

Daniel ran through the roster in his mind. If his memory failed he could always go downstairs and take attendance. There was Andrew. Daniel had felt sorry for him. He'd run into him at a bar one night when he'd stopped in after filming. He was an actor Daniel had worked with in a few commercials. He'd said he was between jobs and needed a place to stay.

Then there was Donelle, the bodyguard Daniel had hired years ago after the stalker started calling and leaving notes in front of the house. After she scaled the fence and left a love letter on the front porch, Donelle had brought in his cousin Tyrell to patrol the grounds. He was down there, too.

And, of course, there was Esperanza, his wonderful housekeeper, though she went home at night, and there was the landscaper and his helper. There was the trainer, who came four times a week. And they all had friends who seemed to have some reason for hanging around, too.

And now Denise was here more often than not, and she had a regular army of assistants of one kind or another. It cleared out a little when she went back to her own place, like tonight. And then there were the legitimate visitors. People popping in for a signature or to deliver a quick message but who always seemed to hang around for a drink or a meal.

He left his clothes in a heap on the floor and stepped into the shower. He felt the water like sharp hot needles on his back. It felt good. Ordinary.

He supposed the thing that made him and Bobbie Garrison alike was that for one reason or another they weren't part of the flow of ordinary life. Ordinary life. He wasn't sure he knew what those words meant anymore, but for a moment he tried to think.

Ordinary life would be waking up to an alarm clock, showering, and going to some job where you did something, made something, waited on people. You would have something to show at the end of the day of an ordinary life. Cars you'd sold, airplane doors you'd riveted, fences or houses you'd built. Ordinary life. That would be coming home to a family, to one person, maybe two or three, counting your children, but the same ones every day. You would do some ordinary thing like cook dinner—a whole meal beginning with some raw meat and vegetables that you yourself had bought at the grocery store and ending with steaming bowls and platters and dishes and silverware and napkins and sitting around a table. Not little things you microwaved, or ate off a napkin standing up or riding in a car or in an RV that doubled as your house. Real life. That would be where you snuggled up against someone warm but imperfect, maybe with sharp shoulders—he still smiled when he thought of how thin she'd always been. Where you slept with the same one every night and woke up beside her every morning and enjoyed the warmth of your bodies close in the cocoon of the covers before it was time to wash faces and brush teeth.

He finished his shower, stepped out, and dried himself. He looked into the mirror. His face stared back at him, stark and lonely. He missed the little disciplines. The regularities. The boring mundane things that actually led to a product other than himself. He dried off in front of the mirror and barely glanced at the tanned, lean body. He almost felt as though it belonged to someone else.

He was doing well, he told himself, taking out the tattered but comforting thought. His career had recovered after the mess with the DUI. Serena and his agent had been right. Their wedding and subsequent divorce had seemed to distract everyone. His jail sentence was old news now, and he had gotten several important parts since then. He was a success. He had climbed the ladder of the minor leagues and was ready to step across to stardom. This next picture would be the one that would vault him to the upper climes. Everyone said it, and he knew it wasn't just ego-blown hype. It was the truth. He knew it himself. He felt the same surge of excitement he always did when he thought of it, yet another part of him knew the whole thing was a fraud. An elaborate hoax.

They were a town full of egos. He saw that now. Everyone saw themselves as alone in the room, mentally cropped every picture until only their own face remained, perfectly lit and smiling into the eye of the camera. He thought of the myth of Narcissus, the boy who had turned away the girl who loved him and had been cursed to fall in love with his own reflection.

But lately he had the oddest sensation when he saw pictures of himself. It was as if he didn't recognize that person. He would know it was he, of course, but at the same time there was the sense that he was looking at someone else, with an almost complete detachment. Which was odd, because at first it had been almost the opposite.

He remembered at first feeling that he *was* the person in the picture, in the ad, in the movie. And for a while he had enjoyed it. He could be whoever he wanted. It had relieved him of some pressure, but now a cold dull fright had gripped him. The fear that when the game was over he would not be able to remember who he was. The real Daniel Monroe.

He poured himself a glass of liqueur and took a sip. It was as smooth as hot glass going down. He sat in the chair by his bed, leaned his head back, and tried to remember something real. A scene popped into his head, one that surprised him.

The memory arrived with sound first, the picture following later. A piano reverberated, echoing in his mind, building in a crescendo. He could hear reedy voices joining high and wailing out the notes as if in lament. *"If I gained the world but lost the Savior, were my life worth living for a day?"*

He remembered listening to them sing the plaintive question and wishing he could leave, but as always, he was trapped between his uncle's solid coal miner's body and his three well-behaved cousins. He saw his own thin legs kicking the back of the pew, his dirty, bitten nails as he used the stubby pencil to draw on the small visitor card, his thin arms as he counted the hairs on them. Anything to pass the hours. He could smell the hymnal, musty and old, could see the filtered sunlight coming through the colored window, through its bright mosaic of Jesus praying in the garden. He could see it all again: the wooden back of the pew, the offering envelopes, the tally board telling how many had attended Sunday school. Sunday morning at the Baptist church.

"Could my yearning heart find rest and comfort in the things that soon must pass away?"

It all passed away, he realized, listening to the words of the song play in his mind. Nothing was stable. He'd known that even then. He closed his eyes and felt as if he were resting his head on the back of that pew as their voices queried him.

> If I gained the world but lost the Savior,
> Would my gain be worth the lifelong strife?
> Are all earthly pleasures worth comparing
> For a moment with a Christ-filled life?

Just words, floating and washing, and voices and kind hands. His memories flooded together, not just of church, but of his uncle and aunt's home. His life with them. It was a good place, as places went. But not permanent. And certainly not his. He was a guest there. A visitor. And even though he was washed and bathed and fed and clothed in his cousins' outgrown jeans and shirts and pajamas, although he sat at the table with the five of them, slept in the bottom bunk, even though Aunt Dorothy combed his hair each morning and handed him his lunch in a brown paper sack like the other three, he hadn't been one of them. Not really.

He hummed the rest of the song, surprised he remembered the words, but his aunt had loved it, had sung it as she cooked and cleaned, almost as if she were preparing him for the question he must someday answer.

> Had I wealth and love in fullest measure,
> And a name revered both far and near.
> Yet no hope beyond, no harbor waiting
> Where my storm-tossed vessel I could steer.
> If I gained the world but lost the Savior
> Who endured the cross and died for me,
> Could then all the world afford a refuge
> Whither in my anguish I might flee?

He felt suddenly very weary. He took another drink.

Lenore's face appeared in his mind, replacing the earlier scenes. He had been thinking of her often lately, her thin face and thick brown-red hair bobbing up before his eyes at odd moments. He remembered how she had been, warm and breathing and alive, and he had felt something warm and alive inside himself when he was with her. Sometimes hesitant and fumbling, but real. It was odd that he, who could have had and had had any woman he wanted, would be longing now after a memory of sharp shoulders and chin. Even now, all he would have to do to end this solitary musing would be to pick up the telephone. He did not have to be alone. Ever. He could have a woman here, almost any woman he wanted, in the space of an hour.

Lenore Vine. He remembered her telling him once about the meaning of her name. Lenore. It meant soothing. Soothing vine. Yes. That was right. For that's what she was, and that's what he yearned for now. To be soothed. To sit beneath a cool vine. Now, that would be pleasure.

He slugged down another inch of the liqueur and realized the truth. He had gained the world. A large and buzzing world, full of important deals and publicity and lots of money and people who told him that everything he said was clever and funny, even when he knew it was dull or meanspirited. The world he had gained was miles and miles away from the little rooms they'd started in. But he still wondered, every time she sent him a birthday card or a Christmas card with the pictures of Scott that showed him going from sweet-faced child to gangly boy. Every time he heard her voice on the telephone.

It was always there. That question. What would happen if he were to call? It had been years and years ago, but he knew he had never settled it. He wondered if she still felt he owed her something. An apology. An explanation. He thought about picking up the phone and offering one now, but the very thought shamed him. The thought of calling her when he was drunk. He shook his head, poured himself another glass of liqueur, and sat in the chair drinking until he fell asleep.

Twenty-five

2000

$\mathcal{S}$COTT DIDN'T KNOW EXACTLY why he had stayed at Kidd Valley with Jason and Tyler until eight o'clock. Maybe it was because Mr. Caputo had frowned at him this afternoon when he was leaving, had looked at his hair and shaken his head, and Al had pointed his finger at him like he was scolding and said, "You just be sure you're back here by five o'clock, my friend."

"You just be sure you're back here by five o'clock, *my friend*." Scott repeated it to himself for emphasis. As he sat by himself in the dark kitchen waiting for everyone to get back from Mom's surprise birthday dinner, he was rehearsing all the reasons he'd decided not to do what they had all told him to do. He wondered if she would be mad, and he felt a little twinge of guilt.

But he was tired of her, and he rehearsed that, too. "Scott, have you done your homework? Scott, Mr. Jackson called again today about your tardies. Scott, why weren't you in school last Friday? Scott, where do you go when I drop you off for youth group?" Always questions and nagging and trying to set him up with some guy to take the place of his father.

He *had* a father. He didn't need all these cheesy substitutes his mom arranged. He had his own dad, and he'd be here just like that—Scott snapped his fingers, the only sound accompanying the whirl of thought—if Scott needed him. He was thinking of going to L.A., anyway, of going to live with his dad. He was sixteen now. Old enough to make his own decisions, and living with Dad would be better than staying here. Seattle was totally for losers.

He heard his mother's car pull up in front of the house, and he rolled his eyes again, then got up quickly and flipped on the lights and tried to look as though he hadn't been sitting here waiting. He knew it was them. He could hear that car coming a mile away. He shook his head just thinking about it. He was embarrassed by the car, an '81 Lincoln his mom had gotten cheap because it had a dent that ran the length of one side. Al was always saying how he was going to go to the junkyard and find another quarter panel, but then Mom would argue with him and say it didn't matter, and if he replaced it they'd have to repaint it, and then they'd start arguing, and meanwhile every time she picked him up from school his friends would say, "Hey, Scott, your cruise ship's here. Hey, Scott, the Love Boat's docking. Hey, Scott, the Queen Mary's circling the block." Why couldn't they have a normal car? Or a cool car like the one Dad drove? If his dad drove up in front of Queen Anne High School, nobody would laugh when Scott got into his Porsche. He was tired of being laughed at.

The front door opened. Mr. Caputo came in. "Where were you?" he said, doing that stupid whispering that's really shouting. He was mad, but he looked funny. His face was all twisted up, and the little bit of hair he had was all blown around his dome. Scott didn't laugh, but he couldn't help smiling.

"This is not funny, young man," Al said from behind Mr. Caputo's shoulder.

Angie came in behind them and gave Scott a sympathetic look. She rolled her eyes at Mr. Caputo's back, then went to the sink and poured herself a glass of water. Angie knew how to show them all. She sneaked out every weekend and went to parties with her friends. He was going to go with her next time. And if he got caught, big deal.

Al glared at Scott and went downstairs, which Scott had to admit was a relief. He was never quite sure what Al would do. Mr. Caputo gave him a cold look, and Scott felt bad for a minute. It was like Mr. Caputo didn't even like him anymore.

Mrs. Callahan came in and plugged in the coffeepot. She gave Scott a shake of her head and clicked her dentures at him. He could hear his mom and Edie talking in the dining room. He thought about slipping through the hall and trying to make it upstairs, but just as he was getting ready to make his move, the voices got louder, and his mom came into the kitchen.

"Scott, where were you?" Mom sounded more hurt than angry, and Scott felt another little stab of guilt and then a rush of irritation.

"I was just a little bit late," he lied. "You guys must have just left. Sorry." Another lie.

Mom didn't say anything, just looked at him for a second or two longer than she needed to and gave her head a tiny shake, so small nobody else probably even noticed it, then went to hang up her coat. Edie looked at him, too. But at least she didn't look mad at him, just curious or something, like she was going to ask him a question she really didn't know the answer to, not the bogus questions that the rest of them asked, which were really just excuses to chew on him. But then Mom came back, and Edie gave him a little smile, then went back to talking to Mom. After a few minutes Scott realized nobody was going to chew him out or do anything at all. At least not tonight. Mr. Caputo and Mrs. Callahan were uncovering the cake and arguing about how to cut it. Angie had gone into the study and turned on the TV. Al had gone downstairs, and now the doorbell was ringing, and his mom went to answer it, and he could hear it was Dr. Ashland. A few more people came. Carlene. Derek had a basketball game tonight. Scott hung around a few minutes more, and then feeling a little disappointed, though he couldn't exactly say why, he went upstairs.

He was planning on coming down when they cut the cake, but nobody came and got him, and after a while it would have been embarrassing to go downstairs, so he just stayed in his room. He felt a little bit mad at them then. They seemed to be having a good time down there, probably doing something stupid like playing games or something. He put a tape in his boom box and put on his headphones.

"You should really turn those down, Scott," his mom had told him yesterday. "When I can hear it from across the room through your headphones, it's too loud. You'll damage your hearing."

"*Whatever,*" he had said, but now, remembering, he turned the volume up a hair.

———

Lenore lay in bed the next morning and listened to the birds' wild chatter outside her window. She got up, pulled up the blind, and looked outside, feeling weary in spite of the fine day. Everything had that sunny, scrubbed look—Seattle's peace offering when the sun shone. A day off and sunshine. What were the odds of that combination occurring together? It made her feel slightly guilty, as if she now had a moral obligation to enjoy the June morning, but she hadn't the heart today. She dropped the curtain, and her mind adjusted itself to its default position. Worry. Over Scott.

Where had he gone? She blinked her eyes and felt as if someone had died. He had been so precious as a little boy. Soft brown hair, huge brown eyes, and the warm skin that looked like he had a little bit of a suntan even in winter. She could feel the beginning of tears, and she sniffed hard and cleared her throat.

She had a vision of him around the age of four, wearing jeans and a flannel shirt and some cowboy boots she and Daniel had gotten him for his birthday. Every day he put them on the wrong feet. "So my feet won't get tangled up," he'd said.

Where had that boy gone? He *was* gone, she realized, and again she felt just as pierced and bereft as if he had died. In a way he had. He wasn't coming back again. Not that little boy.

Lenore cleared her throat again and looked around for a tissue. She found one, blew her nose, and knelt down beside her bed. She prayed with a vehemence that had become her habit. Sometimes it was almost as if she could feel the darkness surrounding her son. He carried it with him. He wore it as an aura. She cried out to God to come against it, to pierce it somehow. She wept, finally ending the prayer as she ended most. "Please, God, save my son," she pleaded, and she meant it literally, as if he were in some mortal danger and these whispered words his only lifeline.

She remembered with great comfort the words he had spoken to her a few months after they had arrived in Seattle. "I asked Jesus to come into my heart," he'd said. "You can, too."

What God had begun, He would finish. She held on to that promise.

She dried her eyes and blew her nose again. A familiar guilt assailed her. Maybe if you hadn't been so busy with school and work, you could have given Scott the attention he needed, it accused. But even while she felt the familiar sinking and gnawing in her stomach, a part of her argued back. She somehow felt that more attention from her wasn't what Scott had needed. In fact, she had a suspicion it was exactly what he was going to so much trouble to break free from.

"Ain't nothing easy," Mrs. Callahan had said to her last night when they'd had to cut the cake without Scott, and Lenore guessed she was right. There was especially nothing easy about a single mother raising a son, in spite of all the moral support she got from her friends and adopted family.

She had even thought about calling Daniel. Just lately, since Scott had started in with the attitude, with the grunge music and grunge clothes and grunge hair that swung down over his face in lank, grungy strings. He acted grungy, too, and she felt her guilt become muddied with anger as she remembered the multitude of little insults he'd aimed her way during the course of the last few months.

She pulled on a pair of shorts and a T-shirt, went into the bathroom, and washed her face. It wasn't that she didn't know what the problem was. She could write a paper on it, but that didn't make it any easier to deal with. Scott was sixteen and entering the whitewater part of adolescence, trying to navigate between the rocks and keep his boat upright, trying to figure out how to be a man and paddling through it all basically alone. Because that was one job Lenore couldn't help him with. And neither, apparently, could Mr. Caputo or Al. She had thought she had a plethora of male role models, and she had even tried fixing him up with Erik, but that had failed miserably. She wasn't sure why. Erik hadn't confided in her, simply saying their rafting trip was "fine," and all Scott had said was that Erik was a loser. Along with the rest of the world.

She dried her face and went downstairs. The kitchen was empty. The coffee was made, and a box of Danish pastries was sitting on the table along with the remains of last night's birthday cake. She seemed to be alone. There was no sound except the whine of Al's power saw from the basement. Scott and Angie were in school, for a few more days, at least. This was Mr. Caputo's morning at the food bank, and Mrs. Callahan volunteered at the nursing home today. She had the house to herself. Ordinarily that would have been an occasion worth savoring, but today she felt unsettled. She brushed the hair out of her eyes, poured herself a cup of coffee from the carafe, and took her Danish out onto the patio.

The air was fresh and held a bit of moisture, like a hint of some flavoring. She pulled out a lawn chair and surveyed her garden. The grapevines were already covered with their broad, flat leaves. She loved to look at them. Their little curling tendrils were like suction, covering the trellis Al had made, and underneath it was a fine place to sit and read or just listen to the wind chimes on a summer afternoon.

The vegetable garden was in full leaf. The cutting garden she had planted this year was doing well, too, but there was a new crop of weeds. She finished the sweet roll and licked her fingers, then took a last swig of her coffee and tossed the rest of the cup onto the clematis vine that curled around the deck railing.

"There's an article here about a guy in Parkland," Al had said last week, thumping the paper. "Says every morning he tossed the last of his morning coffee onto the clematis vine by his porch and that sucker grew forty feet long last summer. This year he's going to try to do it again."

"We could do that," Lenore had suggested.

"Was it black or with cream and sugar?" Mr. Caputo had asked.

Al checked the article and shook his head. "Didn't say."

"Well, I'll give it a try," Lenore had promised. So far the clematis looked fine, but it hadn't become an overachiever yet. She bent down and pulled a weed or two. She noticed another patch. She bent down and got those, too, then finally abandoned herself to the job. As she worked, she could feel the muscles pull and tighten in her arms and back and the backs of her legs. By the end of summer her skin would become darker, her hair wilder and coarser and redder. Ah well, what did it matter?

She dug a little harder, wondered again about calling Daniel, but then put the thought from her. At best, Daniel would tell her to send Scott to live with him, and even in her wildest dreams Lenore couldn't imagine that solving anyone's problem. From what she read in the papers, Daniel was going through the same kind of adolescent nonsense as his son. Married to this one, seen with that one. Divorced now from this one. Linked to that one. On this. Using that. She was almost afraid to let Scott visit, but he had assured her it was all hype and lies.

"Mom, whenever I go there, it's just fine. Just me and Dad and sometimes his friends, but nothing bad. Really."

"What friends?" Lenore asked, and Scott would shrug and clam up, until she'd finally shaken her head and entrusted the little visits to God. They were infrequent enough. Scott had only gone down twice in the past two years. Once last summer for a week, and a few days last Christmas.

She weeded for several hours, watered everything down, then went inside to take her shower. She felt better. There was something about digging around in the dirt that gave her a feeling of satisfaction like nothing else. Not even her nursing. Maybe it was that planting and growing were so elemental and so simple. You dig, you water. Things grow. No agony. No worry.

She wished she could take the same attitude toward Scott. Just provide the right ingredients and trust that everything would be all right. But somehow she knew things were not that simple.

Twenty-six

SIX WEEKS LATER their little family got two new members. Benjamin Kaplan was stocky, medium height, with a full head of gray hair, a bushy round beard, and piercing eyes. He reminded Lenore of Abraham. He arrived, delivered by Edie, on a Saturday afternoon. His apartment had caught fire when he had put on a pot of noodles and then fallen asleep. The only things saved were he and his cat. He had heard about the clothing bank at the church and while there had ended up telling Edie his story. The rest followed naturally. He shook his head, his eyes misty with gratitude as he surveyed his new family. "I thank God for you."

"We're so glad you're here," Lenore said. The others echoed her assurances. They gathered in the dining room for lunch—a simple meal of tuna sandwiches and apple slices—while Mr. Kaplan shared his story.

He had been born in 1930 in Germany just as Hitler was coming to power. His parents had decided to emigrate to America. "Their emigration number was very high because they had no U.S. citizen to sponsor them. Forty-five thousand. Meaning that many left before them. Things were bad and got worse. So much so that they often doubted whether they would make it out alive. When I was eight years old, our synagogue was destroyed. Jewish children were expelled from schools. The Nazis began the deportations to concentration camps then, but our number finally came up. We left Germany in 1941. We barely made it out in time," he said, his face looking grim. "Most of our family didn't."

They had settled in New York. His father was a cantor. "We were Orthodox Jews, completely kosher. My mother kept two sets of dishes and another completely different set to be used for Passover."

Lenore looked down at the tuna sandwiches in dismay. She didn't remember reading about tuna in the Bible, but Jesus had eaten fish, hadn't he?

"Not to worry," he assured her, smiling and shaking his head. "I began to have questions about our customs when I was a young man. After reading Leviticus, I began to see that the things we did weren't even what God had prescribed. My doubts grew until finally I became an agnostic."

Lenore set down her sandwich, his story more interesting than her food.

"I was trained as a chemist," he continued. "My co-worker was a passionate Christian. I told him I wasn't interested in his faith and asked him to please refrain from discussing it around me. He said I had no intellectual integrity to make a request like that, which was probably the one thing he could have said that would have forced me to listen. He challenged me to read the Scriptures for myself, the Old Testament and New."

"Did you?" Scott asked. Lenore was slightly encouraged that he was paying attention. Al looked intrigued, as well.

"No, but the hound of heaven was after me." Mr. Kaplan smiled and stirred his tea. "Now came one *coincidence* after another. A few weeks later I got sick and went to a clinic. The doctor there was from Madras, India. I thought I'd be safe, since she was probably a Hindu, and told her about my personal struggles as well as my physical ones. It turns out she was a Christian, and before I left she gave me a New Testament." He grinned and shook his head.

"I didn't read it," he confessed. "But soon after that a Jewish friend came over. I told him all that was going on. We began talking about the problem. 'There are so many coincidences,' I said. Just then the telephone rang. The caller wanted to speak to my former roommate. I said he had moved. The man mentioned he was calling to invite my friend to a Hebrew Christian Bible study."

Lenore felt a shiver. She loved stories like this, where God's hand, invisible, moved people and events inexorably toward His goal.

"I gave up," he said with a smile. "I went."

"And?" Mr. Caputo asked, his satisfied expression anticipating the answer.

"I found Yeshua," Mr. Kaplan said softly.

Lenore felt a warm thrust of joy. Al narrowed his eyes as if he were thinking. Scott sank down farther in his chair. Mr. Caputo beamed.

"Praise God!" Mrs. Callahan exclaimed.

"Huh," said Angie. "Cool story."

———

Nathan Delacroix's arrival was announced two hours later by a tele-phone call from Edie. "It never rains, but it pours," she said.

"What is it?" Lenore asked. "Or rather, who?" It was her turn to cook supper, and she was stirring a huge pot of vegetable beef soup. It would stretch as far as it needed to, she thought, pleased that she had chosen it. But then again, as Mr. Kaplan had reminded them, there were no accidents.

"His name is Nathan Delacroix, but only if you can manage another person," Edie cautioned. "I know you're getting full."

"Of course we can manage," said Lenore. "Al is fixing up one of the rooms in the basement for himself. Nathan can take the last empty room on the second floor. It's funny. All these years with no one but us, and now two more people are added to us in the same day."

"Isn't that just how it seems to go? You can never imagine what a day will bring."

"Who is he?" Lenore asked.

"He's a country boy," Edie said, "from Georgia. He just got out of the navy, and he wants to stay around here for a while, earn a little money while he decides what to do. He asked if we knew of any reasonable places to bunk."

"Well, we're about as reasonable as they come," Lenore said. "And he's welcome."

"He'll be there in time for supper," Edie promised.

Lenore hung up the phone and finished her supper preparations. She was setting the table when Scott descended the stairs. She was fairly certain it was Scott, though it was hard to tell. He had dyed his hair black. His clothes were all black. The look he gave matched the rest of him. She gathered her strength for another confrontation. "Where are you going?" she asked, keeping her voice calm.

"To a show."

"What kind of show?"

"A concert?" He had a way of speaking the words that made her seem like an idiot for not reading his mind.

"What group? With whom? Where?"

He closed his eyes and breathed out his frustration. "Sister in Chains. With some kids from school. At DV8."

She was shaking her head before his words were completely out. "No," she said.

"Why not?" Scott was angry, and he didn't even care if she knew it.

"Scott!"

Mom's face was red, which meant she was mad, too, and the knowl-edge gave him a little feeling of satisfaction.

"What kind of people go to a place called deviate?"

Scott shook his head and rolled his eyes. She was really so weird, he was surprised she wasn't embarrassed. "It's just a *music* club, *Mom*. I'll explain again, and I'll try to keep my words short so you can understand." He had used that line on Jason last week, and it popped out of his mouth before he really thought about it.

"You'll watch your tone."

Mom was really mad now. Great. Now he wouldn't get to go. "Sorry," he muttered.

His mom gave him another look and started lugging a great huge pot of soup to the table. Scott knew he should help her, but he didn't, just stood there with his arms crossed over his chest.

"The last time I let you go there, it looked like Dante's inferno when I came to pick you up."

"What are you *talking* about?" he asked, then wished he hadn't. She hated it when he did that. Sure enough, she turned to him, and her face was hard and angry again.

"Scott, the guy taking tickets had a piece of cork the size of a coaster in his earlobe."

Somebody started knocking on the front door.

Scott couldn't think of anything to say, so he just shook his head and gave her another dirty look.

"Go answer the door," Mom said, giving him one back. "We've got a new housemate."

"Great," said Scott, giving his pants a pull with one hand. They were a little long, even for him, and kept getting caught under his shoes, some Vans that he had gotten at the outlet mall. They were the same kind everyone else wore. "Just what we need," he muttered as he went to the door, "another loony for this nuthouse." He pulled open the door with a jerk, making the brass knocker rattle.

"Hey."

The guy wasn't what he'd been expecting. His hair was buzzed, but other than that he actually looked pretty cool.

"I'm Nathan," he said, sticking out his hand.

Scott looked him over once more. Nathan did the same back to him.

"How ya doing?" Scott finally said. He stuck out his own hand, then opened the door and let Nathan in.

Lenore put on water for a cup of tea and thought about the events of the day. Mainly the arrival of Nathan Delacroix. As soon as she had seen him, she'd had the feeling he was the answer to her prayers, the whispered, urgent reminders to God that He had promised to be a father to the fatherless.

"Please take care of my boy, God," she had asked fervently again last night, then reminded herself that He had ways she couldn't even imagine. And now, not even twenty-four hours later, she'd been greeting this tall, skinny boy from Georgia, whose name was Nathan Delacroix.

She thought he looked about eighteen, but she guessed he must be at least twenty-three if he'd already been in the navy for four years. He was quiet and respectful when he was introduced to Mr. Kaplan, Mr. Caputo, Mrs. Callahan, and Angie, but he lost his stiff politeness when he talked to Scott.

"I had four brothers," he'd told Lenore moments ago before retiring to his room. After she had thanked him for the attention he'd paid.

"I enjoyed it," he said and seemed to mean it. He and Scott had talked about bands after supper, Scott apparently having forgotten or given up on going to the concert with his friends. Nathan had gone to Scott's room with him and listened to some music, and then the two of them had gone outside with Scott's skateboard.

"Nathan says there's room for a half-pipe out there, Mom," Scott had told her when she'd pulled his face down and kissed him good-night. Lenore didn't know what a half-pipe was, but it was the first time in weeks Scott had spoken to her without the tone and the eye roll.

"That's great, honey," she'd said. "What's a half-pipe?" She had only grown a shade doubtful when he'd explained it was a huge half-circle contraption that kids shot from on skateboards. "Derek's got one in the skate park by his house."

"That's great," she'd repeated and kept her doubts to herself. She made a note to make sure he wore his helmet.

She looked around now for her favorite mug—the one with Scott's face laminated onto the side. He had given it to her for Christmas when he was eight. It was in the dishwasher now. She took it out and washed it by hand, then filled it with hot water so it would be warm for the tea. She needed to unwind for a little while before going to bed. Decompress, although today had definitely been less stressful than yesterday. Suddenly she didn't feel so alone. It was as if someone had crawled into the little raft that she and Scott were desperately pushing away from the rocks and submerged stumps and had taken up a paddle to help them. Why was being a mother such a mix of things? she wondered for the hundredth time. Pride and sadness, joy and regret, and always the thinly disguised terror that marked the voyage.

She wondered briefly about Daniel. Again. She never heard from him, and he communicated with Scott only rarely these days. She wondered where he was, right now, this very moment. She looked at the clock above the sink. It said ten-fifteen. Lenore didn't even know what coast Daniel was on. What continent he was on. And for one wild moment she had the urge to call him.

Instead she prayed.

The urge passed.

She finished cleaning up the kitchen, gave the countertop one last swipe with the rag, poured the merrily boiling water over her herbal tea bag, added a spoonful of honey, turned out the light, and climbed the steps. She sank into her chair, sipped her tea, and read a few pages of her novel, then got up to take her shower.

Her mind was still on other things, which was why, when she found the lump, she shook her head, resoaped her hand, and felt again.

It was still there. It was tiny, hard, didn't budge when she tried to move it, didn't hurt when she pressed it. All bad signs.

She tried to stay calm, to not jump to conclusions. It could be a benign cyst. But it didn't feel benign. It felt mean and little and hard. It felt like cancer, and she felt another chill when she realized that even though it was just the size of a pea, barely palpable, by the time she could feel it with her hand, it could well have spread. She thought of her grandmother who had died of cancer. Breast? And there had been an aunt, as well.

She was overreacting. It was probably a mistake. An ultrasound would prove it. She tried to pray, but her mind was slick and clean, and the thoughts slid off its walls along with the sheets of water. She got out of the shower and put on her gown, climbed into bed, turned out the lights, and tried to go to sleep, but she lay awake for a long time, staring into the warm night, thinking how odd it was that one small thing could be so huge. How one tiny pea-sized fear could displace so many others.

Twenty-seven

LENORE CALLED HER gynecologist first thing Monday morning.

"Come in right away," Dr. Forrest said and worked Lenore in that afternoon. The doctor hadn't liked the feel of the lump, either, and what followed was two weeks of mammograms, ultrasounds, and biopsies.

Edie went with her to the appointment with the surgeon after all the tests had been completed.

"There's no metastasis," he said. "That's good news. The bad news is the multiple foci."

He looked her in the eye. Lenore nodded. She had a feeling she knew what he was going to recommend.

"Translate all this for me," Edie said sharply. She sounded impatient, almost angry.

"The cancer hasn't spread," the doctor said. "But we found more than one tumor. That's not a good thing," he said, his voice gentle.

"Oh." Edie's voice went from angry to small.

"What do you recommend?" Lenore asked him. She was surprised at her own reaction. She seemed to be moving and making decisions on some level above her emotions.

"Because of the multiple foci, and with your family history, I'd recommend a mastectomy. But waiting a few weeks probably won't affect the outcome if you'd like to get another opinion."

"No," she said. She had had days to think, and ever since the mammogram had shown there was more than one tumor, she had known what the outcome would be. The important thing wasn't whether she had one breast or two. The important thing was Scott. She needed to be here for him. "I'll accept your recommendation." Her voice shook, and that was the closest she came to losing her control.

Edie squeezed her hand.

Dr. Simons said nothing, just looked at her with large, sad eyes and nodded.

Scott was in the kitchen making nachos when she arrived home.

It was only four in the afternoon, but more than anything she wanted to crawl into her bed and pull the covers over her head, as she had done when she had first arrived in Seattle. Instead, she told Scott about the cancer. She let him keep fussing with the nachos instead of making him sit down and look her in the eye. It was easier for him to talk if he was doing something with his hands.

"Do you have any questions?" she asked when she was finished.

"No." He drizzled melted Velveeta cheese over the tortilla chips. "Not really."

"Well, if you do, or you want to talk . . ." Lenore's voice trailed off.

Scott poked at a packed can of green chili peppers with the tip of his fork, and they fell out onto his nachos still in the shape of the can. He began to spread them over the chips and cheese. He didn't answer. Lenore didn't have the energy to press the issue. She went over to him, stood on tiptoes to reach his cheek, and kissed him softly, feeling his body rigid like a board.

She called her mother and sister, who reacted about as she'd expected. Her mother offered to come and seemed intensely relieved when Lenore thanked her and said no. Leslie asked a few questions, then launched into a tale of her own woe—something about a boyfriend in jail and a stolen checkbook. She told the rest of them after dinner. Mr. Caputo, Mr. Kaplan, Nathan Delacroix, Mrs. Callahan, and Angie, who was uncharacteristically quiet, watching Lenore with wide eyes. But of all the people in the house on Chestnut Street, oddly enough it was Al who took it the hardest.

He stalked away from the table, leaving the others staring after him. Lenore followed him into the kitchen after a moment.

"It's not fair," he raged. "Why you?" He seemed to want to say more but restrained himself. With a terrible face, he leaned over and kissed her softly on the cheek and then excused himself and walked to the basement stairwell, holding himself tight and stiff. She could hear him slamming things and stomping down there, the floor shaking slightly under her feet.

Lenore woke up at five-thirty, ready to climb out of bed, shower, and go to work. Then she remembered. She had taken a leave of absence.

She had no work, at least for a month. Tomorrow morning she would have her surgery. She shoved her fear back behind its wall, rolled over, and went back to sleep, and when she woke up the second time she could smell something cooking. It was eight o'clock. She pulled on her robe and walked down the stairs, and the predictable creaking on the second step from the top and the last three was the nicest thing that had happened to her in days. She almost climbed them again for the sheer pleasure of hearing that familiar squeak. Instead, she went into the kitchen and greeted Mr. Caputo, who was making spaghetti sauce. According to him, it had to simmer at least eight hours or it was unfit for consumption. His face creased into lines of anxiety when he saw her. She cringed.

He put down the long-handled spoon, not even bothering to aim for the spoon rest, and covered her with his arms. He felt warm and solid, and she leaned against him for a minute and rested her head on his shoulder. "Our prayers will make it right," he said. And then when she sat down at the table, he poured her a cup of coffee and handed her the cream and sugar, then offered his own brand of therapy. "Let me fix you something to eat."

Lenore sat at the oak table and sipped a cup of coffee and made his day by requesting eggs and bacon. He carried on a chipper little conversation, and she had a sudden feeling of being back at the Lakeview Apartments, sitting on the stool in his kitchen, watching him make rolls and stir polenta. She'd been so downhearted over Daniel then that she thought dying would have been better than life. That had been nearly twelve years ago. That was a long time.

Mr. Caputo set a plate of sizzling eggs, crisp bacon, and buttered toast in front of her. She ate.

The rest of the day went by in sort of a numb progression. She packed her things—a housecoat and gown, a pair of sweats, a button-up blouse to wear home, an extra pair of socks, some underwear. No bra.

Dinner was a stiff little meal, and that was the moment when Lenore almost wished she hadn't told anyone. Then at least she could have gone to the hospital in the morning with their happy voices lingering in her memory. Mr. Caputo's squinting smile and his banter with Mr. Kaplan, his new best friend, Mrs. Callahan's proper grace, Al's gruff kindness. She could have remembered Nathan Delacroix and Scott insulting each other good-naturedly and even Angie's bright little eyes and forthright assertions. As it was, Al glowered, looking as though only a great effort of his will prevented him from upending the table, as hot in his pure, white anger as Jesus was when He drove the money changers from the temple.

"You're only making it worse for her," she heard Mrs. Callahan say to Al in a stage whisper when she went to help Mr. Caputo fetch the cobbler and ice cream. She didn't even have the energy to smile.

She hadn't told Erik, though she'd spoken to him several times since her diagnosis. She'd instructed the others to say nothing, as well. At first she'd told herself she would tell him after the tests were completed, but there never seemed to be a good time. They'd both been busy, and she hadn't wanted to tell him over the telephone. But she knew the real reason had more to do with the way he had looked when he talked of his wife, of God separating the light from the darkness. She didn't think she could bear to carry her own fears and his, too. She would tell him later. When it was all over.

After they finished dessert, Angie finally broke the tension. She got up from her chair, crossed over to Lenore, then got down on her knees and clasped Lenore's hands inside her own. With a deep sigh and all her fifteen-year-old drama, she said, "Pray with me, Lenore."

Lenore had laughed. The others, as if freed from some great tension, had done the same. She had bowed her head, and Angie had given her a benediction.

"Jesus, take care of Lenore, and for crying out loud, *don't let her die.*"

"Angie!" Mrs. Callahan protested, mortified.

"Amen," Lenore answered firmly, laughing again.

"Amen," the others repeated.

Angie looked at her and beamed, then walked airily away, as if the problem had been taken care of.

———

The next morning was busy, a flurry of activity. She checked into the hospital at six, was offered a lemon glycerin stick to swab her mouth with instead of breakfast, then she was given her pre-op meds and wheeled to the operating room. Mr. Caputo and Edie were waiting in the hallway with Scott. The gurney paused long enough to let her speak to them.

"Hi, honey." Mr. Caputo stroked her arm. She was sleepy from the drugs they'd put in her IV, but she could see that Scott looked angry and close to tears. She had the fleeting thought that she should have tried harder to make contact with Daniel, persisted after her one call was unreturned, but she didn't know if having his father involved would be a help to Scott or just another stress.

"Come here, sweetie," she said to Scott. "Give me a hug." She searched his face for a glimpse of the fine-haired, brown-eyed baby, but his jaw was long and scratchy, and when she looked at him, she saw Daniel's muddy eyes and dark skin.

He bent over and awkwardly put a hand on each of her shoulders.

"Love you, Mom" came out slurred and in a rush, as if the words burned and their corners were sharp in his mouth.

"I love you, too." She felt too sleepy to say more.

"We're praying for you." It was Edie, her face behind Scott's shoulder. Lenore gave a nod and closed her eyes. It was too hard to keep them open.

The next thing Lenore heard was a high-pitched wailing, like a siren, and she wondered where she was and what the sound was coming from. And she was afraid.

"Enough already!" she heard someone say.

"She's been wailing like this for twenty minutes," another voice complained.

She felt a hand on her wrist. She clutched it, but it pulled away from her gently. More fussing with the covers. Then a voice said, "How are you feeling? Lenore?" Loud and insistent. "Lenore, are you waking up?"

As the voice got louder, Lenore realized she was there, inside her body, and it hurt. Nothing more than that. Then the wailing started again.

"I'll get her some morphine," the voice that had pulled away the hand said.

In just a moment or two—or was it an hour?—the pain was blunted, as if someone had inserted a wad of cotton between its sharp edge and her chest. She fell asleep suddenly, a dark curtain falling between her and the voices and the pain.

Twenty-eight

"PHONE FOR YOU, Scott." Nathan jerked his head toward the kitchen. "I think it's your dad."

Scott got up and went to answer it, his head pounding, his stomach a tight ball. He didn't feel good. He hadn't felt good since Mom had told him about her lump. About her cancer. His stomach was upset. But what was he supposed to do? Ask her to make him feel better after he'd been such a jerk to her? There was no way he could do that. He couldn't talk to anybody here. They all thought he was a jerk. So he had called his dad and gotten the machine, of course. He'd left a message. "Hello," he said now, his voice flat.

"Hey, buddy," Dad said. "How's it going?"

"Fine."

"Hey, who was that who answered the phone?" Dad asked, his voice sounding forced and tight, and suddenly Scott wished he had never called his dad. Here we go. Same old drill. Dad wanted to do whatever he wanted but got all bent out of shape whenever he thought Mom had a life.

"Nobody," he said, not telling Dad the truth, that it was Nathan Delacroix who had answered the phone, someone not much older than Scott himself. "Just a friend of ours."

Long pause. "Oh. Well, what's up?"

"Nothing," Scott said and had the feeling that he couldn't say more even if he wanted to. That the words were tight, sewn to his lips and throat.

"How are you guys doing?" Dad tried again.

"Fine."

He could hear Dad's even breath in the silence, and then Dad said something that shocked Scott out of his sullenness.

"Let me talk to Mom for a minute."

Scott felt surprised and then angry, though he couldn't say why.

"She's busy," he said. "She can't come to the phone right now." Well, that was the truth. She was in the hospital. They'd taken off her breast.

"Well, will you tell her that I called?" Dad asked. His voice was smooth and calm, not annoyed the way Mom and the others got with him.

"Sure," said Scott, without any intention of doing so.

He hung up the phone and glared at it. He wasn't sure why he had lied to Dad. He only knew he felt angry at him for not knowing what was going on. He didn't deserve to know, Scott told himself.

He felt a little ashamed of himself. He knew he wasn't being fair. If Dad knew what was going on, he would have tried to help. He might have invited Scott to come and stay with him or maybe have volunteered to come up here. But maybe he wouldn't have. Scott admitted that possibility to himself, and suddenly he was mad again. Mad, and glad he hadn't told Dad anything about Mom. Dad didn't deserve to know, he repeated.

Daniel sat and looked at the telephone after he hung it up. Why do people do that? he wondered. Keep staring at the telephone after a call, as if it is going to somehow interpret what just happened for them, like newscasters after a presidential speech.

Scott sounded hostile tonight, he half expected the telephone to say, *and about the guy who answered—I think there was a shade more to all that than Scott let on.*

He wondered if he was losing it.

"Who was that?" Denise came downstairs. Her suitcases were already lined up in the foyer.

"Nobody."

"I thought I heard you talking to someone on the telephone."

He didn't answer her, just looked at her curiously, as if seeing her for the first time. Now, on the day she was leaving him. Just now seeing her long legs and golden skin and wide-set limpid blue eyes, which gave her a helpless, pleading sort of look. Her only flaw was her too-wide mouth, but even that just came out girlish and cute when she smiled for the cameras.

"What?" she demanded.

Daniel shook his head. "Nothing."

Denise sighed, exasperated, and dug around in her purse. "What is *with* you?" Daniel could hear her muttering.

The idea that she would understand, even if he told her, was ludicrous. She had the emotional experience and maturity of a sixteen-year-old. Of

Scott. And he had married her. Well, that mistake would soon be rectified. As soon as she called her lawyer. She said it was because of his drinking, but Daniel knew it was because she smelled failure. She, like everyone else around here, would distance herself as far and as quickly as she could.

Daniel leaned over the little desk and rubbed his forehead with his hands. Lenore had been out. She had plans. She was busy. Well, of course she was, and he wondered again why it had seemed so important to return her call, to discuss Scott's situation now. She had left her message a week ago, and he had been dreading the conversation until now. Until he felt the need for consolation. He shook his head at his ridiculous, pathetic neediness. Or was it the last shred of sanity he had left? The death grip on the last true thing he had known? He laughed out loud at the thought. At the sheer irony of the thought. He could see Denise out of the corner of his eye, watching him.

He had left Lenore to find life. Life in capital letters. And he had gotten all the things he had wanted. If he had scripted his life like one of the dramas he starred in, it couldn't have gone any better. Until now. His last movie had tanked. His series had been canceled. Just setbacks, he had told himself. But people were deserting now, scuttling away like rats on a sinking ship.

"What are you doing?" Denise's tone was irritated.

"I'm *thinking,* Denise." He could hear the sarcasm biting through his words. He didn't add anything unkind about her not recognizing signs of the activity, though he was tempted.

"Well, you're creeping me out."

"Sorry." He got up and went upstairs. He pulled on a jacket and a baseball cap, then reached for his sunglasses and smiled at the triteness of it. Wearing sunglasses so he wouldn't be recognized. He probably didn't need to worry if the public was as disinterested as the ratings and box-office take seemed to indicate.

"Where are you going?" Denise demanded as he came back through the foyer. Her voice had gone from querulous to petulant, a far more familiar tone.

"Out."

Denise made a sound of exasperation, probably miffed that he was spoiling her grand exit.

"I used to think you were something," Denise said to his back, unable to resist a last cruelty. "But now I know the truth."

He paused, turned back to allow her this one last thrust.

"You're just one more of those guys who almost made it."

———

Daniel called from the car. Robert Pasquale was at home and said of course he would be glad to see Daniel. Daniel drove to his house, not quite sure why he was making the trip. He had spoken to Pasquale months ago at a birthday party for Eldon Heywood, the game show maven, one of the last social events he'd been invited to. He had worked with Pasquale before on a film, and though Robert had never attained the status of superstardom, he was a good actor and had accumulated a solid body of work. A few of his films had received high critical acclaim, and most did well enough at the box office. Daniel envied him.

"You look a little gray around the edges," Robert had said to him at the party. "You all right?"

"Sure," Daniel had assured him. Pasquale had eyed the drink in Daniel's hand with a raised eyebrow.

"Come and see me sometime," he'd invited and had jotted his phone number down on a scrap of paper, which Daniel had carried in his wallet for months. And here he was.

Now Daniel pulled up in front of the gate, and after a moment, seemingly of its own accord, the huge wrought-iron gate swung slowly inward. He drove through, and it closed behind him. He followed the drive up to the house, which was curiously unimposing after the huge gate and driveway. A simple rambler. It seemed Robert Pasquale wanted privacy, not opulence. Pasquale himself stood in the doorway, a warm light behind him.

He invited Daniel into the living room and offered him an overstuffed chair. The room was comfortable. The furniture looked old, and a German shepherd, sleeping by the couch, lifted his head, gave Daniel a sorrowful stare, then went back to sleep, his tail giving one thump.

"So you've got the movie star blues," Pasquale said. Daniel squirmed, not sure if the question was serious or sarcastic.

"Fading movie star," corrected Daniel.

Pasquale didn't argue. "Have a Coke?" he offered, indicating his own. Daniel blinked. Not what he'd been expecting. "Yes, thanks."

Pasquale disappeared and came back in a few minutes with a juice glass. Mickey Mouse was on the side. Daniel took it, smiled, and had a sip. It was Coke. Nothing more.

Pasquale sat back down in what was obviously his favorite chair. It was an old green recliner, and the upholstery was ripped on one arm. The book he had been reading was lying facedown on the table beside it. The title was something Daniel hadn't heard of. Not anything Oprah had picked for her book club. Pasquale smoothed his beard, crossed his legs, and settled back into the huge old chair. He looked curiously at Daniel, waiting for him to speak. Daniel took another sweet, fizzy sip and leaned his head against the back of the chair.

"Your fifteen minutes running out?" Pasquale asked.

Daniel raised his head and looked at him. Pasquale was smiling but not cruelly. Daniel shrugged. "Maybe."

"It hurts to see the brass ring in the rearview mirror."

"Yeah."

"Plenty of people are going to be the next big thing, then things kind of fizzle. Everybody says, 'Whatever happened to that guy?' "

Daniel thought of what Denise had said. He was just another one of those guys who'd almost made it.

"You've had a good run, though," Pasquale said. "A lot of films. One of them did all right."

"Several were high grossers," Daniel corrected. "Three, actually."

"And don't forget the TV show."

Daniel nodded.

"You working now?"

He shrugged. "My agent's negotiating."

Pasquale's turn to shrug. He knew that could mean anything.

"You using?"

Daniel shook his head.

"So it's just the booze."

Daniel nodded.

"Me too." Pasquale held up his Coke glass. "Ten years sober this Christmas."

"Congratulations."

He tipped his head modestly. "Of course, you know the drinking doesn't help. People get to thinking you're a drunk and they don't want to give you parts. They start wondering if you're going to show up. And in what shape."

Daniel nodded. Pasquale could have heard the rumors, or he could have just read the tabloids. They were both exaggerated. He had never come to the set drunk. Hung over a time or two, but he'd never held up production. It was gossip. That was all.

"Ready for rehab?"

Daniel shook his head. "Don't need it." He didn't. He wasn't an alcoholic.

Daniel expected a smirk from Pasquale. His look was serious, though, almost sorrowful. "Whatever," he said quietly.

They sat in silence for a few minutes, and Daniel remembered guiltily that he was the one who had come to Pasquale. For advice. "Have you got any wisdom?" he joked, hoping Pasquale wouldn't bring up rehab again.

Pasquale considered for a moment. "You got any money?"

"Some," Daniel allowed. He had some money, and he hadn't exactly fallen to the bottom of the pond, just partway. After the divorce was final, he would probably end up back in the hills somewhere instead of Bel Air, would drive one Porsche instead of three. But he wasn't broke.

"You could do the comeback routine," Pasquale suggested. "Hollywood loves the whole phoenix-from-the-ashes deal. Go to rehab—whether you need it or not," he added quickly. "Come back and call a press conference. Then take whatever part you can get, work hard, and see if you can build your career again."

"I've already done that once," Daniel admitted.

"Do it again, then. Do it as many times as you need to. Or, you could get over the idea you have to prove something. You don't need to be a superstar. Just be satisfied putting food on the table and start building a life." He indicated his book, the room. The dog raised a quizzical eye.

"And how would I go about doing that?"

"You quit chasing after the things that are killing you. It's a game," Pasquale said, shaking his head with a knowing little smile. "You just tell them you don't want to play anymore. Get yourself away to someplace where nobody knows you and wouldn't care if they did. Someplace like Montana, where they'll just tip their hat at you when they pass you on the road. Somewhere as away from here as you can get."

"That would mean the end of my career." The very thing he'd been saying he wanted, he realized. But what would he do without it? Who would he be?

Pasquale shrugged again. "So?"

"Doesn't sound like much of a life," Daniel said, making little swirls and whirlpools in his glass.

"Apparently," Robert Pasquale said, giving him the eye and making a wry face, "it would be an improvement over the one you have now."

Daniel stared into the fire.

"It's not an easy decision," Pasquale agreed, and they were both silent for a while.

—————

By the time he arrived back home after a quick stop at the liquor store, Daniel had decided not to do anything rash. Following Pasquale's advice would mean giving a lot of things up. And in real life, it wasn't as simple as just walking away. There would be two houses and cars to sell. . . .

His thoughts trailed off, exhausted. When he thought of the work peeling himself free from his life would involve, he felt as if he was at the foot of some great mountain, looking upward, with only a coiled rope in his hand. It would be different if he knew something he wanted to do instead. Somewhere he wanted to go. He sighed and walked slowly up the steps to the back door, getting his key ready. He was too tired tonight. He would start thinking about it tomorrow.

He went inside. Denise and her luggage were gone. He poured himself a glass of Scotch and turned on the television. That show was on. The one where they interviewed the actors about their craft. He wondered if he would ever be invited on. He snorted. Probably not. *Ninja Darkness* was his biggest grosser, and it wasn't their idea of great art.

He pretended anyway, that he was the one being interviewed by the pompous host. He answered the questions along with the guest. An exercise in improvisation.

What's your favorite word?

Rest. Yes, that would be it, and the picture he conjured up in his mind was a tall, dim building with smooth stone floors, still corners draped with heavy, rich curtains, the faraway sound of trickling water. Rest.

What is your least favorite word?

Sunlight. So bright and vulgar. Glaring in his face and eyes. He longed for respite from its ceaseless heat and assault.

What turns you on?

He briefly flashed on the women he'd known before the answer distilled. Kindness. He realized that now. Kindness and faithfulness and joy and sweetness. Not body parts exquisitely arranged, but virtue. An old-fashioned word for what he longed for. Virtue turned him on. It reminded him of those old reading books his aunt Dorothy collected. Every story was intended to drill home a character quality. Maybe they were on to something, he thought. He smiled and puffed out a bitter little laugh, realizing that no one with virtue would want him.

What sound do you love?

Scott's voice. Not the way it sounded today on the telephone, dull and flat, more and more like his own, but the sound of that child's voice in his memory. Thin and excited. Loud. He smiled.

What sound do you hate?

Chatter. He had had enough chatter, that low buzz in the background at every function, the meaningless, vapid blather that came out of everyone's mouth. For once he would love to hear truth, spoken simply, even if it was brutal.

What is your favorite curse word?

He laughed at the unlikeliness of it, his voice a harsh grating in the silent room. Beautiful. Oh, you're beautiful. He's so beautiful. He could see now, blandly, almost disinterestedly, that it was a curse.

What profession other than yours would you like to attempt?

Garbage man would be okay. House painter. A clerk at the all-night gas station.

If heaven exists, what would you like to hear God say when you arrive at the pearly gates?

He laughed again. He knew, beyond a shadow of a doubt, what God would say. He would search His guest list carefully, then give His head a slight, cold shake. "Not on here, buddy," He'd say and jerk His head back the way Daniel had come. He wondered idly if he would be able to slip God a few bills and have Him look the other way as he sneaked past.

Twenty-nine

WHEN LENORE WOKE UP, her entire chest felt raw and screaming, and the pain traveled like hot needles under her arm and up her shoulder to her neck and head and all the way down to her fingers and side. She was awake, but her head felt fuzzy and unclear.

"How are you feeling?"

Lenore opened her eyes and saw Dr. Simons. "It hurts," she said.

He nodded and made a notation in the chart.

Lenore moved her fingers and was rewarded with shooting pains that traveled from her armpit through her chest.

"We'll get you started on some clear liquids today, maybe some soft foods. You should be out of bed walking. We'll switch you to oral pain meds."

"When can I go home?"

Dr. Simons shrugged. "Tomorrow. The next day. Any questions?"

"No." Lenore shook her head and felt the needles travel the other way this time, from her neck down her shoulder to her fingers, the same hot little points of pain. Dr. Simons gave her a smart nod and turned on his heel. She pushed the call button before his white lab coat was out the door.

The nurse who answered was not one Lenore remembered having seen before. Not the ones who left the door open or the one who had pulled away her hand.

She was young and sweet, with blond hair and dimples, probably Swedish or Norwegian and the Lucia queen every Christmas. And fresh out of nursing school, Lenore thought. Lenore read her name tag—Kristin Knutsen, RN.

"I'm glad to see you're awake this morning, but I'll bet you're in some pain." Kristin spoke in a normal tone, not shouting like the nurses in recovery had. But, of course, she wasn't hollering now.

"I am," Lenore said, every word an effort. Even breathing hurt.

"Let me get you some medication for that. There's no reason for you to hurt more than you need to. And after you're feeling better from the meds, I'll see what you'd like to eat."

"I'd like something to drink," Lenore said, still thirsty in spite of the IV. The inside of her mouth felt parched to the point of cracking, though she could see the used glycerin swabs on the bedside table and could faintly taste the lemon on her tongue.

"I'll get both right away." Kristin Knutsen turned on her heel and was back in a minute with a syringe that she injected into the IV and a cup of ice chips. "Keep those down, and I'll bring you some water." She smiled at Lenore, and her eyes were soft, and the dimples were deep in each cheek.

Lenore progressed through ice chips, water, soda pop, and soup, even got up several times that day with Kristin's help. She went to the bathroom, hunched over her wounded arm and chest, Kristin supporting her and bringing the IV pole along like an uninvited guest. By the end of the day she'd worked her way up to oatmeal and egg custard.

She looked up from her supper tray to see Nathan Delacroix with Scott in tow.

"Hi, guys." She smiled, very cheered to see them, and saw Scott's face release a little of its tightness.

"Come and give me a kiss. Right there." She pointed to her cheek with her good arm. "That should be okay. It's one of the few places that doesn't hurt."

"Are you doing okay, Mom?" Scott's forehead creased. That was a long speech for him these days.

She smiled at him. "I'm feeling better by the minute."

Nathan Delacroix peered at her tray. "Well, it's not mashed potatoes and gravy, but I guess it could be worse."

Kristin came in, saw Nathan, smart and tall. Lenore saw Nathan perk up at her entrance.

"Kristin, this is my son, Scott, and our friend Nathan Delacroix."

"Pleased to meet you," Nathan said in his smooth Georgia drawl, his honest, handsome face beaming with pleasure.

Kristin blushed furiously. "I'm glad to meet you, too."

Scott grinned at Lenore, and it was the best part of her week.

Kristin was off the next day, and Lenore wasn't able to thank her because Dr. Simons came by, read her chart, looked at her sitting up in bed eating scrambled eggs, and said she could go home. By lunchtime Lenore was pulling up in front of the house on Chestnut Street and being helped from the car by Al and Edie as if she were made of glass.

Lenore didn't know why, but she felt out of sync, as if she were dancing with her feet out of step to the music. Nothing was right. The house seemed too quiet. Angie and Scott weren't around. She didn't see Mr. Kaplan. But she could see the preparations they had made, and she tried to be cheerful. Mrs. Callahan had put clean sheets on her bed and flowers on the bedside table, and there was something good-smelling in the kitchen.

"I made a vegetable soup for you." Mr. Caputo beamed at her, his eyes disappearing when he smiled.

Al carried in her suitcase while Edie helped her walk up the stairs.

But still, everything felt odd. Things looked unfamiliar and out of place, even though they were just as they had been two days ago when she had last seen them. She finally decided it was she who was out of step. She wasn't doing what she normally did. It reminded her of the days of her childhood when she'd stayed home from school. There were different things on the television than she was used to, different amounts of light coming in the window, different sounds, the delivery trucks and garbage trucks and mail trucks outside, the daytime feel of a house she was only used to seeing in the evening and at night. She shook her head, too tired and ill to diagnose her malady further. She had cancer. She was missing her breast. It hurt. She felt odd.

She told Edie she needed a glass of water and took a pill. She went to sleep.

Scott felt bad. Everything was all messed up. That was the best he could do, and he didn't even try to be more specific. It was just all messed up. His mom was sick, maybe even dying, and he felt bad. Really bad.

He thought about it awhile, then went and found Nathan, who was sitting at the kitchen table writing something on a piece of paper. Maybe a letter or something.

"I'm feeling kind of bad," he mumbled.

Nathan looked up, his eyebrow raised. "I'm sorry. I didn't hear you."

"I said I'm feeling kind of bad," Scott said again with emphasis, irritated he had to repeat himself.

"Oh," Nathan said mildly, giving a slight shrug. "You *should* feel bad." He didn't raise his voice a bit and didn't seem mad at all.

Scott was off balance, wondering if one of them wasn't understanding, but Nathan went on and cleared up any doubt he might have had.

"When are you going to cut out this attitude of yours and grow up?" Nathan asked the question just as nicely as if he were asking Scott if he wanted to take a ride with him or shoot some hoops.

Scott was surprised. Stunned.

"Here's a news flash for you, sport," Nathan said, and now his voice sounded brusque and clipped. "You may be pretty special, but the earth still revolves around the sun. Think about somebody else for a change."

Scott felt anger well up, deep and hot. He was getting ready to say something when Mr. Caputo came down the stairs. His face looked different than Scott had ever seen it. It was cold and angry and he had a baggie in his hand. *The* baggie.

"What's this?" he asked, his voice flat. "I went in to put your clean clothes in your drawer, and I found this."

Scott tried to take it, but Nathan snatched it out of his hand.

"Give that here!" Scott reached for it, and Nathan grabbed his arm. Held it hard and wouldn't let it go. Scott started to say something, then remembered Mom was sleeping right above him and changed his mind.

"Come with me," Nathan said and pulled him outside, back by the garage, behind the grape arbor. He could see Mr. Caputo and now Al, too, in the window, watching like two old ladies the whole time Nathan was yelling at him. It was no big deal, but the way everybody was acting, you would have thought he was an ax murderer. A tiny bit of weed and all of a sudden you were a junkie. Scott felt a strange mixture of emotions. Hard, hot anger, fear, and dead, cold bitterness—at Mr. Caputo, at Nathan, at Al, even at Mom for some reason he didn't understand.

"Don't you have any sense?" Nathan bit the words out.

Scott didn't listen to much of what Nathan was saying about drugs and guys in the navy who'd tanked their whole careers from using them or about the people who ended up losers because all they wanted to do was get high. He just stood there. Nathan had come in and acted like his friend, and now that he was going through a tough time—his mom had cancer, for crying out loud—he was making a huge deal about something really stupid.

"If I catch you with this again, any drug, or even a beer, I'll take you out behind this garage and part your hair on the other side. Are we clear?"

Scott didn't answer. He glared at him.

Nathan got about an inch away from his face. "I spoke to you," he said.

"Yeah," Scott answered.

Nathan stared at him for a minute, and a new emotion added itself to the mix. Scott felt hurt well up and threaten to spill out. He blinked his eyes hard and bit the inside of his mouth.

"All right, then." And Nathan, still shaking his head, turned to walk away and leave him there by the garage. But he only got a few steps away before he stopped again. "One more thing," he said. "I don't want you out here sulking all day with your mama laying sick in bed. You get your butt back inside in five minutes, and you'd better be working at something and not mooning around, or I'll take you out, and *I will* tan your hide."

Scott stared at him, trying to make his face as dead as he wanted to feel inside.

"I care about you." The look on Nathan's face was fierce. "And I'm not going to let you tube yourself. *You got that?*"

Scott didn't answer. Nathan didn't make him.

He waited a minute until Nathan was gone, then went inside, walked past Mr. Caputo and Al, still in the kitchen, went upstairs, and found his stash of money. He shoved all he had—about a hundred dollars—into his pocket and didn't bother to take any clothes with him. He passed his mother's door, hesitated, even reached for the knob, then thought again and withdrew his hand. She'd be happier without him here messing up her life. He went back down the stairs as silently as he could, avoiding the steps that squeaked. He could hear Mr. Caputo and Al now talking to Nathan in the kitchen. He went out the front door as silently as he could and then broke into a run, caught the bus on its way to Seattle Center and was just sitting down when Nathan's five minutes were up. He got off at Fifth and Pike, transferred, and walked the last few blocks to the Greyhound station. He spoke to the guy at the ticket window and shelled out ninety-one of his hundred dollars to buy a ticket to L.A. One way. He swallowed hard, but it wasn't a difficult decision to make. He didn't have enough money to buy round trip. He thought about calling his dad and decided against it, not going into the reasons, even in his mind. He would just show up. He would surprise him.

Sylvia took three phone calls while Daniel sat in the waiting room. She was dreading what was to come. She hung up from the last one and checked her watch. She hated this part of her job.

She steeled herself. It wasn't personal. She buzzed Kari, had her send Daniel in. The door opened. He looked terrible in spite of the pressed pants and silk shirt. He was hung over again. He took off his sunglasses, and she could see that his eyes were bloodshot. She sighed with regret. There came a point in every drinker's life when the cosmetics didn't cover the evidence anymore. And all the aftershave in the world couldn't disguise that slightly fruity, mellow fragrance of yesterday's Scotch.

"Sorry to keep you waiting," she said.

Daniel smiled. The wattage was dimmer but still there. She felt another stab of regret. It was a shame. Such a waste. She steeled herself.

"Did you hear from them?" he asked, making it easier for her. It was the first sentence that was the hardest, the introduction of the subject.

She nodded. "They passed." His last three films had been box-office bleeders. She hadn't really held out much hope that he'd be offered another major role, but she had walked through the motions with him.

Pssew. He blew out a little stream of air.

She tensed herself, waiting to see what he would say, if he would make it any harder than it needed to be. He said nothing. She took a deep breath. One thrust and it would be over. "Look, Daniel. The last four roles you've read for have gone south. I think you should think about adjusting your expectations."

He nodded, the smile back again, slightly mocking, though she couldn't tell if it was her or himself he was amused by.

"I think you should explore doing some more television," she continued. "Maybe another series, some guest appearances. I'm not really connected well for those, but I have some associates who do excellent work."

He stood up and came toward the desk. She froze, suddenly afraid, but all he did was extend his hand.

"Thank you, Sylvia, for everything. It's been a good ride."

She extended her hand and felt the regret again. It really was a shame. "Good-bye, Daniel."

He gave her the full smile this time, still dazzling in spite of the booze and disappointment, then turned and walked out.

Thirty

LOS ANGELES WAS HOT. Scott blinked his eyes, groggy from the half sleep he'd been in when the bus had pulled into the station, and looked around him at downtown L.A. This wasn't what he'd expected, and he wasn't sure what he meant except that he was remembering those trips to see Dad when he was a kid. Dad would meet him at the airport. He'd have Donelle driving and a present waiting in the back seat of his fancy car. Scott didn't remember even driving through any places like this. The streets Dad had taken him down were clean, breezy, with palm trees and nice cars everywhere, clean sidewalks and fancy shops. Not like this.

He looked up and down the street from the Greyhound station. There were chain link fences with razor wire everywhere, just like a prison, and all the buildings had bars on the windows and were covered with gang tags. There was garbage everywhere. Scott took off his jacket and started walking.

"The city bus stop you need is up the street," the guy had said, bored, not caring whether Scott found what he was looking for or not. Scott thought about calling Dad from the pay phone, but somebody was on it and two more people waiting in line. He walked a ways, found a gas station with a phone booth, but the telephone there was broken. Somebody had stolen the receiver. The cable hung limp from the box. Scott walked on. He was starting to sweat. He smelled bad. He passed a bum and realized he probably looked just that bad. Mom would have a cow.

Mom. His stomach churned when he thought about her. He felt guilt twist him up like a vise, then anger when he remembered the way Nathan had treated him. And Al and Mr. Caputo. Where did they get off? Who did they think they were? He tried to whip his anger up to its original heat, but it was no good. It had fizzled and cooled as he had made the long bus ride. As reality had set in. He felt really bad for going off and leaving Mom. He should have talked to her, but what good would that have done? She was already going to be upset and mad when Mr. Caputo showed her the baggie. He had already hurt her. Leaving would probably just make things easier for both of them. Now, without him around, she could just concentrate on getting well. And he would be happier here, he told himself, eyeing the clump of guys on the street corner as he turned and headed in the opposite direction.

He finally found the bus stop, and when the next bus came he asked the driver how to get to the address he had written down—225 Canyon Springs Drive. He followed her instructions, got on the right bus, then watched with relief as the streets became cleaner, the people less frightening looking. He got off at Sunset Boulevard to transfer. There were tourists walking around taking pictures. Business people wearing suits and carrying briefcases. Now people were staring at him, and he realized he was the one who looked scary and dirty, out of place and threatening. He was hungry, but he didn't have any money left. He would be at Dad's soon, he told himself, and then all this would end. He could have anything he wanted at Dad's.

He took the last bus, stepped off when the driver told him to, followed the directions he'd been given to Canyon Springs Drive, then followed the winding streets until he found the right address.

It was a different place than the one before. He couldn't see the house, but this time there was a buzzer by the gate. He pressed it.

"Yeah." A voice he didn't recognize answered after a minute.

"Donelle?"

Silence. "Donelle don't work here no more. Whatcha need?"

"I want to see my dad."

More silence for another minute. Then the big black wrought-iron gates swung open. Scott walked in, and by the time he turned around to look the way he'd come, the gates were already closing behind him.

Thirty-one

I T WAS INTERESTING HOW one problem could be completely eclipsed by another. The part of her mind that remained calm and analytical—a very small part—thought about that. Everything had changed in just an instant. What had seemed a life-shattering loss twenty-four hours before was now just a bandaged wound on her chest. Its foreboding threat seemed hazy and obscure, distant and trivial.

Lenore paced around the living room, going compulsively to the window to look out every few minutes. The view was always the same. Overcast day, well-groomed front yard with a few maple leaves scuttling across the green grass, cars parked in an orderly line out front. But no bedraggled boy opening the gate and coming up the sidewalk. She dropped the curtain and began walking again. Her chest hurt, but she didn't take a pill. She needed her head clear. She had abandoned her bed long ago, early this morning when Mr. Caputo had come in and woken her to tell her Scott was gone. And why.

She went to the telephone—the other step in this dance—and tried Daniel's number again. Got the answering machine. No woman this time. Just Daniel's voice saying in flat tones to leave a message. She left another one, her own voice shrill and panicked.

She had called the police, of course, only to be told that since the state of Washington had deemed running away a personal problem, there was nothing they could do unless she suspected foul play. "Did he steal your car?" the officer asked hopefully.

She had called Edie and Matt, who had both come over and prayed, finally leaving at her insistence but promising to come back later. And promising to pray. Of course to pray.

"Honey, I'm sure that's where he's gone," Mr. Caputo soothed again.

"Where is Daniel? Why doesn't he call?" Lenore chafed. "What if Scott gets there and no one is home? Maybe Daniel's off somewhere doing a movie. Then what will happen? Scott will be in L.A. by himself."

Al stopped his own pacing and faced her. His face was terrible. "I'm going after him. I still know some people on the force. We'll find him if he's down there."

"I'll go with you," Nathan said. He looked terrible, too. He blamed himself, a fact he had told her over and over again. She had tried to reassure him. She would have reacted exactly the same. And this had been coming for months, she admitted to herself. Perhaps even years. She was constantly being compared to Daniel, the glittering father. Daniel, the cool one. Daniel, the one who would understand. And she constantly came up short. Well, he had probably gone to his father. He had made a choice, and for the first time Lenore faced the very real possibility that Scott would not be coming home. Perhaps from now on she would be the one who received the visit at Christmastime and the two weeks in the summer. Her throat caught. She swallowed down the lump and promised herself she would not borrow trouble. She would not jump ahead. She prayed quietly. *Give me wisdom,* she pleaded. Her chest throbbed along with her pulse.

"Wait a little longer," she said. "Daniel is sure to call soon."

If Scott wasn't at Daniel's, Nathan and Al wouldn't be able to find him, no matter what they thought. She stared at the wall bleakly, now in the despair phase of the cycle. She saw her son, thin and vulnerable, standing forlornly on an L.A. street corner. She closed her eyes, as if that would block it out.

Nathan left the room. Al grumbled and peered out the window. Mrs. Callahan murmured something, her dentures clicking forlornly, then went to see to Angie, who was calling her loudly from the kitchen. Lenore sat down. Her body felt shaky and tired but wired and unable to rest. Mr. Caputo disappeared in the direction of the kitchen, then came back with a tray. A bowl of soup, a piece of toast, a glass of milk. One of her pain pills. She didn't argue, but neither did she go to bed. She sat on the couch, covered up with the afghan Mr. Caputo draped across her, and waited for the telephone to ring.

———

This place wasn't much like the mansion Dad used to have, and the guy who had let him in was nobody Scott had ever seen before. He was tall, muscular, dark-skinned. He didn't bother to introduce himself, just jerked his head toward the sliding glass door that led to the pool. "Your dad's out there," he said. "If he wakes up, tell him he owes me a check."

He put on a pair of sunglasses and left through the door Scott had just come in.

Scott stood there for a minute, not sure what to do. He looked out toward the pool and could see Dad lying in a lounge chair. He wondered if the guy had told Dad he was here. He glanced around the house. No one else seemed to be here. Not like it used to be, with people everywhere. The air was heavy, and all the windows were covered with dark curtains. The light on Dad's telephone was blinking. Scott opened the slider and stepped outside, the heat hitting him again like a fist in the face after the relief of the air-conditioned room.

His dad turned at the sound. He didn't sit up, but he set down the glass he'd been drinking from and took off his sunglasses.

Scott got a little closer.

"Scott?" Dad asked.

Well, at least Dad recognized him, and Scott felt an unaccountable relief. *Of course he would recognize me,* he told himself. *I'm his son.* Still, it had been a couple of years since Dad had seen him in person. Not many visits since the DUI bust. He glanced at what his dad was drinking now, at the short, stubby glass beside the chair. Something brown. He looked behind the tumbler and saw the bottle. Scotch whiskey and a brand he'd never heard of, not the bottle with the wild turkey on the front—the "special drink" he hadn't been allowed to sample when he was a kid.

"Hey," he said, waiting for Dad to get up and hug him or something.

Dad stood up, rubbed his face, and now that Scott was closer he could see that his dad looked terrible. Probably about as bad as he did himself. Dad hadn't shaved in quite a while. His eyes were bloodshot, and he smelled like what he was drinking. Dad gave him an awkward hug and a pat on the back, then rubbed his face again.

"Sit down," he invited, motioning Scott toward the other lounge. Scott found a chair instead. He sat down. The pool looked good. Calm and aqua blue. The sun was starting to go down, but instead of feeling happy that he'd arrived at his destination, Scott suddenly felt sorry he'd come. This reality wasn't the one he'd imagined. Things felt empty and dark. Weird. Off balance.

"What are you doing here?" Dad asked it pleasantly enough, but Scott could tell he was uncomfortable. His arrival hadn't brought the joyful reaction he'd imagined. A stupid idea, he could see now, and childish to even think it might. Dad might jump up and down to see him when he was six, but not now. Nobody wanted a trouble-making sixteen-year-old showing up on their doorstep. Dad would probably get rid of him as soon as he could.

Scott thought about how to answer Dad's question. What was he supposed to say? *I got busted for having some weed and thought I'd come here where you would understand?* Well, that much was true. He glanced down at the bottle. "Just thought I'd come see what you were up to," he said.

"Mom know you're here?" Dad asked, maybe not as clueless as Scott had thought.

He shook his head. Dad nodded his.

"We'd better call her," he said. "I've been bad lately about listening to my messages."

"You call her," Scott said, wanting to avoid that conversation. "Can I take a shower or something?"

"Sure," Dad said, smiling, like it was no big deal that Scott had ridden the bus for twenty-six hours and shown up at his door. "Upstairs and to the right. Take some of my clothes."

They both walked into the house. Scott went upstairs and took a long time showering, put on a pair of Dad's shorts, which, though still too big, weren't as bad as the pants. When he came downstairs Dad had put on a T-shirt and some jeans and had made a pot of coffee. The light wasn't flashing on the telephone any longer.

A buzzer sounded. Dad punched a button, and a few minutes later the doorbell rang. Dad went to answer and came back with a pizza box. He set it in front of Scott and opened it. Pepperoni with extra cheese. His favorite. He smiled at his dad, the first time he'd felt good since he'd gotten here. He ate. Dad said he didn't want any. He sat and watched Scott scarf it down, and after he'd eaten, the two of them faced each other across the table.

"Mom okay?" Scott asked, wiping his face with the napkin. His stomach felt tight and unsettled, and he wished he hadn't eaten all that pizza.

"She's okay," Dad answered. He didn't say anything about the operation, and suddenly Scott didn't want to tell him. He didn't want to talk about that. Didn't want Dad to know what a louse he was to walk out and leave Mom alone when she was going through something like that. He felt a surge of bitterness when he realized that maybe he shouldn't mind. After all, Dad had left both of them. Maybe they'd actually been the ones who left, but he knew it wasn't what Mom had wanted. He remembered how it had been, how sad she had been. How sad he had been. He felt angry at Dad now. And it made him even angrier that there was nothing specific he could say. He was angry about everything. Angry that he had had to ride the bus for a day and a half to see his father. Angry at not knowing how to find his house. Angry that when he finally did find it, he needed someone else's permission to even get to the front door, and angry that his dad had been sitting by the pool drinking instead of doing something, well, something important. Something good.

"Is this all you do?" Scott bit out, jerking his head toward the pool.

Surprise lit Dad's eyes for a minute, then he smiled, though it looked a little strained. "Pretty much," he said.

"Don't you work anymore?"

"Sure I work. Today's my day off." Dad's voice was mild, but his eyes dropped down to the floor.

Scott stared at him a little longer, then dropped his own eyes. He felt silly and immature.

"Look," Dad said.

Scott stiffened. Here it came. This was it. "You don't have to tell me," Scott said. "I know I have to go home."

There was silence for a minute. When he looked up, Scott couldn't read the expression on his father's face. It was sadness mixed with something Scott didn't recognize.

"I'm not a good role model right now," Dad said with a sort of quirky smile. It sounded like he was repeating something someone else had said about him.

"Mom say that?"

"She's right."

Scott shrugged. "Whatever." He couldn't analyze his feelings. They were a muddy mix. Wounded pride at being sent home like a little kid, guilt for leaving in the first place. Dread at what would be waiting for him when he got there. Bitter disappointment at what he'd found here, but a little relief. Yes, he admitted it to himself. He was relieved. He wanted to go home, he realized. Had wanted to since the first moment he'd stepped off the bus and realized he might be running away from something but there was nothing here to run to. He had known that even before he'd arrived at Canyon Springs Drive and found Dad hung over by the pool.

"Crash here tonight," Dad said. "In the morning I'll put you on a plane. You can come back and visit at Christmas if you want."

"Sure," Scott mumbled. He darted his eyes away from his dad, back out to the pool. The water was stirred up now, a little breeze passing over it. It rippled across in tiny waves, then dissipated into smooth blue again. "That's fine," he said, and suddenly he wished it were morning already.

The flight took two and a half hours, and when he arrived at Sea-Tac, they were almost all there to meet him. Mom looked a little pale and was wearing her sweats, but she grabbed him and gave him a one-sided hug. She was crying. She kissed him and then yelled at him, then cried and kissed him some more. Al glared at him, muttered something about pulling stunts and tanning hides, then went to get the car. Mr. Caputo kept saying, "Oh, you gave us a scare, young man," over and over again. Mrs. Callahan kept clicking her tongue and shaking her head at him, and Angie rolled her eyes and gave him a look of sympathy.

"Where's Nathan?" Scott asked.

"He went to work. He said for you not to take off. He wants to talk to you when you get home," Mom said. Then her face got a little angry again. "I told him that wouldn't be a problem, that you'd be around."

Scott nodded. He knew he would be grounded for the rest of his life. And that wasn't a problem. He had been expecting it. And he had had some time to think. All the way home in the cool plane, sipping his Coke and pointing his eyes at the in-flight magazine, he had really been thinking. Remembering. It had never been that great in Dad's world. He had always wanted to come home before the visit was up, but somehow he had thought it was because he was five years old, or seven, or nine. Now he knew it was something different. It had to do with who he was and who Dad was. Who they all were. He looked around him at the chattering crowd of people. This weird family that he really disliked sometimes didn't seem so bad now. At least they cared about him, he realized, his throat getting tight again. He thought of Dad by the pool, and he knew Dad cared about him, too, but there was something wrong. Something missing, and he didn't know what it was, but he knew he couldn't fix it.

"You and I are going to have a little talk when we get home," Mom promised, her mouth a thin line but her arm around him like she didn't ever want to let him go.

"Okay," he said, and he felt good, as though he had come back to earth from floating, as though his foot was on something solid again.

Thirty-Two

IT WAS AS IF THEY HAD gotten together and planned it, though Lenore was reasonably sure they hadn't. For the next few weeks the whole houseful of people closed around her in a tight, warm embrace. Mr. Caputo and Mr. Kaplan were lords of the kitchen. They were having conferences about the Jewish High Holy Days, which were coming up. Mr. Kaplan had asked everyone's permission to celebrate them.

"Of course," said Lenore. Scott had shrugged, but he seemed to have lost that angry smolder, and Lenore didn't even care to analyze why. She just felt relief like a melting iceberg in her chest. He had accepted his punishment—three months' grounding—without protest and actually seemed happy to hang around the house or have his friends come over instead of the constant round of concerts and hanging out that had been the norm before his flight. Angie, who was learning about different religions, wondered if she could get credit for it at school. Al said that was fine with him as long as he didn't have to *do* anything religious. Mr. Caputo, of course, had suggested it, and even Mrs. Callahan, who didn't stray very far from the Southern Baptist Convention's idea of sound doctrine, said that it would be fine. "I'd like to get a glimpse of what the Savior did. It's almost like going to the Holy Land," she had quietly enthused.

So the two men began the first of many discussions, scratching shopping lists on the backs of envelopes. Lenore liked it. It made the house seem more alive, created a little buzz of enthusiasm in the air that had been hushed and still before, cowed by her illness. The cancer, she corrected herself.

Al had taken it upon himself to overhaul the car engine since Lenore would not be driving it to work for a while. He spent every morning and afternoon hunched over the engine. Lenore could see him from the front window, orange rag draped out of his pocket, tools in a red metal box at his feet, or sometimes he would be underneath the car and all she could see were his legs.

Mrs. Callahan had taken over the cleaning, which she had done most of anyway. But she seemed happy, and Lenore could hear her vacuuming and singing as she dusted and worked. She would bring the laundry into the sitting room and watch soaps while she folded it.

"Do you know Jill is still seeing Andrew?" the woman on the screen would demand, and Mrs. Callahan's head would shake. Even as her eyes were alight with interest, she would shake her head and say, "Lord, have mercy."

And Nathan seemed to have taken over the care of Scott. The day of Scott's return the two of them had shut themselves up in the study for forty minutes, and when they came out they were friends again. No, better than friends. Mentor and follower, and Lenore breathed a silent prayer of thanks. They had been friends before, but it was as if there had been a barrier between them. Scott had been holding back, and she didn't understand what had happened, but since Scott's return from his father's, the wall between the two of them seemed to have been removed.

Nathan wanted to be a fire fighter and was on the list to take the test, but in the meantime, he had taken a warehouse job. It paid good money, and he was home from work every day by two-thirty, the same time Scott finished school.

"I'll swing by and pick him up on my way home," Nathan told Lenore. "It's no trouble." Then the two of them would go work on the car with Al for a while, or sometimes Lenore would hear them in the back yard, their basketball bouncing off the side of the house for hours at a time. Scott was definitely more like himself. His eyes were clearing, and he actually smiled once in a while. Every time she heard the ball bounce, Lenore closed her eyes and said, "Thank you, Lord."

And Lenore herself was feeling better. Physically and otherwise. Her incision had healed. She looked at it thoroughly, not sparing herself. She had cried a little at first but made herself keep looking at it. Made herself love it. As if it were her foot or her hand. Maybe not beautiful, but her reality. She took to bringing up the cancer every day at least once when they were all together and made a point of saying the word: Cancer. Their faces had gone from the shocked stillness the first time she had said it to calm acceptance now.

"I'm reading a book about living with cancer," Lenore had said last night at dinner.

"How is it, honey?" Mr. Caputo asked.

"Pass the green beans," Nathan had said.

It was getting better. Easier for all of them.

She had finally told Erik. He had been compassionate and kind, but something had hooded itself in his eyes when she had said the word *cancer,* and she knew he had switched from Erik the quasi-boyfriend to Erik the physician. He had quizzed her as to details, had come to see her the next day with a box of chocolates and a bunch of daisies, and had visited every few days since then. He was attentive and kind but did not ask why she hadn't told him sooner, a fact she thought odd.

"This is a special night for Jews. And for me, a completed Jew who has been redeemed by Yeshua Hamashiach, Jesus the Messiah, it means even more." Mr. Kaplan wore a skullcap and fringes on his clothes. The table was set beautifully. Lenore had heard Mr. Caputo and Mr. Kaplan arguing about whether or not to use the good china. Mr. Caputo must have won, because there it was, his own Royal Doulton, the good Waterford crystal glasses, and the lace tablecloth.

Lenore felt a warmth settle over her. She had dressed for the occasion, the first time in weeks she'd worn something other than sweats. She smoothed her dress and took a sip of her water. The dark wine Mr. Kaplan had poured each of them, even Angie and Scott, sat waiting for its time in the ceremony. She didn't know the cause of her good feelings—whether they were due to being here at the table with someone else's holiday prepared and served up for her, being back in the land of the living, having Scott here and coming out of his deep unhappiness, or just the fact that she felt safe and cared for. She didn't really care. She just settled back into her chair and nestled in the feeling.

Mr. Kaplan picked up his Bible and adjusted his glasses. "The prophet Isaiah, over seven hundred years before Jesus was born, wrote this about the one who would be the Messiah." His voice was deep and sweet, like ripe fruit. " 'Who has believed our message and to whom has the arm of the Lord been revealed? He grew up before him like a tender shoot, and like a root out of dry ground.' "

Lenore thought about the tender heart of Jesus and the dry, violent world.

" 'He had no beauty or majesty to attract us to him, nothing in his appearance that we should desire him.' "

He was plain, too.

" 'He was despised and rejected by men, a man of sorrows, and familiar with suffering. Like one from whom men hide their faces he was despised, and we esteemed him not. Surely he took up our infirmities and carried our sorrows. . . .' "

She remembered the raw pain of her wound.

" 'Yet we considered him stricken by God, smitten by him, and afflicted. But he was pierced for our transgressions, he was crushed for our iniquities; the punishment that brought us peace was upon him, and by his wounds we are healed.' "

She felt the deep, rich peace flow through her again as she remembered that.

Mr. Kaplan closed the Bible and recited the last of the passage from memory. " 'We all, like sheep, have gone astray, each of us has turned to his own way, and the Lord has laid on him the iniquity of us all.' "

There was silence around the table.

Lenore looked down at the plate that had been set before her. Two slices of apple and a tiny bowl of honey. A symbol of a wish for a sweet new year. She watched Mr. Kaplan dip the apple in the honey and put it in his mouth. She did the same. The sweetness mixed with the tart green apple. She dipped it again, bowing her head and closing her eyes.

"L'shanah tovah," Mr. Kaplan said.

Lenore raised her head.

"L'shanah tovah," he repeated, his face shining brighter than the candles in front of him. "For a good year."

Thirty-three

BY THANKSGIVING WEEK THE house was happily awash with holiday preparations. Lenore began working half time at the hospital. Her strength and cheer had returned.

No one knew exactly when Al had gotten the letter from Arvid Chamberlain. Lenore had seen the envelope lying on the telephone table, picked it up, and noticed it was addressed to Al. The smiling, well-groomed, bushy-haired face of the television evangelist had beamed up from the envelope. To her surprise, she had found Al watching his program now and then when they returned home from church on Sunday mornings.

Thanksgiving Day Miracle Prayer, Thursday, November 23, the envelope proclaimed in bold red print. *What longstanding prayer request have you been believing God for?* Lenore had given her head a shake, knowing that inside would be a return envelope and a letter, which among other things would contain boxes to check: $30, $50, $100, $1000, other. She'd gotten a few like it herself. Not from Arvid Chamberlain. Hers had been Reverend Ewing's Church by Mail and had included a piece of paper featuring a rug in a colorful Oriental pattern. *Your authentic prayer rug,* it had announced and assured her that if she would send a contribution, then join with Reverend Ewing in praying for her request while kneeling on the rug, her petition would be granted.

At the time she had seen Al's envelope, Lenore hadn't thought much of it. But later Al had approached her in the hall, said he needed to talk to her, and sat down across from her at the kitchen table. His face was taut, tight-lipped and strained. "I made a prayer covenant with Reverend Chamberlain about you," he said.

"You did?" was all she could think to say.

Al nodded. "I did an exchange covenant. Reverend Chamberlain wrote me personally and told me about it. He said I could offer myself as a sacrifice for someone else, and God would honor it."

Lenore shook her head. "I don't understand."

Poor Al's face had flushed a brilliant red, but he went on stoically. "I offered my life to God in exchange for yours. I promised I would serve Him and then die your death if He would spare you from any more cancer."

Lenore was struck dumb. She gave her head a little shake and went on looking at Al, her mouth a slight O.

"I called and sealed my covenant with Reverend Chamberlain. The proof of it is that I have to tell you what I've done and then speak no more about it."

"Al . . ." Lenore felt her way around what he had just told her, as if she were walking through an unfamiliar house in the dark. "Reverend Chamberlain told you that you could be substituted for me, that you could die my death—like from the cancer?"

Al nodded, his icy blue eyes never leaving hers. "Yes. That's it exactly."

But, Al, Lenore wanted to say, *that's impossible.* But she could see the fire in his eyes and the slight smile behind the flushing face. Al looked happy. He looked energized. She said none of the things she thought of saying. Her mouth went from the O to a flat line. She opened it, took in a breath, closed it again.

"Thank you," she finally said, feeling somehow that it was the least she could do for someone who claimed he had just purchased her life.

"You're welcome," Al said grandly, expansively, as though he were a great king bestowing a holy gift.

"You're right," Matt said. "That's what he thinks." He gave his coffee a stir and gestured down toward the basement where they could hear Al's table saw start up again after a short spell of silence, during which he had made short work of answering Matt's questions.

"He's convinced he's entered into some kind of bargain with God." Matt shook his head. "He's convinced he's offered himself up as a sacrifice instead of you. Said he's going to go to church from now on and has promised to read the Bible. He says he's a new man and you're going to live because of it."

"Did you explain to him that that's not how God works?"

Matt nodded and smiled a little ruefully. "I tried."

Lenore smiled in spite of her aggravation. She could imagine that conversation. Al was not a person who was open to new ideas once he'd made up his mind.

"Let's just leave it up to the Lord," Matt finally suggested. "He has a lot more finesse than we do. If Al sincerely draws near to Him, He'll take the responsibility to correct him."

"I don't know what to think." Lenore shook her head. She had never had someone treat her so gallantly, so burning-eyed sacrificially. Al had laid down his life with the panache of a gentleman spreading his cape over a puddle.

"Greater love has no one than this . . ." Matt murmured.

Lenore stared back, her eyes burning as well as her heart.

Thirty-four

2003

$\mathcal{D}$ANIEL WOKE WITH A JERK. His pulse shook his chest and rattled through his head. There was a sour taste on the back of his tongue, and he tried to swallow it down, but his mouth was too dry. He pulled himself upright and went downstairs. It was bright and sunny, as usual. Nearly noon, he saw from the clock on the stove. He went to the window and looked outside toward the gate. There were no tourists. No crowds, as there had been at one time. No vultures perching, their cameras pointed in his face, their shutters whirring, documenting his despair. For a while they had followed him everywhere, chasing him in their cars, even cornering him once in a blind alley. He'd slammed his tanklike SUV into reverse and rammed the photographer's little sedan, bouncing it back a few yards with each crash until he could drive out and away.

He smiled, thinking of how he'd defeated them. Every morning he would come down here to the wrought-iron gate where they congregated. He'd stood motionless, aimless, sometimes strolling around the yard, and finally just standing, a cigarette hanging from his lip, unshaven, wearing old sweats and a torn T-shirt. Smelling bad.

After that they began calling him unhinged. "Daniel Monroe Has Psychotic Break" screamed the *Enquirer* and the *Sun*. "Monroe Files for Chapter Eleven," the *Los Angeles Times* reported. But that had been a while ago. No one seemed to care now.

Maybe he *was* coming unhinged. He could almost feel something swinging loosely, flapping and creaking and slapping up against the sides of his head. He'd come unhinged. He let the curtain drop.

He swayed for a moment, thought about what his stomach would tolerate, then chose a cup from the collection in the sink. He ran the water until it was lukewarm, not waiting until the coffee rings on the bottom disappeared, then filled it, turned off the tap, and stirred in some instant coffee from the jar on the counter. He took a few tentative sips, ignoring the undissolved globules that floated on the surface. He licked one off his lip.

Those small sips sent his stomach reeling toward nausea. He tried to remember when he'd last eaten and failed. Last night had been finger food and drinks. Mostly drinks. Esperanza had made a real meal sometime last week, before he'd given her his heartfelt thanks for all the years she'd cleaned his house and cooked his food, before he'd sent her away with his heartfelt thanks and a little nest egg. He smiled, remembering how her eyes had bulged when he'd pressed the thick wad of bills into her hand.

He opened the refrigerator. The light spilled blue and cold onto the kitchen floor. No milk, no juice. There were meatballs on toothpicks, leaning sideways like fallen soldiers, some little pizza turnovers on a paper plate, each one lying in its own oily circle, and some cheese dip sporting a fuzzy blue cap. He closed the door and hesitated only a moment before taking a clean glass and the bottle of Drambuie from the cupboard beside the sink. He went to the living room and sank into his chair.

There was no sound in the room. Nothing but the creak of the old leather wing back as he dropped into it. He caressed it with his thumb, shifted a little inside it, and felt it mold to the contours of his body.

"At least get it reupholstered," Renee had nagged.

Serena had said nothing, just had it moved to the basement. But he'd brought it back up.

Denise had been more adamant. "It's a relic. Throw it away."

He'd ignored all of them and held on to it steadfastly, like a piece of wreckage that was keeping him afloat.

He took a sip of the syrupy drink and followed its hot trail from mouth to gut, where it landed with a warm little splash. He licked the sweetness from his lips and thought about his mother going in and out of rehab. He had never understood it then. He did now. How many times had he said he could quit if he wanted? He wondered now if that was the truth or just what people like him said.

The telephone chirped like an electronic bird, stopping abruptly when the answering machine clicked on. The light was blinking. He waited until it clicked off, then listened to the messages.

"Daniel—" He recognized his new agent's voice. A guy he had never met, just talked to on the phone now and then. He took another sip and braced his arms against the chair, as if for impact.

"I'd rather not do this over the telephone," he said with a slight hesitation, "but I heard back from Lifetime about the movie. They're aiming for the younger viewers, and unfortunately they said your look isn't right. But call me. QVC approached us about doing a half-hour weekly on ab toners."

Daniel blew out his breath, exhaled in a whoosh of air, almost as if the agent had given him a stiff jab in those abs instead of just knocking the wind out of him with his suggestion.

He'd lost the part. His last hope and the only movie he'd even gotten a shot at in the past year. A made-for-TV Lifetime original about a guy who has three wives. So this was it. The final gritty end. He was down to selling hair restorers and exercise machines. He rasped out a humorless laugh and took a deep draw of the Drambuie. And the reason was fitting. It was perfect. Cosmic justice if he believed in such a thing. His looks weren't right. He shook his head and closed his eyes, and when he did, he could see Lenore's thin face and huge eyes when she had told him she was leaving.

Two clicks and the next message played. "Mr. Monroe, this is Kelly Newton at Bank of America. Could you give me a call?"

So the clock had run out on that front, too. He was actually a squatter, he admitted as he looked around the hacienda-style house, the last in a downward cascade of real estate. He had climbed his way up. Lou's couch, the apartment in Santa Monica, the house in the hills, the one in Bel Air. And he had stepped back down the same way. They would probably chain the door soon, since he hadn't made a house payment in five months. He would have to see if Lou was still around, he thought with a humorless laugh.

He listened to the next message. The finance company about his car payments.

The next was American Express.

One last message. He flinched, then asked himself how much worse it could get. Still, he decided to wait a moment before he listened to it. He stared into space and meditated on the cause of his demise after a meteoric rise and was again struck with the irony. His look wasn't right.

The currency he had traded in all his life—the arrangement of bone, the connection of tendon and muscle, the placement of connective tissue and fascia that created the hills and valleys of face, the rolling landscape of arm and leg and shoulder—had just been declared unfit for circulation. So this is what a person's worth could boil down to in the end—whether the eyes were placed another millimeter apart or close together, whether the melanin arranged itself evenly or in spots, whether the blood vessels were close to the surface of the skin of the cheeks or deeper. All of life could finally come down to the angle of a jaw, the width of a nose. Who would imagine so much could hang on so little? He should understand it. He, of all people.

He remembered Lenore's eyes, greenish gold like a choppy sea, her thick shock of brown hair, her cleft chin. She had been thin to the point of pain, her skin milky in the age of bronze, her ribs more prominent than her small breasts.

He focused his eyes and let himself grind back to the present, then shut them again for a second or two as if he were drawing strength. He rose up with some effort, crossed the room, and rummaged around in the drawer until he found what he was looking for. He brought the gun back with him to the chair, settled himself comfortably, then put the barrel into his mouth. He tasted the oil and the sharp powder on the back of his tongue. It sent a chill all the way down to his bowels, and he felt them wrench and twist. He gagged. Took the gun out and rested it on his leg, took another sip of Drambuie and sloshed it around his mouth to get rid of the oily taste. He asked himself another question. What would he leave behind if he were to die?

"If I were to die." He said it out loud, and his voice sounded strange to his ears. He felt a yawning sense of being unprepared. He let the gun slide to the floor and sat doing nothing for a while.

Finally he played the last message. He recognized her voice at once, though he hadn't heard it in years. But he would never forget the soft tone, the gentle mountain accent.

"Danny, it's Aunt Dorothy. Your uncle George went home to be with the Lord yesterday."

He didn't hear much of the rest of the message. Had to replay it later, in fact, to get the funeral time, to hear the details of the accident that had taken his uncle's life, which were sketchy even on a third listen. He called his aunt, heard her voice, and the thought that struck him then was that he had been reprieved. Something real, something tragic, someone else's life—actually, his death—had just intervened between him and his own. He did not know exactly why, but he knew he must go. He put the ticket on his one remaining credit card, slept a little, then packed, showered, shaved, and left for Kentucky.

Thirty-five

THEY BURIED DANIEL'S UNCLE on the mountaintop, not deep inside it where he'd spent most of his life. At the graveside Daniel stood beside his aunt and cousins, a place of honor he felt he didn't deserve, as the mortal remains of George Monroe were committed to the ground. The grave was in the churchyard, not the small Monroe family plot he remembered. A pickup truck rattled by, popping the gravel. A flock of starlings swooped down and landed in the grove of pines that edged the cemetery. The crowd of mourners pressed in close to the grave, men stiff and uncomfortable in shiny suits, women in hats and heels holding tissues against quiet tears. The wind was sharp coming off the ridge. Daniel hunched down a little deeper into his suit coat. He thought of his last glimpse of his uncle, lying pale and waxy in the satin-lined coffin. He wondered where his soul was and hoped it was where they all testified it was with shining faces and tearful eyes—safe in the arms of Jesus.

The minister, a round, red-faced man, read from his Bible in the familiar mountain accent. " 'Unless a kernel of wheat falls to the ground and dies, it remains only a single seed. But if it dies, it produces many seeds. The man who loves his life will lose it, while the man who hates his life in this world will keep it for eternal life.' "

A murmur of amens followed.

"Let us pray."

All heads bowed.

"Father God, into your hands we commit your son George." The minister's face was heavy, his voice quiet but confident. "Father, we thank you that at this very moment he looks upon your face. Comfort us, Father, until we join him in your heavenly kingdom."

Another amen.

The crowd dispersed as they began preparations to lower the casket. His aunt was surrounded by her sons and daughters-in-law, and Daniel suddenly felt out of place. His presence felt like more of a distraction than a comfort. What had he thought? He looked at the family that had raised him and felt no sense of recognition even though their faces were familiar, all variations on the same theme.

A few people stared at him, flashed tentative smiles when he met their eyes. He smiled back briefly, ill at ease. He went back inside the church, walked slowly through the painstaking exhibit his cousins' wives had put together—Uncle George's life documented in pictures and words. He examined the snapshots, read the handwritten text. His uncle hadn't done much, really, except graduate from high school and go to work in the coal mines. Raised his family. Raised his brother's boy. Gone to church.

"You're coming back to the house, aren't you, Danny?" His aunt's hand touched his arm.

He covered it with his and nodded. "Sure," he said. "I'll be there."

She gave him a pat and followed the others out.

He waited until they had gone, then went back outside. A light mist had begun falling. It made him damp and cold. The wind was still sharp. He got into the rental car, drove a bit down the road to the place he wanted to see once more. The hills and hollows rose and fell before him in gentle rhythm. The trees were bare scratches of gray against the smoky sky. Here and there an ancient barn or cabin dotted the landscape. It was stark but beautiful, just as he remembered.

He parked his car on the shoulder, got out, and chirped the door lock. He found the path. It was grown over with weeds and brush. He pushed past bare branches, and just when he was thinking he'd made a mistake, that he'd chosen the wrong spot, he saw it.

The wrought-iron fence looked incongruous out here in the woods. He opened the rusty gate and stepped inside. It closed behind him with a squeak and the clack of iron. His eyes flicked across the rows of graves. Monroe. Monroe. Monroe. Monroe. Monroe. Monroe. Monroe.

He finally found the one he was looking for, his father's, but somehow when he read the name, the sensation came over him that it wasn't his father's grave he was looking at, but his own. There it was, engraved in cold marble. *Daniel Joseph Monroe.* His heart thumped wildly. His throat became dry and tight. He swallowed. Turned and left.

It was odd driving up to his uncle's house. It still looked the same. Exactly. A small brick rambler on a sloping hillside. Dogwoods and azaleas in the yard. Bare now, of course. A car parked in the impeccably tidy carport. The truck gone, totaled in the collision. Daniel entered through the carport and kitchen door, years of habit dying hard. Aunt Dorothy hadn't liked the boys coming through the living room. He hesitated, then knocked. One of his cousins' wives opened the door. Her face flushed pink when she saw him.

"Oh. Come on in. You don't need to knock." She smiled nervously.

"Thanks." He came inside and got his bearings. It was warm. The smell of coffee and baking bread saturated the room—probably Aunt Dorothy's cinnamon rolls. He remembered them, huge soft pillows of dough covered with icing, erupting cinnamon and sugar. The kitchen was full of women of all ages and descriptions. A few great-aunts were at the sink, their white hair swept up into formal dos or curled into iron gray cork-screws. The next generation, Aunt Dorothy's sisters—sixtyish—fussed around the table. Verna still looked the same—she'd looked sixty thirty years ago and had therefore not needed to accommodate the passing years. Jo had been pretty once. She hadn't worn well. Age had improved Mattie, added softness and tempered her hard edges. His cousins' wives were there in force, not just George's sons, but the extended family, as well. George had had four brothers, not counting Daniel's father, and each of them had married at least once and sired countless offspring. Daniel had no idea who most of them were except a few whose faces he vaguely recalled without accompanying names.

Conversation halted as he came in. They greeted him. Too warmly. He imagined them seeing the headlines about him in the line at the Piggly Wiggly and Winn-Dixie. He felt a surge of shame and wished he had said his good-byes at the graveside. It was too late now. The great-aunts had come to greet him. They had to have hugs. He found himself enveloped in soft bosoms, his face patted by veined, arthritic hands. Aunt Dorothy herself took his coat. She was holding up well, considering. Daniel thought again how strange it was. How odd that his uncle could be here one day, going to work, washing his truck, fishing, going to church, and then be gone, a decision as simple as changing lanes destined to be his final one.

He waited for their attention to shift away from him, then slipped into the hallway. His picture was hanging there beside the other boys'. The house seemed much smaller than he remembered, but that could be because right now the entire membership of Hillside Baptist Church was packed in here. Forty years at the same church, another testament to his uncle's fidelity. He went into the living room. The men were in there with the television turned to a football game, the sound muted. His uncles were all accounted for and quite a few of his cousins. He had better luck here at matching names with faces.

For the next hour he shuffled from one group to another, talking sometimes. They were a kind bunch. No one asked him directly about the rumors of his fading fortunes. Perhaps they didn't know, but he thought a few might. He could tell by their hesitant manner, as if they were screening conversation for anything hurtful or embarrassing and winnowing it out. There were a few who were obviously clueless, clapping him on the back, making awkward, self-effacing jokes about having a Hollywood star back home in Kroger. He responded to a few well-meaning conversational attempts about acting, Hollywood, movies. Mostly he listened. They talked about ordinary things: their jobs, their children, church. They gossiped. Two of his aunts had a spirited conversation about the merits of counted cross-stitch versus traditional embroidery. His uncle's accident was replayed at great length, each detail cemented now, a certain comfort coming from at least understanding the what if not the why.

It felt strange to be out of L.A. It was as if he saw himself differently. And it was especially strange to be around all of them, so like him. So much the same raw material, yet such different end results. Ten years ago he would have felt differently. He didn't think he would have sneered. For all his faults he didn't think he'd ever been an unkind person. But he would have felt superior. As if by staying here, working at the mine or the grocery store or the insurance agency, they had failed somehow to glimpse the bigger picture. That smooth certainty was gone. He listened to them talk. Joe was going hunting with someone named Charley this weekend, to Big Bear Creek. Jack had to put the snow tires on his car. The wives chatted softly in the kitchen. Tina laughed, a loud, contagious guffaw like a machine gun. He smiled in spite of the emptiness he felt. He would have been familiar with that laugh if he had stayed Danny Joe instead of becoming Daniel Monroe. By the time he'd listened for a while longer, the suspicion he'd been carrying in his gut for weeks—months? Years?—grew to certainty. He had made a mistake. He knew it with a deep conviction and felt dread overtake him, filling him with a regret that rose like oily liquid inside him.

He found his cousin Jack, Uncle George and Aunt Dorothy's oldest son, the one he supposed he'd been closest to. Jack had been stoically accepting when Daniel had moved in with them. He had suffered the addition of bunk beds to his single room, a privilege of being the oldest. He hadn't complained, and if he had never been affectionate, well, he had never been cruel, either. Their paths hadn't crossed much even then, the three-year gap in their ages too wide to cross. Actually, Daniel remembered, he hadn't hung out much with his younger cousins, either. In fact, this entire day the feelings of his childhood had swept back over him. A rushing current of not belonging, of being out of place, the stranger among fast friends.

Now Jack was looking at him straight on, refreshing after the sideways glances and nervous conversational bullets of the other family members.

"What are you working on now, Danny?" His voice was strong, deep, reminding Daniel of his own except for the accent, a feature Daniel had worked hard to eradicate.

"Nothing," Daniel answered. A straight question deserved a straight answer, didn't it? "Work seems to have dried up."

"That happen now and then?"

"Now and then." When you were on your way out. "How about you?"

"Still at the finance company. Probably put in my thirty."

"What do you do the rest of the time? When you're not working?" Daniel asked, aware that it was a ridiculous question but wanting to know.

His cousin answered with a slight shrug. "We go to church on Sundays, morning and evening, and again on Wednesday nights. Jack Junior plays football on Friday nights. We go to the games. I hunt in the fall and fish in the spring. Nothing special. Most days I just get up and go to work. Sounds pretty tame compared to your life, I imagine." No apology. Just acknowledgment.

"What do you do when you come home?" Daniel asked, suddenly hungry for the details of his missed life, the one he might have had.

His cousin gave him a pointed look. "You researching a part or something?"

"Something like that."

Jack shrugged again. "Well, let's see. Most nights I get home around six. We eat supper together, all of us."

He had three boys and a girl, Daniel remembered. He couldn't remember their names, but he could imagine them all around the table. Could almost smell the steaming platters of roast beef and mashed potatoes, see the glasses full of milk.

"Then the kids do their homework. Colleen and I read the paper, watch a little TV. Used to watch *Court of Law* on Tuesdays," he said with a wry grin.

Daniel smiled back. Colleen came in from the kitchen and joined them. She was a plump, sweet woman whom Daniel wished he thought pretty. She leaned against her husband and pressed a frayed tissue against her nose. "Every now and then it just hits me, you know? Just now I thought of something I wanted to tell him." Her eyes spilled over. Jack put his arm around her and gave her a squeeze. Her head came to the middle of his chest. After a moment she recovered her composure, dabbed at her nose. They chatted a little more, and as usual things trailed off.

She cast about for a moment, looking for the lost conversation. "Have you got a picture of your boy?" she finally asked, relieved she had landed a question.

"Scott," Jack put in. He rested his hands on her shoulders. She reached up and covered one with her small plump hand.

"That's right," she said, smiling. "Scott." She had dimples, Daniel noticed.

Daniel pulled out Scott's high school graduation picture. He glanced at it. The long, lanky hair was gone, as was the earring. He handed it to her.

"Ohh." She smiled and shook her head. "He looks like Robbie." She tilted her head up toward Jack for confirmation.

"Sure enough does," he agreed.

Daniel's eyes flicked to the group of boys on the sofa. Robbie, the youngest, looked to be about sixteen. He did look like Scott. Scott, the missing cousin. The one who had never met the rest. The face like theirs on the other coast who had no idea they existed. The creeping dread took hold of him again, caught on to his gut and pulled hard.

He said good-bye to Jack and Colleen, then found Dorothy and said his good-byes. He was sorry he'd come and now wanted only to leave.

"Let's get a few pictures before you go," Dorothy urged. "Everybody together."

Daniel shrugged in resignation.

"Over there," she said. "Just the boys this time." Daniel took the place they'd assigned him. The rest of them had shifted together perfectly, grouped according to age, he guessed, probably veterans of many such photos. Daniel stood beside Andrew, just to the left of Jack, in front of Merle and Dwight, a few squiggling little boys lined up in front of him. The flash sparkled twice.

"Let me get one more." Another flash. Two.

"I'm going to take one with the instamatic," Great-Aunt Lucille said. She took five.

When they were finished, he slipped away as they began lining up for more photos according to family groupings.

Lucille caught him on his way out the door. She grabbed him by his arms and gave him a fierce hug. Her plain, honest face was grieved when she patted him on the cheek. "I'm praying for you," she said. "Have been for quite a while."

"Thank you," Daniel said, and it reminded him again of his childhood. That's what they had all said to him. When his mother left. When his father died.

"You take this." She placed one of the snapshots in his hand. "I'll get your address from Dorothy and send you one of the big ones when they come back from Snappy Photo."

He thanked her again, bent and gave her a hug, brushed his lips against her cheek. It was soft. She smelled like hair spray, and oddly, it was a comforting smell. Associated with kind, if clumsy, affection. Church. Food.

He was in the car before he looked at the picture. It was ridiculously small, all twenty or so of them in a four-inch square. He picked himself out. There he was, but looking at the whole, he didn't look so different from any of the others. A few were better looking. There was nothing special about him.

He started the rental car and drove toward the motel, his heart tapping out a thready staccato rhythm. He focused on the scenery, on his driving, anything to keep a step ahead of the awareness that was hot after him.

Nothing about the town looked familiar. The sleepy main street had become a strip mall. He saw a Blockbuster Video store, Office Depot, McDonald's, a liquor store, a Pizza Hut. He shook his head. He drove by the place he had lived with his mother—one of the places, at any rate. He remembered it well—a run-down apartment complex, lots of poles and railings, more like a motor court than an apartment building. A U-shaped building with everyone's living room window fronting the parking lot. His childhood home. It was still there. Unchanged.

He drove back to the liquor store and bought a fifth of Scotch, drove to his motel, let himself into the room, inserting the plastic card and waiting for the green light to flash. It was bare, empty, cold, and smelled faintly of cigarettes. He sank down into the lone chair, set the bottle on the pressed-wood table, and stared at it. He could open it and start drinking and once again blunt the edge of truth, stay a step ahead of the realization that was dogging him. Or he could face what he'd been trying hard not to see. For years, he realized.

He flicked his glance toward the blank walls and thought about mistakes. Some were so huge that to admit them meant that everything that had followed them was wrong. That everything in his life had been wrong, like a math problem with a mistake near the beginning. Like a song started out in the wrong key.

He glanced back at the bottle, and the urge was strong, a steady beat behind his pulse.

He rubbed his face, leaned over, and rested his head in his hands. After a moment he sat up straight, and quickly, before he could debate and reconsider, he got up and took the bottle into the bathroom. He broke the seal, twisted the cap, and poured the brown liquid down the sink. He set the empty bottle on the back of the toilet, then sat down on the edge of the tub.

He admitted it then. For the first time.

He had made a mistake. A huge, deep crevasse of a mistake, a fault that was now quaking, widening, threatening to swallow him up. He knew only one thing. He couldn't fix it. It was too deep, too long, too late for that. He could acknowledge it, though, he realized, staring at the stack of white towels on the cold metal rack, the stark white of the wall behind them. He owed her that much.

———————

He flew back to L.A. and stopped at his home only briefly. He surveyed the dark rooms one more time, stopping in front of the chair, the empty bottle of Drambuie on the floor beside the gun, the expression "nothing left to lose" becoming blindingly clear. He went toward the bedroom but stopped to check his messages. He had a sense of portent as he pushed Play.

"Hi, Dad." Daniel's chest tightened when he heard his son's voice— deep now, sounding like his own. He was nineteen. In college now. "Dad, I got approved for the semester abroad," Scott said. "I'm leaving for Europe after Christmas, and I don't know when I'll be back. I'd like to see you before I go. That's all. I'll talk to you later."

He felt pain, deep and heavy. But behind it a sense of destiny. It was a sign. He didn't stop to analyze, just moved. He went to his bedroom, took off the suit he'd worn to the funeral, put on a pair of jeans, a sweatshirt. He took the old rucksack from the floor of the closet and filled it with whatever clothes were within reach. He took the wallet from the suit, counted out the last of his money, all he'd been able to save from the bill collectors. Two thousand dollars in hundreds and twenties. It would have been more, but the trip to Kentucky had cost him. He shoved the cash into his pocket.

He paused on the way out, rested his hand on the chair, the only thing he would miss. He didn't touch the gun, even to put it away.

He drove the SUV into town, left it parked on the street, phoned the finance company from a pay phone to tell them where to find it, then walked to the Greyhound bus station and bought a one-way ticket to Seattle. He climbed onto the bus, aware of a few curious glances, but no one spoke. He found a seat. The bus began to move, and Daniel closed his eyes and leaned his head against the vibrating window. He worked the problem of his life again, reviewing it the way he'd heard dying people do. It turned out the same as always, like that math problem with a hidden mistake. In his retracing he could see that he'd been fine up to a certain point, and then the road had forked. He had taken one way instead of the other, and nothing had been right ever since, no matter how it seemed otherwise.

He slept, ate orange crackers with peanut butter, drank soda, used the small, smelly bathroom on the bus, then slept again. The Greyhound streamed past San Francisco, curved and groaned its way up the Siskiyou Mountains, through the dark forests of Oregon, aimed for Seattle. But Daniel knew he was aimed toward a destination not found on any map. When he'd begun the journey, he might have thought he was going to Seattle to say good-bye to his son, but now he realized the truth was much simpler. He was looking for the last true place. He was going to find Lenore.

Thirty-six

LENORE TURNED HER FACE UP toward the sunlight. Tomorrow would be the first day of autumn, and already it was deepening to gold instead of yellow. Still bright but without the beating heat of the summer. It slanted through the burnished leaves of the maples, through the gnarled pines and rustling bamboo, onto Mr. Kaplan's bonsai, which were lined up like little soldiers by the fence. Her own reflection shimmered back at her from the blue gazing ball, from the pooled rainwater in the birdbath. In fact, all around her was still and quiet. Even her footsteps on the walkways were muted on the thick green carpet of moss. She closed her eyes and stood as still as she could. She heard the faraway tinkling of a wind chime, a guttural crow, the soft rustle of the first leaves falling to the brick walkway, water running, dripping from the bamboo pipe into the carp pond.

She had a sense of life hovering, poised for some kind of movement, and for a moment she felt a twist of anxiety. She quickly reassured herself that everything was fine. She tallied the evidence, went down the list of loved ones, checking each one off in her mind.

Scott was in college at Seattle Pacific just down the hill, Daniel's generosity over the years being put to good use. He had qualified for the semester abroad, and though Lenore would miss him, she shared his excitement. Mr. Caputo was healthy and happy. In fact, his daughter had invited him to visit this week, a rare but welcome occurrence. Angie had settled down from her rebellious phase, although a few consequences remained, specifically in the form of Joey, her one-year-old son. The entire household doted on him, and Mrs. Callahan had not been as devastated as Lenore had feared; perhaps her years of coping with Angie's mother had given her a certain resilience. And there had even been some healing on that front. Angie's mother had contacted them not long ago. She had gone through drug treatment and was back in Tennessee. Angie, Joey, and Mrs. Callahan were visiting her there now. Lenore still missed Nathan, but she smiled when she thought of him now working as a fire fighter for the city of Everett, married to Kristin, her long-ago nurse, the two of them expecting their first baby. Mr. Kaplan still told jokes, cooked for them, and exuded his calm, peaceful encouragement.

The only cause for concern was Al. His appetite had been poor lately as well as his energy level, and she had a feeling his diabetes was becoming harder to control. He had promised to see the doctor. She would corner him soon and see if he had followed through. She smiled, thinking of how he still growled protectively when anything threatened to harm her. But he had changed from the hard-eyed loner. He didn't talk about Arvid Chamberlain any longer, but he had attended church with her since the bargain had been struck, and Lenore was sure his faith was genuine even though his theology might have a few wrinkles. Her mother had, amazingly, married a man and was living in Arizona in relative normalcy. For now. Her sister had come for a visit last year—a week that seemed like a month—and she was just as she'd always been. Yes, Lenore reassured herself again. They were stable and firm, the ones she loved. Everything was fine.

She had the image of her world as a perfect bubble floating on the air. She tried not to think about what inevitably happened to those bubbles, and once again she felt a sense of foreboding, a persistently knocking anxiety that she didn't understand.

She remembered living in Oklahoma for a year during tornado season when she was a child. She recalled one hot and sticky afternoon. She'd heard the ominous rolls of thunder far away, and she and her mother and sister had joined the neighbors out on the lawn.

"It's so quiet," one said.

"Eerie."

"The sky is a funny color," said another.

"It's so still."

And that's how she felt now. Insulated. Encased and quiet, but with a sense of portent.

She opened her eyes, took in a deep breath of the wet, musky air, then scuffled through the leaves to the potting shed, its homely appearance grounding her again. It could use a coat of paint. The gray cedar siding showed through the peeling white, but you could hardly notice, she told herself, the way the ivy climbed across it. She jiggled the rusty latch and pulled open the door, lifting it slightly over the raised place in the walkway. She went inside, then just stood for a moment, smiling and breathing in the perfume of damp earth and stone and the thin green smell of the herbs and flowers drying over the bench. The roses were already crisp, blooms gone from yellow to parchment, tips shaded pink. Hydrangeas clumped on the floor in a weightless mass beside the bunches of baby's breath and sunflowers, twine, peppers, stacks of clay pots, a galvanized pail, an old ax handle that she always meant to sand and refit, a trowel that needed sharpening and oiling, a box of metal labels, a bucket of broken pot shards, a bundle of bamboo canes she was saving to stake pea vines next spring.

She took longer than she needed to gather her things—the leather gloves a gift from Al last Christmas, the spade that had been a birthday present from Scott, the rake that Mr. Caputo had bought her when they first moved in and made their crazy-quilt family. She rubbed her nose with the back of her hand and went out to work.

She glanced at the sky again. A bank of gray clouds hovered threateningly. The wind picked up. No rain yet, but it would come, and soon. She swept her eyes like the hands of a clock over the whole yard and stopped on the day lilies. She strode over and, like a surgeon, plunged her spade into the ground, almost hearing the roots slice neatly under the sharpened blade. She dug in a careful circle around the root ball, then under, loosened it, then set down the spade and lifted the plant out of the ground. The leaves were discolored and papery, the long dry stalks all that remained of the bright orange flowers. She dug up another and another until the ground around her was littered with the earthy balls. Then she took her spade and stood on it, slicing the root balls into halves, then fourths, and soon there were whole crowds of them. It took two trips with the wheelbarrow to move them to the empty spots by the fence and another while to plant them all. Next spring each of the quarters would have strong new roots. Then she would dig them up again and take out the old parts. Their job would be finished.

She stopped and rested. The bamboo behind her rustled like paper in the breeze. She leaned on her spade for just a moment, then went on to the tomatoes. The vines were sagging with the remains of the crop. The tomatoes that remained were a rainbow of every possible color between green and red: puce with yellow streaks, gold with green patches, neon orange, spicy red, a few new green bumpy buds that wouldn't have time to mature. She pulled the plants up by the roots and carried them, one by one, to the potting shed, secured them upside down to the line Al had strung across for just that purpose. They would ripen or not, and those that didn't would become green-tomato relish. She dusted her hands on her overalls and looked up.

The sky was darkening, the wind constant. The wind chimes sang. She smelled the rain. It would begin soon. It wouldn't stop until April.

She hesitated, flickering her eyes across the thick gray blanket of clouds and then across the yard. She tried to think if there was anything that still needed to be done. She began at the back porch and walked around, doing slow inspection, ignoring the drop of rain that landed on her cheek.

Everything was lovelier than it had been in summer, easier on the eyes, the colors more muted. The flowers had ripened, going rusty around the edges, the foliage gone from sassy green to muted golds and oranges, beautiful dark spicy colors. Her scientist's eyes knew it was the chlorophyll breaking down, but her heart said it was ripening, fruition, mellowing like tart grapes sweetening into smooth, potent old wine. Some might love the summer garden, full blown and in full flower, but she preferred this. Nothing glaring or shocking, but soft and soothing. Easy and peaceful, their colors the truest.

Soon everything would go to seed. Some with huge bursting pods, some with seeds so small you could hardly see them, no larger than a grain of sand. The lamb's ears would be heavy with pink seeds, the ferns brown-edged, ready to sleep, roses leggy, gone to hips; the vegetable garden would soon be bare, even of the drooping tomatoes. The holly, ash, pyracantha, and dogwoods would be jaunty with red berries.

She walked slowly back toward the potting shed, her feet making imprints in the damp, sparse grass and the brown earth underneath. She passed their one little bed of annuals. A cheery little garden, but dying. Red geraniums were missing some of their blossoms, but their leaves were still deceptively green. Marigolds were bright yellow in spite of the fact that they were not long for the world.

She brushed the dirt from the wheelbarrow and leaned it under the eaves beside the bed of nasturtiums, their leaves imperfectly round with the stalk in the center. They leaned toward one another like gossiping women. The blackberry vines arched behind the shed, making wicked, thorny arbors, the last of their berries dark and shriveled, the leaves turning scarlet and gold. She needed to cut them back, but that would be another day's job. She wiped her forehead with the back of her hand and pulled off her gloves. She was finished working. She had dinner to fix, and everyone would be home soon.

She took her time showering off the garden dirt, put on a pair of jeans and a sweatshirt, and barely glanced at herself in the mirror as she brushed the knots out of her hair. She had savored her garden, the one spot of poetry in her life, but now it was time to turn her thoughts to the mundane. What should she fix for dinner?

By the time she'd gone down the creaking stairs and reached the kitchen, the rain was pelting the roof and she'd settled on a menu. Chili, if she had enough beans. And she would make a pie—an apple pie, she decided, eyeing the box of Gravensteins on the floor by the sink. Their trees had been productive this year, and besides the fourteen quarts of applesauce that stood beside peaches and pears on the pantry shelves, there were three boxes of apples that remained even after Lenore's determined gifts to everyone she knew. She eyed them and knew one pie wouldn't even make a dent. She would make a few extra to freeze.

She pushed the box over to the sink with her foot and started picking around for the biggest and best apples. She filled the sink with them, little brown-spotted peelings side by side with the uncut apples. She peeled, quartered, cored, sliced. Peeled, quartered, cored, sliced.

She lost track of time and found an easy rhythm to her work. There was no hint of threat in the air anymore, just the steady pelt of rain on the roof. Her earlier apprehensions seemed silly now, fanciful and fleeting. Her life was well ordered, as regular and consistent as the clock on the wall. There were changes coming, but they were good changes, and she thought of Erik. Their relationship was a standing joke around the house. Mrs. Callahan called them Barney and Thelma Lou after the long-running but slow-moving romance on the *Andy Griffith Show*. She deserved their ribbing, she supposed. But she was ready to commit now. And she thought Erik was, too, though he had waited patiently until Scott was through school, more patiently than any other man would have done. Soon she would launch her son and be ready to begin a new phase in her life.

They had talked of marriage, in general terms, of course, but no doubt by summer they would marry. She felt a twist of sadness when she thought of leaving here, but everything had to end, didn't it? And she couldn't very well ask Erik to move into the house with all of them. She had brought up the subject, and his lack of enthusiasm had said what he had not. She felt a twinge of regret but told herself again that Erik was the right man for her and now was the right time. Everyone agreed, especially Carlene, who was overjoyed at their progress but still annoyed at their level-headed planning.

"For crying out loud," she had exclaimed, "people in love are supposed to do stupid, impetuous things. My grandmother is more impulsive than the two of you."

Lenore smiled every time she thought of Carlene, sassy and confident in her thrift-store clothes and acrylic fingernails, and she felt the tiniest twinge of unease at the point she had made. But there were all kinds of love, weren't there? There was the impassioned kind, the kind that dug down into your heart and latched on. And then there was the grown-up kind.

She opened the pantry door and brought out the twenty-pound bag of sugar, added some to the apples, shook in some cinnamon, then stirred, tossing the slices around in the sugar and spices. The kitchen was starting to smell good. She tossed in a handful of flour, stirred the apples again, and went to work on the crusts.

She cut the shortening into the flour patiently but for just the right amount of time. Too long and the crust would be hard and flat-tasting. She rolled it out, then lined the pie pans. There was enough for four. She scooped the apples into mounds on each plate, dotted the tops with blobs of butter. Not margarine—butter—five or six curly slices of it would go under the top crust. She divided the dough into parts, then rolled it out again and draped the top crusts across the tops of the pies.

She went around the edges expertly, turning the top crust under the bottom: turn, pinch, turn, pinch, turn. Then she made little dents with her fingers. She took the fork, made little vent holes in two, cut slits with the knife in the other two for variety. They sat grandly on the counter, stout kings and queens holding court. She smiled, satisfied.

She checked the rest of her dinner supplies. She would need to buy canned beans since there wasn't time to cook the dry ones. And now that she'd decided on pie, she would need vanilla ice cream. The good kind, with the brown flecks of vanilla bean. She checked the clock and went to the closet for her jacket and umbrella. There was just enough time to walk to the store.

After her shopping trip she put away the last of her groceries and put on some sweet music to listen to while she chopped onions and put together the chili. By the time she went to set the table, the house was filled with the pungent aromas of cayenne and onion wrapped around the cinnamon from the pies bubbling in the oven. She wrapped the ones she intended to freeze, then took the others out of the oven.

She glanced out the window. The wind had picked up. Quite a lot, in fact. The yard was dark, but she could see the outlines of the trees bending low in the wind, could hear it rushing, pressing against the house, causing it to creak in protest.

She heard the front door open, and Mr. Kaplan and Al came in together. Then Scott came home from class, dumped his backpack in the den, and clumped up the stairs. Mr. Caputo called and said he was coming back from visiting his daughter the day after tomorrow instead of Saturday and could she pick him up at the bus station. She said of course, and then the doorbell rang just as she was realizing she had set the table for one too many. She couldn't get used to Nathan being gone, and she wondered, in a flash that she would later call precognition, if the person at her door waiting for her to answer would be his replacement. She almost picked up the extra plate as she passed the table, but indulging her fancy, and more practically, not wanting to carry it to the door with her, she left it where it lay. She didn't realize until she had her hand on the doorknob that she still clutched the silverware.

She swung open the door in time with a stiff gust of wind, then stood still and stared.

Thirty-seven

IT WAS DANIEL STANDING on the porch. His head was bowed as though in prayer. His clothes were soaked through. She felt as if someone had turned her to stone.

"Lenore?" he asked hesitantly, looking up at her.

She stood there, frozen, taking in the details even as her mind tried to make sense of the fact that Daniel was here. On her porch.

He had been thoroughly soaked. Droplets of water were dripping off his hair onto the collar of his shirt. He wore no jacket. He looked cold and miserable. She stared. For years she had imagined what she would do if she were to see him again, her scenarios ranging from tearful to violent, and now she fulfilled none of them. She stood and stared.

He coughed, and she came to herself. She swung the door wide open and stepped back, a part of her surprised that her arms and legs still moved.

He started to come inside, paused, then propped his bag in the corner of the porch.

"You'd better bring it inside," she said. "It'll get wet there."

He picked it up. He came inside. He set the rucksack down. The rain dripped from it and puddled on the oak floor.

She shut the door behind him. The wind was making a low moaning sound now. They stood there facing each other, and she felt winded, as though she had just run a great distance.

"What are you doing here?" she finally asked, the words coming from that numb place inside her.

"I . . . uh . . ." He cleared his throat. "Scott called."

She widened her eyes. "Scott asked you to come?" she finally asked.

"Well, not exactly."

There was silence for a few minutes. He looked down at his feet, and

she followed his eyes. The hallway was littered with little maple tree helicopters that he'd carried in on his shoes. He raised his head, and she met
his eyes. They were full of misery. He was thin and haggard. His face was
sad.

"Dad?"

They both turned. Scott came down the stairs, his eyes wide. "Wow.
This is a surprise."

"I thought you called him," Lenore said before she thought not to.

Scott frowned. Looked at Lenore, then back at Daniel. "Yeah," he
said. "I did."

Daniel's mouth was open again. He took another breath and closed it.

Scott reached the hallway, began a handshake with his father that
turned into a hug. A fumbling, awkward, man-type hug, with as much
pushing away as pulling toward.

Lenore set the silverware down on the table in the hall. Her hands
were shaking, and she felt a little light-headed.

"So where are you staying?" Scott asked.

Daniel seemed to have recovered a little of his charm. He smiled, but
it was a strained, weary smile compared to the dazzling brightness of yesterday. "I haven't exactly firmed up my plans yet."

He looked sad. He looked weary. Cold and wet. And if the tabloids
were right, he was broke and friendless. She crossed her arms, suddenly
cold herself.

"Can he stay in Nathan's room?" Scott asked.

There was a stiff, tense silence during which several possibilities presented themselves to Lenore, all involving Daniel on the other side of the
front door. But there was Scott, looking—what was that in his eyes? It
wasn't bright enough to be hope. But it was more than simple compassion.
No. This situation, this turning up of Daniel here on their doorstep, was
not simple in any way. This was a complication. A complication in the
form of a person. And there were two approaches to those kinds of com-
plications, she had found. You could refuse them, turn them away and let
them take their problems somewhere else, or you could let them in and
sort through them—a messy affair, with lots of snarls and knots and tangles.
She had never taken the first option, though she had been tempted many
times and never more than now. Never more than when the bag of trouble
was dragged into the house by this one she'd thought she would never see
again. She lifted her shoulders in a shrug, the best she could manage at the
moment. Her mind was still anesthetized but slowly coming awake, little
prickles of pain beginning to stir, and it reminded her of her surgery. She
wondered when the wailing would start.

Scott nodded, aiming his eyes somewhere between her nose and chin. "Come on upstairs, Dad," he said.

Daniel looked at her, a question still on his face. He needed words, she supposed.

"Sure. Take him to Nathan's room." One night, she assured herself. Two at the most. Then life would go back to the way it was. Before she'd looked out and seen that face she had thought she would never see again. Before Daniel had come back.

"You can shower and put on some dry clothes," Scott said to his father as they left the room. "Eat some dinner. Then we'll talk."

Daniel nodded and followed Scott wordlessly up the stairs.

She followed, too, wanting to go to her room. To be alone for a moment. To gather herself back together from where she had spilled out.

Scott led Daniel to Nathan Delacroix's old room. It was freshly painted, all the little bits of paper and lint cleaned from the drawers and closet, clean, sweet-smelling sheets on the bed. She had even put a fresh towel on the bedspread, since she never knew who would be coming or when. She felt a wild urge to laugh as the humor of it struck her. She had cleaned out those drawers for Daniel. Washed and folded the quilt. Smoothed the clean sheets onto the bed for him.

Daniel crossed the doorway, then turned back, looking as surprised as a child who comes downstairs on Christmas morning to find a pony munching on the lower branches of the Christmas tree. The rucksack thumped behind him disconsolately. He dragged it into the room.

"The bathroom is down the hall." Scott pointed in the right direction. "There's plenty of hot water. Why don't you warm up and get out of those wet clothes?"

"I will. Thank you," Daniel said.

She went to her room before Daniel could turn and speak to her, before he could say anything else. She didn't want to speak to Scott now, either.

She went inside, shut the door, and stood with her back against it, as if to protect herself, wanting some small bit of safety between her and what had just come through her door.

Daniel. Daniel had come. She fixed a filtered gaze on the far wall. Daniel had come. And not at all as she might have imagined.

She had imagined his life there in Hollywood, as she had her own quiet one here. She had imagined him wearing dark suits, sunglasses, a tuxedo like the pictures in the magazines. She had imagined him in a limousine, sleek and dark, or in his little pointed sports car. She had imagined him buying tiny, expensive, glittering gifts and flowers and wine for those women he squired. She had imagined.

That was what he had done for them. For those women she had seen in the pictures. Tall, lean, willowy women. Blond, luminous women who wore gossamer clothing and changed with the phases of the moon. Dark, lustrous women who gleamed and glowed like dark, deep-cut gems. That is how he had been with them.

And this is how he had come to her. To Lenore, who was not.

She felt something begin to stir. She walked to the desk and sat down in the chair.

Once she had seen a picture of a volcano in Iceland that threatened a village. The people had devised an ingenious solution to the problem. They had sprayed it with seawater, and she still remembered the strange sculpture of frozen fire. She had wondered at the time what would happen if it erupted again. Would it break through the controlling layer to become molten fire again? Would it melt the frozen cap? She felt like that now. Something was beginning to stir under the ice. A little crevice was opening. A little curl of steam escaping.

She gave a small half laugh and pressed her wet eyelids together, surprised that this well wasn't dry. She had thought herself wrung, spent. How amazed she felt at the tears this man could still wrest from her heart. But of course he had waited until it filled again.

"No." She said it aloud. "I won't. Not again." She saw Daniel, but his name was Disruptor, coming in to twist away her hard-won peace. "No," she repeated, her throat tight against tears, and she wondered to whom she was speaking, for the room was silent, and the quiet voice that sometimes spoke inside her was quiet, as well.

She sank her head down, felt the cool wood of her desk beneath her cheek. It seemed that no time had passed at all since that day she'd watched him walk away. And now he had walked back.

After a while she got up, went into the bathroom and washed her face, then went downstairs and finished setting the table, moving automatically, swiftly, efficiently, as though nothing had happened. She found the silverware on the hall table and placed it beside the extra place— Daniel's place, she knew now. She felt an impulse to pick it up and fling it against the wall. The urge competed with the desire to sit down and weep.

She brought another glass from the cupboard, gave the chili another stir, and mixed up the cornbread. She gave the salad a final toss and, without even noticing, shook almost a whole box of croutons onto the top of it. She tossed it again and took it to the table, then checked the cornbread, and without knowing what else to do, she went to the sink and stared at her own reflection in the dark window. She remembered a night like this, fifteen years ago at another sink, peeling potatoes. The evening their happy little life shattered. The evening Daniel couldn't answer her question. Wouldn't say yes.

Daniel and Scott came down together. Scott began heating water, getting out cups to make tea, trailing conversation behind him in spurts, catching up his father on his life. First year of college completed and almost finished with the first semester of year two. Six month study abroad in Europe beginning in January. English Lit, he thought. Not sure, though. Lenore examined Daniel in swift glances. He looked more like himself now after his shower and change of clothes, though not as glamorous as the images Lenore had seen in the checkout lines over the last few years and nothing like she had imagined. But he had shaved, and the face under the whiskers was still familiar. It was a bit thinner, more gaunt, the eyes a little bloodshot, but those were just temporary things. There was no way to tell about the man inside. He wore a simple chambray shirt and jeans, both wrinkled. She could imagine, knowing his habits, how he had packed. The Daniel she knew had chosen these clothes. Not the Daniel Monroe of the limousine and tuxedo. For just a moment her certainty faltered. Then the door from the basement opened. It was Al.

Oh no. She had forgotten.

Al, apparently, had not.

The look on his face was terrible. Not fury. It was too cold for that. Not disdain, for there was something alive and electric in his eyes. A cold, dangerous voltage. Enough to kill or maim and aimed at Daniel, the one who had hurt his loved ones, who had left them alone and vulnerable. The one who had struck down a child in his dissipation and carnality. The one who had come back now to do who knew what damage. He stood there, reminding Lenore of a fierce, warrior angel. He looked toward Lenore as if inspecting her for damage. Then at Scott. Then back at Daniel.

Daniel was going through gyrations of his own. Lenore could see his confusion play out. Al's face must be familiar. How could it not be? Al had personally testified at Daniel's sentencing hearing. Had made sure that Daniel would get the stiffest sentence possible under the law. Made sure he didn't skate away clean because his face was on the cover of *People* magazine. But Daniel hadn't been expecting to see him. Not here, at any rate. Lenore watched his eyes move through confusion, then to realization. His jaw went a little slack, but he recovered quickly. The consummate performer.

"Al has lived with us for several years now," Lenore said. "He took care of Scott when you . . . after . . ." she finally trailed off. There were so many potholes.

Daniel nodded. "After I was arrested. I remember you now," he said. "Thank you for taking care of Scott."

Al seemed to take offense at Daniel's gratitude. "I didn't do it for you," he said.

Lenore felt her face heat up, but she couldn't take her eyes away. It was painful to watch but fascinating.

Daniel's face was still grim. "Thanks all the same," he said. His hand was still extended. After an agonizing three or four seconds, Al took it. They shook quickly, then dropped hands.

Mr. Kaplan came into the room, and Lenore felt relief come in with him. He broke the stiff standoff, and if he noticed the awkwardness, he didn't mention it. He was gracious as always, but then, he knew little of their history. When they all gathered around the table and eased into their chairs, Lenore was heartily glad that neither Angie nor Mr. Caputo was there. Angie would have made things uncomfortable by the depth of her adoration. She was always asking Scott about his father and said often that she thought he was the sexiest man alive, prompting many reprimands from her grandmother. And though Mr. Caputo was the gentlest of souls, she wasn't sure how he would react to the man who had, in his mind at least, caused the sorry state she had been in when he had found her. Al's cold anger was bad enough.

Mr. Kaplan said the blessing. The meal was uncomfortable. Silent. Mr. Kaplan looked from Al to Daniel to Scott to Lenore, then down at his plate. Lenore didn't taste much. She was too conscious of Daniel across the table. It had never broken, she supposed, that invisible thread that bound them together, whether it was across three states or simply across a dining room table. She could feel it binding them now, and she looked up to see him looking back at her. She gave her head a little shake and almost laughed out loud. The situation was the stuff of soap operas.

The dinner conversation was limited. Pass this. Thank you and please. Mealtimes had been considerably quieter anyway with Mr. Caputo gone and not there to play straight man to Mr. Kaplan's jokes, and of course Mrs. Callahan, Angie, and now little Joseph added to the normal frenzy. This meal was quiet and subdued, tense.

"Excellent chili," said Al gruffly.

"Would you like some more?" Lenore asked him and then noticed that he had eaten only half of the bowlful she had served him. She frowned and looked at him. His color was bad, and he had a strained, tense look about him. He had been that way for days, even before Daniel had come. She would corner him soon and ask about his diabetes.

He shook his head. "I'm saving room for some of that pie." He gave her a tight smile, and she was touched by his blundering effort at comforting her, taking his role as her guardian seriously, as always.

"I'll get it," Lenore said, eager to escape the tension.

She busied herself slicing the pie, which was still warm, then scooped the ice cream. She served it to their murmured thanks. They ate in silence, the clacking of their forks on the plates the only sound.

Al finished and excused himself after carrying his plate to the sink. He'd only taken a bite or two of his pie. Mr. Kaplan began putting away the food. It was his and Scott's turn to wash. Scott began scraping the plates and loading the dishwasher. Lenore went back into the dining room and gathered up the last of the dishes.

"Lenore, could we talk for a moment?" Daniel asked, and she tensed. He wouldn't—he wouldn't dare barge into her life, eat her food, then thrust an apology onto her, another unwanted thing she would have to cope with somehow, would he? Could he be so prideful? So arrogant? And even as she thought it, she knew it was false and prideful of her to feel her forgiveness so prized, something to be earned rather than freely given.

She stopped, the dishes in her hand, and looked at him, expectant.

"Do you have a moment?" he asked.

She sat down without answering. Set the dirty plates back on the table.

"Thank you," he said, then didn't speak, just watched the candle flicker in the center of the table.

She got up, gave the swinging door to the kitchen a nudge with her foot. It swung in and out a few times, then settled closed. She sat down again.

Daniel smiled at her, and she could still remember how her heart used to lurch when he looked at her with those smoky eyes. "I guess I owe you an explanation." His voice was somnolent, sweet, like a drug, and for a moment she could imagine herself succumbing to him again. She steeled herself and felt angry, as if he had taken advantage of her in some way.

"Well, I suppose you don't have to explain if you don't want to." The words came out hard, a little bitter.

The tender look went away. Daniel suddenly looked tired, and his face tightened into drawn lines. "I want to," he said quietly.

She felt a little flush of shame and waited for him to go on.

He started in a couple of times, backing up, grinding verbal gears as he did so. He said he felt as if he had nothing to show for his life. He halted and began again. The second time he began to say something about her and Scott, but then he began to choke up and had to take a few minutes to clear his throat and cough. Lenore felt her heart thump an extra beat, though as a nurse she knew it hadn't actually done that. It was probably only a reaction to the surge of adrenaline she felt when Daniel said their names. She was glad he hadn't gone any farther down that road.

Finally he seemed to realize what Lenore already suspected. He wasn't going to be able to put words to exactly what had drawn him here. Not for a while. He slumped forward onto the table with a look of such exhaustion that Lenore felt pity move her heart past its tense stall. Pity even for Daniel. Even now. Even here.

"I'm tired, Lenore," he finally said. "I needed to see you."

She nodded, and with her pity of him came the memory of how she had once loved him. She had loved him as a child loves, with no understanding or patience. She had been a bottomless cup, always needing to be filled. He had been so beautiful, so shiningly beautiful, and she had been so plain. And she had needed to know again and again and again that he loved her. It was as if each day her memory was erased, at least her memory for his love, and each morning she had needed to refresh it. To go over it once more. She looked at Daniel's weary eyes and for the first time could imagine how that would have felt to him. It would be like carrying a burden to live two lives, as if his one body supported two souls. And to think that hers was the best love he had had. The one he had come back to. No wonder he was tired.

"We'll talk later," she said, not thinking even to herself when that would be, what that would mean, but feeling a deep sadness settle over her as she said the words, as though she had just promised something that would cost her dearly.

He nodded and kept his eyes on her. She could feel him watching her as she rose up to leave. She didn't blow out the candle, though, just left him sitting there. She glanced back as she left the room and saw him sitting quietly, watching the flame burn.

———

It was fitting, somehow, that the events that would set their lives onto a new course would be accompanied by a tree-cracking, wind-whipping storm. By the time Lenore crawled into her bed, the wind was crashing by her window, sounding like a freight train. Still she slept, probably out of sheer emotional exhaustion, until around three in the morning. She sat up in bed then, not sure at first what had woken her. She heard a huge pop, pop, then crack and the sound of splitting wood, and then the crash of its landing. Felt it, as well. The bed rocked under her. She ran to Scott's room, met him and Daniel in the hallway, then found Al and Mr. Kaplan in the kitchen, obviously dressed in whatever had been closest to their beds. The power was out. Lenore picked up the candle from the dining room table and found the matches.

The tree, a huge Douglas fir, had fallen across the neighbor's yard and landed on the fence. Al went outside to check. Lenore looked at Daniel across the room, their faces eerie in the flickering light of the candle. He

was frozen, as if listening for some far-off sound or aware of some significance to the scene that escaped the rest of them. She looked outside,
away from his eyes, and saw herself reflected in the window—long nightgown, hair in one long plait down her back, holding the candlestick high,
Daniel beside her, still and wary. They looked like some Victorian tableau
vivant, two characters who had been violently wrenched from their normal
lives and thrown together in a moment of great drama and import.

"I'm going back to bed," Scott said, breaking the mood.

Al chose that moment to come thumping back in. He assessed the
situation in his usual terse style. "Everybody's all right. Fence is down.
We'll deal with it in the morning."

Lenore followed the rest of them back to bed, but the wind still
whipped and groaned outside her window, and she dreamed restless, disturbing dreams all night long, all of Daniel.

Daniel didn't go to sleep right away after the little excitement with
the tree. He lay in the bed and felt as if his mind had begun to wake up,
as if it had been asleep under anesthesia. He felt the same sharp pricks of
first awareness and the unpleasant premonition that there might be real
pain to follow.

The first twinge had come when he had seen her through the window,
but looking back on it, that had been a self-indulgent little dramatic pain,
comforting in a way, compared to what came later. For as soon as she had
opened the door, he had felt less noble, less like a tragic figure in some
sad story, albeit of his own making, and more like a common, garden-
variety heel.

Standing in her hallway he had seen the sign, *He has set the lonely in
families,* and it had struck him then that the word *lonely* had applied to her
and Scott. And he had made them so. Had left them unprotected, alone,
at the mercy of the storms of life. He didn't feel the seductive comfort
of depression anymore, the drawing, cloying melancholy, the self-pity. He
didn't even feel the dread, the emotion that had propelled him here. He
felt shame.

He lay there in the borrowed bed and thought of his uncle George,
his cousins. The mundane work they did. The small acts of faithfulness
they performed every day—getting up, going to work, coming home,
playing with their children, listening to their stories, going to bed. Then
getting up to do it again. He couldn't imagine Jack going off and leaving
Colleen, no matter what the enticement. Couldn't imagine Jack letting her
leave him. He lay there listening to the wind lash the window as the
thoughts lashed his mind.

Lenore had changed. Her physical body had changed. He had noticed that right away. She was fuller, stronger, calmer. But something had changed inside her, as well. He could see it in her eyes. They used to look hungry. But they didn't look like that anymore. Now they were calm and settled, and he was the one who was hungry. He wondered if it showed in his eyes, on his face, the way it used to in hers.

After supper, after Lenore had left him at the table, he had wandered upstairs and talked to Scott. But there wasn't much to say. There were too many years to cover, and besides, Scott had been busy at his desk studying. He had gone back downstairs to the living room where the Jewish man, Mr. Kaplan, had been watching television and had invited Daniel to sit down, but Daniel didn't want to watch television. He had taken a book down from the shelf in the living room, gone up to the little room Lenore had given him, and read until he had gotten tired of reading. After that he had just lain on the little bed under the handmade quilt—he wondered if Lenore had made it—and listened to the rain on the window.

He hadn't been able to picture their household when Scott had described it. What little information he had been given made it sound like some kind of retro sixties commune. But this was just a big old house, and the supper had felt just like a family dinner, with perhaps a cousin or an old uncle or two thrown in. A strained family dinner, perhaps, with the black sheep relation having shown up without an invitation. But a family, nevertheless. And there were others who would be here soon, Lenore had said.

He wondered if they would mind his being here. If they would want him to leave. The temptation enticed him to bundle up his shame and regret along with his wet clothes and slink off in the morning. He could be gone before anyone even woke up, and Lenore, certainly, would not be sorry. But there was Scott. And on examination, running away seemed as selfish and indulgent as demanding that they forgive him.

He could see now that that had been his hidden motive—to ask forgiveness. That had been the thought in the back of his mind when he'd climbed onto that bus—that he would resolve this burdensome thing that had hung like an albatross around his neck for so many years. He had envisioned a scene in which he had the lead role, in which they would recite the appropriate lines and release him from his guilt. He was ashamed of even thinking it now. He had no right. He had no rights here at all. That had been manifestly clear from the moment Lenore had opened the door and, instead of welcome, had exhibited that stony shock.

In fact, as the evening had worn on, his initial hopes had changed into something else. Instead of wanting something from them, he began to feel a weight of responsibility pressing onto his shoulders. It pressed upon him now, and he knew he must stay here long enough to see if there could possibly be anything they needed from him. He must determine if any part of the debt he owed might be repaid from what few resources he still possessed. It was probably too late even to try, but he knew, in a way he couldn't explain, that this was his mandate. His mission, so to speak.

He turned on the bed, still restless, punched the little pillow under his neck and pulled the quilt up over him. He listened. Everyone else must have gone to bed. He'd heard some footsteps on the stairs a while ago, but now everything was quiet. The only sound was the wind, still loud as the night wore on, and the old house creaking as it stood against it, busy sheltering the ones who slept inside, who were trusting it to keep them from the storm.

Thirty-eight

DANIEL WOKE AT FIVE-THIRTY, glad the long restless night was over. He dressed, washed, then walked down the stairs, through the dim house, and into the kitchen. He was the first one up. He wondered if he should go back to his room, then heard feet behind him.

"Hi, Dad."

Daniel listened for nuances in Scott's voice and found little to go on, either positive or otherwise.

"Hey, buddy." Daniel found a glass and turned on the water. "You're up early."

"I have a test in my eight-o'clock class. I'm going to go meet my study group for one last review. Help yourself to anything you want to eat."

"Should I make breakfast for everyone?" Daniel asked. He would hate to have Lenore find him sitting here as if waiting for her to feed him. But then again, maybe it would seem an affront to find him cooking. She might think him presumptuous. He felt off balance. Unsure. "Do you suppose your mom would mind if I started a little breakfast? Maybe made some coffee?"

"I think she would wonder if she'd died and gone to heaven. She hasn't changed that much."

Daniel smiled. The expression felt almost painful as it drew his face into an unfamiliar position. Lenore had always hated to wake up in the morning. And he had been the designated breakfast cook.

"I'm not taking anybody's job or anything?"

Scott reached over and put his hand on Daniel's shoulder. "Today's my day to cook breakfast, Dad. And because I want to make you feel welcome"—he smiled—"I'm going to donate it to you."

Daniel felt something ease. At the touch. At the words. "You're a champ," he said lightly. He opened the refrigerator and rummaged around. He found a few slices of ham, eggs, some mushrooms, and onions.

"Flour, stuff like that is in the cupboard there, more stuff in the pantry." Scott was on his way out of the room. "Coffee by the coffee maker."

"Have a good day," Daniel said.

"You too."

Lenore woke up at five forty-five as usual. In one of those delayed assaults, she remembered what had happened the night before and felt that the weight attached to her middle had plummeted a few feet. Daniel was here. She sat on the edge of her bed for a minute and waited for her heart to quit thumping. She hated it when her adrenaline flowed this early in the morning. It made her feel nervous and skittish.

She showered and dressed and decided to have a bowl of cereal since Scott was assigned to breakfast this week and wouldn't have made anything. She gave her head a little shake. Next time she would give him dinner duty. But the closer she came to the kitchen, the more hopeful she grew. She smelled coffee and fried onions. Daniel was sitting at the little table in the kitchen, reading the paper and drinking a cup of coffee.

"Good morning," Daniel greeted her when she came into the kitchen.

"Good morning." She felt cautious, on her guard.

He looked better this morning. His eyes weren't as red. He was wearing sweats, a pair just like the ones he used to have. Lenore poured herself a cup of coffee. "Are those the same sweats?" she asked him.

"No. These are expensive brand-name sweats that look, feel, and are exactly the same as the ones you bought at Kmart."

Lenore smiled, then immediately regretted it. She was on dangerous territory, and one false step could send her careening over a precipice.

Daniel set the paper down, rose, and pulled her chair out for her. "You sit. Scott generously gave me his turn to cook today. Would you like an omelet? Pancakes?"

"No, thank you," she said, unwilling to do anything as intimate as eat food he had prepared.

He looked at her intently for a moment, then sat down again. After a moment she took the chair he'd offered. Neither of them spoke, but Daniel began rocking his coffee cup softly, creating small waves, whirlpools, miniature oceans. She watched, transfixed.

"Lenore," he finally said.

She tensed.

"I know my coming here is awkward. I'm not exactly sure why I did it."

She blinked. Took another sip of coffee. "Are the stories in the *Enquirer* true?" she asked bluntly.

He gave her a wry smile. "Which stories? The ones that said the First Lady is pregnant with my child or the ones that said I was abducted by aliens and cloned?"

She didn't feel like smiling. "I was thinking of the ones that say you're drinking too much and owe everyone money and can't get any parts anymore." She hurled the words at him. He didn't react.

"Ah, those," he said. He met her eyes, and if she was expecting him to flinch, she was disappointed. He smiled briefly and nodded. "Yes. Those are true."

His honesty disarmed her. She took a breath and another sip of coffee, glanced at her watch, but unfortunately she had plenty of time.

"But I didn't come for money," he said. "I have money. A little. And I don't expect you to let me stay here."

"Why Seattle? Of all the places in the world, why here?" Her grievance came out in her voice.

He opened his hands, let them fall back onto the table, gave his head a small shake.

It was Scott, of course. Scott had called him. "I never thought he'd come," he'd told her last night. "I planned to go there." Well, they had both been surprised, hadn't they?

"Listen," Daniel said, "I know you have a life, and if I'm causing you a problem, I can leave. Just say the word and I'll disappear." He smiled briefly. The wrinkles at the corners of his eyes still crinkled.

She felt the anger begin to smolder then. The volcano burst through the ice. She stood up and left her coffee. "I have to go to work," she said shortly. "We can discuss it later if you want."

He didn't answer. She didn't look back, but she could feel his eyes on her back as she left the room.

Lenore put Daniel out of her mind, which wasn't difficult, as her patient was very sick. She worked her shift, but afterward, instead of going home she walked the short distance from Harborview to the church, her head down against the rain. The lights were on, as usual, warming the windows with welcome. She pushed open the door and stepped inside. The heat felt good. The secretary's desk was empty, the light off. She checked her watch. It was nearly four-thirty. She went to Matt's office, tapped gently on the door, which was slightly ajar.

"Come in," he invited, then smiled when he saw it was her. "What a pleasant surprise."

She stepped inside.

"Sit down," he invited. "Want a cup of coffee?"

Lenore eyed the pot and shed her cold, wet coat, wondering how long the coffee had been sitting there.

"Just made it fresh. I promise," Matt said, reading her mind.

"Okay." She smiled. "Half a cup."

He poured it for her, and she sipped. It was strong and hot. She felt herself begin to relax a little. Matt let her take her time. After three or four sips she lowered the cup to her lap. "Daniel showed up yesterday."

She didn't need to explain any further. Matt's eyes lit with surprise, then narrowed in concentration. "Really."

She nodded.

"This is the first time you've seen him in all these years?"

She nodded. Sipped her coffee again. "Talked to him maybe three times on the phone."

"And he just showed up."

"On my doorstep. Looking like something the cat dragged in."

"Wow."

Yes. That about said it.

"What did he say?"

She thought back to the tortured monologues, the halting speeches, to the one coherent conversation they'd had this morning. "I think he'd like to stay around."

"With you? At the house?"

She shook her head. Shrugged. "He made noises about getting his own place."

"So this isn't just a visit."

"I don't know. He can't seem to put two words together right now, but he admitted his career has tanked and he's broke. He looks—" she thought about how to describe him—"down and out. He did say he came to see Scott."

"Just Scott?"

Lenore's jaw tightened. "I don't know. I certainly have no desire in that direction. Anyway, I was wondering if you had any advice."

Matt shrugged. "I don't know. How do you feel about all of this?"

She didn't have to cast her mind back to locate the emotions she'd felt when Daniel showed up. They washed back over her like a breaker in a storm. "I'll tell you how I feel," she said, biting the words out as if they were hot in her mouth. "I feel angry. I feel used. I feel like the backup plan. I wish he'd go away. I never want to see him again. I wish I would go back home and find him gone and never see his face or hear his name again. He's a child," she said, her voice a ragged rasp. "A self-absorbed, self-indulgent, undisciplined, narcissistic child. He's never cared for me. I hate him."

The words shocked her, but there they were, hot and burning on their way out of her mouth like a spew of acid.

Matt's face was grieved but not shocked.

Lenore bowed her head, covered her eyes, and moaned, appalled at what she had revealed. What she must deal with now that the truth was out splattered into the room. She felt the same overwhelmed feeling as she had the day Scott had upended a gallon of grape juice, splashing it all over the kitchen. The same sense of overwhelming mess. Someone must clean it up.

"Okay," Matt said slowly. "At least it's good to know what we're dealing with, isn't it?"

She sniffed. He passed her a Kleenex. She blew her nose and raised her head.

Matt didn't speak for a minute or so. When he did, it wasn't what she'd expected him to say.

"You know, when you told me he'd shown up, my first impulse was to put the kibosh on the whole thing. Advise you to send him packing, at least make him stay somewhere else, and that may still be advisable. I don't know. But now that I've seen the depth of your feelings for Daniel—"

"I don't have feelings," Lenore interrupted.

"Hatred is a feeling," Matt said quietly.

"I was upset. I don't really hate him." She wondered if she told the truth. Apparently Matt had the same question.

"I think you have some things to work out," he said. "I'm wondering if that's not why the Lord led Daniel here."

"The Lord didn't lead him here," Lenore pronounced positively.

Matt didn't argue, just looked at her again. "Anyway," he said pointedly, "if you were looking for my opinion on what to do, I think you should take this opportunity to make your peace."

"But I don't want him here," she argued.

"Then why did you come and ask me what you should do? Why didn't you just send him away?"

She stopped. Opened her mouth and closed it again. "Because I want to do what the Lord wants me to."

"But I thought you said the Lord didn't send him. If He didn't send him, surely He wouldn't mind if you sent Daniel away."

She couldn't decide whether to laugh or be angry. She finally chose neither one. She rose, set the coffee cup on the counter. She felt chilled, and suddenly she just wanted to go home and get warm.

She pulled her Bible toward her. The leather was soft and pliable under her hand.

"Talk to me, please," she whispered. She closed her eyes and opened up the pages, part of her feeling foolish, the other part hoping. When had He ever dealt with her in linear, logical paths? Their entire relationship had been built on the chance, the importunate, from the first time she had knocked on a door for help. She opened her eyes. She had opened to the book of Isaiah. She read the first words her eyes fell upon. She shook her head and would have laughed if she hadn't felt so full of darkness.

Forget the former things; do not dwell on the past. See, I am doing a new thing! Now it springs up; do you not perceive it? I am making a way in the desert and streams in the wasteland.

A mistake. She tried again. Her eye fell on Matthew ten, verse eight. *Freely you have received, freely give.*

How could it get worse? One last chance. Deuteronomy chapter thirty-two, verse thirty-nine. *I have wounded and I will heal.*

She shook her head again, the tears flowing freer as it became clear she was not struggling with Daniel. "No. Please, God. It's too much." It was too much to ask to feed him and clothe him, to shelter him, mend him. And for what? To watch his back again when the siren sang? To see him leave as soon as he got a better offer?

Leave that part to me, He said quietly into her heart, and she knew in that certainty He gave what it was that He wanted. She could almost feel the heavy cross of wood on her back pressing her into the ground, could almost feel the rough splinters tearing into her soft shoulder and the piercing pressure of it dragging behind her, buckling her knees. *It's too much to ask,* she almost said, the words forming but never getting past her lips. From anyone else it would be too great a request. But not from Him. Not from the One who had already done the unthinkable for her.

She remembered her fervent prayers. *"Do whatever it takes,"* she had whispered, *"but don't let me go."* Would she have asked that if she had known?

She remembered the days when God's hand had been the one guiding hers, His face before her. The sweet intimacy of His love. Did she want to lose that now? Over this? By saying no?

"All right," she whispered. "I'll do it. Because you asked."

The hatred she'd felt for Daniel festered like a boil. She admitted it to Him, agreed with Him that it was noxious, poisonous, and asked Him to remove it.

She laid her head down again and felt hot tears course silently down her face. Her shuddering breath was the only sound in the silent room.

She remembered Edie's words to her—years ago now. *"Your turn will come to say thank you,"* she had promised. *"Don't doubt that for a minute."* This was it, she realized with an irony that ran down her heart like a thin, sharp razor. She raised her head, blew her nose, went into the bathroom and washed her face, then went downstairs just as Mr. Kaplan was putting the finishing touches on dinner.

Scott came in. He and Daniel chatted. She set the table and avoided both of them. They ate, the conversation still stilted but not as bad as the night before. Al left as soon as the meal was over. Daniel began clearing the table. Lenore felt a heavy sense of duty come over her like a garment she put on. She felt like a soldier, one who had trained all her life for a mission and could execute it automatically without having to consider or decide.

"Daniel," she said as soon as the room cleared, "could I speak to you for a moment?"

He nodded, his face full of dread. He sat down across from her and waited.

She sat down and took a few moments to compose her thoughts. His face was tight as he waited.

"I made a promise a few years back," she finally said, again tracing the patterns in the tablecloth with her spoon, "that I'd do the best I could to pay back the kindness other people have shown me. I decided that I would never turn anyone away if they needed a place to stay, and that includes you."

"So what are you saying?" Daniel asked carefully.

He waited as Lenore took a deep breath. "You can stay here. For a while. See Scott. Tie up your loose ends."

He tried to read her face and saw nothing on it but stoic determination. No doubt she was regretting that long-ago promise now. He had an idea what it was costing her. Rather than pricking his pride, it made him even more humbly thankful that she was allowing him to stay. "Thank you," he said.

"You'll need to talk to the pastor, though," she added. "I think in this case it would be good to get his approval."

His approval. That sounded ominous. "Okay. Where do I find him?"

She got up and started rooting around in a very messy drawer in the buffet. He smiled, remembering that she had always kept the drawers messy. Finally she found a pencil and a piece of paper. She wrote something down and handed it to him. "Here's the church phone. You can call and make an appointment. If he says yes, you'll have to work," she said, "around here, as well as getting a job. And no drinking. We don't need that here."

"Of course." His relief bubbled up. He hadn't realized how badly he wanted to stay.

"And I was wondering if you would do something for me," she continued. "Mr. Caputo needs someone to pick him up at the bus station at two o'clock tomorrow, and I'll be at work. Could you take his car and go get him? I'll draw you a map."

"The bus station," Daniel answered, "is the one thing in Seattle that I know how to find. Anything else?" He felt eager to be of service, to make her glad she had decided to let him stay for a while.

She shook her head.

"Where do you work?" he asked, ashamed. He knew she was a nurse. That was all. There was so little of her life he knew.

"Harborview Hospital," she answered, her face blank of expression. "I'm a nurse in the Trauma Intensive Care Unit."

He felt another slam of reality. He looked at her with wonder. Who knew this person had been there? All along.

She sat there a few more moments, indulging his paltry attempt at conversation, then excused herself. Daniel watched her go and felt a strange mixture of emotions—regret and a sense of the immensity of the task that lay before him, and hope bobbing up, determined.

Thirty-nine

$\mathcal{D}$ANIEL MADE BREAKFAST the next morning and was pleased when Lenore actually ate what he prepared. Only half the omelet, though, and with small, wary bites, as if he might have poisoned it. She left for work. Mr. Kaplan and Al came in one at a time and had breakfast, thanking him but refusing his offer of an omelet. They each had a bowl of cold cereal; then Al said he was going to do some woodworking. He went back down to the basement, and in a minute Daniel heard an electric saw start up. He shook his head in amazement. It had been a long time since he had heard that noise. Since he had seen any kind of normal, everyday activity.

"I have cooking to do today," Mr. Kaplan said, interrupting his musing. "Tonight is my night to do supper, and I need to start my bread if you don't mind."

"No problem," said Daniel, stepping out of his way. "I'm lucky to even be here."

"Aren't we all?" said Mr. Kaplan.

Daniel called the church, made an appointment with the pastor for the next day, then worked on the yard most of the morning, cleaning up the storm debris and quieting his nerves. He discovered to his amazement that after so many years of having his needs anticipated and met before he even felt them, he liked doing work. After he picked up the loose limbs and boughs, he went next door to the neighbors and introduced himself as a friend of Lenore's and volunteered to cut up the Douglas fir.

"Oh, that would be wonderful," the woman enthused. "We were afraid we'd have to pay somebody to haul it away. We're on a fixed income, you know."

He nodded. "Do you want it for firewood?"

"No, if you can use it, go ahead and take it," she said, then paused.

"You know, you look just like that movie star. What did you say your name was?"

"I get that a lot," he said and didn't answer her question. "I guess we all have a twin somewhere."

She nodded, satisfied, and went back inside. He worked until it was time to drive to the bus station. He was far from finished with the tree, but Lenore's chain saw was pitiful. He would find a hardware store and get another one, a gas-powered one so he didn't have to keep tripping over the cord. He'd buy a good ax, too. He realized he was making plans, and that fact made him uneasy. It felt good in one way but unsettling in another. He had no idea if he would be here to carry them out.

He started Mr. Caputo's car, drove to the bus station, then waited. He wasn't sure how he would find Mr. Caputo, but the problem was solved for him when an old man with a big mustache and shiny bald head made a beeline for the car. He smiled. There weren't that many '79 Chevy Impalas in the parking lot, after all.

The old man's face darkened when Daniel hopped out to help him with his suitcase.

"Ah . . . I'm Daniel. Lenore sent me to pick you up."

"I know who you are," he said, and Daniel was not under any illusions that that was a good thing.

Daniel nodded, forced a smile, and took the suitcase from Mr. Caputo's hand. Handed him the keys and wondered if he would need to find his own way back to the house.

"So get in," Mr. Caputo ordered.

Daniel obeyed.

Mr. Caputo took a moment to move the seat forward and adjust the mirrors.

"You're here for a visit?" he growled after a moment or two.

Daniel nodded.

Mr. Caputo gave his head quick little darts to look at Daniel and then back to the road. Finally, when they had pulled up in front of the house, Mr. Caputo turned off the engine and faced him. Daniel braced himself.

"I'll be honest with you, young man," Mr. Caputo said. "Our girl was in pretty sorry shape when you got through with her."

Daniel felt his face heat up.

"I wouldn't want anything or anyone to hurt her like that again, not after all she's been through."

"What has she been through?"

Mr. Caputo frowned darkly. "Never mind that. I just want your assurance that you aren't here with any funny business. Because if you are, it would be better to just turn around and go back to *Hollywood*," he said with heavy sarcasm. "She's happy now. She's dating a decent man. Scott is raised, and he's a good boy, and she's in good health. She's happy." Mr. Caputo gave Daniel another hard stare. "And I want her to stay that way."

Daniel listened. The words were painful. Especially the part about her dating a decent man. He hadn't anticipated that. He should have. He breathed in. Out. He looked at Mr. Caputo, who seemed to be waiting for an answer.

He swallowed. His tongue stuck to the roof of his mouth. "I was wrong to do what I did. I don't deserve her kindness."

Mr. Caputo's wary look relaxed a fraction.

"I don't want her to be hurt anymore, either. I'm glad she's happy." He meant it, though the words cut a channel though his chest.

Mr. Caputo gave him another hard look and, with a little nod of his head, opened the car door. Daniel fetched the suitcase and followed him inside, and neither one said anything more about it.

———————

"Where's Al?" Lenore asked, noticing his empty place at the supper table.

"I'll go check," Scott said. He disappeared and came back after a few minutes. "He said he's under the weather."

"I'll go check on him," Lenore said, rising from her seat.

"He said for you to eat your supper first," Scott said. "But that he'd like for you to come down later."

"I'll make him a tray," Mr. Caputo offered. "I have some vegetable soup in the freezer."

Lenore nodded, but she was concerned. Her worries over Al's appearance during the last few weeks came back in force. He had lost weight and seemed irritable and restless. She berated herself for not insisting he go to the doctor. She would take him herself tomorrow if she had to miss work to do it.

They ate. It was a quiet meal. She was alone with her worries. Daniel was subdued. Mr Caputo eyed him warily, and if Lenore had had the energy, she would have been amused. When Mr. Kaplan served the jelly roll for dessert, she excused herself and went downstairs. She felt like everything in her body was on high setting, and her chest tightened with dread.

She knocked on Al's bedroom door. He called for her to come in. He was lying on his bed in the dark.

"How are you?" she asked gently.

"I'm all right." He sat up and turned on the bedside lamp. His book slid off the bed onto the floor. She picked it up and set it on the bed beside him.

"What's the problem?" she asked, hoping he would say stomach flu or a simple fever but somehow knowing that would not be the case.

"Just a little under the weather," he repeated.

"You've been under the weather for quite some time," she pressed. "Did you go for your checkup yet?" She examined him closely, her dread increasing. He was jaundiced, and she wondered how she could have not noticed.

"As a matter of fact I did," he said, and something in his voice made Lenore's stomach tighten.

"What is it?" she asked, dreadfully hoping and praying it would be something minor. Something correctable.

He gazed at her with steady eyes, then spoke, his voice quiet and calm. "Doctor says I have cancer. In my pancreas."

Her limbs went cold, and for a moment she was afraid she might faint.

"Do you need to put your head between your legs?" He leaned forward solicitously.

"No." She could feel the blood drain from her face, and she sat down beside him on the edge of his bed. The dinner shifted dramatically inside her stomach. There was silence for a good two minutes as Lenore processed the information. "What kind?" she finally asked.

Al sighed deeply, then gave her a look. "I knew you'd ask." He picked up a piece of paper from the bedside table. "Adenocarcinoma."

She felt the bile rise in her throat. There could hardly have been a worse diagnosis. Pancreatic cancer was deadly and quick.

"What about chemo?" she asked.

"Do no good."

"Surgery?"

"Sounded more like hari-kari to me."

"Have you had a CAT scan?" she asked.

"And an ultrasound. It's in my lymph glands and liver, too."

"Oh, Lord Jesus," she whispered. She closed her eyes and berated herself. How could she have been so stupid? The symptoms had all been there. How could she not have seen them?

"He's in charge of everything," Al reminded her, and the fierce look was back. Daring her to argue. He gave her a rare smile, and he looked so firm and straight as he sat there, ramrod stiff, that she couldn't help herself. She put her arms around him, and in a rare moment of approachability, he let her. She cried. Sobbed like a baby on his shoulder. He patted her awkwardly. She thought she heard him murmur "there, there" a time or two. When she finished, he handed her the handkerchief from his pocket. How ironic, she realized, that he was the one who was comforting her.

"It's all right," he said, his hands on her shoulders, and he looked so earnest, his clear blue eyes lit by a fire she could not even dimly understand. "It's really all right," he said. "I wish I could make you understand that to me this isn't sad. It's like . . ." He struggled again. "It's like this is the most important thing I'll ever do in my life. Like dying well is the job I'm supposed to do now. Maybe the whole reason I've been put here. It makes me feel proud and strong. I can't explain it. I just feel like that's what God is saying to me."

She thought about the vow he had taken and wondered if that was at the root of it. If he thought he was fulfilling it, somehow—dying the death she was meant to have.

Lenore hugged him again, and he patted her back. She remembered what Edie had said when they'd discussed it.

"His life has been such a shipwreck, Lenore. It doesn't surprise me that he's come up with this idea. It's probably given him the sense that all of this has meaning somehow and that everything that led him to you had a purpose, even the drinking and wasted years."

She could see now that Edie was right. She wondered again if they should attempt to talk him out of it. To point out the truth. She decided to save that decision for later. She gave Al's chest a final pat and let herself out the door, leaving him, she supposed, to go calmly back to reading his book. She climbed the basement stairs and thought again about Daniel, who had just come to this house, and Al, who would probably very soon be leaving it. An arrival had occurred, and a departure had been announced.

She could hear the wind hurling the rain against the window in little icy needles. She didn't see Daniel on the way up, and the candle on the table was out but still smoking. She climbed the stairs to the second floor— why did they have so many stairs? She went into her bedroom and closed the door. She picked up the Bible from the bedside table and sank into the chair. She buried her face in her hands and tried to pray. For Al. For Daniel. For herself. For Al. She opened her Bible and found the verse she was looking for. *Unless a kernel of wheat falls to the ground and dies, it remains only a single seed. But if it dies, it produces many seeds.* Then she flipped back to Matthew. *What good will it be for a man if he gains the whole world, yet forfeits his soul? Or what can a man give in exchange for his soul?*

Then it came again—the comfort. In the midst of her trembling and weeping, her questions and dread, He came. The warm oil of His presence spread through her heart, spilled out into her chest. She laid down her Bible, climbed into her bed, pulled up the covers, and slept.

Forty

THE THIRD DAY HAD ARRIVED, Daniel realized upon awakening. The day that would decide his future. That would move him out of this odd, awkward limbo into the status of semilegitimate visitor or give him his walking papers. He got up and pulled on some clothes. He started to leave the room, then went back and pulled the covers up over his pillow. Shook his head. Started over, beginning with the bottom sheet. He pulled it tight, then smoothed out the blanket and bedspread, folded them neatly over the pillow, picked up the quilt from where it had fallen on the floor, refolded it and laid it neatly across the foot of the bed. There. That was better. He looked around for dirty laundry, found some socks, added them to the small pile on the floor of the closet. He would have to find out about laundry today. There was no Esperanza running around picking up after him here. He walked softly so as not to wake the others, then went downstairs to make breakfast. By the time Lenore came down, he had her omelet ready, the hashbrowns nicely golden, the toast buttered, coffee done. Another day or two and he'd have his skills back in top form.

Lenore was wearing jeans and a sweater, a pair of suede clogs. She changed into her scrubs at work. He'd learned a little about her routine. She was getting ready to leave, to do what she did, to be who she'd become. She was a nurse. He felt humbled when he thought of it. He had always been the one with important things to do, and Lenore just along for the ride. Now the roles were reversed. Her hair wasn't in a braid today but up in a clip. Her eyes had a little hint of sadness. They were tight at the corners, as if she was using up some energy keeping something inside that wanted to get out.

She made Al a breakfast tray—a pot of tea, toast, and part of the eggs he'd made. She took it downstairs, and when she came up, she looked sadder.

"You eat now," Daniel said.

She eyed the stove, the food he had prepared for her. "Oh, my goodness. That can't all be for me."

"I'll help."

She darted a glance his way but said nothing. He felt embarrassed, as though he'd overstepped a boundary. He wondered suddenly if he should eat in another room, but she took down two plates and set them on the table, poured herself a cup of coffee and refilled his. He served the food. They sat facing each other, and Daniel could feel her wariness. He ate, keeping his eyes down. Every conversational start he thought of felt loaded. He finally thought of something, a legitimate question that would fill the tense air.

"Where's the nearest grocery store?" he asked. "And is there anything I should know about the washer and dryer?"

She looked a little relieved, as if she, too, had found the empty silence threatening. "The Queen Anne Thriftway is just a few blocks north on Queen Anne Avenue, the street you walked up. It's a great store. Rows and rows of vegetables and fruits, all kinds of exotic foods, and they have their own coffee roaster. I love to go there." She got up, scraped her plate, put it in the dishwasher, washed her hands, and squirted some lotion onto them from a frog-shaped dispenser on the windowsill. "Christmas past. A gift from Scott," she said, following his gaze to the frog.

He smiled and wondered in a flash how many Christmases he had missed.

"The washer is pretty straightforward, but the temperature control on the dryer doesn't work," she continued. "It's always on scorch, so be careful you don't leave things in too long."

Daniel nodded. "I want to give you some money," he said, thinking of his two thousand dollars and how long it would last.

"Okay."

Daniel smiled. He had thought she might make some polite argument against it. It was refreshing that she hadn't.

"The bankbook for the house is in the drawer over there." She nodded toward the cupboard. "You can deposit whatever you want. The bank is right next door to the Thriftway."

Daniel nodded, got up and took the bankbook from the drawer, tore out a deposit slip, then carefully replaced it. He put the slip in his wallet, then sat back down at his place and helped himself to a slice of bacon from the platter on the table and a piece of toast. He was enjoying his own cooking. Surprisingly. He couldn't remember feeling hungry for a long time. Probably the alcohol had filled him up. He hadn't had anything to drink for nine days, though the desire to rectify that situation had been strong at first. Like a drumbeat during the plane ride from Kentucky to L.A. Like a dull throb on the bus from L.A. to Seattle. Now it was more like—like what? Like hunger pangs, he supposed, coming in a burst every now and then. But he could resist them. It seemed as if there was a reason to resist now, where there hadn't been before.

"How do you guys work things with your finances and your jobs?" he asked, happy to force his mind onto another track.

"Well, Mr. Caputo chips in from his pension," Lenore said. "He's a retired Boeing engineer. I contribute from my salary, and Al gets a retirement from the LAPD. Mrs. Callahan used to get Aid for Dependent Children for Angie." She made a little face and shrugged. "Now Angie gets it for Joseph. Long story there. Anyway," she said, finishing the last of her coffee, "we get by. As far as the housework goes, we divide it up." She checked her watch and put her cup in the sink.

Daniel scraped the plates into the garbage. "You need a dog around here," he said.

Scott scuffled into the kitchen, went to the coffeepot, and poured himself a cup. "Bye, Mom," he said.

"Bye, honey." Lenore pulled Scott's face down for a kiss. Daniel smiled and remembered what a tiny little bunch of drawn-up knees and diaper Scott had been as a baby and almost could not relate the memory to the long-boned young man who towered over Lenore.

"Have a good day," Daniel said, and Lenore darted a last furtive glance toward him. He wondered if she would ever look him in the eye again.

"Check on Al after a bit," she asked him.

"Of course," he agreed, eager to help.

After Scott and Lenore left, Daniel finished washing the breakfast dishes. By the time he was finished, Mr. Caputo and Mr. Kaplan were having breakfast. The two men were discussing the habits of Canada geese as though they really cared. Far from feeling left out, Daniel realized he was enjoying himself.

This little group was so different from the seven or eight bodies that had been assembled at his house in Bel Air. This place seemed to have a life in common, something that lived and breathed. Living together had made them something different than living apart would have done.

He listened to them for a few more minutes, then checked his watch. Not even eight o'clock. His appointment at the church wasn't until after two. Daniel went downstairs to check on Al. He knocked gently on the door, then pushed it open when no one answered. Al was asleep, his tray untouched on the table beside him. He went out into the back yard and worked on the fir tree a little longer, stacking the wood he had already split, raking up the mess. He stopped at eleven. Time enough to go to the grocery store and buy the things he needed.

He walked, following the directions Lenore had given him. He found Thriftway. It was just as Lenore had described and just like the upscale grocery stores he was used to. He left without buying anything and went to the ancient Safeway store across the street. He bought some laundry detergent, deodorant, razors, a paper, took a *Little Nickel Want Ads* from the wire rack of giveaway papers by the door. Maybe he could get a job, rent a room if the pastor didn't approve his visit. He felt a sagging sense of hopelessness at that thought, a desperation at the prospect of being told he must leave.

Only one clerk, a young girl, said anything to him, but he noticed a few heads turning as he walked by.

"Are you Daniel Monroe?" she asked in a whisper as she rang up his groceries.

"I used to be." He smiled at her. She looked fourteen, but she must have been older.

She giggled, her face awestruck. "Could I have your autograph?"

He stared at her for a moment, then sighed and nodded.

She giggled again. He signed the back of his cash register receipt and handed it back to her. *To Audrey,* he wrote, copying the name from her tag, *the nicest grocery checker on Queen Anne Hill.*

She turned pink and must have been too embarrassed even to giggle this time. "I can't wait to tell my friends," she breathed.

"Now, Audrey," he said, gathering up his bag.

"Yes?"

"If too many people find out I'm hanging out here, I'll have to start shopping at Thriftway." He gestured across the street.

Her face instantly became serious. She made a crossing motion over her chest. "I'll only tell two people."

Daniel laughed. "Well, if that's the best you can do."

"Okay, I'll just tell one person."

"Thank you," he said.

He stepped outside into the drizzle, found the bank and deposited two hundred dollars, folded the receipt carefully and put it in his wallet, then started the walk back. He passed a liquor store. He kept walking. He remembered the taste of the Scotch on his tongue, the blessed numbness it had brought. He didn't need that now, he repeated. The memories faded. The hunger subsided from pang to dull rumble.

He walked back to the house, went upstairs to the room they'd given him, set the bag on the bed, and gathered up his dirty clothes. He went downstairs to the basement to wash them. Al was up and in his shop. He looked awful, but he was standing upright, working on a piece of wood, tightening it into a vise. Daniel started the washing machine and paused by Al's workbench on the way out.

"This is quite a setup," he said, hands in his pockets. Al looked like the kind of guy who wouldn't want anyone touching his things. Especially not Daniel Monroe.

Al gave him an upward jerk of his chin that passed for a nod, pulled his goggles down, and drilled a hole in the wood he had clamped.

Daniel stayed, waited a minute or two for the drill to stop whirring, watched Al blow wood shavings from the hole and wipe it smooth with callused hands.

"What are you making?" Daniel asked.

Al took the goggles off, gave Daniel a brief glance that he was sure was meant to encourage him to be about his own business. "It's going to be a pie cupboard," he said shortly. "It's a Christmas gift for Lenore, so don't say anything."

That was a long speech, especially from Al. Especially to him. Daniel shook his head. "I won't," he said. He watched Al sand the smooth pine with long, fluid strokes, then brush the powdery sandings away with his hand. Over and over again, each time finding a spot that was too rough to suit him, going back to it again with the fine-grit sandpaper. After a few moments he stopped, sat down in the chair, wiped the sweat from his forehead, and leaned forward, arms resting on his knees.

"Are you all right?" Daniel asked.

"Be fine if I could get a little peace and quiet," Al answered.

Daniel took the hint.

He went back upstairs, called the bus line and found out how to get from where he was to the church, his stomach beginning to tighten as the time grew closer. He supposed he could have asked someone for a ride, but he didn't want to do that. He wrote down the instructions, figured when he would need to leave to be at the church by two. He cleaned up, carefully pressing his pants and shirt. He dressed as well as he could under the circumstances, then left to walk to the bus stop.

He waited, the drizzle feeling good on his face. He realized again that this man whom he had never met would probably decide his future. Two things struck him from that realization. First, that he was helpless, at the mercy of someone else. A new feeling, and different from what he was used to feeling, that leaky, listing, or not, he was captain of his own ship. But he wasn't. He saw that now. Clearly. He never had been. He felt small, not masterful and powerful. He felt humble and suddenly hoped very much that Pastor Matt Reynolds would take pity on him. If he didn't, his money would hold out for a few weeks, and then he would be on the streets.

Then the second thing struck him, and the prospect of homelessness underscored it. It wasn't that future calamity worried him much. He had reached a sort of Zenlike acceptance of whatever came his way. It was the thought that it would be over. That any possibility of connecting with his son or with Lenore would be gone. He knew then how badly he wanted to repair it. To have that part of his life in some semblance of order. The ruins at least arranged neatly.

The bus pulled up to the stop and the door opened. He boarded. He rode through the rain-slicked streets. After a bit he saw the street sign he'd been told to look for. He got out when the bus stopped, followed the directions the church secretary had given, and after a moment he was there.

He stared at the building. At the worn red brick, at the cross on the spire, at the boulder by the door. *Proclaiming Truth. Extending Hope.* He read the sign. *Greater Grace Tabernacle.* He felt a twinge of unease. He would have preferred something mainstream. Something predictable. He climbed the steps and pushed open the door.

Matt Reynolds was about Daniel's own age. A little older, maybe. His face was kind and unlined. His hair was thinning a little, combed back from his forehead. He had an intense look about him, a flash of something in his eyes. Passion, Daniel realized. He smiled at the incongruity. The average body, the fire inside. He wondered how Pastor Reynolds saw him and realized the opposite was probably true. Nice package, burned-out flame.

"Daniel, nice to meet you." Matt shook hands with a firm, earnest grip. "Sit down," he invited, and then he joined Daniel at the chairs in the corner. He didn't sit behind the desk as if he were interviewing him. "Would you like some coffee?" he offered.

"Yes, thank you," Daniel answered. He was cold and worried he might shake. "Coffee would be nice."

"How do you take it?"

"Black is fine." He liked cream, actually, but didn't want to be any trouble.

Matt smiled, left the office, came back in a moment with two cups, then sat down again. They each took a sip, then Matt set down his cup.

"This must seem odd to you," he said after a moment, "having to come here and get permission from a stranger to visit your son and his mother."

Daniel shrugged. It did seem odd, actually, but then, what hadn't seemed odd about this whole adventure? "The house belongs to you," he said. "You have the right."

Matt shook his head. "It's more than that, actually." His face was still pleasant, but his tone had a firmness to it that Daniel hadn't noticed before. "Our congregation considers Lenore to be our special responsibility, as we would a widow."

Daniel swallowed hard. The comparison jolted him.

"Lenore and Scott were both hurting when they joined us. We're protective of them, as I'm sure you understand."

Daniel nodded, and oddly he felt no thrust of anger. Instead he had a surge of gratitude. These people had been here when he had failed. They had picked up the pieces and protected Lenore and Scott. All those years. "I do understand," he said.

Matt examined his eyes and seemed to find whatever he saw there acceptable. He leaned back in his chair and relaxed a little, took another sip of coffee. "So what, exactly, is your intention?"

Daniel fumbled and felt like a teenager being interviewed by a date's protective father. He swallowed again. He thought about giving some vague answer about rebuilding bridges and immediately rejected it. The very walls of this place demanded truth. He met Matt Reynolds' gaze and laid it out, raw and plain. "I walked out on them fifteen years ago," he said. "I know there's nothing I can do about that now, but this is my last stop."

Pastor Reynolds looked at him with a question. Daniel chose not to answer it. He didn't know himself what he had meant by that statement. "I don't know exactly what I want to accomplish. But this is my unfinished business. I'd like a chance to do whatever it is I'm supposed to do."

Matt eased back in the chair. He didn't say anything for a long time, then he leaned forward and rested his elbows on his knees. "How are things with you and God?" he asked.

Daniel shook his head. "I don't know how to answer that question. I don't know Him. Not the way you folks do." He thought of his aunt and uncle, of his cousin and his wife, of their shiny children and happy homes. He shook his head again.

"Would you like to?" Matt asked.

Daniel's mind felt like sucking mud, confusion and despair vying for his attention. "I don't know."

Matt nodded and was silent. "I'd like to have you stay," he said after another moment or two.

He said it like he meant it, but Daniel's stomach dropped. The phrasing gave away the "but" that would follow.

"But there are other factors besides your intentions. As you said, the church owns the house, and it's a ministry of our congregation. You're certainly welcome as a person in need of a home, but your former relationship with Lenore is a complication. We try to avoid even the appearance of impropriety."

Daniel nodded. He set down his coffee cup. "I'll make other arrangements. Thank you for your time."

"Just a minute," Matt said, holding up his hand. "I feel there may be a solution. We just don't know it yet."

Daniel looked at him skeptically.

"Why don't you plan on staying at least a couple of weeks. That will give you time to look into other arrangements, and it will also give the Lord time to communicate whatever He wants to say. To all of us."

Daniel stared at him. The man didn't look crazy, but he'd made the last statement with the matter-of-factness of someone expecting a phone call from his wife.

"Okay," Daniel said simply. *Let me know when you hear from Him,* he wanted to add. He didn't.

"In fact, let's ask Him now," Matt suggested with the same ease.

"Okay," Daniel repeated again. Matt closed his eyes and began talking to God as if He were in the chair beside them.

"Lord, you know Daniel's here. You know what brought him. You know what you intend to do. Would you show us your will in this matter, Lord? That's all we want. Thank you, Jesus."

Daniel raised his head, but Matt wasn't done.

"And, Lord, I ask you to rest your hand on Daniel. You promised in your Word that you would rebuild the ancient ruins in our lives if only we would let you. Father, bring your mighty power to bear on Daniel's life. Breathe your healing spirit into it. Thank you, Lord."

Daniel squinted open one eye. Matt was looking at him. He opened both. "Thank you."

"You're welcome." Matt stuck out his hand. They shook again. Daniel stood up and took his leave, anxious to be out of that place. Uneasy with the thought of God's heavy hand upon him.

He rode the bus to Lenore's home silently. The visit had disturbed him. He wasn't sure why, and he didn't want to analyze it to find out. He tried to put it behind him but couldn't. And the verdict he'd been given weighed on him, as well. He had two weeks. Unless, of course, the Lord intervened. He counted down the days and thought about the impossibility of erasing a lifetime of neglect in fourteen days.

Lenore was sitting in the kitchen when he came in. Mr. Caputo was stirring a pot, and Daniel could smell tomatoes and basil and oregano. He greeted them and went upstairs to his room. After a moment he heard footsteps and a gentle tap on the door.

"Come in."

Lenore poked her head around the door. "What did he say?" No preamble. He tried to read her eyes and saw something guarded. He couldn't tell what.

"He was concerned about the situation. Said I had two weeks, barring divine intervention."

Her eyes became troubled, the gold and green flecks looking stirred up like an uneasy sea. It warmed him, somehow, that she cared about his fate, but just as suddenly he was stabbed with condemnation. He didn't deserve for her to care. She nodded. "I'll pray, too," she said.

He opened his mouth but had no answer to that. It didn't matter. She had gone, closing the door gently behind her.

———

Supper, as he had expected, was delicious, but there was a subtext again, a tension, a sadness that was almost palpable. Al was back, but Daniel noticed Mr. Caputo and Mr. Kaplan darting glances his way every now and then, and Lenore had the tight, strained look. Al himself ate little and didn't speak. Daniel wondered again if it was his presence that was causing the trouble. Afterward, Daniel and Scott had dish duty. They worked together for a while, then Daniel volunteered to do the pots. Scott left the room for a moment, then came back and sat down at the oak table. He was looking at the yellow newspaper Daniel had brought home from the grocery store and left on the coffee table in the living room. The *Little Nickel Want Ads*. Now and then he circled something.

"What are you looking for?" The obvious question. The one Scott must have wanted him to ask.

"We need another car around here," Scott said with studied casualness, "and we were thinking of a truck. People move in and out from time to time, and Mom could use it for hauling stuff for her garden. Here," Scott said, handing him the paper. "What do you think about these?"

He had circled three. A '92 Ford F10 in someplace called Fall City, a '90 Nissan, and a Chevy in someplace called Magnolia. "The Nissan might be a little small," Daniel said.

Scott nodded. He swallowed and Daniel could see his Adam's apple go up and down. "Want to go with me to look at them?"

Daniel drew in his breath. "Sure." His heart was thumping. His throat felt tight. "The best one looks like that Ford in Fall City." He cleared his throat.

Scott nodded. "Fall City is a little ways away," he said. "We can go tomorrow. I don't have anything else to do. My classes are Monday through Thursday."

"Sounds good." Daniel handed the paper back.

"Good," Scott repeated. "I'll call the guy and see when he's home."

"Good," Daniel repeated, nodding again. Scott flashed his eyes into Daniel's briefly, then left. Daniel turned back to the soapy pot and scrubbed hard.

Lenore came in after a moment. He sniffed and cleared his throat. She was busy examining a list in her hand.

"Do you care what days I give you for chores?" she asked him.

He gave her a questioning look.

"You're here for two weeks. You didn't think we were going to wait on you, did you?"

"No. No, of course not."

She flashed him a smile. The first one, he realized.

"I was kidding, Daniel," she said.

"Oh. Okay. Whatever works."

She sat down at the table. He wiped down the counter and watched her work for a moment. Her hair was loose and brushed the paper while she wrote. Her face was serious with concentration, but at least she'd lost that sad, tight look. She'd made a grid and was filling names in the blocks, last month's schedule, rumpled and stained with cooking splatters from where it had hung beside the stove, beside her on the table. After a moment she looked up, her eyes troubled again.

"There's something you should know," she said, "about Al."

Daniel tensed at the mention of Al's name. His animosity toward Daniel still fairly glowed. And to be honest, Daniel wasn't exceptionally fond of him. He still remembered seeing Al testify at his trial, straight and honorable in his blue uniform, arguing that the cause of truth and justice would be best served if Daniel were put away for a long time.

"He has cancer," Lenore said, her voice rough and tight.

Daniel felt a quick stab of guilt for resenting the man, even momentarily. As if he had any right to resent anyone here. "I'm sorry," he said.

Lenore gave her head a little shake and cleared her throat. Daniel remembered how tenderhearted she was. This must be hitting her hard.

"Anyway—" she cleared her throat again—"I expect I'll have to cut down my work hours when he starts to get bad. The kind of cancer he has progresses very quickly. By the time it's diagnosed, there are usually only a few months left."

"What kind is it?"

"Pancreatic."

Daniel nodded. "How's he doing with the whole thing?"

Lenore shrugged. "Al is . . . Al."

Daniel nodded. Nothing he could say would comfort her.

"I haven't told Scott yet," she said.

"I won't say anything," Daniel promised.

She nodded and went back to her list. "I guess I'll put him on the chore list." Her eyes were troubled when she looked up.

"I'll fill in for his jobs if he gets too sick."

"Maybe I shouldn't." She tapped her pencil on the table. "If he sees his name on there, he'll be mortified if he can't do his jobs."

"Is he that sick?"

She nodded. "I went with him to the doctor this afternoon, which was quite a step for him."

Daniel thought of Al's taciturn ways and could imagine that it was.

"It's already advanced. It probably won't be long."

"How long?"

"Months." Her eyes filled with tears, and Daniel felt ashamed of his insensitivity.

"He said he would go into a nursing home. That he had the money saved." She looked grieved to even be discussing the possibility.

"What will you do?"

She shook her head. "I'm praying about it."

There it was again.

"But I won't send him away if there's any other option."

Daniel thought of Mr. Caputo, seventy if he was a day. Scott was at school most of the time. Lenore worked. Maybe they were counting on the absent Mrs. Callahan or Angie. "I think you should put his name down," he said quietly. "Otherwise he'll feel as if you've written him off. I'll help him if he needs it," he repeated.

Lenore met his eyes for a moment. She nodded gratefully, then wrote Al's name in a few squares. "Angie and Mrs. Callahan will be back in a week or so." She looked up and smiled at him. Her face rose out of its worried lines, and he felt warmth start at his chest and spread outward. "Things will definitely liven up around here then."

"I was enjoying the peace and quiet." He smiled back at her.

"Well, enjoy it now," Lenore said, quirking an eyebrow, "while you can."

He sat there for a few minutes longer, asking her what she had done that day and listening to her tell about her patient, and for a moment it was easy to pretend that this was a life they shared together, that all the years between them hadn't happened at all.

Forty-one

"DON'T HAVE IT RUNNING," Daniel told the man on the phone when they called and arranged to look at the truck. He remembered a little bit about buying used vehicles. "I'd like to start it cold."

The man said that was fine and didn't grumble, which made Daniel optimistic about the state of the engine.

Lenore turned down his invitation to go with them, even though she had the day off. "Don't you remember all the fun we used to have buying used cars?" he asked, daring to tease.

She rolled her eyes. "Thanks," she said, "but I need to run some errands and do some shopping." He suspected she was wanting to stay close to Al, as well.

Daniel and Scott jammed into the front seat of Scott's little car and took off. Fall City was a fair distance from Seattle, as Scott had said. They chugged away, but it still took a good hour to get there. Daniel enjoyed the drive. They went through Seattle, then Mercer Island, another rich enclave according to Scott, then Issaquah, ten square miles of strip malls and upscale urban sprawl that had once probably been a nice place to live, Daniel cynically assessed from the window of Scott's car. But past Issaquah, at a little town called Preston, they left the big highway, and after that Daniel felt at ease. With a few hills and hollows added, it could have been Kentucky. With different trees, of course. There were knobby pines in Kentucky, not the tall dark firs and cedars of Washington. But he liked them. He liked the others, as well, and recognized the gnarled branches of oaks, moss covered, their twisted limbs looking like lace against the sky. He liked the way everything was covered with vines and moss and lichen. The way everything was green. He even liked the rain. It was refreshing after the monotony of sunshine every day.

They found the guy's house easily enough, a brown rambler on a few acres of car hulks and chain-link fence. A dog came out of nowhere and chased their car into the dirt driveway.

"Kobuk! Get down!" A man, tall and thin in loose jeans and a Seattle Seahawks sweatshirt, came out of the house and called off the Siberian husky that was now doing his best to make Daniel and Scott get back into the car. The dog skulked away.

"That's it." The man pointed to the blue Ford pickup parked by the garage. I just pulled it out of the garage. That's all," he promised.

Daniel nodded, wondered if the guy was telling the truth. He rested his hand on the hood. It was cool. He walked around the truck. The body looked pretty straight except for the tailgate, which was held on with a piece of baling wire.

"What happened here?"

"Aw, just caught it on some pole in a parking lot. Cost too much to fix. I thought I could straighten it out but never did get around to it."

Daniel nodded. Scott had popped the hood. Daniel paced back and forth and tested wires and plugs. The engine looked okay. Clean, at least.

"You start it up, Dad," Scott said, so Daniel did.

"Runs a little rough," said Scott. "Looks like it needs new plugs and the timing adjusted."

Daniel ducked his head under the hood beside Scott's and lowered his voice. "What do you think?"

"I like it," Scott whispered. "What do you think, Dad?"

"What's he asking?"

"Eight hundred."

"Offer him six."

Scott nodded and made his offer. The guy in the droopy jeans countered with seven fifty. They settled on seven hundred, and Scott pulled a wad of hundreds from his pocket and paid him.

The man signed over the title, all the while glancing at Daniel and frowning. "Hey, aren't you that movie actor?" he finally asked.

"Guilty."

The man shook his head in disgust and looked at the wad of bills in his hand, obviously wishing he had asked for more money.

Scott drove the Ford back down the road, Daniel following behind him. They stopped at Schucks, as they'd agreed, bought points and plugs and a timing light, and after they got home the two of them spent the afternoon in the drizzle in front of the house tuning up the truck. When they were finished, they took it around the block, and it ran a lot smoother.

"That car of yours could use some new plugs, too." Daniel said. "How about tomorrow or Sunday?"

"Sure," Scott said. He cleared his throat. "If you want to drive the truck while you're here, you can," he offered.

Daniel couldn't read his face. When they parked, Daniel walked around the truck one more time, took another look at the tailgate. It would be easy to fix. He would do it tomorrow.

Watching Scott warm up to his father was like watching a loaf of bread rise up until it was ready to bake, Lenore thought, watching the two of them from the living room window. After the first stiff awkwardness had worn off, it was as if being around Daniel gave Scott something he had been missing. It was as if Scott had needed something that he was finally getting, something that she'd been unable to give him, no matter how she hovered and worried. Something no one else had been able to give him, either. She shook her head, not wanting to get too ethereal. But it was good to see the two of them together, heads bent, back ends sticking out of the hood of the car. She felt a little uneasiness, though. What would happen to Scott when Daniel decided it was time to disappear again? But then, she reminded herself, Scott would be leaving himself after Christmas, and she felt a surge of relief. He would leave Daniel this time. He would leave both of them. She looked one more time, then let the curtains fall.

———————

Daniel enjoyed the evening meal, which, as it turned out, had special significance. At least it did to Mr. Kaplan, who was, as he put it, "a completed Jew." It was the beginning of the Jewish new year, Mr. Caputo told him as they waited for supper, when Jews remember and make atonement for what they've done that was wrong over the past year.

"Or their entire lives," Mr. Caputo said, not looking at Daniel when he spoke.

The meal was quiet and peaceful, and if Daniel felt he deserved to, he might have enjoyed it. The table was covered with lace, and the candlelight shone through wine the color of black cherries. In every glass but Al's, which contained grape juice.

"I'll have juice, as well, please," Daniel said, and Lenore took his glass away and replaced it without comment.

Mr. Kaplan, wearing his cap and tassels, said prayers that sounded like music, and Lenore wore a dress the color of russet leaves. She looked at Daniel twice, and though she didn't smile, neither did she frown.

"Tomorrow begins the Days of Awe," Mr. Kaplan said, explaining to Daniel and reminding the others, he supposed, "when Jews remember the way they have lived and plan the way they would like to live in the coming year." Mr. Kaplan's voice was deep, and his face was sober. Mr. Caputo beside him looked at Daniel with a glinty stare, and Al's face was tight and hard. It was probably Daniel's guilty conscience, but the three old men seemed like ancient judges, spare and severe, all looking at him, with Lenore and Scott to the side as the plaintiffs.

Daniel took a sip of his juice and listened as Mr. Kaplan explained that all their names were written in God's books, who would live and who would die, who would have good and bad times for the next year, and that perhaps our actions during this season of repentance could alter God's decree.

Daniel looked at Al, but he was watching Mr. Kaplan now and looked attentive and sober, someone content with, not looking to alter, God's decree.

"Repentance, prayer, good deeds—these are the things God loves to see in His children." Mr. Kaplan beamed, now looking like a happy father himself. "It pleases Him when we make things right with ones we may have wronged"—his voice sobered—"when we forgive those who have wronged us."

Mr. Caputo was still looking at Daniel with a meaningful stare, as though he hoped the message of the holiday wasn't lost on him. Daniel watched them. They watched him. Only Lenore seemed oblivious, sipping her wine, her eyes shining in the light, listening intently to Mr. Kaplan's words.

At the end of the meal, Mr. Kaplan dipped a piece of apple in honey and put it in his mouth. "L'shanah tovah," he said. "For a sweet year."

Daniel did the same as the others. Dipped, tasted. "For a sweet year," he said, repeating the words but knowing they didn't apply to him.

After supper Lenore went to her room, and everyone else was busy with their own things or watching television, which Daniel still couldn't bring himself to do. He was half afraid he would see himself, like some grotesque parody of a person. Looks alive, talks, moves, but is strangely dead. As a child he'd read a book like that, about a horrible scientist who could make dead people walk around, talk, and move. But they were still dead, their bodies rotting and decomposing all the while. That's how he felt. As if he were the walking dead, and only since coming here had he even vaguely remembered what it was to be alive. To chop wood, to eat a simple meal with kind people who might have been friends. In some other life.

Forty-Two

SUNDAY NIGHT ENDED what had been a long, tense weekend. Lenore had finally told Scott about Al's illness. He had taken it as well as could be expected. She had gone out to supper with Erik, but by then her emotional reserves had been emptied. She hadn't told him about Daniel. She'd intended to, but he'd been called to the hospital before she'd gotten a chance, a happenstance for which she had to admit she was extremely grateful. She knew she couldn't put off that discussion indefinitely, but she toyed with the hope that Daniel would go away after the two weeks and she could frame the announcement in the past tense. She stepped into the shower now, happy to relax, to unwind, to think about nothing.

She stared at the tile wall of the bathroom, ignoring the nagging voice that reminded her she was supposed to be praying about Daniel's future, not making a unilateral decision and setting it in stone. She soaped her hand and made little circular motions, beginning with her armpit and moving down toward the center of her breast, the one breast she still had. All the stress of the past weeks had made her sloppy. She had forgotten to do her breast exam. She moved her hand, pressing downward in circles, noting absently that she should get the soap scum remover and give the shower a good going-over. She stopped and frowned. Backed up, performed the same movement again. Felt it again. A hard little knot, no bigger than a pea, a centimeter or so, she noticed with clinical accuracy. It didn't move when she rolled over it. It didn't hurt.

She continued to assess her findings with the clinician's cold eye, but her body was already beginning to respond to what her brain hadn't gotten to yet. What it meant. Her heart was beating unnaturally fast, and her stomach felt jittery and nauseated. She was hot. She turned off the shower and stood leaning against the tile, water dripping off her naked body, off her white skin, off her whole breast, running in tiny rivulets down the channels left by the ropy scar tissue where the other breast should have been.

"Aren't you overreacting a tiny bit?" Daniel used to ask her years ago when she would overestimate the potential for some disaster. She was doing it again, she told herself.

She dried off, pulled on her flannel nightgown, and lay in bed. After a while she got up and went downstairs for a cup of something hot. She settled on herb tea, brought it back upstairs with her, then took the quilt from the foot of her bed, wrapped it around her, and sat in her chair, thinking through the implications of what she had discovered. This small knot, this earthshaking event.

And oddly enough she thought of Al. She remembered his joy, his beaming face after her first round with cancer. *"I've purchased my life with yours,"* he had said. They hadn't spoken of it in months, years, but the longer she sat and considered, the more certain she became. Al must not find out.

Find out what? she chided herself, only her galloping heart belying her thoughts. *It's probably nothing. A cyst. You'll get the whole household in a panic and for nothing.* She was still seeing Al's shining eyes as he told her like some chivalrous knight that he had sacrificed himself for her in a covenant with God. That was the truth he clung to, that made his dying meaningful. Al must not know. He would be gone in a few months, certainly not more than three, and maybe in only weeks. If the lump didn't disappear, there would be plenty of time then for the round of doctor's appointments, biopsies, and exams that would follow. What was a few days or weeks when a soul's peace was at stake? She would keep quiet, and she would wait. It was probably nothing, anyway.

Daniel went down the stairs, carefully balancing the lunch tray Lenore had asked him to deliver.

Al was at the workbench, pasty with pain and fatigue, trying to change the paper in a palm sander. Daniel set down the tray on the bottom step.

"Can I help you?" he asked. He waited for Al to answer. Al's jaw tightened, but he nodded grudgingly. Daniel repositioned the paper, flipped down the clamps. Al sat down, leaned over again, and held his head. When he sat up, Daniel inspected him. He looked terrible.

"I'm not going to be able to finish it," he said.

Daniel was surprised that Al made the admission to him. He didn't know what to say. He had no glib answers.

Al gave him a brief glance. "I'm dying, you know."

Daniel thought about the polite noises people make when faced with that fact and decided to respect Al enough not to do that. He nodded. "Lenore told me."

"I wish I could finish that cupboard." His breath came in pants, as if the effort was painful.

"It's almost done, isn't it?" Daniel asked.

"Except for sanding, staining, putting it together."

Daniel stood, considering. Al caught his breath from the exertion of talking. Daniel picked up the sander. He had done a little woodworking as a kid growing up. His uncle had taught him, and he'd made a few things. A birdhouse. A stool. A small table. But it had been years ago. He glanced at Al, who didn't speak, just watched him with those wary eyes. Daniel turned on the sander and began making long, fluid movements along the grain of the wood. He stopped after a moment, turned it off, felt the surface, waited for Al's reproof.

"Now you need to go over it with a fine grit, by hand," Al said gruffly. "Sandpaper's over there in the drawer." He pointed toward the workbench.

Daniel took out several sheets of the sandpaper. He sanded the piece— a long piece of the back, he guessed, looking over it now. "How am I doing?" he asked Al.

Al gave a shrug. "Hard to tell from here."

Daniel suppressed a smile.

"There's the rest of the back," Al said, pointing to a stack of boards leaning against the wall. "I guess you won't hurt it much. Just sand it smooth, and I'll watch you."

Daniel took the next board, set it on the work surface, and started sanding. It felt relaxing, natural. He sanded, smoothed, sanded, smoothed. He liked seeing the grain of the wood and feeling the rough imperfections glide away with the movement of the sandpaper. When he finished, Al rose painfully, came over, and inspected his work.

"That's pretty good." He jerked his chin toward the stack of boards in the corner of the room. "You can do the rest. Wake me up when you're finished, and I'll look at what you've done."

Daniel kept his amusement to himself. He helped Al into his small bedroom. Al took a few sips of soup, swallowed a pain pill, and lay down on his bed.

"You're going to do that now, aren't you?" Al asked.

"Sure, I can if you want. If the noise won't bother you."

His answer seemed to ease Al's mind. He lay back and closed his eyes.

Daniel went back to the shop and sanded the rest of the cupboard. By the time he finished, nearly four hours had passed, and he had enjoyed every minute of it. He couldn't remember when he had become so engrossed in an activity that he had lost track of time.

He peeked through the crack in Al's door when he was finished. Al was awake, sitting on the edge of his bed. He got up and made his way painfully to the workbench and examined Daniel's work.

"You didn't do half bad," was Al's assessment. "You can come back tomorrow, and I'll let you do the front."

That was it. No fluffy praise. No false gushing. No "That was beautiful, Daniel." No "You nailed that character, Daniel." None of the false and inflated cheering he was used to. And oddly enough, that little bit of left-handed praise from Al and the hours he'd spent sanding pine for the back of Lenore's pie cupboard combined to make the most rewarding experience he had had in months—maybe years.

He nodded, his eye on the jigsaw and router. "I'll be back."

Forty-three

DURING THE DAYS THAT FOLLOWED, if Daniel wasn't with Scott, he was in the basement with Al, working on the pie cupboard, which was nearly finished. Lenore usually ignored him, and he felt a pang of grief at what was becoming obvious. His presence here might be bringing him comfort, but it was bringing her only pain. Well, in two days he would leave. The two weeks were up.

He felt as if he were waking up from a beautiful dream to a grim reality, and he still didn't know what he would do. He had tried thinking about it many times, but his options seemed meager. He could go back to L.A. Face his creditors. Get some kind of work—maybe opening shopping malls or filming infomercials. He hardly cared anymore, but somehow going back there had the feeling of death about it, as though it would seal his fate.

He could go home to Kentucky, but there, in that very phrase, lay the problem. It wasn't home. Perhaps it could have been, even should have been. But it wasn't.

He could stay here, get a job and a cheap apartment. In fact, that had been his intention in the beginning, but he thought about that now in the light of reality instead of the conveniently vague glow he'd come here with. Scott would be leaving in a couple of months, and though he might come home again, there was no guarantee he would stay. Daniel's only tie to this place would be Lenore, and he had no reason to think she had any desire but to sever it.

He put his thoughts aside, as he had been doing for the last weeks, as if he could keep tomorrow from coming by refusing to think about it. He went down to the basement, his feet thumping hollowly on the wooden stairs. He thought about the cupboard, almost finished, and the thought gave him pleasure. It would be a gift from him as well as Al, although Lenore would never know it. It gave him pleasure to imagine her soft hands on the wood he had sanded and oiled and polished.

Al was waiting for him, sitting on the straight-backed chair by the workbench, leaning slightly forward. It made Daniel hurt to look at him. Now that he knew what to look for, he could see the signs of his illness. Al's skin had a yellow cast, and the whites of his eyes were also discolored. He winced as if every movement hurt him. Al gave him a slight nod as a greeting and pointed toward their project, now ready to assemble. "Get the hardware from that drawer over there," he said, never one to waste words or time, least of all now. His voice was still strong, a little gravelly, and Daniel could imagine him thirtysome years ago when he'd first joined the force, lean and trim in an LAPD uniform, smoking and driving, prowling slowly up and down the streets.

Daniel obeyed, followed Al's instructions, and the cupboard took shape before his eyes. He was beginning to screw on the drawer pulls when Al spoke again.

"Time's almost up for both of us," he said. A statement, not a question.

Daniel looked up briefly and nodded.

"You out of here soon?"

"Guess so," Daniel answered shortly.

There was a pause. Daniel glanced up at Al. He appeared to be catching his breath, looking off to the side of the workshop, then back at Daniel. "Where you going?" he asked.

Daniel shook his head. "Don't know."

Al gave him a stare. "Not good."

"Why's that?"

"You're a drunk, aren't you?"

Daniel stared at Al for a moment, then went back to the drawer pull. "I haven't had a drink since before I came here." Even he could hear how paltry and meager that sounded.

"How many days?"

He didn't answer.

"Since you had a drink," Al pressed. "How many days?"

Daniel stopped working on the handle and looked hard at Al, who was looking just as hard back at him. "Twenty days," he said quietly.

Al nodded. Didn't laugh or scorn him as Daniel had thought he might.

"You been in rehab." Another statement. He knew quite well that Daniel had been in rehab. Had been sitting in the courtroom the day it had been ordered along with six months in the L.A. county jail.

Daniel nodded.

"You know the drill, then."

Daniel shrugged and went back to his work. He had no faith in their programs and affirmations. "Yeah. Twelve easy steps and then I'm fixed."

"Nobody said they were easy, and you can get by without all but one."

"And which one would that be?"

"The one about surrendering your life to God, only forget all that stuff about Him being whoever you conceive Him to be." Al snorted in derision, then winced again in pain. "He's who He is, and you'd better deal with it if you know what's good for you." He paused for a minute, apparently letting that sink in or catching his breath, Daniel wasn't sure which. He was trying to sort out what he felt and was alternating between anger and raw pain.

"You never answered my question," Al said, slicing through his thoughts. "Are you a drunk?"

"I don't know," Daniel answered, wishing Al would leave him alone, the prospect of being gone from here suddenly seeming more attractive.

"You don't know?" Al demanded.

"Yes," Daniel said hotly, "I'm an alcoholic. All right? Does that make you happy?" but surprisingly, saying those words, facing that fact, didn't bring the wrenching pain he'd expected but rather a rush of relief. "Yes," he repeated, and his anger at Al evaporated when he looked at Al's face. He didn't see the condemnation he expected but a look of poignant compassion, of remembered pain.

"So was I," Al said quietly. "I was a drunk just like you."

Daniel stared.

"All the time I was looking down on you and telling them to throw the book at you, I was doing the same thing."

Neither one of them spoke for a minute. "You go to rehab?" Daniel finally asked.

Al shrugged. "Yeah, but that's not what really changed me. I was washed," Al said simply before Daniel could even ask, "washed, sanctified, and justified in the name of Jesus."

Daniel listened to the archaic words. He didn't understand what some of them meant, but they felt full of power.

"Do you want help?" Al asked after a long, silent pause.

Daniel hesitated.

"You know as well as I do that if you walk out of here tomorrow, the bottle's gonna be waiting for you on the corner out there."

There's nothing you can do to help me, Daniel wanted to say, but it felt cruel to call attention to Al's pitiful state.

"I can hook you up with a program here, and I can pray for you,"

Al said firmly, as if he had guessed what had been in Daniel's mind. Then, before Daniel could consent or refuse, Al rose to his feet and placed a big, callused hand on Daniel's head.

"Precious Savior," Al began, his voice surprisingly firm, and Daniel closed his eyes, years of training kicking in. "I call on you today in all the authority of your name and ask you to rescue Daniel from the destroyer, who has taken him captive to do his will."

Daniel felt Al's hand pressing down, heavy and insistent on his head.

"Make him sorry for the wrong he's done, God," he said.

Daniel was surprised. He thought he'd *been* sorry. Thought everyone must know that, and he had the feeling again that these Christians were a strange people. He had never been able to satisfy them, no matter how carefully he had mimicked their words and actions.

"Help him, Jesus. I'm crying out to you on his behalf," Al said, and his voice grew louder. "Help him, God."

Daniel felt something inside him shift and turn at hearing his enemy pray for him with such passion. Al stopped speaking. Daniel still felt the pressure on his head.

"Jesus, I beg you," Al said, his voice low but insistent. "Protect him. Seal him. Love him to yourself." He paused a minute as if he might be thinking about saying more. "Amen," he finally finished and lifted his hand, but for a moment Daniel could still feel it, heavy on his head.

"Thank you," he said after another moment of silence.

Al gave a half nod and sat back down in his chair, obviously drained. "I'm going to rest awhile," he said. "Over there is something for you."

Daniel followed his glance. On the workbench was a book of wood-working plans.

"Thought you might want to make something of your own," Al said, back to his customary gruffness.

Daniel looked at him questioningly. He'd be gone in a couple days.

"We prayed, didn't we?" he growled. "Anything's possible."

Sure. Sure it was. "Thanks," Daniel said again.

"Take the book upstairs with you."

Daniel didn't bother to argue. He picked up the book and leafed through the pages.

"See anything you like?" Al asked.

"The jewelry box is nice," Daniel said, participating in the fantasy. "Lenore might like that." He watched for Al's reaction. Al didn't even blink, just nodded.

"Need some nice wood for that. Some cherry or mahogany. Hardware store don't have nothing like that, but I know a place."

Daniel nodded again. Al rose to his feet, and Daniel moved to help him, wondering if he would be rebuffed, but Al seemed grateful to take his arm. Daniel helped him to his bed, took off his shoes, arranged his pillows, and turned out the light for him.

"Shall I bring you some lunch?" he asked.

"Maybe later," Al answered, his eyes already closing.

Daniel closed the door gently, went back to work, and by the time he climbed the stairs, the gift was assembled, oiled, polished, and under blue tarps in the corner of the basement. Daniel felt a warm pride and a sharp sense of loss. He would have to tell Scott where it was and remind him to bring it up on Christmas morning.

———————

"Lenore, I think we should move Al upstairs," Daniel told her that night after supper. He had a sense that he should take care of what he could, help them all as much as he was able before he took his leave.

She looked at him suspiciously, as if he might have an ulterior motive in suggesting it. Or perhaps it was his use of the pronoun *we*. He felt irritation this time instead of his usual shame.

"Look, it's up to you, but I'm telling you, he's not going to be able to get up and down those stairs to use the bathroom much longer," he said bluntly. Twice this afternoon Al had called, and fortunately Daniel had been within earshot both times. He had helped Al up the stairs and back down again, supporting most of his weight. "If you want me to help you get him moved before I go, tonight's probably the night."

Her face took on a sober look, whether at his departure or Al's illness, he didn't know.

"Are there any rooms on the main floor he could use?" Daniel asked.

Lenore nodded. "He could use the study. It's plenty big enough. The TV can go into the living room."

"Tell me what to do," Daniel said.

"Let me talk to him first."

She went downstairs, had a brief conversation with Al, then came back and said she thought he was right. Daniel went downstairs while she prepared the study. Al's light was on. Daniel could see it coming out from under the door. He gave a knock.

"Come in."

"Let me help you upstairs before we start moving things," Daniel suggested.

Al allowed it. They climbed the steps for what would probably be Al's last time. Al didn't glance at the tools on the way out but kept his eyes straight ahead and leaned heavily on Daniel.

There was an overstuffed chair in the corner of the study into which

Al sank gratefully. Lenore fussed over him, promised to rent him a hospital bed tomorrow so he could be more comfortable.

Daniel went back downstairs and within a half hour had moved up the bed, dresser, the chest of drawers, the small desk, the box of personal belongings. Lenore began arranging them. He noticed she had hung curtains over the glass study doors and windows to give Al his privacy. He sat on the edge of the chair now, bent slightly forward, hands on his knees, obviously in pain.

Daniel went into the kitchen and, for lack of anything better to do, put on a pot of coffee. After a few minutes he went back to Al's room. Lenore was gone.

"She had a phone call to make," Al explained.

Daniel nodded, touched that Al thought he had the right to know. "Do you need anything?" he asked.

He expected the same answer Al usually gave: *"Don't need nothing. Thanks all the same."* But his time Al rubbed his thinning scalp with his gnarled fingers and said, "I could use a cup of that coffee I smell."

Daniel doubted he would drink it, but he nodded smartly and returned with a freshly brewed cup for both of them on a tray with the cream and sugar. Al added a large dollop of half-and-half to his cup and two spoonfuls of sugar, then stirred and took a tentative sip. Another.

"Ahh." He closed his eyes and gave the look of sweet satisfaction that only another coffee lover could understand. Daniel smiled.

"I miss my coffee."

"Why don't you drink it?"

Al shrugged. "Don't settle too well, but I still love the taste."

Daniel nodded and neither one of them said anything for a minute, just sipped their coffee. Listened to the rain drip down the gutters.

Al set the coffee down on the desk and opened the top drawer. He pulled out a sheaf of papers he had clipped together. They sat right on top, as if he took them out often and looked at them.

"These," Al said, "will explain everything when I'm gone. What to do with my retirement account and such, the addresses and phone numbers of my daughters and my wife."

Daniel noticed he didn't say ex-wife, though he knew Al was divorced. Lenore had told him that much, and he wondered if that was the way it always was. You were tied to the woman you'd loved first, had children with, no matter who or how many came after. He wondered why Al was showing him.

"It upsets Lenore," he said, answering his unspoken question.

"I'll make sure the right people find out," Daniel promised. He would tell Mr. Caputo or Mr. Kaplan.

Al nodded. He took off the paper clip awkwardly and handed Daniel the papers. Daniel looked through them. There was a simple will. Lenore was the beneficiary of his tools, personal belongings, and savings account. An insurance policy with a woman's name Daniel didn't recognize. A list of funeral instructions. A sheet of paper with names and addresses printed out. Daughter written beside two of them, sister by one, wife by the other. The last sheet of paper was a sensational advertisement for some evangelist whose picture gleamed at him from the upper right-hand corner. Arvid Chamberlain promised, with white-toothed, smiling sincerity, that if the recipient would agree with him and seal the prayer agreement with a token of remembrance—Daniel used all his concentration not to frown at the blatant manipulation—then any "longstanding prayer request you have been believing God for" would be answered. It was dated November three years before. Underneath the printed copy was written *Covenant with God* and the date, a few days after the letter had been received. Underneath it was Al's signature in a tight, cramped hand and the words *I purchase the life of Lenore Vine with my own.*

"What's this about?" Daniel asked, his chest tightening even though he had no idea what the cryptic words meant.

Al frowned and looked at the paper Daniel held up.

"Oh." He gave his head a small shake. "That's from when I first found the Lord," he said. "When Lenore had her cancer."

Daniel's gut plummeted. His chest tightened. He nodded slowly, not asking questions for fear Al would know he had divulged something Daniel hadn't known. "When she had her cancer," he repeated, and Al nodded.

"When was that, exactly?" Daniel asked, as if the exact date had some-how slipped his mind.

"Right when it says there," Al pointed out.

Daniel read the date. Three years ago. Lenore had had cancer three years ago, and no one had told him.

"Here," Al said, holding out his hand. He took the papers from Daniel, clipped them back together, hands shaking, clumsy, and put them back in the top drawer. "You'll know where to find them," he said, "when the time comes."

———

"How could you know all this and not tell me?"

Scott faced his dad squarely. Dad was angry. That much was obvious. And Scott felt the same emotion stir in him. Cruel answers popped into his head, words having to do with the fact that people who left other people didn't have a right to any explanations at all. He kept those to himself. At one time he would have loved to hurt his dad. But not now.

"Scott." His dad's voice was less angry now and sounded more anguished. "She had cancer?"

Scott nodded.

"What kind?"

"Breast."

"When?"

"About three years ago."

Daniel sat down on Scott's bed, leaned over, and rubbed his head with both hands, elbows on his knees. Finally he gave a great sigh and sat up. Scott wondered if he still loved Mom. He was sure worked up.

"Tell me everything. Please."

Scott was about to tell his father that if he wanted to know about Mom's cancer he should ask Mom; in fact, he had his mouth open to say the words when he remembered his own behavior during that time. Dad might have treated Mom badly, but he hadn't done much better. Neither one of them had any right to pride. He took a breath, sighed it out, and told his father what he wanted to know.

"About three years ago Mom found a lump in her breast," he said. "They did tests and found another smaller one, too. They were cancerous, but the cancer hadn't spread to the lymph nodes. Because there were two locations they decided to remove her breast."

"Is she cured?"

Scott shrugged. His father putting words to the question they all carried probed a painful spot. "What does that mean, Dad?" he asked quietly.

"I mean, is the cancer gone?"

"As far as they know."

Dad shook his head again and ran his hands through his hair. Scott felt guilty for not telling his father, but he knew he would have felt just as guilty if he had. He felt something else, as well—a tiny flare of anger toward his father for not knowing. For not being in a place to have known. For just a second even his own hurtful deeds seemed as if they could be laid at his father's feet. The struggle, familiar if not comfortable, returned in force: to forgive or to hold back. To hate or to love. Soon his father would leave. He felt a bitter regret at that in spite of his conflicts, a hollow emptiness at the thought. He gazed at the wall.

Finally Daniel stood up from the bed. "Thank you for telling me." His voice was humble, sad.

Scott remembered something else now. That night so long ago, the night Mom was in the hospital after her surgery, Dad had called and Scott hadn't told him. It weighed on him afresh now, and he wondered in a brief flash of torment what might have been different if he had. "Wait, Dad," he said.

Daniel paused at the door and turned back.

"I'm sorry for not telling you." The words seemed skimpy, inadequate, covering years of possibility, miles of missed time.

Daniel gave a long sigh, and his face looked so bleak and bereft that Scott felt regret and remorse pierce him again. "I'm sorry, Dad," he repeated.

"That's okay, son," his father said, the lines in his face drawing it down. "That's okay."

Forty-four

LENORE DROVE HOME from work. Slowly. Carefully. The lights of the cars gleamed on the wet streets. It was already getting dark and only four o'clock. The thick, cold raindrops splattered with a pelt and slid down the windshield. She turned on the wipers and the heater. The warm air toasted her knees, but it did nothing to really warm her. She felt so odd. Ever since Al had gotten sick and Daniel had come and she had found the lump, she had felt odd, and whether the cause was from one or all of those events, she didn't know. But lately she seemed to be afraid of the strangest things. She would be driving and she would have a sudden fear that the car was going to fly out of her control—veer off into some unpredicted direction, or perhaps even lift off like a plane—and she would be helpless to do anything about it.

Or sometimes she would become terrified when she stopped thinking of it as "riding in the car" and saw the reality of her situation. She was hurtling forward. Going fast—very fast—fast enough to take the flesh from her bones in seconds if she were to come into contact with the pavement. She could see it happening, her flesh coming from her bones like filleting a chicken, and the only thing separating her from that fate was a few feet of air and a thin shell of metal.

She had told no one about the lump; in fact, she tried to keep it out of her mind, and for the most part she had been successful. She had convinced herself it was common and benign, a fluid-filled cyst. In the daytime she barely thought of it, pressed it resolutely back to some closed-off part of her mind. It was at night, when she was tired and her mind was tired, that the panic built, the fear began whispering.

Her lunch with Erik today had done nothing to comfort her. He had changed lately. Or was it she who was different? She didn't know. She just knew that lately he seemed foreign, unfamiliar, like someone she barely knew. She had suggested lunch at the Russian Samovar, a carefully calculated strategy. She wanted to see him but needed the time to be limited, thereby also limiting the chance of the conversation veering into dangerous Daniel territory.

She had been staving off Erik for two weeks and actually had found it surprisingly easy to do—a bothersome fact, now that she considered it. One would think her almost-fiancé would be more insistent about seeing her, would pine, object. But in truth, Erik was so busy he seemed to barely notice her absence, considerably lessening her guilt for not telling him about Daniel's visit. Oh, they had grabbed a quick bite of lunch at the hospital one day, had a few telephone conversations, always ending with the promise of quality time to follow. But she hadn't really seen him in weeks. Perhaps longer. So today she had suggested the Russian Samovar, a warm cocoon of Oriental rugs and worn velvet. They had sipped tea and borscht, eaten cabbage rolls.

"Where have you been the last few Sundays?" she'd asked. "I haven't seen you at church." She regretted the words as soon as they were out. Who was she? The attendance police?

Erik had given his head a slight shake. "I haven't been around."

"Working?"

He shook his head.

She didn't know what to ask after that, just waited for him to explain or tell her to mind her own business.

He set down his fork and knife, and there was a look on his face she hadn't seen before. It was flat, exhausted, defeated. "I've been visiting other churches."

"Oh." She felt as if he had slapped her.

"You're upset."

"No," she said quickly. "Well, maybe a little. I just thought you would have told me something like that."

"I'm telling you now."

"After I asked," she pointed out.

"I haven't made a final decision." His voice was a shade defensive.

"Whatever," she said but felt a twinge of hurt. Completely hypocritical, she realized on consideration.

"I'm tired, Lenore," he said bluntly.

She looked again at his exhausted face, his dulled eyes. She wondered how long that weariness had been there and why she hadn't seen it before now. She felt a pang of guilt mixed with deep disappointment.

"I'm tired of the endless pain and illness," he continued. "But I can't quit. What would I do? Become a mailman?"

Erik had been practicing medicine when she was in high school, she realized. When she was in college. When she was having Scott. She thought of the sick children who had come through his clinic. The ones born incomplete and flawed. The ones in the hospital with serious, often fatal, illnesses. He got up early and made his rounds. Went back again later after the office closed. She could see the weariness, the bone-jarring fatigue in his eyes and face.

"I can't buy the philosophy of Greater Grace anymore," he said.

She hadn't thought about them having a philosophy. "What is that?" she asked.

"That God fixes everything." He shook his head. "I've seen too much," he continued. "We live in a world where chaos reigns. Every day it doesn't happen to you is a good day."

She felt stunned at his words, though his voice had been soft, delivering them tenderly. She was put in mind of the time she had taken their old, sick dog to the vet, a job that had fallen to her since her mother and sister couldn't bear to do it. She had held it as the shot put it out of its misery. That doctor had had the same jaded eyes she saw across from her now. The same soft flatness in his refusal to offer any hope. Something in her lurched in despair, then rose up against it.

"I'm not sure I agree with that."

Erik shrugged slightly. "Doubt is the normal response to the fallen world we live in. We weren't created for this. Despair is inevitable, the only rational way to feel when evil triumphs."

The words he'd spoken felt sharp and hot. She pushed back against them. "Yes, there is evil and chaos in the world. But does it reign?"

He shrugged and smiled another of the tired smiles. "It sure feels that way to me most days."

She felt a flash of anger. "So what will you do? Wait to be beamed up?"

He didn't answer, the slight rise of his brows the only indication he'd heard her at all.

They had finished their lunch in silence. He had kissed her softly when she'd left.

She felt ashamed now when she thought about it but also still angry, as if he had taken something that was precious to her and left it outside in the rain.

She steered the car across Denny Street now, up Queen Anne Avenue. She tried to imagine Daniel walking back down this street, back the way he had come. He was leaving tomorrow, she realized, her heart heavy at the thought. She hadn't spoken to Matt again, but it was up to her, really, wasn't it? He wasn't going to intervene. Her reaction had been another

ironic twist. For the past seven days she had counted down the time to
Daniel's departure. Now that it was here, it felt like a fresh loss, a grief,
a tearing off of a bandage on a barely healing wound. Did she want him
around? She didn't know. She didn't want to hope again. And she had
been praying, but she'd sensed no answers.

She drove up to the house, grateful the lights were all on. She liked
it like that. Too many days of her childhood she had come home to a
dark, empty house. She liked it warm. She liked it bright. She parked, got
out, walked to the door, and went inside.

Scott's coat wasn't on the coatrack. He must still be in class. She heard
no voices from the kitchen and wondered where Mr. Caputo and Mr.
Kaplan were. The study—Al's bedroom—door was pulled almost shut.
She peered inside. Frowned. Stepped a little closer to get a better look.
The hospital bed she'd ordered for Al had arrived. Mr. Caputo and Mr.
Kaplan were putting sheets on it. She didn't see Al. She pushed open the
door. Mr. Caputo acknowledged her arrival with a quick smile and a nod.

It took her just a moment to see what had happened. A wad of soiled
sheets was on the floor.

"Al's in pretty bad shape, honey," Mr. Caputo confirmed. "Daniel's
giving him a shower."

Mr. Kaplan was folding a piece of plastic over the mattress. She helped
him, and then they spread out the old blanket they would use as a temporary mattress pad. They put fresh sheets on and were finishing just as
Daniel and Al entered the room. Al's hair was wet. He wore a terrycloth
robe she thought was Mr. Kaplan's. Daniel was practically carrying him.
He was obviously in misery and bent forward in pain.

"I'll call his doctor," she told them. "See if I can get something
stronger for pain."

"And for vomiting and diarrhea," Daniel said. He gently lowered Al
into the chair and went to the dresser to find him some clean pajamas.

She took the dirty things to the washer. She would have to buy a
plastic mattress liner and some Attends. Someone would have to stay here
with Al full time. Someone strong enough to lift him, or he would have
to go to the nursing home. Her stomach lurched again. She went to the
phone, following the instructions for paging the doctor in case of an emergency. She had trouble dialing. Her hands weren't working. When she
was finished, she looked up to see Mr. Caputo and Mr. Kaplan standing
by anxiously, waiting for their next assignment.

"How can we help, honey?" Mr. Caputo asked.

"Make supper?" It was her turn, but she couldn't focus on it.

They nodded and went to work, snapping orders to each other as if
they were planning D Day instead of putting a meal together. At least that

was a relief, and Lenore felt a ridiculous sense of lightness as she relinquished even that small part of her burden.

The doctor finally called her back, listened quietly for a moment, then ordered medication for the pain and nausea.

"Where shall I call it?" he asked, his voice weary.

Lenore gave him the number of the Rite Aid on Queen Anne Hill. Scott came in just then, and before he even had his coat off, Lenore had sent him out again.

"Al's worse," she told him briefly. "I need you to go and get some prescriptions."

He nodded, set down his books, and turned to leave again. "Hey, Mom," he began hesitantly.

"What?" She tensed, hoping whatever he had to say was not another problem.

He paused. "Never mind," he said, and Lenore didn't even ask what it had been. She didn't want to know. She left him, went back to check on Al. Daniel was easing him into the bed when she returned. He had fresh pajamas on. His hair was combed. Daniel settled him on the pillow and pulled the blanket under his chin. Al shivered. Daniel took another blanket and added it to the first.

"I'm sorry," Al said wearily. He hardly had enough energy even to be humiliated.

"Oh, honey," she said, "don't be sorry."

He closed his eyes. His face was skeletal, the color of parchment.

Scott came back with the medicine, and then she was faced with another situation. They were all in suppository form. Of course she could administer it. She had done so a hundred times. But for Al?

"I'll do it," Daniel said quietly. He listened to her instructions, then disappeared into the room and came out a few minutes later saying Al was going to try to sleep.

Mr. Caputo and Mr. Kaplan served dinner, but no one was very hungry. When Lenore thought about Angie and Mrs. Callahan coming back the next day, she wanted to weep. Instead, she left everyone at the table, looked in on Al again, who was sleeping, breath slow and regular, mouth slightly open, and went upstairs.

She sat in the chair by the window a few hours later and shook her head at the humor of the situation. It had been like a sitcom. No, like an old comedy from the forties. One by one they had crept to her room, knocked on the door, delivered their messages with varying degrees of toe digging, foot shuffling, ums and ahs.

Mr. Caputo had been first. "Honey," he had said, "I just wanted you to know that I think I may have been a little harsh. In my judgments, I mean. If you want Daniel to stay, well, that's all right with me. I understand. I mean, I can even see the good in it. Anyhow, it's up to you."

Then Mr. Kaplan came. "I know I'm a newcomer here, but it occurs to me that we could use someone around right now with a strong back." He had held up his hands, looking for all the world like Tevye in *Fiddler on the Roof.* "He's already here, and as I understand it, he has nowhere else to go. Forgive me if I'm speaking out of turn."

Scott had been the one who had torn at her heart. "I'm not telling you what to do, Mom. But I'd like him to stay. At least until I go." And that had been the thing to undo her. Scott deserved that, didn't he?

"It's not just up to me," she had answered. Scott had nodded and left, his dark eyes not difficult to read at all. Full of sorrow.

She stared at the pictures on her wall, at the quilt on her bed, and thought how strange things had become. Another tap on the door. It was Mr. Kaplan who peered around the corner.

"Dr. Ashland's here, honey," he said quietly. "Shall I tell him you're resting?"

She closed her eyes. This was beautiful. What a perfect ending to this day. "No," she said. "I'll come down."

Mr. Caputo was visiting with Erik in the living room, entertaining him until she arrived.

"Shall I get you two some coffee or tea?" Mr. Caputo was getting up, making himself scarce like a good parent when the suitor comes to call.

"I'd love some coffee," said Lenore.

"Sure, coffee would be fine," Erik agreed.

Lenore listened for Daniel but didn't hear him. She breathed a sigh of relief. The time had come for her to tell Erik, but she would do it in her way. It would take a little finesse.

She sat down on the sofa, and Erik sat down beside her, a few inches away. He always did that, she realized. Sat near but not touching. He leaned across and gave her a kiss. She stiffened.

He leaned back and examined her face. His own eyes were troubled. "Listen," he said. "I feel bad about today."

She frowned and tried to remember. Oh. The conversation at the restaurant where he'd expounded his personal chaos theory. She shrugged.

"You're upset."

"Upset is too strong a word."

"Bothered."

"Sure," she agreed. Tonight is not the night she would have chosen to iron out the fine points of semantics. She stifled a yawn.

"You seem more than that."

"Maybe I'm a little disappointed."

He drew back. "In me?"

She gave another shrug. She reminded herself of Scott in his rebellious phase. Everything was shrugs and I don't knows. "It's easy to give in to despair. It takes muscles to have faith. To—what's that verse?—set your face like flint?"

He leaned back and crossed his arms. He opened his mouth to speak, but they were interrupted by Mr. Caputo with the coffee.

"Here you go." He set down a tray with two thick mugs of coffee, a small pitcher of cream, the sugar bowl, and a plate of shortbread he must have made today. He gave them each a quick glance and left the room.

Neither one of them touched the refreshments.

"I'm sorry if I don't live up to your expectations," Erik said stiffly.

"Come on, Erik," she pleaded. "Don't do this to me right now."

His face softened. He knew about Al. He didn't know the rest.

He nodded and took her hand, and just then Daniel came through the doorway. He saw them there, and Lenore watched his face go through its changes, and she saw why he had been a good actor. He saw her first. His eyes lit, the smile began, then he noticed Erik, and his face went blank. Wiped clean of all emotion, only to be replaced within seconds by a professionally pleasant expression.

Erik's eyes went from Daniel to her and then back to Daniel, and a light of understanding dawned in them when she introduced him. Inevitable that he would guess their connection. Now that Scott was grown, his resemblance to Daniel was striking.

"Daniel's been staying with us" is what she actually said, but she could see Erik's eyes hood and his face grow tight as he shook Daniel's hand, and she knew that he knew Daniel was much more than a casual guest.

Daniel excused himself, and she heard him go up the stairs.

"Daniel is Scott's father." Erik said it as a statement.

"Yes." Lenore nodded. "Yes, he is."

"And now he's back."

"Yes," Lenore said. Obviously. *Back how?* she wanted to ask, as if Erik might actually know.

"Daniel Monroe is Scott's father." Erik said it again, seeming to want to nail down that fact.

"That's right," said Lenore wearily.

"I see." He was angry. His face did look like flint now. His eyes gray granite. "Were you planning on telling me this at some point?"

"You knew Scott had a father, didn't you?"

"I didn't know who he was."

"What difference does it make?" Her head hurt. She massaged her temples. "You're acting like a child. He's my son's father. I come with baggage."

"What is that supposed to mean?"

"Nothing. It just means I have a child. He has a father. He will always be a part of our lives."

"That's not what you used to say."

True enough. She had no answer for that.

"How long is he staying?"

"I'm not sure," she said.

"A day? A week? Indefinitely?"

"Indefinitely, I guess."

"Well, I don't think that's a good idea."

Her anger flared. "I don't recall asking your opinion."

They stared at each other for a moment, then Erik stood up and took his keys from his pocket. "I'll call you tomorrow," he said. "I don't want to talk anymore tonight."

Suits me fine, she wanted to taunt him. *Go ahead and leave. See if I care.*

He turned and left. He did not say good-night. He most certainly did not kiss her good-bye.

She watched the front door close on his back and didn't know whether to be distraught, angry, or amused. She rose up and climbed the stairs, then walked to Daniel's room, each step seeming like a journey in itself. His door was open. He was folding clothes carefully and packing them into his rucksack, and suddenly her weariness turned to dismay. She had assumed so much. What if, in spite of all their condescending permissions, Daniel himself did not want to stay? She hadn't realized she wanted him to stay until just now. She swallowed, then knocked softly.

Daniel greeted Lenore with a smile and saw her face relax a little.

"I guess it's that time." He put in the last pair of pants and shoved the stack down. It would close but just barely. He took his wallet from the dresser. He knew without counting how much was left—four hundred dollars. He'd left another five hundred dollars in an envelope in the plastic bag in the kitchen where they kept their household cash. He stopped packing for a minute to give her his attention. But it hurt. He felt like someone had died, but the facts were plain. He needed to leave. He took down his jacket and set it on top of the rucksack. He would go tonight. Before he could change his mind. "I know my being here is making you even more stressed out," he told her. "I'll get out of your hair." He tightened the string on the duffel and tied it into a knot. When he looked up, he saw that she was crying. The tears were making crooked little rivers down her cheeks, which had gotten a little thinner since he'd come. He dropped his hands to his sides and felt a lurch of emotion toward her. Longing mixed with frustration. "I thought that would make you happy," he said. Her face contorted. He took a step closer. "What is it you want?" And even though he was frustrated, he could hear tenderness in his voice, like the old days.

It made her cry harder. Pretty soon they were great digging sobs coming from deep within her. She sat down on his bed. He moved toward her. Stopped, afraid that any comfort he offered would be perceived as taking advantage of her distress. Finally he couldn't stand just listening without doing something, so he sat down beside her, reached out, and touched her hand hesitantly. She grabbed it hard. He held it, pressing and murmuring until her crying eased off. She started talking then, her words pouring out of her, one on top of the other.

"It's okay. It's okay," he said to her over and over again. "Slow down and tell me what's wrong."

And then she told him some things he already knew and something he didn't. Her words still ran together in a lump, like racers neck and neck. She told him she'd had cancer and that Al had made a bargain with God to save her and now he was going to die and that agreement with God was the only thing making him happy. Then she told him that she had found another lump, and though his mind—it felt like his heart, as well— stopped and stalled there, his ears heard her say she felt that she was being pulled in too many directions, and she didn't want to tell anyone.

He heard everything she said, but that one thing, that she had another lump, rose up in front of him like a mocking enemy, standing in his face and taunting him. He felt a fierce anger well up inside him, and he felt determined to go head to head with it, vowing he wouldn't let her go again without fierce fighting. He tightened his hand over hers.

"Don't go, Daniel."

Those words landed on his parched heart like a sip of cool water.

"I won't," he promised.

"I don't know how I feel." Her voice sounded small and hoarse.

"You don't need to know. It's okay."

"I'm scared." She sounded scared, her voice was thin and trembly.

"Don't be scared. I'm here. I'll stay with you."

"I'm scared for Scott."

"Don't worry about Scott. I'll be here for him, too."

"I have to take care of Al."

"I can take care of Al. You show me how, and I'll do it." Some of the tenseness seemed to leave her. "I'll take care of things, Lenore." He loved saying those words. "You just let me take care of things. Let me carry you for a while."

She breathed a deep breath in, then out, then pulled her hand away. His own suddenly felt empty.

She wiped away her tears and took control of herself again. "I'll need to ask Matt," she said. Daniel remembered the sober-eyed pastor, the firmness of his warning when he told Daniel how protective he felt toward Lenore. He realized he wasn't home free yet. Not by a long shot.

"Let me know what he says," Daniel answered. "I'll leave my things packed just in case."

Lenore nodded. She looked swollen and red around the eyes.

"Daniel—" she sounded exhausted, as if the crying jag had taken the last of her energy—"you can't tell anyone. About me. About the lump. Al doesn't have much time left, and a few weeks or a month one way or another won't make a difference to me."

What if it does? he wanted to shout at her. He kept silent instead.

"Al thinks he's bought my life. It's what's giving him the courage to die. I don't want him to know otherwise, and if I start going in for tests and maybe another surgery, he would find out."

Keeping a lid on his frustration took all his self control, but Daniel didn't argue with her. "I don't know if I can make that promise," he finally said, and he wondered if she would tell him to leave then. It was the second time he had said those words to her, he realized, and it hit him how different this circumstance was from the first time.

Her face tensed for a moment, then she gave a slight shrug, as if she had decided not to fight that particular battle tonight.

"I'll get things checked out as soon as it doesn't matter to Al," she promised him.

And feeling ashamed of himself, Daniel hoped that it would be soon.

He received his special dispensation of grace just before nine. He was called to the dining room to find Pastor Matt there himself. In the flesh. Calmly sipping a cup of tea, another cup waiting at the place across from him. Daniel sat down. It was the mug he liked best, and he wondered which of them had recognized that small fact and served his tea in it. It was one of those souvenir items with a photo of Scott glazed onto it. Scott at age nine or so, all big teeth and cowlicks.

"How are you, Daniel?" Matt asked, and he looked interested to hear the answer, not just framing his speech.

"Good," Daniel answered and realized it was true. "Considering."

Matt nodded. "I hear the situation has changed since we spoke."

Daniel raised an eyebrow.

"Al's illness."

"Oh. Yes."

"The members of the household seem to be agreed that your presence here is helpful."

Daniel felt touched. In fact, his eyes smarted. He sniffed hard.

"However," Matt said, "my original concerns remain."

Daniel nodded.

"Would you be willing to help care for Al if you stayed for a time?"

He blinked. Was he being given a chance? He was shocked at how desperately he wanted the answer to be yes. He nodded. "Yes. I would be willing."

"It may be hard. Emotionally as well as physically."

Daniel nodded again. He could see that already.

"If you're willing to sleep downstairs and promise to make yourself accountable to the other members of the household, I'll allow it."

Accountable to the other members of the household. Daniel thought of Mr. Caputo's unpredictable appearances, his wary looks. He smiled. "I could do that."

"All right," Matt said, his tone careful. "We'll give it a try."

Daniel finished his tea and the visit. He went to Scott's room. Told him. Watched his son nod and smile. "Thank you," he told Scott softly. He found Lenore in the living room, reading. Mr. Caputo and Mr. Kaplan, like ancient fathers in their respective recliners, smiled benevolently at him tonight. The cold disapproval seemed to be gone. "Thank you," he said. They, too, nodded and smiled. Beneficent, benevolent monarchs.

"I'm glad you're staying," Lenore said briefly before returning to her book.

He took the rucksack downstairs, where Al's bed, returned to the room after they had rented the hospital bed, was the only furniture left in the small square room. He didn't care. He looked at the little bare space, like a prison—no, like a monk's cell—and felt a holy joy.

He lay down but didn't sleep. Just lay there, eyes closed, thinking how precious it was because he had been away for so long, and maybe he had come back for the closing moments of the play.

Forty-five

"WELL, I THOUGHT WE would like to never get back!"

Daniel watched the blue-haired lady with a round-cheeked baby in tow unwrap both of them from yards and layers of clothing. The baby's cheeks were red with heat.

A short, rounded, adult version of the baby came through the front door. She had a ring in her nose. Her mouth dropped open when Daniel held the door open for her. "I. Cannot. Believe this," she said, face lit with amazement.

"I don't believe we've met," said the blue-haired lady, the infamous Mrs. Callahan, Daniel assumed.

"I'm Daniel, Scott's dad," he said. "You must be Mrs. Callahan."

She nodded graciously, extricated one hand from under the baby's rump, and gave him a quick shake. "I'm just so pleased to meet you."

"And you must be Angie," he said to the younger woman. She looked ready to swoon. Scott was grinning from the bottom stair. Lenore came in from the kitchen and joined them, and soon everyone's comments were lost in a flurry of jackets, handbags, and greetings. Daniel escaped to the car to bring in their suitcases, and when he came back, Lenore apparently had made explanations, because there was a little more order, and Angie had gotten control of herself, though her face was still somewhere between awe and adoration. Daniel hoped she'd get over it.

The baby, Joey, was oblivious to it all, his attention focused on breaking free of Mrs. Callahan's vise grip by squirming and going limp in turn.

"This *child* has like to *driven* me *insane,*" the old woman said, and the minute she put him down, he made for Lenore, walking stiff legged in his new-looking sneakers.

"Well, hey there, JoJo." Lenore got down on one knee and put her face near the baby's.

"Up," he commanded. Lenore obeyed, and Daniel was reminded of the good times they'd had when Scott was a baby. He caught her eye, and she smiled back at him, and to him at least, in that frozen moment, it seemed as if no time had passed at all.

Mr. Caputo and Mr. Kaplan came in, and the whole throng eased their way into the living room, where they spent the next few minutes catching up. Lenore gave them all an update on Al's deterioration. She'd warned them on the telephone what to expect, but they seemed shocked by how quickly he'd gone downhill, their voices shushing and becoming solemn when they spoke of it.

Daniel had his own theories. "I don't think his condition changed that much," he told Lenore. "I think he's just been denying it by sheer force of will, and he finally ran out of gas."

"Could be," Lenore admitted. Neither of them doubted the force of Al's willpower, and Daniel marveled again that Al had such courage in dying a death he believed was for someone else.

"We'll try to be quiet," Mrs. Callahan was saying now. "Won't we, Angie?"

"Sure," said Angie, never taking her eyes from Daniel. He sighed and gave her a small smile, causing her to turn crimson.

There were benefits to their return. It turned the rest of the household's attention from him and gave him time to think. Once he had been granted asylum by Pastor Matt, once Lenore had told him he could stay, once the initial glow of victory had faded, it had hit him. What had he done? he asked himself. How had this happened? His situation, in all of its ramifications, was starting to dawn on him. Somehow he had been thrust into the realm of selflessness, and like a lowlander on the heights, he wasn't sure if his lungs were equipped to breathe the air.

He was doing his duties, of course. He'd paid attention as Lenore had shown him how to take care of Al. He performed those rituals carefully, if a little clumsily. But he had a feeling of constriction in his chest, as if he couldn't get a breath. He tried to remember when he had felt this way before, and it finally came to him. It was when Lenore had told him she was pregnant. Yes, that was it. Well, that had turned out all right, hadn't it? For a while, at least. Yes, he could do this, he reassured himself. For the thousandth time. This morning. He could. He would not renege. He would not back out. He would not leave.

He had done something else, as well. He had phoned Al's sponsor and made arrangements to attend an AA meeting with him tomorrow.

Joey had found his laundry basket of toys that Lenore had stashed in the corner and was busy reacquainting himself with old friends. Daniel smiled, remembering how Lenore would keep half of Scott's toys packed away in a box, and every six months she'd rotate them "so they'd be fresh." And it had worked, too. Scott would be just as happy to see the old favorites when they reappeared as he was on Christmas morning.

It struck him then that they were all here now. Everyone had gathered back except the legendary Nathan Delacroix. They were all there. Mr. Caputo, who'd been the first one, who'd rescued Lenore from her distress. There was Al in the study down the hall, dying here in the same house that had offered him refuge from the streets. There was Mr. Kaplan, who apparently had come for a temporary stopover and had never left. Mrs. Callahan. Angie, who had multiplied. And he himself. The last wanderer, who had shown up on the doorstep cold, dripping rain, and hungry, for all his money and fame no better off than any of the others. And of course Lenore and Scott, who'd been taken in and then had set about returning the favor. Again. And again. And again.

His eyes were smarting. He gave a sniff, turned, and left the others, their voices a happy buzz in the background. He let himself through the French doors, closed them quietly behind him.

He checked on Al, consulting the written instructions Lenore had pinned to the bulletin board. He was clean but in pain. Daniel checked the glass of soda on the table beside the bed. Still nearly full. Lenore had said if Al didn't drink more, the hospice nurse might need to start an IV.

Daniel gave him another dose of pain medication, a patch this time, which was less humiliating than the suppositories. He had been unwilling at first to take the narcotics, his years of alcohol addiction coming back as a bad memory. But he had relented.

"I guess it won't hurt," he'd said. "Lenore said when you use it right, you don't get hooked."

"That's right." Daniel heard his voice, and it sounded like the calm, reassuring tones he used to take with Scott. "This is what it's meant for," he said. He didn't point out the obvious.

The medicine took effect quickly, and Daniel saw Al's face relax from its tight stiffness.

Forty-six

Scott walked up the hill from the college, his feet scuffing through the piles of leaves on the sidewalk. He loved that smell, that damp, sweet dirt smell of autumn. He would miss it here, he realized, looking around at the hilly streets lined with old houses, past them to the skyline, to the islands out in the bay, covered with green smudges of fir, cedar, and pine.

He remembered hating Seattle, and not so long ago if he counted back the years. But those emotions seemed distant, as if they belonged not to him but to another person in another lifetime.

He knew when he had changed. At least when the change had begun. In fact he could pinpoint the exact moment. He had been riding for the longest day on that dirty bus, trying to get to Dad's, running away from everything. He had hiked to Dad's house, managed to get through the gates, and he still remembered the feeling of anticipation as he had walked through the silent house to find his father. But he had seen him there from a distance, sitting in his lounge chair, his bottle on the table by the chair. He had finally risen up from the lounge chair, looking at Scott with a look that tore Scott's heart. His eyes had been empty, full of his own pain, and Scott had realized that was what he could look forward to if he followed in his father's footsteps. He had known then that his father couldn't help him, that he didn't have what Scott was looking for. The rest of the short visit had been confirmation of that, the plane ride home a long time to think.

He had been hurt, angry, disappointed, but humbled, too. Then he'd had nothing but a jumble of feelings. Now he could put words to what had taken place. He had seen in his father the fruit of rebellion. In fact, that verse Mom liked to quote had kept running through his mind the whole ride home. "The rebellious live in a sun-scorched land." He had seen his dad, tanned and empty by the smooth aqua pool. His own heart had been broken then. He'd been angry and hurt and empty. He had cried out to God there on that airplane. If you're real, show up in my life, Scott had challenged Him. He smiled now, thinking about it. That was a prayer that was bound to get an answer.

He couldn't exactly point to any one thing that had turned his life around after that. Things had just sort of lined up. Or maybe he was the one who'd been facing the opposite direction and had finally lined himself up with the rest of the world. Anyway, he'd gotten closer to Nathan. He'd felt less angry at Mom and Al and Mr. Caputo. He'd started going to youth group and really listening to what they were saying. Little by little things had gotten better.

He could see the house up ahead, huge and welcoming. The lights were on. He smiled. The lights were always on. He thought about the fact that he would be leaving in just a couple of months and felt the usual mix of anticipation and regret. The regret a little sharper now that Dad was here, though it was anyone's guess how long he would stay. Scott was under no illusions, and he still was amazed that he had made the call to his father that had brought him here. But he had felt the need to finish things, to settle them, or at least to try one more time. But he had never expected him to show up on their doorstep.

He opened the gate and stepped over Joey's Big Wheel. Actually it was his old Big Wheel. Mom never threw anything away. He stood still on the porch for a minute, remembering the Christmas he'd gotten it. It was a dim memory, but he still could call it up. He remembered Dad. And he remembered how Dad had seemed to him then. Huge, solid, smart. Someone who would always be there. He felt something tight in his chest. He thought about Daniel Monroe and wondered if the man he remembered was still inside somewhere. He supposed they would all find out soon enough. He swung open the door. He walked carefully past the study, now Al's bedroom, and as he came closer to the kitchen he could hear the warm sounds of pots clacking, water running, Joey's chatter, and familiar voices.

Forty-seven

I T WAS ODD TO HAVE LIFE carry on so steadily in spite of someone in the process of dying, but that's the way it seemed to Daniel. October passed, and most of November. After Mrs. Callahan's and Angie's first day back, the house had settled into a new normal. Always a new normal, Daniel thought, remembering when Scott was born.

"I keep thinking tomorrow we'll get back to normal," Lenore had said, weary from being up at night, looking at Daniel, the wailing baby on his shoulder. "Now I don't think we'll ever be normal again."

"We'll find a new normal," he'd told her. And they had. They'd never been the same again, but the new was better. The three of them instead of the two of them. And now here they were together again. He still felt amazed at that fact and a little uneasy, as if the situation might change suddenly and with little warning.

He kept getting up early and making breakfast for Lenore and Scott, and now he added Mrs. Callahan and Joey. Angie went off to her job at True Value Hardware with a cup of coffee and an adoring good-bye toward him. He could just imagine what she said to her co-workers as they stocked tire chains and antifreeze. "Daniel Monroe makes me coffee every morning." He cringed just thinking about it.

The triumvirate of Mrs. Callahan, Mr. Caputo, and Mr. Kaplan seemed to have worked out a faultless method of corralling Joey and spelling each other so that one or the other of them was always free to watch their soaps and game shows, or work their crossword puzzles, or refresh the birdseed in the feeders in the backyard.

And someone always sat with Al. It was never formally arranged, no sign-up sheet or anything like the chore lists for the kitchen, but Daniel noticed that whoever wasn't watching Joey usually brought their crossword or whatever book they were reading into the sickroom. There was a small television that Al seemed oblivious to, and the guests watched it. Al mostly slept, which Daniel realized was a blessing.

Daniel had overcome his initial unease with the two challenges he had taken on—AA and taking care of Al. With both, the solution seemed to have been simple. Just doing the right thing seemed to have been the key, rather than having a huge insight or change of heart. His decision to give up the alcohol seemed more solid now after six weeks of meetings. More of a real possibility than an empty wish. And he was glad to be caring for Al. He was good at it.

It was incredible when he thought about it. After all the things he'd done—the movies he'd made, the premieres, the guest appearances, the trips to film festivals and to Europe, the talk show circuit promoting movies—he had found the most fulfilling work of his life to be in caring for Al. Preparing hot cereal and tea for him, helping him eat, seeing to his medications, changing linens, bathing Al's sweaty body, and easing him into clean gowns.

"You're a nurse's aide," Lenore had said to him just last night. "You could walk out of here and get a job anywhere." And he had felt as proud as he ever had at landing a role. He had even slept by Al at night for a while, but after a few days Lenore said that wouldn't do and had insisted on arranging for a hospice nurse to come in the evening. The woman, tall and thin with a short cap of gray hair, was adept and quick and seemed genuinely kind. Daniel had come upstairs and spied a few times the first night. He'd peeked around the corner and seen Karen sitting quietly, looking at a magazine in the dim light of the one small lamp she kept burning. He stood there and watched for ten minutes or so, long enough to see her put down the magazine, peer over at Al, lean over to check his breathing, pull the blanket over his shoulders, and only then go back to her reading. He slept after that, satisfied he could trust her.

Now that the end of November had come around, he thought Thanksgiving would be ignored because of the circumstances of Al's dying. He was wrong.

"Oh no," Mr. Caputo answered him when he asked. "We'll have Thanksgiving. We need it even more this year, don't you think?" His face was kind. He'd mellowed toward Daniel in the last two months, though Daniel wasn't sure why. Maybe he noticed Daniel's tenderness toward Lenore.

She was different. He felt a little awed by her. She had changed in the years he'd been gone, gotten bigger and better. Now there was even more substance to her. Before she'd been made of good ingredients. Now they'd been boiled down, distilled into a thick, rich mixture, and just a drop of it was enough to warm him. And since he'd learned about the cancer and now the lump, she seemed inestimably precious to him, and he was sure it must show in the way he talked to her, looked at her. He found himself watching her sometimes, just storing her up against a future time of leanness. The thought pained him, and he didn't follow it to its ending. Just knew that there didn't seem to be enough time.

Her secret was eating away at him. He thought of it constantly now, and he wasn't sure how much longer he would keep it. Let her get angry and send him away. That was the worst that would happen if he told. And if he didn't tell? If she waited until Al's death and that proved to be too late? He couldn't think about that.

He was excused from Thanksgiving duties because of his work with Al, but everyone else was discussing their assignments now as they finished supper.

"Nathan and Kristin will be coming," Scott said. "You'll like Nathan, Dad."

Daniel had nodded, passed the peas, and said he was sure he would. Mr. Caputo brought the subject back to the meal.

"Kristin is bringing pumpkin pie and whipped cream," Mr. Caputo said and made a careful check on the back of the envelope he was using for a planner. "And Nathan said he would make his famous gravy."

"Nathan is from Georgia," Lenore explained to him, "where gravy reigns supreme."

"Ah," Daniel said.

Mrs. Callahan sniffed.

"I'll do the turkey and stuffing." Mr. Caputo made another check.

"I'll peel potatoes," said Angie, then blushed when Daniel smiled at her. Scott grinned.

"I'll make rolls," Mr. Kaplan volunteered, "if Lenore will do another dessert."

"Deal," she said.

"Will Edie be coming?" Mr. Caputo looked up from his list, pencil poised.

"Edie will be coming," Lenore confirmed. "She's bringing a vegetable."

"What about Dr. Ashland?" asked Angie, then looked at Daniel and turned an even deeper shade of crimson.

"Yes, he's coming," Lenore answered, smooth as glass, the only hint of emotion the slight weariness of her tone and a pinking of her cheeks.

Daniel thought of Lenore's beau, the tall, raw-boned, serious doctor Erik, and felt a surge of something he didn't care to analyze.

The day came and went in a buzz. The kitchen was full when Daniel got up at six o'clock, and the smell of cinnamon and nutmeg, allspice and sage filled the house all day. Angie and Scott vacuumed and cleaned the bathrooms, and Mrs. Callahan watched the Macy's Thanksgiving Day Parade and entertained Joey. Everyone else was jammed into the little kitchen except Daniel, who took care of his patient.

"Sorry it's so loud," Daniel said to Al. Scott was vacuuming the hall, and even through the French doors it was a dull roar.

"I don't mind." Al was sitting up, hunched over. "I like to hear their noises."

Daniel could imagine why. The idea of life going on around him was comforting to him, too.

Al was awake for much of the day on Thanksgiving. He looked frail and thin, and his skin was as yellow and tissue tight as parchment. He refused his afternoon pain meds and visited with Nathan Delacroix and a hugely pregnant Kristin.

"The baby's middle name will be Alan," Nathan said in the stiff way men showed that they loved one another. Daniel smiled and thought if Nathan could punch Al's shoulder he would feel better.

Al merely nodded soberly and said, "Thank you." Then smiled. "I hope he's worthy of the name."

There wasn't much meaningful conversation. Daniel realized that all the ideas he'd had about dying were myths. It was long and arduous and hard work, and if Al's experience was typical, it left little energy for conversation, light or otherwise.

Erik had been the first to arrive and seemed annoyed when Daniel answered the door. He hovered around Lenore. Daniel stayed clear.

Lenore's friend Edie came. She greeted Daniel with warmth and kindness, none of the sulking suspicion he had grown to expect. He liked her immediately.

He spoke to Nathan Delacroix himself, catching him alone when his wife was in the kitchen with the other women.

"Thank you for what you did for Scott when he was growing up," he said. Lenore had told him how this young man had mentored his son. He felt shame, but actually it had morphed into something else. Humility? The awareness that he hadn't been there, but others had, and an acceptance of that fact. It was mixed with gratitude that someone else had done what he had not.

Nathan examined his face. Nodded. Stuck out his hand. "You're welcome. He's a fine young man."

"You'll be a good father."

"Thank you," Nathan said. "That's my goal."

Karen came a little early that night and sat with Al so Daniel could join the others for supper.

"Would you like a plate?" Daniel asked her.

She looked up and smiled at him pleasantly, shook her head. "I had dinner with my family this afternoon. You go ahead. I'm here for the duration."

Daniel nodded, passed the word, and one by one the group stuck their heads in the door and said good-night and good-bye to Al before they sat down at the table. Al took a dose of his pain medication then. Daniel hoped he would sleep. Many of them came to the table fighting back tears.

"I know it'll probably be the last time I see him," Nathan said, and Kristin squeezed his arm. "He won't last till Christmas," he said, halfway between statement and question.

"Probably not," Lenore said, and Kristin, also a nurse, Daniel learned, shook her head, as well.

Erik said nothing, just stirred his coffee, but the expression on his face looked more angry than sorrowful.

Mr. Kaplan waited a few minutes, then as he often did, Daniel noticed, he knitted them together. His words were rich and textured, like a strong, beautiful thread that caught each person and knit them back into the weave of the whole. "It's so often like this," he said now. "So often thankfulness and grief are all tied up in the same package. Let's pray."

Carlene came over to visit the day after Thanksgiving, and Lenore wished she had told her to wait. She was exhausted, and the house was still a mess from the day before. They'd done most of the dishes, but the dining room table was piled with platters and china ready to be put away, the refrigerator was too full of leftovers, and everyone was tired and crabby. But even though it sounded like a contradiction, she knew she was feeling better. Deep down. This was just a surface ripple. Underneath she felt that sharing her dread with Daniel had taken its weight from her shoulders. But today she was grouchy and out of sorts.

"For every action there is an equal and opposite reaction," Mr. Kaplan said after Angie barked at him when he asked her to move Joey from the hall outside the study where he was pounding on the wall with a pot lid. "Yesterday was a high point. Today's the low." He quirked his head philosophically in Angie's direction and went back to his chopping. He was helping Lenore make turkey soup. Carlene came in, sat at the table, and watched, every now and then going out onto the back porch to smoke.

"Where is he?" Carlene asked.

Lenore resisted the urge to roll her eyes. Carlene was just as smitten with Daniel as Angie, but she disguised it a little better. In some ways there wasn't a dime's worth of difference between the two of them, she realized.

"He's in the study with Al," Lenore said.

Carlene picked at her nail and changed the subject. "Well," she said, with the air of an announcement, "Rick and I are going to Vegas next weekend. We're getting married."

Mr. Kaplan looked up and smiled. "Congratulations," he said.

Lenore dropped her handfuls of celery into the soup pot and wiped her palms on her apron. "Last time you were here you said he was a jerk, and you were going to break up with him."

Carlene shrugged and finally succeeded in chipping off the last of the pink polish from her thumbnail. "I was just mad that day. But now I want to marry him. Besides, he'll be good for Derek."

That was true enough, Lenore thought as she crossed the room and gave her friend a hug. Derek had turned around a few years ago when Rick had come into the picture, and even though Rick was gruff and no-nonsense toward Carlene, that approach seemed to have pulled Derek from the brink of trouble. He'd been on probation at school, but Rick had quickly let him know what he thought about that. Now Derek worked alongside Rick at his body shop. Lenore went back to her soup, smiling. Carlene went to work on the index finger. Mr. Kaplan finished peeling the potatoes and excused himself.

"What about you?" Carlene asked after a few minutes, not looking up.

"What about me?" Lenore asked, knowing exactly what she meant but not intending to answer any questions.

"Are you torn between two lovers?" Carlene asked with a sly grin.

Lenore gave Carlene a look and didn't answer her question directly, though she did feel her life was a seesaw ride lately. Her dates with Erik were strained, and she had no doubt that the time would come, and probably soon, when she must make a choice. His unspoken ultimatum hung in the air like imminent rain.

Her relationship with Daniel was that of a fellow worker, and the oddness of it struck her then. Years ago it had been Erik with whom she had worked side by side. But more than either of the men in this drama, the lump in her breast had been weighing on her mind. Even though she'd promised herself she wouldn't, she'd felt it every day of late. It was always there, a little pea-sized reminder that it could all be gone in a week, a month, an instant. Love triangles seemed hugely irrelevant.

"Let me be a little more specific, then." Carlene was nothing if not persistent. "How are you and Daniel getting along? Or you and Erik?"

"We're all getting along fine," Lenore answered, not answering.

Carlene heaved a great sigh, dramatic and annoyed. "Oh, for crying out loud."

Lenore put in the last of the vegetables, tossed in a handful of salt, and put the lid on the pot.

Forty-eight

I T SEEMED TO DANIEL that Al was dying quickly. His abdomen was distended, which Lenore said probably meant the cancer had spread to the abdominal cavity. He had terrible pain in his back and stomach, and the hospice nurse had mentioned surgery to cut the nerves, but Al had refused it. The jaundice and nausea remained. He had lost weight and his muscles had wasted. He no longer fought the pain medication but took it regularly and asked for more. The doctor and hospice team were happy to oblige and instructed Daniel and Lenore on how to keep Al pain free.

"There's no reason for him to suffer any more than necessary," Lenore said. And for that, at least, Daniel was grateful.

Al was in and out. Sometimes completely lucid and sometimes someplace else, talking to Trudy, the wife who'd left him, or Michelle and Darla, their daughters. Occasionally he was fighting criminals, and Daniel would play the part of some long-ago partner and reassure him that everything was under control.

A few days after Thanksgiving, during a lucid time, Al asked Daniel to phone his sister. Daniel told her the situation, then she and Al had a brief conversation.

"Would you like me to call your daughters or your ex-wife?" Daniel asked afterward.

"You can call if you want," Al said, "but don't tell me one way or the other." And he looked toward the wall.

Daniel could understand why after he made the calls.

"My father left us thirty years ago." Darla's voice still sounded freshly angry, as if the offense had occurred that morning. "Why should I come see him now?"

"He's dying," Daniel said, keeping himself calm and reminding himself it wasn't his place to judge but feeling a cold chill, nevertheless, when he imagined that if he hadn't followed the trail of old wounds, he might have been the subject of some future phone call and Scott and Lenore on the other end of a similar conversation. "I'm not telling you what to do," he told Darla. "I'm just telling you that if you want to see him again, you should come soon." Darla had tartly said she wouldn't be coming, and he had no better reception from Trudy, the ex-wife.

Michelle, the other daughter, said she would come, and she did, two days later, carrying a yellow chrysanthemum. She showed up on the front step, a thin, pale woman, her eyes wide and frightened.

Lenore met her at the door and took the flowers while Daniel helped her off with her coat.

"He's this way," Daniel said. "He's been very sick, and he's not eating much." He wanted to prepare her as best he could, though he could see from the shock on her face when she entered the room that he hadn't done a very good job of it.

"Dad," she'd said, and fortunately Al was having a lucid time. He accepted her hug and put a hand on her head. "Dad," she repeated, and Daniel saw Al begin to cry before he shut the French doors and left them alone. Then he went into the bathroom and dealt with his own tears.

Al's daughter stayed an hour or so and then left, her face red, nose swollen, refusing their offer of tea or coffee. "Thank you for taking care of my father," she told them as she left.

Daniel crept back in to check on Al, but he was already asleep, the potted plant on the bedside table the only evidence that the visit had happened. Who knows, Daniel thought, tomorrow Al would probably think he had dreamed it, and he thought again of how dangerous it was to wait to do anything. These last times were not times to make anything right, so focused was the mind on simply drawing the next breath or letting it go.

Al was getting ready to go.

The hospice nurse called them together the next day. The members of the household gathered solemnly together in the living room. Even little Joey sat quietly as he sucked on his fingers in Lenore's lap.

The nurse told them what to expect, the same thing Lenore had said to him yesterday. Daniel imagined her saying it to many people during her work and marveled again at the woman she had become.

"He'll be sleeping more and more now," the nurse said, "for the next few days or weeks, and he might not wake up at all at the end. He'll probably gradually quit eating and drinking, and then he'll die."

She said the word out loud, and even though he was staring it down every day, Daniel still was startled to hear it spoken so loudly. Only Lenore seemed unafraid. Her eyes fixed calmly on the hospice nurse, she gave a slight nod.

Daniel didn't usually remember his dreams, but that night he did. He dreamed about seedpods, little helicopters like the ones from the vine maple tree that used to be planted beside the front porch of his aunt and uncle's house when he was a boy. He dreamed he was back there again, watching them come loose from the tree—those little pods, each carrying a seed. His whole dream was watching them fly away and seeing where they landed. They'd whirl and twirl their way on the wind and finally settle on the hard rock of the garden or on the dandelion-choked lawn or perhaps, with great fortune, onto a soft patch of rich soil.

He lay there in bed, quiet inside himself just as the old house was quiet around him. This old creaking barn of a house reminded him of a pod and everyone living here the little seeds. They were all like travelers in that pod, whether comfortably seated by a window watching the scenery like Mr. Caputo or white-knuckled, belted in, and hanging on like himself. Nevertheless, they all glided their way toward landing.

Daniel reached over to his bedside table and took the scrap of paper on which he'd written the Bible verse Al wanted him to read at his funeral. He'd given Daniel and Lenore all the instructions during one of the long days the two of them had sat by his bedside.

Daniel read the verse out loud now. " 'Unless a kernel of wheat falls to the ground and dies, it remains only a single seed. But if it dies, it produces many seeds.' "

How much fruit could he claim? Daniel wondered. There was Scott. But the truth was, he had only fathered Scott. Someone else had done most of the work of raising him. The ones here in this house had raised his son. Lenore, Mr. Caputo, and Nathan Delacroix, Mr. Kaplan, Mrs. Callahan, and Al. But what he was doing now, well, that was fruit. That was something he could be proud of when his time came.

One day his turn would come to die, to relinquish his body, his pod. He wondered if there would be anything left behind or if all of him would vanish when they returned him to the ground. Would his body just return to the elements from which it was made? Or would there be something substantial and alive that would burst free when his pod broke?

The house quieted over the next few days, almost as if it were preparing for Al's death. Edie or Matt came often and talked or read to Al, usually from the Psalms, and Daniel, after asking if they minded, would sit and listen, too, taking it all in, the steady, lilting rhythm of the words, sometimes groaning out the soul's pain, sometimes soothing it.

Daniel waited for Al to die and dreaded it and wanted it to come, and he was not even ashamed. If Al had known that Lenore waited, he would have hastened himself on if he could. Daniel knew it wouldn't be long, and he wanted him to hurry and get his things together and leave so Lenore would go to the doctor. So Lenore would see to her breast. The secret he carried with her was hot and burned him every time he thought of it. It didn't seem to bother Lenore, though. She was better since she had told him, and that made him happy. "I'll take care of things," he had said, and she had seemed to take comfort in that.

One night after supper he came in to hear Lenore reading to Al, her voice soft and low. " 'Now we know that if the earthly tent we live in is destroyed, we have a building from God, an eternal house in heaven, not built by human hands.' "

Al's face was set and firm, his mouth a straight line of agreement. He shifted his head in a nod against the pillow. "That's the truth," he said, as if daring someone to argue with him.

" 'Meanwhile we groan, longing to be clothed with our heavenly dwelling.' "

Daniel listened, hovering in the shadowed hallway. Lenore read on. He caught phrases here and there. " ' . . . God who has made us for this very purpose. . . . Therefore we are always confident . . . at home in the body we are away from the Lord. We live by faith, not by sight. . . . For we must all appear before the judgment seat of Christ. . . .' "

At that, Daniel's gut gave a twist. He felt as if cold, dark water had risen to his knees and was continuing to climb. And it wasn't Al's fate he was dreading, he realized. It was his own. For sometime in the last three months—he tried to think when and failed—all of this had stopped being pablum, rhetoric, religious claptrap, and had moved into the realm of truth. A truth observed, perhaps, but truth nonetheless. He felt the ground shifting, cracking into huge fissures under his feet. He would not be able to stay in this place for long. He must find safer ground or be swallowed up.

He put off the decision until one week after Thanksgiving, when Daniel knew it was time. Al was ready to let go, just like those little whirly pods breaking free of the branch. Daniel sat with him because Karen had needed the night off. They had one last conversation, and Daniel should have known, should have been prepared.

It started out with his thanks. "I appreciate all you've done," Al said. "You've been a good friend to me, Daniel."

Daniel resisted the impulse to wave away the tribute, but instead he received the words, let them settle into his heart. They felt good and right. "You're welcome," he said. "It was a gift to me, as well."

"There's some letters there. Karen wrote them for me."

Daniel followed his eyes. There, leaning against the bedside lamp, tucked beside the pile of medical supplies, was a small stack of envelopes.

"See that they're delivered, won't you?"

"Sure I will," Daniel promised. His throat felt tight. He cleared it.

"I wish I'd done more with my life," Al said quietly, his voice tight with pain and regret.

"You've done good things," Daniel reminded him. "You took care of Lenore and Scott."

"That part turned out right," Al admitted.

"And you loved her so much, you offered your own life instead of hers. Doesn't the Bible say something about that?" He vaguely remembered a verse. Something Jesus had said. Al's next words jolted him out of his concentration.

"That was foolishness," he said. "She's got her appointment, and I've got mine. I could no more die for her than she could for me right now."

And Daniel closed his eyes and felt the absurd desire to laugh mixed with the strong urge to weep. Here they had been creeping around, hiding Lenore's condition from Al, and all along he'd known the truth. They just hadn't given him credit.

"That fellow was a huckster. What he said was hogwash."

Daniel felt the urge to get up right then, wake up Lenore, and take her to the hospital. He calmed himself. Tomorrow was the soonest anything could be done. He would wait. He could. Another day one way or the other, he said to himself, reciting a tired refrain.

"Now I have a question to ask you, Daniel," Al said, his voice clear though soft, and Daniel nodded, still distracted by his thoughts.

"If you were to die tonight," Al began, and for a moment Daniel was confused, wondering if he'd missed a crucial piece of the conversation. Wasn't it Al who was dying tonight? "If you were to die tonight," Al repeated, fixing those hot blue eyes on his, "do you know where you would spend eternity?"

Coming from anyone else at any other time, Daniel would have dismissed it, been irritated by it. But this very night Al might step from his body, make his own journey into that eternity. Daniel shook his head.

"You can know," Al said. His voice was an urgent whisper. "If you ask Jesus to forgive your sins, He will. Give your life to Him. He'll know what to do with it." He reached a hand toward Daniel, and Daniel took it. It was thin and trembling. "This is the most important decision you'll ever make. 'For what shall it profit a man,' " he quoted, " 'if he shall gain the whole world, and lose his own soul?' " He closed his eyes, as if the effort had exhausted him. He slept after that, too spent to even close the deal.

His words unsettled Daniel. He felt a sense of doom. Somehow being here this close to death, sitting across from it, made Al's question real and urgent. And there was something else at work, as well. He couldn't say what. Just that as he sat in the chair, his past played itself out for him, as if he were watching himself on film. He saw himself, hurt, lost, but also self-absorbed, even from childhood. Every selfish act, every coldhearted deed, and every indulgence stood out against his mind, an ugly scar.

Mr. Caputo came to the door in his robe and slippers to relieve him halfway through the night. Daniel went downstairs to his room. To bed. He dozed, but even in sleep he couldn't escape whatever was after him. Whoever.

Behold, I stand at the door, and knock: if any man hear my voice, and open the door, I will come in. . . .

Who had said that?

It had been a memory. Nothing more. A voice from his childhood had called it out. Perhaps his aunt or uncle with their urgent prayers on his behalf. Or perhaps it was his own voice, thin and childlike, standing in a serpentine line with the other sixth graders, shouting out their verses to win a prize.

Daniel felt as if he were dreaming, had taken leave of his senses. Yes, that was the closest to the truth. He felt as if he had taken leave of them—he was numb and empty. He hesitated, then challenged. "If you're real, show me," he whispered.

He waited for the warm wooing he expected, the feeling of serenity and peace. Something like the warm buzz of alcohol when the first few sips went down. But instead he felt as if a rough fist gripped him from the inside, and a dread, no longer nebulous, settled over him.

Badness was the only word he knew to describe it. He felt bad. His pulse rattled away. He could feel it in the artery by the side of his Adam's apple and in his chest as a weak, fluttery thing, like a bird imprisoned between cupped hands.

And then he was visited—not by the calming spirit he had desired, but by his sins. They came to him boldly and without invitation and with a clarity he had never appreciated before. His sins. He saw them as that for the first time, these little vignettes this troublesome Spirit seemed intent on showing him. And oddly enough, the thing that struck him most about them was their lack of originality. They were neither unique nor particularly creative. Nor all that grand, for all his delusions.

He had the flashing thought that he would be unable to explain any of this later. The only thing that could come close, he would say, was a nightmare. That peculiar sense of the ordinary becoming horrific. That is what happened to him now. As the Spirit, or whatever it was, began to grip him. He saw, like clips from his movies, the women, their perfect plastic bodies. They had been willing, but now, from this odd view, they seemed but the last in an endless parade of objects he used, like the alcohol and fame, to blunt the slicing edge of his emptiness.

He thought then of that sin he had committed against Scott and Lenore and felt the sheer weight of it fall on him. And then he forgot about himself, for now it was as if he were Lenore, and for just a moment—a mercy, for he didn't think he could have borne it longer—he felt through her heart, saw through her eyes. He saw himself walking away, looked down and saw Scott clinging to his legs. He felt the searing grief, the jagged wound of rejection, the sheer terror of the yawning choices that faced her. Where to go. What to do. He felt small and powerless, and then when he couldn't stand any more of that, he looked up through Scott's eyes. Saw the one he loved walking away. He began to weep, deep, racking sobs, and he wished desperately, with an impotent remorse, to be able to travel back, to offer a different answer to her question, one that would alter everything.

He opened his eyes and was himself again. Still here. Still now. But as the enormity of his life's sin began to grip him, he knew he would die. He must. He felt no terror. No longing to have things be otherwise. He saw that it must be. Justice required it. Looking over the vast and barren scape of his life, he saw the grasping greed. The numbing alcohol. But most of all, he saw that the evil that had him by the throat was the detached, bored conviction that the life was his. To be lived by him. To be enjoyed by him. Even to be ended by him. Everyone else a player on his stage. In his play. In his world. And for once he felt the pain it had caused the others. Saw his aunt's and uncle's kind, honest, bewildered faces. Everyone he had used and abandoned.

Somehow he moved from the bed to his knees and finally to his stomach on the basement floor. His face burned hot against it and he could feel tears on his cheek. He knew he must die. He would die, and he fully deserved it. He lay there for some time, accepting of his fate. Then the thought occurred to him that he should ask for help. Again, the thought assailed that he deserved no mercy, but he saw that even that was a pride of sorts—putting himself above the pale of everyone else. Making himself special and unique, even in his sin.

"Jesus. Have mercy," he whispered.

Just those three words. Then all was silent again except for his own ragged breath. Daniel could touch that silence. It gradually expanded and began to fill him. He didn't move, just repeated the words over and over as though his very soul depended on them.

And oddly enough he began to calm. And that calm was as potent as the horror of the torment had been. Clinging to that peace, he fell into his bed, still repeating the words.

Whatever death was, it was not the loss of the self, for he was aware. He was himself. Only gradually, with a sense of awe, did he realize that he was, in fact, alive. He had not died. Almighty God, for whatever reason, had spared him. Anything more than that would, forevermore, be unexpected gain. More than he deserved.

He lay in his bed with his eyes still closed, and he saw an image of himself, a mass of atoms held together only by the breath of God. Cell by cell, he gave them back to their maker. He began at his feet and worked his way up to his head, giving everything back. When he was finished, he was crying again. He wiped his face, blew his nose.

He dressed, then went downstairs and looked in on Al. He was sleeping but breathing shallowly, irregularly. There was a thin film, almost a dust, on his skin, as though his body had already begun to separate itself into its parts and give some up. It wouldn't be long now. Daniel placed a hand on his arm. Al's eyes opened, and after a moment they cleared in recognition.

"I did it," Daniel said. "I gave my life away."

Al's face creased into one last smile, and he gave his head a slight nod.

He slept after that and didn't wake again. He took one breath, two, quickly in succession, then would come a long, silent pause, then one breath, long pause, then another. Daniel sat down and waited.

Forty-nine

AL DIED ON MONDAY EVENING, and on Tuesday afternoon Lenore went to her doctor. Daniel was furious the biopsy couldn't be scheduled for a week and a half, but Lenore held up her hand to him. "Daniel," she said, taking a tone she'd never have used with him in the old days, "I've waited this long. Another week and a half won't matter one way or the other."

Except it might, he kept thinking.

"It will be all right, or it won't," she said to him. "It's already decided somewhere. Just let it go." She softened her words by resting her hand on his just for a moment before she removed it again to her lap.

The instructions Al had given for his funeral were carried out to the letter. His body was placed in the small, plain casket he had selected and buried in a nondescript plot he had bought and paid for himself. The service was held at the church. By his request, there were no flowers, except a simple arrangement of white roses and ivy that Lenore placed on the altar.

"He was used to my willfulness," she said with a smile. "He'll forgive me."

The choir sang Al's favorite hymn, and Daniel closed his eyes, letting the words penetrate deep. "Out of my bondage, sorrow, and night, Jesus, I come. Jesus, I come."

"Al Younger was a man with eternal vision," Pastor Matt said. "He saw beyond the boundaries of this life."

Daniel thought of Al's burning, fervent convictions, and he realized that they had given birth to that same kind of hope in him. That defiance of reality in which anything seemed possible if God willed it to be. He closed his eyes. He listened intently to Matt's words.

"Al lived according to the truth that there's another set of books being kept beyond those we tally here on earth. And one second after this life ends, those books are opened."

Matt went on talking, but Daniel was thinking about something else. He was thinking about what his book would say. Daniel Monroe, movie actor? He didn't think so. Television star? Doubted it. What would it say? Scott's father? No. That would go in someone else's book. A realization settled over him. He had nothing to his account in that kingdom. He was bankrupt there as well as here.

They stood. They sang, and Daniel smiled, a wry acknowledgment that even now the Voice was speaking, listening in on his thoughts. The words to the song were aimed with fine irony.

"In my hand no price I bring. Simply to thy cross I cling."

He felt humbled. Overwhelmed. He had been stripped of everything, yet something had been born in that moment of death. He closed his eyes and sang, the words coming from somewhere deep in his memory. He thought of the picture in Lenore's hallway. The woman clinging to the cross as the waves crashed around her, and now he understood what had sustained Lenore through the years of her loneliness. He opened his eyes and turned his head toward her. She was looking back at him, green eyes sharp and bright. With hope? Or some other emotion? He turned his face back to his hymnal and sang the song with the others.

It was three days later that he went back to the church. He took the bus, stepped off at James Street, and walked up the hill. Al's coat just fit him. It was warm. Plaid wool with sheepskin lining and collar. Lenore had given it to him after the funeral, and he liked wearing it. He turned up the collar now and lowered his head against the wind. He turned the corner, saw the red brick building, the sign. The rock. *Proclaiming Truth. Extending Hope.* He climbed the steps and opened the door, grateful it wasn't locked. He should have called first. On a Friday afternoon they might all be gone. But he felt he needed to talk to someone, to chart out his next movements on this unfamiliar journey.

The hallway was dim, no light in the church office. He went down another hallway. The doors were closed. No light shining from underneath. Not even under the one that said *Matt Reynolds* on the door. He stared at it, feeling bereft.

"Daniel!"

He turned. It was Edie, Lenore's friend. She was a short little thing, her grayish brown hair cut in a cheerful bob, her face happy, interested, as if coming down this hallway and finding him here was the nicest thing that had happened to her all day.

"Hello," he said. "I was just looking for Matt."

"Gone, as you can see," she answered. "Can I help you with something?"

"Yes," he said, taking only a second to decide. "I hope you can. Do you have a minute? Could I talk to you?"

She gave him an examining look, as if she were debating, and for a moment, Daniel worried that she would say no.

"Of course." The smile returned. "Come on back to my office."

He followed her through the dark sanctuary, only the altar lights glowing on the cross. Her office was at the far end of the building. It was cluttered and warm and smelled like fresh coffee. He identified the source: a small pot brewing on the end table.

"Would you like a cup?" she asked. "This was my Christmas present from Matt and Jenny last year."

"Sure," he said. "I'll have a cup."

"You take cream," she said.

He nodded, surprised she remembered. They had shared only two meals—Thanksgiving, which had been such mayhem he was surprised she could even remember he was there, and the funeral supper of three days ago. She handed him the cup. He sipped. Neither one of them spoke for a few minutes. He wondered where to start. She gave him no help, just watched, the pleasant expression still in place.

"I gave my life to Jesus," he blurted out.

Her eyes widened, and the smile became bigger. "Why, Daniel, that's wonderful. How? When?"

He told her as simply as he could. "It was Al," he said. "The last thing he did."

Edie stared at him for a moment, then threw back her head and laughed loudly, as if something was really funny. Daniel stared, mystified. She laughed, and then he realized she was crying, as well. He handed her the box of tissues from the end table and waited for an explanation.

"I'm sorry," Edie said, dabbing at her eyes. "But just after you came here, Al asked me to pray for you. He confided to me that he had claimed you. Another one of his bargains, I guess. He said he was going to lead you to the Lord *if it was the last thing he did*." She smiled and shook her head. "I guess God took him literally."

"Wow." Daniel thought about that. "Wow," he said again. It gave him a strange feeling to know he had been in Al's sights from the first day he had walked through the door of the house on Chestnut Street. It made him feel like a player in events bigger than himself. And all along he had thought he was their author.

"Humbling, isn't it?" Edie asked, suddenly serious.

"Yes." He nodded. "It's becoming a familiar sensation."

She nodded again, her face solemn.

"I don't know what to do next," he admitted. He set his coffee cup down and rested his hands on his knees, palms open. "I don't know whether to stay or to leave. I don't know what to do with myself now that Al's gone. My vision is better," he said, feeling once again the sharp pain that fact brought him. "I see the trail of wreckage I've left behind me. Scott. Lenore. My family. I didn't even take care of things when I left L.A.," he admitted. "I just walked out on my life."

She pursed her lips and leaned back in her chair. "Have you prayed about what you should do?"

He nodded.

"Any answers?"

He shook his head and felt the burden return. "I feel that I'm supposed to talk to Lenore and Scott. To say I'm sorry. But I don't know how."

"I think the Holy Spirit is prompting that," Edie agreed.

"What am I supposed to say? 'Sorry about the lifetime of pain I've caused. If I had a second shot I'd try to do better'? I don't have any right to ask her to forgive me. Or Scott."

Edie gave him a calculating look. "That sounds like pride to me."

He frowned. "I'm not sure I follow you."

She shrugged. "Pride says, 'I'll bring an offering to appease you.' Humility says, 'I come empty-handed and throw myself on your mercy.' It's dangerous," she said, reading his thoughts. "It's radical. They may be fresh out."

He nodded. "That's all right," he said, understanding now. "That's her right. That's her decision. That part isn't up to me."

"That's right," Edie agreed. "It's not. You're responsible to be obedient. What Lenore and Scott do after that is between them and God."

He nodded again. "All right," he said. It felt good to decide. To know his next task. Good and terrifying and heavy and dreadful. All at the same time.

"Have you thought about what you'll do now?" Edie asked.

"I guess that depends on Lenore and Scott."

She hesitated, then spoke. "The church is looking for a janitor to start after the first of the year," she said. "The pay isn't much, but it would be enough for you to get by on for a while at least. I could put in a word for you if you're interested."

At one time even the suggestion would have burned like a corrosive. A janitor. That was the kind of fate he'd run to California to escape. He thought of his uncle, mining coal. His cousins, changing tires, overhauling engines, approving car loans, being faithful to their wives and raising their children. Burying their father with dignity and a life full of memories. "I'm interested," he said. "But let me talk to Lenore and Scott first." About whether he would stay. About whether they would want him to.

Edie nodded. "Let's pray before you go."

He bowed his head and listened to her soft voice calling on the powers of heaven to mark his way, to guard it, to be a wall of fire between him and the powers of darkness and death that might seek to ensnare him again. At one time he might have written her off as crazy, unbalanced. Not any longer. He listened, his heart joining with hers in fervent petition. "Yes, Lord," he whispered as she blessed him. "Yes, Lord. Please."

Lenore was gone when he got home.

"I think she went out with Dr. Ashland," Angie said with careless cruelty.

Daniel turned down her invitation to watch TV, left her and Joey in the study, and went into the living room. Scott's car was out front. He was in his room, studying, most likely. Daniel took down one of the photograph albums from the bookshelf and opened it. The albums had drawn him for weeks, but he'd avoided looking inside them, not willing to freshen the pain. They had felt it, he realized now. Why shouldn't he? He opened the book.

There was Scott, looking just as he had the day Daniel had said good-bye to him, had held him, had felt the sharp shoulders, the small hands clutching at him, begging him not to go. He was smiling in this picture, his tilted eyes the only hint of Lenore. His hair was dark and cut in that familiar bowl shape, his face round and soft. He felt grief overtake him, deep and dark, a crevasse at his feet. And then, just as it was threatening to swallow him up, he remembered.

"What should I do?" he prayed aloud. The answer came immediately, a sure, swift voice in his mind. He took one more look at the picture, imprinting it on his heart, that child he had lost, and it was just as if that child had died. By Daniel's neglect. Had languished and hoped and finally died.

He set the book down, rose heavily to his feet, and climbed the stairs. He tapped gently on the door of Scott's room, then pressed open the door when Scott called out for him to come in. Scott was studying. He looked up and nodded. "Hey, Dad. What's up?"

Daniel stepped inside, shut the door behind him. He stared at his son, searching for some trace of the boy who had been. He was tall and lean. His face had matured into sharp planes, high cheekbones like Lenore's. The broad jaw was his own. The high, wide forehead. Scott needed a shave, and Daniel realized suddenly, in an insight that took the breath from him again, that there was no going back. The boy was gone, and if he had expected to come here and find a semblance, a footing to build upon, he was wrong.

Scott was looking at him sharply. He frowned. "What's wrong? Is Mom okay?"

Daniel nodded and sniffed, brushed at his eyes quickly so as not to draw attention. So as not to gain unfair advantage by sympathy.

"I wondered if I could talk to you for a minute."

"Sure." Scott's face was kind, and Daniel realized again what he had missed. He had missed it all. Every birthday and report card. The first date. The first restriction. Someone else had raised his son, and he thought again of this houseful of odd, beautiful characters, and he realized for the hundredth time what a debt he owed them.

"Sit down," Scott invited.

Daniel shook his head, wiped at his eyes again, and cleared his throat. *Help me,* he cried out silently, and the cry must have been heard. He cleared his throat again and found he knew what he must say.

"I left you." The words lay bald and raw between them. Scott's face went suddenly blank, and Daniel could read nothing on it. "I left you because I wanted other things more than you and your mother. It wasn't just foolish. It was wrong. It was evil."

Scott still stared. No words, no hint of expression.

"As I think about it now—" and even as he said the words, Daniel saw the child Scott running toward him on that last day, could feel the soft, shiny head under his hand, the thin arms and heaving chest as he held him close, only to pry him off and walk away—"it's unforgivable." He stopped then, turning his face away from his son in his grief, waiting for Scott's anger. His cutting words. His revenge.

There was silence for only a minute before Scott spoke. "Offenses aren't just against the universe, Dad. They're against a person. And if that person forgives you, then they aren't unforgivable."

The silence lengthened. Daniel looked up. His son's face was earnest, his eyes kind. "And I forgive you."

How could that be? Daniel wanted to ask. There must be some mistake. Instead he shook his head and squinted his eyes shut, and then he felt his son's hand on his arm, and he was embracing him, crushing him against his chest. "I'm so sorry," he cried out, voice hoarse. "So sorry. Oh, how I wish I could go back and do it over."

Scott didn't answer, just hugged him tightly. His own chest was heaving, too. They stayed like that for minutes that seemed like days. When they finally stood apart, Daniel reached across and touched his shoulder. It was firm and hard, a man's shoulder. "I love you," he told his son. "I'm so proud of you. You're a fine man."

Scott's eyes filled again. He brushed them with his palm, a gesture so like Daniel's it was like a gift, another gift, undeserved. Scott was his son. Nothing could change that.

"It's not too late, Dad," Scott said. He shook his head. "It's not too late."

Fifty

LENORE LOOKED TOWARD the house and wished there was some way out of this situation, that she had thought of some kinder way to say the words she'd just said. Instead, she just repeated herself. "I'm sorry, Erik." The situation between them had become completely tangled. Only recently had she realized she did not have the will or the desire to do the necessary work to straighten it out. This was a conversation she'd been destined to have for weeks. Perhaps even years.

He gave a bitter smile. "Well, I can hardly compete with Daniel Monroe." He gave a short laugh and started the car engine. "You'll forgive me if I don't walk you to the door."

"I'm sorry," Lenore repeated again, not bothering to tell him it wasn't just Daniel. It was the differences in their philosophies. The distance they were both content to keep between them. Their mutual lack of passion. "You've been a good . . ." She paused. "You've been good to me."

He nodded, taking it as his due, then leaned over and kissed her cheek. "Take care of yourself, Lenore," he said. She got out and walked to the door. He waited until she had opened the front door and stepped inside before slowly driving away. She knew she wouldn't be seeing him again.

She went upstairs to her room, shut the door, went to the chair, pulled the blanket over her, and looked out the window. It was bare, stark outside. The leafless branches of the maple brushed against the window. The heat came on, taking a little of the chill of the room away. Lenore saw the fat candle Scott had gotten her for her birthday. She lit it, waited just a second until the flame took hold and it was burning steadily. She took down her Bible from the shelf, her notebook. She set them both on the table beside her. Opening the pages seemed to require too much energy. She prayed instead, and immediately Daniel's face appeared on that interior screen of her mind. She sighed.

Daniel was different. Daniel had changed. He hadn't told her yet, but she knew all the same. How? she wondered. His face came to her mind again. It was different, she realized. Not in the features, of course, but in the expression. It was different from the Daniel of twenty years ago. Those eyes had had a gleam of ambition, the mouth a slight curling of arrogance. It was even different from the dejected face he'd worn a few months ago, the eyes flat and hopeless, the mouth a flat line that looked as if it would never again lift in surprise or joy or mirth. No, this face was different. The eyes were lit with something, but he showed no trace of ambition. His mouth was often curved into the shape of a smile, but different from the ones of years ago. This one was tender and gentle, not mocking or slightly amused at something only he could see. Something was coming into the room with Daniel when he came through the door. Someone. She felt something twist inside her, another hurdle rose up to cross. First she had opened the door to Daniel, then her life. Now, it seemed, she was being asked to open her heart.

"Lord, the last fifteen years were hard," she objected. They flashed back to her now, the loneliness, the torn heart, the aching nights and windswept, cold days.

I was there, wasn't I?

She nodded, remembering that fact, too. She stared at the flame of the candle, and countless other times came to her memory. She remembered the feeling of fear or loneliness or sorrow welling up in her, tightening her, threatening to twist her crooked, and then He would come, and something warm, like oil, would begin at her heart and spread out through her chest. "You were there," she whispered.

Were you damaged? He asked her.

She blinked in surprise. Yes, of course, waited on her lips. But had she been? Had she really? Was she, in fact, damaged now? She shook her head. No. She was whole in every way. Much more complete and healed than she had been with Daniel. His leaving had actually moved her into a better place than she'd been before. She stared at the bright flame of the candle, at the shimmering pool of melting wax underneath it. "No," she admitted.

Still, the years needed to be accounted for, didn't they? The deeds?

You dealt with that already, a part of her reminded herself. She recalled that tearful session with Edie, calling up the festering blisters of bitterness and draining them. If Daniel had never returned to her doorstep, she supposed she would have gone to her grave believing that their business was finished, transacted, done. She knew now that it wasn't. This churning in her gut was proof of that. She wondered if forgiveness was more like peeling an onion than breaking an egg. That had been top-layer forgiveness. This would be deep forgiveness, boring down to the bedrock, to the taproot, to the core of who she was and what Daniel had done.

She opened her Bible and looked at the first verse her eyes landed upon in Ezekiel. *Do I take any pleasure in the death of the wicked? declares the Sovereign Lord. Rather, am I not pleased when they turn from their ways and live?* She felt a burst of shame. She, who had no right to holy anger, was grudgingly holding back forgiveness.

She launched out before she could reconsider, pitching her small boat into the rough waters of mercy. "Father, give me a new heart toward Daniel. Give me a heart that completely and earnestly desires for him to be free, for his life to be transformed. Give me joy that you've begun that work. Thank you for your mercy to both of us."

It is new every morning.

The tears came then. They always did when He did this kind of work in her. She found herself fervent, hot in her haste to hand over to Him the burdened contents of her heart. "Mend Daniel's heart as well as mine, Lord."

I have done it and will continue.

In that instant she saw, as if someone had flipped on a light, that the reason Daniel had wounded her so deeply was because he was wounded himself. She saw it for the first time. It wasn't about her. Or Scott. It was and always had been about Daniel, about his aching need for something she couldn't give him. Something only one person could.

"Thank you, Father. Thank you, Lord." She felt awe and a twinge of fear. Who was she to have withheld mercy when He offered it to her? How had she dared? But His solidness was as real beneath the soles of her feet as the hard oak floor. His love as pure as the steady flame of the candle. She caught her breath and felt like Moses. She should take off her shoes, for she was standing on holy ground.

She came down to breakfast early the next morning, not able to break her habit just because she had a weekend off. She saw the back of his dark head, his broad shoulders under the sweatshirt. He turned when he saw her, gave her the smile. The new smile—gentle and kind, not simmering and seductive. She helped herself to a cup of coffee and sat down across from him. She had no makeup on. Her hair was wild around her shoulders. She wore a sweatshirt, too, over an old T-shirt of Scott's, her baggy jeans, and a pair of wool hiking socks. She smiled to herself, thinking how she would have rather died than appear like this before him at one time.

"Good morning," he said.

"Back at ya," she answered, stirring in the half-and-half. He was writing something. Rows of figures, she realized when she snooped further. She looked away. None of her business.

He set down his pencil but made no move to cover up the papers. "I've been wanting a chance to talk to you," he said. "Is now a good time?"

"Sure," she said, her stomach becoming tight, realizing the truth. Scott would be leaving after Christmas. Daniel had paid his penance with Al, and after he saw her through her biopsy ordeal, he would leave. He would pave the way now.

"What?" he asked, scanning her face, as if for clues. "What did I say?"

She shook her head and took another drink of coffee. "Go ahead," she said shortly. "What was it you wanted to talk about?"

He took a deep breath. Now it was he who looked tense and unsure. "I've given my life to Christ," he said, "though I'm not sure why He would want it."

Once again she was off balance, suspended between suppositions. She took another sip of coffee and warmed her hands on the cup.

"But that doesn't exactly have to do with what I have to say, except that I probably wouldn't be saying it if I hadn't . . . well, at least not in quite the same way."

She stared at him. Her heart softened. Her certainty that he was making a good-bye speech evaporated. The cues were wrong.

"Anyway," he repeated, clearing his throat, "I see a lot of things now." His eyes darkened and twisted with pain as if he were seeing them at that very moment. "I see how badly I hurt you and Scott. How wicked it was. How wrong and evil."

She looked at Daniel, but she was seeing past him, remembering those years but casting them against last night's transaction.

"I don't deserve your forgiveness," he said, "but I want you to know how sorry I am. That if there's anything, anything at all, I could do to help . . . I don't know." He finished. Trailed off, sorrow on his face and in his voice. His hair was gray at the temples and the little Y-shaped wrinkles deeper and wider than they had been years before.

"I forgive you." Her words came out sure and swift. She cast them out before she could think of some reason to hold them back.

He looked up, his face full of disbelief mixed with hope.

"I forgive you," she repeated, "and I'm very glad you gave your life to Jesus." She said it simply. Without tears. She looked into his eyes, deep with gratitude, swimming with release. She held out her hand, laid it flat on the table between them. He clasped it with his own.

Fifty-one

THE BIOPSY WAS SIMPLE. There wasn't much pain. It would take a week to get results. Right after Christmas. Lenore dressed quickly, anxious to leave the exam room, the hospital.

Daniel was waiting for her when she arrived at home, hovering around the front door. He looked at her anxiously when she came in, then, as if forcibly wrenching his attitude in a different direction, he smiled. "How do you feel?" he asked her.

"I feel fine."

"Results?"

"A week."

He clenched his jaw. Another determined smile. "Let's go Christmas shopping, then."

She considered for a moment. She had the day off and had nothing else to do. And she needed to do her shopping. She should have been finished by now, but life had intervened. She shrugged. "Okay," she agreed. "Why not?"

When they'd settled in the car, she had an inspiration. "Let's just do all our shopping on Queen Anne," she suggested. "If they don't have it here, we won't buy it."

"I like that idea," he said. He turned the car toward Queen Anne Avenue, and Lenore remembered that first day in Seattle when she had wandered around and found herself in the neighborhood of the old trees and buckled sidewalks. She smiled and felt amazed again at what God had given her. She was conscious of Daniel's presence beside her, though, a huge, ungainly thing she didn't know what to do with.

She looked out the window. The streets were crowded. The lights were glowing merrily in the dull, gray morning. Wreaths and garlands festooned the street lamps. It was beginning to feel like Christmas, Lenore realized, even though Al was gone and there was an emptiness where he had been. Even though there was the lump and the question that hung over their heads.

Daniel parked the car behind the bookstore. "It looks like snow," he said, and with a careful look at her eyes, he took her hand. She allowed it, feeling wild and dangerous, as if she were taking a great risk. But something else felt safe and comfortable as she felt his warm fingers close over hers. Their shoulders brushed companionably.

"We can pick out some things together if you'd like," she offered. She glanced sideways to gauge his reaction.

"I would like that," he said.

They chose a set of the works of Shakespeare that Scott had been wanting, leather bound with gold-leaf edging, from the bookshop on the hill and a guidebook to Europe. They picked out a couple of pop-up books for Joey, found a sweater for Angie in a nice shade of red that would look good with her dark hair. They split up for a while, then met at the coffee shop. They drank cocoa piled high with whipped cream and topped with chocolate shavings. It started to snow on the way home, and Lenore thought it was like a story. Like a movie. Like something that wasn't real. That couldn't last.

"Where are we going?" Daniel asked with a smile. Scott was being absolutely mysterious.

"You'll see," he said.

Scott drove toward the university district and then, consulting the scrap of paper in his hand, pulled up in front of a modest house decorated wildly with Christmas lights.

"I'm Scott Monroe," he said to the woman who came to the door.

"Come right in," the woman said, "Rudy's waiting."

Daniel wondered who Rudy was. His question was answered a few minutes later when the woman came out carrying a chocolate Lab puppy with a pair of reindeer antlers on his head. "Here you go," she said. "He's Rudolph, you know, like the reindeer." Scott exchanged the puppy for a check, then handed the dog to Daniel.

"Merry Christmas, Dad," he said. "You're always saying we need a dog. If you don't want it, though, she said she'd give us back the check."

The woman nodded, her eyes resigned.

Daniel held the squirming puppy and knew it was a test. His son's eyes examined his face. The dog licked his hand, chewed on his finger with razor teeth.

"He'll be a good dog for us," Daniel said quietly, meeting his son's eyes. "Of course we'll keep him. If it's okay with your mom."

Scott nodded. His face relaxed.

Joey loved the puppy and chased it around until it wet all over the living room floor. Lenore asked Daniel to clean it up since she was trying to get supper on the table, and after all, it was his dog.

"What were you thinking?" she asked Scott, and Daniel couldn't tell if she was perturbed about the dog or about something else.

"He'll be a good dog for us," Daniel repeated, reaching around her for the paper towels. "After I get him trained."

She looked at him, her eyes cautious and wary.

Daniel completed his preparations for Christmas, taking a calm pleasure in them. He went to the Christian bookstore. He selected cards. One for each of his cousins' families. For his aunt he chose a small plaque similar to ones he'd seen on her walls. He stopped at the mall on the way home. Bought gift wrap, a small gold cross necklace for Lenore, a poinsettia for the living room. He went to Eddie Bauer and chose a sturdy backpack for Scott. Too bad he couldn't get hold of his own leather luggage, but it was in California. In his padlocked house.

He needed to go back. The thought had been worrying and nagging at him lately. Reminding him that as much as he enjoyed this life here with them, he had another that he had left behind in shreds. He had spent a grim morning sorting through a stack of papers and bills. It was a snarled mess, that life he had run away from, and it had caught up with him. There were letters from the bank, the car financing company, the credit card companies. An apologetic note from Esperanza saying that when she had gone to clean out the house as he had requested, she had been met by a padlock on the door and a repossession notice on the window.

He had walked out on his life. He felt a rumbling guilt, a nagging tug that he should go back and face it.

There was one good piece of news. *Court TV* had bought the rights to *Court of Law*. When he'd seen the ads, he'd called his agent, and he had verified it. Daniel would be on television again. The thought brought him no joy, but at least it would bring him a check. Not a huge amount but definitely more than he'd seen in a while. As long as it ran, the residuals would make a nice addition to his budget.

He had listed his bills. The IRS. That one came off the top. No discussion there. The others could be discharged in bankruptcy, but after a discussion with Matt, he'd decided to try to pay them off, even if they were initially discharged. It might take years, but he would pay his debts. The totals were discouraging, though. He wondered again why he had never paid anything off, but he knew the answer. If he had, he wouldn't have had as much disposable income. Emphasis on the disposable.

He sighed now and knew the truth. He should go back to L.A., go to the bank, make arrangements, clean out the house. Sort through his belongings, dispose of them, then come back here with a clean slate. It gave him a feeling of regret—no, dismay—that once again, someone else would deal with the consequences of his actions. But he didn't want to go now. Not yet. He drove home through the frosted streets. He would go when the time was right, and he would know when that was.

He felt another sense of uneasiness. He was here in the house on special dispensation to care for Al. But now Al was gone. Soon things would have to be redefined. Would need to go from this comfortable, pillowy state to something with clearer boundaries. He thought of Lenore, of the lump, and felt a strained tension. Would it be better after they knew? Or would they look back on this formless time as the haven, the calm before the storm?

He drove up Queen Anne Avenue, following the now familiar route to the house. All the lights were on, spilling out onto the lawn. He brought in his packages, wrapped his presents. He wrote notes to his cousins and aunt. He wrapped the gifts to Lenore and Scott and put them under the tree. He built a fire and sat there listening to Lenore's voice as she talked to Mr. Caputo in the kitchen. Scott was in the other room talking to Angie. He sat quietly, listening and wishing things could stay like this, frozen in time.

Fifty-Two

"WHY DANIEL MONROE?" Sylvia smiled pleasantly at Kyle Armand and waited for his answer, her heart thumping. She had been thrilled to her socks when the director had called and asked to see her. Now she felt a flash of irony that it was one of her discarded clients who was being sought after and was in a position to rescue or tank her wobbling career. Things hadn't exactly been on the rise for her for the last few years.

Since Armand had called, she had been going through her stable of clients to see whom he might want, for she had known, of course, that was the agenda. He was going to cast one of hers in his next blockbuster, for that, too, was a foregone conclusion. He was the darling now. Whatever he touched made lots of money, and the last two had turned to bald, buff, Uncle Oscar gold. But this conversation wasn't going at all as she'd hoped. In fact, his request had stunned her. Her initial shock had faded now to dread. She had a premonition that her karma had caught up with her. And it was bad karma.

"How about Craig Neely?" she offered. "I represent him, you know, and he's a sure draw. And that's what it's about, isn't it?" Her laugh sounded annoyingly nervous. "Packing them in?"

The director shrugged. "I've got a good script and a part that's tailor-made for Daniel Monroe. I loved *Ninja Darkness,*" he admitted, as one might admit to a hidden vice. "It was my favorite movie when I was ten. I'd like to see him make a comeback." His face darkened and drew into a frown. "You still represent him, right?"

"Oh, sure," she lied. "I was just thinking about box office draw. It's been a while for Daniel, you know."

He shrugged, obviously not worried and for good reason. "If this project does well," he said modestly, "that could all change for him."

"You're taking a risk," she pointed out.

"I think he's solid." He stood, discussion over. He handed her a card. "Call me after you talk to him, and I'll overnight him the script."

She took the card and saw him out, then tore up her office looking for the last correspondence she'd had from Daniel. It hadn't been long. Just a week or so ago, oddly enough, and when she remembered that, she began to think maybe she was in luck, after all. What were the odds that she wouldn't hear from him for years, and then get a letter in the same month as this visit from Armand?

There. She found it stuffed into the back of her correspondence file. A short note. *Moved to Seattle.* Translation, beat it ahead of his creditors. *Thank you for everything you did for me.* It read like a making amends note. *I know I wasn't the easiest client.* Well, you could say that again, she thought, feeling slightly better as she remembered his drinking and his antics. Still. She remembered his face when she had told him she was dropping him. He had left with class, she remembered. No blaming or recriminations.

She picked up the phone to track down his number, then hung it up. A phone call would be too easy to ignore. She read the note one more time. This would take some finesse, she decided. She chewed on her lip and wondered what to do.

"Angie!" Mrs. Callahan said. "That's a fine way for a Christian girl to act."

Lenore was opening the jewelry box he had made her and was sniffling again. She took out the gold necklace and put it on. "Thank you, Daniel," she said.

He nodded, not wanting to speak. Afraid he would break the magic.

"You haven't opened your present yet," Lenore said to him.

"Yeah, Dad, open it." Scott came over and stirred the fire and sat down next to Daniel. And Daniel, who used to tear the wrappings off presents, took the tape off carefully and peeled the paper away, then slowly opened the box. It was a camera. Digital. A nice one.

"You used to like to take pictures." Lenore was blushing. "I thought you might enjoy it."

Daniel didn't answer. He couldn't, in fact, so he dug the batteries out of the packaging, figured out where they went, and took some shots instead. One of Lenore looking pleased, then more of her refilling everyone's cider cups, of Mr. Caputo lounging in the chair, and of Scott, looking just as Daniel had twenty years ago.

The rest of the presents were unwrapped with exclamations and thanks. The paper was fed to the fire. Then one by one they went to bed. All except him and Lenore. Rudy curled up amidst the wrapping paper, his bladder apparently finally empty. The fire was down to a soft glow.

Daniel leaned back on the couch. "Shall I get some more wood?"

"No, I like it like this." Lenore sat down beside him. It was one of those moments he wished he could wrap up and save and just unwrap again and again. *White Christmas* was finishing its strangely bittersweet strains and weaving into *Have Yourself a Merry Little Christmas*.

Daniel sat quietly, listening to the music, the quiet ticking of the clock, the rustling of the embers as they fell through the grate. He looked at Lenore and saw the face that he had never forgotten.

She moved closer and put her head on his shoulder, and he remembered how she used to be so thin it hurt to hug her.

"Lenore, I love you."

She turned her face toward him without moving and put her hand on his cheek. "I never stopped loving you."

"Will you marry me?"

She was silent for a full minute, but when he looked down at her, she was smiling.

"Do I have to give an answer right now?"

He smiled back, then shook his head. It was the right answer, he realized. The one she needed to give. He leaned back his head and closed his eyes.

Fifty-four

CHRISTMAS DAY WAS LOW KEY. They watched Joey open his presents, Lenore made breakfast on the woodstove, and then everyone scattered.

Daniel worked outside for an hour or so, chopping and stacking wood. It felt good, pulling his muscles up and down hard. He looked up a few times, and Lenore was at the sink watching him. He finished, piled the logs up neatly, then filled his arms and went in, kicking the door open.

Rudy looked up, the noise rousing him from his perpetual nap.

Lenore held the door open for him, stood back, and let him pass. He carried the armload of wood to the box beside the old stove.

"Would you like a cup of tea?" Lenore asked.

"Coffee's better," he answered.

She poured him a cup of coffee and took it to him.

"Thanks." He looked at her face. It was tight, filled with tension. He frowned, trying to figure out what was happening. It was as if there was a subtext to this conversation that he wasn't following, a script written in invisible ink.

"I've been thinking," she said, standing back from him and crossing her arms, "about the question you asked me last night."

He nodded and felt his gut clench.

"I think we need some time," she said. "It's been an emotional three months. For all of us. And I'd hate to have you make an impulsive decision because you want to right some old wrongs or because you think I'm pathetic."

"What are you talking about?"

She shrugged and he thought about the breast. The biopsy.

"Lenore, it's not about that."

"I'd hate for you to make a decision you'd regret later," she finished.

"That's not going to happen."

"How do you know?"

Her face looked strained, and he hoped that she wanted him to be right. "I just know."

The stubborn look came over her face. "Then it won't hurt to wait," she said. "If it's real, it will still be there in a month or so. Won't it?"

"Of course it will." He was sure. Her eyes told him she was not.

"Besides, you have loose ends to clear up. You said so yourself. You need to go back to L.A. and take care of your business."

"After the biopsy results we'll talk about it."

She shook her head and he knew that look on her face, that jut of her chin.

"No. You should go now."

He shook his head in frustration. "Why are you doing this?"

The chin rose a fraction higher. "It makes sense. You've said yourself you need to take care of your business."

"But why now? It's waited this long. It can wait another week or so."

"You should go now," she said.

He sighed in exasperation, but he could look at her face and tell it would do no good to argue. "Come with me, then," he said. The simple, elegant solution.

She shook her head again, that stubborn look he remembered still on her face. "No. You have to go by yourself." A pause. "And when you come back, I'll give you my answer," she said softly.

That's when he understood. And when he did, his doubt and hurt disappeared. It was a test. Relief flooded him. He understood now. He knew what he had to do. He nodded.

"I'll come back." His voice was quiet. "Breast or no breast."

She met his eyes, and he saw hope in them. It gave him a quiet joy, a strong and steady resolution to do what he'd promised.

He began to feel troubled and burdened, though, as he prepared for his journey. A sense of unease came over him, as if he were stepping away from his assigned place in the world, embarking on a dangerous voyage from which he might not return. *Of course you will,* he told himself scornfully, but he had the nagging uneasiness that it might not all be up to him. That there were forces at work outside of his control.

He packed the few things he would take with him, leaving the rest of them in the dresser and telling her so. She nodded, eyes full of doubt and hope. He packed his things as Scott packed his, and he felt a lurching worry for Lenore. Who would be here for her? A ridiculous question, he realized, since the house was full of people, yet it seemed that the two of them leaving left her raw and unprotected. Again.

Explanations were made to the others, and they reacted with varying degrees of concern. Mr. Caputo looked as if he might say I told you so, but it could have been Daniel's imagination. Mr. Kaplan wished him a safe journey and said they would be glad for his return. "I'll be praying for you," Mrs. Callahan assured him. Angie looked at him mournfully, as if she, too, feared there might be a buxom starlet waiting at the airport, champagne chilling in the limousine.

He had no such illusions. His plans were simple. He would fly down, take the shuttle to the motel. Tomorrow he would keep his appointment with the mortgage company officer. Make his payment, be allowed into the house. Clean it out, dispose of his things, and be home by the new year. He would, he promised himself, and ignored again that gnawing fear that something would go wrong. Or that she might not be here waiting for him when he returned.

The next day they drove to the airport in silence, and even here Daniel had been overruled. He would have liked to wait until a few days after Scott's departure, but Lenore had said it made more sense for both of them to leave on the same day. It was as if she was determined to feel the full brunt of her situation. No anesthesia. They saw Scott off, and once again Daniel realized what a gift he'd been given.

"Good-bye, Dad." Scott hugged him fiercely. "I'll see you this summer." He met Daniel's eyes and gave him a look of confidence. It cheered him, that look. Daniel saw no doubt in his eyes.

Scott took longer with his mother, hugging her, leaning over to hear her last cautions. Daniel heard her murmurs. "Call if you need anything. Where's your money? You have your passport?" She didn't move until Scott's back disappeared through the security checkpoint.

Daniel thought for a moment that she might relent then, let him come home and take another try at this tomorrow or next year, but she did not. She gave him a sisterly hug. He felt her hair on his cheek. He tightened his arms, but she stepped out of them.

"Your plane will leave soon," she said.

He nodded and realized again that there would be no assuring her with mere words. He must go and do this thing. Perform this labor and bring back the Hydra's head and lay it at her feet. "I'll be back," he promised again. "Take care of Rudy."

"I will," she promised. He gave her a brief kiss, then turned and left.

"So let me get this straight," Carlene said, dumping half a can of Hershey's chocolate syrup over Lenore's ice cream. "The man you've loved *all your life* proposed to you. You said you'd *think* about it, then packed him back off to the land of babes and booze. Sure. Makes sense to me." She gave Lenore a genuinely astounded look. "What were you *thinking*?" she demanded.

Lenore shook her head, too miserable to answer. It had seemed like a good idea at the time, but as she had watched Daniel's back disappearing down the airport hallway, she had been struck with this writhing regret.

Carlene stuck a spoon into the top of the mound of ice cream like Edmund Hilary planting the flag on Everest. She handed Lenore the bowl.

Lenore set it on the counter, took a tissue from her pocket, and blew her nose. "I was thinking I didn't want to be anybody's atonement bride."

Carlene looked puzzled. "What are you talking about?"

"Oh, you know what I mean. I think he's trying to make up for ducking out the first time."

"So? That doesn't mean he doesn't really love you and want to marry you now."

Lenore swallowed down her tears. Just the sight of the ice cream made her feel sick. "I don't know why I did it," she admitted. "Maybe just to get even for the way he'd hurt me. Maybe because I really wanted to see if he'd come back. But when he left today—" she took a ragged breath— "I knew . . . I wasn't . . . going to see him again." She sobbed harder. She heard Carlene's dish rattle onto the countertop and felt her friend's arms around her shoulders.

"Oh, honey. Come on. It'll be all right. Shh, now."

She cried herself out.

"It'll be all right," Carlene repeated, smoothing her hair.

Lenore raised her head, blew her nose again. The tissue was in shreds. Carlene took a clean dish towel from the drawer and wet it at the sink. She handed it to Lenore, and Lenore pressed it against her eyes.

"Do you really think so?" Lenore asked after a minute or so, her voice coming out muffled and congested.

Carlene didn't answer right away. Lenore lowered the towel and looked at her friend. Her face was kind but not exactly hopeful.

"Honestly?" Carlene asked.

Lenore considered. Did she want honesty or did she want comfort? "Honestly," she decided.

Carlene shrugged, picked up her bowl again, and spooned a large chunk of sundae into her mouth. She sighed as she delivered her answer. "It's a toss-up," she said.

Lenore's throat tightened. Possibilities, all desperate, suggested themselves to her. "Maybe I could go down there. Tell him I was wrong."

"No!" Carlene's eyes widened. She made a slashing motion with her hand. Her nails were reddish orange today, Lenore noticed, and she had little rhinestones glued onto the tips.

"Why not?"

"You don't have a clue about any of this, do you?" Carlene asked with an aggravated shake of her head.

"I guess not." Lenore felt miserable. Completely bereft, and it was her own fault.

Carlene took another bite of ice cream. Lenore's was melting, the vanilla Häagen-Dazs following the chocolate river down into the slough at the bottom of the bowl.

"If you go back on what you said, you might as well tattoo *desperate* across your forehead. Now that you've set up the hoop, there's nothing you can do but hope he jumps through it. You'll just have to wait it out."

"Isn't there anything I can do?" Lenore asked, miserable.

Carlene shook her head, the sympathetic look back. "Pray," she advised.

Carlene ate her ice cream. The clock ticked. Lenore could hear the television roaring from downstairs. Rick was watching wrestling.

"You know what got you into this mess?" Carlene asked.

Lenore shook her head.

"Thinking too hard." Carlene gave her a wise look. "I'm glad I'm not a deep thinker." She scraped her spoon around the bowl and licked off the last of the ice cream. "It makes life so much simpler, especially when it comes to men. They came, they went. I married one. He's not perfect, but neither am I. We're pretty happy." She set her bowl in the sink. Lenore's was soup.

Lenore stood up and handed Carlene the towel. "Thanks," she said.

Carlene nodded and walked her to the door.

"Oh no! He didn't!" Edie's sweet face creased into sorrow. She led Lenore to the couch and pushed aside the afghan and paperback book.

"I made him." Lenore's throat tightened. She thought she'd cried herself out, but it seemed she had a fresh supply of tears.

"Oh, honey. Why?"

She tried to explain. "I was afraid he didn't really mean it. I wanted to see if he did."

Edie nodded, a look of dismay on her face.

"Do you think it's hopeless?" Lenore asked.

"Well, what exactly did he say?"

"He said he would clean out the house, take care of his business, and be back within a week."

"That's the last thing he said?"

Lenore nodded.

"You didn't get in a fight after that or anything?"

Lenore shook her head.

Edie looked past her head, considering. "He'll be back," she said, nodding. "He'll see that this is his second chance. He won't let it slip by. He won't." Her face looked hopeful rather than certain, though. Lenore felt the misery rise again.

"Let's pray," Edie said. They did, and Lenore realized then that this was where the hope lay. Not in Daniel's resolve or her own attraction. If He wanted it to be, it would be. And nothing she had done or hadn't done would alter that.

The house was quiet when she arrived home. It was just after nine. Mrs. Callahan, Joey, and Mr. Kaplan were no doubt in bed, Angie out somewhere. Mr. Caputo was asleep in the recliner in front of the television in the study. An infomercial on fat-burning supplements provided background noise. He'd been waiting up for her, no doubt. She quietly pulled the door shut so as not to wake him. She didn't want to speak to anyone. Not even to him.

She stepped away, back into the hall, and picked up the telephone. The broken dial tone told her there were messages waiting. Her heart thumping, she dialed the number, punched in the code, and listened. Message one. Not the voice she'd expected or hoped for.

"Lenore, this is Dr. Simons. Your test results came back. Good news. Everything looks fine. I'll call tomorrow and talk more, but I thought you'd want to know."

A coded message, the real meaning of which was that her biopsy had come back negative for cancer, neutrally phrased for voicemail. Relief flooded her as the meaning of the words sank in. She felt wildly joyous, reprieved from threatened doom. She wanted to tell Daniel. She reached into her pocket, drew out the card with the number of the Econo Lodge. He would be there by now, and she felt an urgency to hear his voice. She halted, hand frozen as it began to dial the number.

If she told Daniel, there would be one less reason for him to come back.

She hesitated, teetered on the precipice of that decision, the card in one hand, the telephone in the other.

She would tell him. She would. She must. How could she not?

She heard footsteps on the porch. A knock. Her heart rose up. She set down the telephone and flung open the door.

It was not Daniel. It was a woman Lenore had never seen. She had silver blond hair. Short. As short as a man's, and she was petite and very stylish in a gray silk suit.

"I'm Sylvia Wiley," she said, handing Lenore a card. Lenore read it. *Sylvia Wiley. Creative Talent Agency, 1920 Wilshire Boulevard, Los Angeles, California.* She looked up to meet the woman's calm blue eyes.

"I hope you can help me," she said. "I'm looking for Daniel Monroe."

Fifty-five

$\mathcal{D}$ANIEL HAD FELT IT as soon as he'd stepped off the plane. As soon as he walked out of the airport. As he smelled the exhaust, saw the traffic writhing across the roadway, blinked at the low spatter of lights over the hills, the dirty haze, the buzz. He felt it. A surging of energy, a flat pressure of depression.

He had found the SuperShuttle, shuffled on board with the others, stowed his rucksack under the rack, helped a woman with two little kids who eyed him suspiciously. The other passengers were let off first: at the Hyatt, the Omni, a house in Santa Monica, and finally they stopped at the Econo Lodge. He paid his fourteen dollars and got off.

The lobby was swept but dirty, the smell of stale food, stale cigarettes, and Pine-Sol faintly hanging in the air. A limp strand of Christmas lights tacked across the desk blinked on and off intermittently. He checked in, his name or face getting a second glance but no comment from the clerk, a jowly, wobbling man. He took the key, found his room. It was about what he'd expected.

He went back down to the lobby, paid the twenty-five-dollar deposit to have the phone turned on. Then went back to the room and phoned Lenore but got no answer. He frowned. That was odd. Someone was nearly always home. He wondered if she had told them not to answer. If her certainty that he would not return was more a desire than a fear. He told himself he was paranoid. He took a walk, bought a burger, then came back.

He took out his Bible and began to read, but oddly, he began to think of Donelle. He could call Donelle and stay with him for the rest of the trip. That would save him the cost of a motel. In fact, he needed the money he had to pay Esperanza and her crew to come in and help him clean out the house. It was eminently reasonable. He followed it out, imagining the course of events, until he got to the part about actually being with Donelle. He remembered what Donelle did for recreation and knew those kinds of things wouldn't further his goals. He shook his head.

He felt as if he should shower, borrow that disinfectant and bathe himself in it. Felt as if he'd been scratched by something vile, and even now the toxins were coursing along his veins, multiplying in his blood, and he would soon feel their effects. He did already. He felt lethargic and stirred up, restless, peaceless, joyless.

"God, help me," Daniel whispered, feeling unworthy for even the thoughts he was having, the slight wistfulness for the life he had left. He picked up his Bible and found a familiar passage.

For we do not have a high priest who is unable to sympathize with our weaknesses, but we have one who has been tempted in every way, just as we are—yet was without sin. Let us then approach the throne of grace with confidence, so that we may receive mercy and find grace to help us in our time of need.

He prayed for a long while after that. Urgent, fervent prayers. Finally he lay down in bed, closed his eyes, and willed himself to sleep. But he did not. The very air around him felt stirred up, swirling with vortices, convergences, and pressures he sensed but could not see and did not understand. He could almost feel the dark angel at work.

Daniel saw the banker at nine o'clock the next morning, signed the papers, and was assured that the property management company would be there to meet him at the house by two in the afternoon to unlock the doors. He called Esperanza and she promised to meet him there, as well. He took a cab to the U-Haul dealer and rented a truck, the drop-off point being Seattle. He felt a little better with something to do.

He went back to the motel room and spent the rest of the morning calling his creditors and making payment arrangements. Most seemed surprised that he bothered. Some were suspicious. A few hostile. He wondered if he was here on a fool's errand. Perhaps he should have left it alone. There was nothing here he wanted, after all. He repeated it to himself, batting down the slight wistfulness that had come over him about his career. He wondered how things might have turned out if he had done things differently. If he hadn't been so ambitious, so hungry for what the world had to offer. He thought of Robert Pasquale and could picture himself in that kind of life. He could call him. He still had the card with his number in his wallet. He took a brief walk instead. Around the block. Past the hookers and peep joints, the bars and porn shops. The liquor stores.

He thought about phoning his sponsor or finding a meeting in L.A. but rejected the idea. He would be home soon.

He had the thought that if this were the movies he would hear the sound of gospel singing, and there would be a storefront church before him. He had read about that once in a book. It had been called the Church of the Second Chance. He liked that. He walked on and passed no churches, just a few kids sitting in the doorway of the youth hostel, smoking.

He went back to the motel, read the Bible, and prayed again, but his prayers felt heavy and dragged in the air, which even in December was thick and warm. He turned on the television and watched a game show. It reminded him of Mr. Caputo and Mrs. Callahan and how they liked to watch *Jeopardy* and keep track of the answers. He wanted to call Lenore, but she would be at work. He had that sense of disconnect, as if there was nothing fixed by which to measure his perceptions. He'd been cut adrift.

He remembered something then—his aunt reading the Psalms, crying out to God. " 'My eyes are ever on the Lord,' " he said loudly now into the empty room, " 'for only he will release my feet from the snare.' "

What snare? he ridiculed himself. He thought and spoke as if temptation were hot on his back, but there was no temptation. He wondered why he had the feeling of urgency and danger. There was no danger. Only a dirty, gritty town and another night alone. He counted the days. It was Tuesday. He would be out of here by Thursday. He comforted himself with the thought.

Lenore felt the two cards in the pocket of her scrubs. She touched them from time to time. Took them out and looked at the cell phone number Daniel's agent had scrawled on the back. She hadn't exactly lied to the woman. She'd just told her that Daniel had left and she didn't know when or if he would be returning. The truth as far as it went.

She looked at her patient now and thought about decisions and their impact. She wondered what he had done or might not have done that would have made a difference. What he might have altered in his schedule. If he had left fifteen minutes earlier, say, or five minutes later. If the traffic light ahead of the one at Fifth and Beacon had been green instead of red. If he had had a flat tire and had stopped to change it, would he have missed the random shot that had pierced his right frontal lobe?

She checked his vitals again on the monitor. The part of his brain that regulated heart and lungs had been virtually undamaged. The part that made this young man who he was had been shattered by the bullet. She administered the next dose of his medication by piggybacking it onto his IV. She checked his drains and bags. She checked the monitor again, made a note of his oxygen saturation numbers, his pulse and respirations.

She tried not to look at the picture above the bed. The families always did that, put up a picture of the patient, alive and vital. It only distracted her. She didn't want to think about this man barbecuing hamburgers or opening his Christmas presents or holding his son. She glanced up in spite of herself. His clear blue eyes stared back at her. She looked away toward his wife. She, his mother, or sister sat beside his bed around the clock. His father and brother shuffled in at regular intervals, stared with red, unblinking eyes, then left.

His wife talked to him. Told him about their son, tears choking off the words intermittently. Her only answer was the soft hiss and thump of the respirator, the artificial rise and fall of the man's chest.

He was gone, only his body didn't know it yet. But the thing that had made him *him* had departed. She was sure. The tests they had planned later today would no doubt confirm it. But his family loved him. They were unwilling to let go of this last bit of him, this warm flesh. It seemed real, but she knew the truth. He was gone.

Lenore went back to the chart. She made her notations.

When she was relieved for lunch, she went to the telephone in the nurses' lounge and made two calls. She dialed Sylvia Wiley's cell phone, then gave her information tersely and hung up without waiting to be thanked. Then she phoned Daniel at the Econo Lodge. No one was in his room. She was put through to voicemail.

"The biopsy came back negative," she said bluntly. "I don't have cancer." She paused, hesitated, came up blank. "Good-bye," she finally said.

She sat there for a moment staring at the wall, then ate a turkey sandwich, which she didn't taste. She went back to work. She disciplined her mind, and Daniel flickered across it only briefly. She set him into that part of life that was outside her control. She turned toward her patient to do what she could do.

They emptied the entire house in hours. Daniel gave most of the furniture and household goods to Esperanza and her family, exactly what they had been hoping, he realized, when he saw the armada of pickups parked outside the house. He sorted through his clothes, gave most away, packed the ones he wanted to keep. He stowed them in the U-Haul along with his golf clubs, an ancient pair of hiking boots, his books, and the leather luggage. Esperanza's husband, Hector, helped him carry out the chair. He placed it between two stacks of boxes, covered it lovingly with a down comforter.

He had thought this would make him feel better. He was wrong. He felt the full impact of what he had been as he walked through that house, as he stepped through the rooms that were just as he had left them, except for a layer of dust. The wide-screen television, the sound system, the pool table, the leather furniture. They were all he had to show for his life, and he didn't even want them. It was no wonder Lenore had sent him packing, and suddenly it became clear to him that that is what she had done. She was probably hoping he wouldn't return. Why had he ever thought otherwise? What did he have to offer her? Debts. Failure. And what kind of a future? He would be a janitor. He looked at Esperanza's family and realized they were more successful than he was. They had jobs. They had trucks. They had families and homes.

"Here, go ahead and take these," he said, handing an armload of pants and shirts to Enrique, Esperanza's brother. He nodded gratefully and carried them off, and Daniel started in on the suits. He tossed them one by one onto the bed, setting aside just a few things to keep for funerals and weddings.

He stopped when he came to the black Armani, the one he'd had his picture taken in when he'd made the magazine cover. He gave a humorless smile, but for some reason, when Enrique came back, he set it aside instead of handing it over with the others. Ridiculous, he knew. What occasion would he ever have to wear something like that again? Still, he kept it and the matching shoes and socks and shirt and tie. He hung them together carefully and put them in the cab of the truck, feeling a whisper of guilt, as if he were putting something precious at risk.

They finished. The relatives drove away with thanks and smiles. Esperanza promised to come back and clean tomorrow, then drop the key through the mail slot. He paid her the amount they'd agreed upon, slipped in an extra fifty, and said good-bye with a kiss on the cheek.

"Mr. Daniel, you're a good man," she said in her broken English. "God be good to you."

"He already has been," he said, but he felt that flat depression again, that heavy sense of failure and loss. He drove back to the motel.

———————

He listened to the message again. Then a third time. He felt a sense of confusion, of emotions mixing uneasily like oil and water. Relief flooded through him at Lenore's words. She didn't have cancer. He felt something cold he had been carrying in his chest thaw and melt away, but something else stirred uneasily.

She hadn't said anything else. Nothing personal to him. He told himself again, for the hundredth time, he was sure, that this was about earning her trust, but the words rang hollow in his mind. He was becoming less and less sure they were true, and for the first time he wondered if he should return. Perhaps she didn't want him to.

He sat down on the bed, rubbed his face, and was wondering what to do next when he heard a tap at the door.

He had the wild hope that it might be Lenore. He opened it quickly, then stood speechless. Of all the people he might have expected to see, this one would have been at the bottom of the list.

"Daniel!" She looked him up and down. "You look—great."

He squinted his eyes in disbelief. "Sylvia?"

Fifty-six

$\mathcal{S}$YLVIA HAD TAKEN the liberty of booking a room in the hotel where their meeting with the director would be, and Daniel was welcome to use it to freshen up. A luxury suite at the Four Seasons when her office was just blocks away. He snorted a humorless laugh. Sylvia must really need this deal. She had baited her hook with a few tantalizing but vague details, the promise of more later, and this suite. He had to admit he was curious. Besides, this place beat the Econo Lodge, and until he talked to Lenore, he had nowhere else to go.

He looked around at the gold walls, the warm coral antique furniture, the black and gold knickknacks so artfully arranged, the fresh flowers in every room. He suddenly remembered his chair in the truck and hoped it would be all right. He wandered to the balcony and looked down at the line of palms, at the tented pavilions by the pool, the dappled aqua water, and beyond to the city and the mountains beyond Los Angeles. He stood there for a moment, then went inside and tried to call again. She still wasn't home. No one knew when she would be. He became more and more certain she was there but avoiding him. He pictured her standing by the telephone, shaking her head as Mr. Kaplan offered her the phone. Daniel thanked him and hung up.

He took off the filthy jeans and T-shirt and called the laundry service to pick them up. He hung them on the doorknob in a plastic sack. He showered. Dried himself with the thick cotton towel, put on the terrycloth robe they provided. He shaved and saw himself emerge, and against this backdrop he seemed different. He saw himself the way he used to be and could imagine his face on a billboard again.

Someone knocked at the door. It was room service with the appetizer tray and seltzer water he had ordered. He sipped the seltzer, licked the lime from his fingers. He had to hand it to Sylvia. Everything had been provided for his comfort. He lay down on the goose-down pillow and pulled up the duvet against the chill of the air conditioning. His earlier feelings of doom were fading, and he realized he was enjoying himself. He thought about the minibar and decided to sleep instead. He dozed for a while, then got up, stretched, and brought the Armani suit out from the closet. It seemed lucky now that he had saved it.

Or was it? The situation reminded him of those silly cartoons he'd seen as a child. A voice whispering into each ear, only here in real life it was harder to tell which was the good angel and which was the bad. Perhaps God was pleased with him. Giving him his career back and restoring what he'd lost. Matt had preached a sermon on that very thing just last Sunday. Only days ago. It seemed like months, years, since he had seen any of them. They seemed far away and distant, like people he'd known long ago in another life. The second voice spoke, pointing out that he might be making a mistake. Another one. He shook his head, put on the suit pants and shirt, and went downstairs.

———

Daniel picked up the script from the restaurant table. He scanned the first few pages, read the treatment again, and felt a little thrum of excitement. It was a good part. The kind of mature character role that could launch his career again. And it was a three-picture series. There would be two more after this, and if the box office take was good, he'd have some money to pay off his debts.

"You don't have to live in L.A.," Robert Pasquale said. "It's like we talked about before."

Daniel hadn't known that Robert was to be part of the deal but realized this was another thing that made him think this offer was a gift for him. What were the odds that his one friend, the one person in this entire city he respected besides his maid, would be the costar?

"This picture could relaunch your career," Kyle said, underscoring what Daniel already knew. "I'll be honest with you. I've already told Robert and Sylvia that I'm having doubts about the whole project unless you sign on. I bought the script with you in mind. I can't imagine anyone else in the part."

The words settled deep down into Daniel. They eased something that had been tight and painful. Kyle Armand wanted him. Only him.

"It's character work," Pasquale pointed out. "You'll never get too old for it."

Part of Daniel realized there could be other motives at work here besides his welfare, that Pasquale had a lot riding on Daniel's decision.

Instead of making him cynical, it made him feel responsible. If he said no, it wouldn't be just his own career he was hurting. His own career. Funny. He hadn't thought about having a career in a long time. But it was back.

"And you know how it goes, Daniel," Sylvia said with a tinkly laugh. "When you've got the green light on this, the phone will start ringing with other things."

The excitement crackled around the table. The air buzzed with it, and Daniel felt it himself, a low current of possibility. He felt that sense of forward movement, that momentum that might at any moment become flight. He had insight now, he pointed out to himself. He had learned so many things. This time he could handle it.

"We'll leave you two to talk," Armand said, giving Pasquale the high sign. They all shook hands, and then he was left alone with Sylvia.

She appeared to be planning her next move. She took a sip of wine and smiled. "It's a great opportunity," she said.

Daniel nodded, troubled. No one needed to tell him that the last two films by the independents' darling had grossed over two hundred million each. "I know that," he said. He took a sip of his seltzer water.

Sylvia tipped her head, probably calculating how much pressure to bear. "Then why the hesitation?" she asked. "I thought you would jump at the chance to work again. And this is not some bit part. It's a major role in a picture that's going to be a hit. Everything Kyle touches turns to gold. You're lucky he's asked for you."

Well, that was blunt enough, wasn't it? But certainly true.

Daniel nodded. Could this be the answer to his prayers for direction? He didn't have to go back to the shallow life he'd lived before, after all. He could still be an actor and a Christian, couldn't he? Others did. Why couldn't he? He chewed on his lip and nodded.

"He's offering two million," Sylvia said. "I know it's not much, but this is just the beginning." Daniel almost laughed out loud. Two million. And he'd just given away all his clothes. He thought about all that money, about the entrée back into the life he thought he'd left behind. He leaned his head on his palm and massaged the bridge of his nose. He had a headache right behind his eyes.

"Think of the good you could do," Sylvia said, as if reading his mind. "You've got a kid in college, don't you?"

He nodded. It was all true. All good reasons for why he should say yes, but still, something held him back, and oddly enough, he saw in his mind Lenore and Scott and Mr. Caputo and Mr. Kaplan and Mrs. Callahan and goofy Angie and Joey and the dog with the reindeer antlers. And Al, his face fierce and righteous.

"It's not that simple," he said, raising his head, and he felt something heavy tugging at him.

Sylvia sighed and said softly, "I can understand if you're resentful."

Daniel focused on her face. "Why would I be resentful?" he asked, genuinely puzzled.

"Because I dropped you."

"I don't hold that against you," he said, remembering the past. It was more than remembering. He could feel it again. The heavy, thick head the morning after. The empty feeling as he sat down in the chair and opened the bottle. The churning and darkness and always wondering where Lenore and Scott were and what they were doing and why he had let them go. "I was drinking too much and on the way down. It was all wrong, anyway."

"Well, I'm sorry." She looked genuinely ashamed.

He shook his head. "We were both the same, Sylvia."

"What do you mean?"

"You used me. I used you."

She frowned. "What do you mean?"

"Just what I said. I used you, and if I could have used someone else more effectively, I would have dumped you first. I was insincere and manipulative." He felt some of the sluggishness lift.

"What's happened to you, Daniel?" she asked, seeming more annoyed than curious.

"I became a Christian," he said, "a follower of Jesus," and as soon as the words left his mouth, his head became clearer.

"Oh no." Sylvia closed her eyes, probably offering up a prayer to whatever deity she served.

Daniel smiled. Suddenly he felt like laughing.

"Look," Sylvia said, obviously lobbing a Hail Mary from the twenty-yard line. "Take some time. Think about it." Her voice had a pleading quality. "Be reasonable. If you turn down this opportunity, that's it for your career, and then what have you gained?"

"What have you gained?" she had asked. *"What have you gained?"* and the words Al had quoted to him came back in full force. *"What shall it profit a man,"* Al had asked, *"if he shall gain the whole world, and lose his own soul?"*

He set down his napkin and stood up, almost colliding with the waiter who was delivering their meals. "I don't need to think about it," he said. "I know what I need to do."

"Why the hurry?" she pleaded.

He put a hundred dollar bill on the table to cover their dinners, leaned over and gave Sylvia a kiss on the cheek. "I have to go," he said. "They're waiting for me at home."

He danced with impatience as the elevator climbed the floors, as he used the electronic card to open the door to his room. Things looked different to him now. Like a stage set, nothing seemed real. There were no worn spots on the carpet, no patina on the silver and brass. Everything seemed polished and fake and only for show.

His clean jeans and T-shirt were lying on the bed. He put them on, swept his toiletries off the bathroom shelf into his shaving kit, and shoved his clothes into the duffel bag. He left, feeling as if he couldn't do it quickly enough, and his last sight was the Armani suit hanging in the closet as he closed the hotel room door.

Fifty-seven

I T WAS RAINING, as usual, when Daniel arrived in Seattle. He had driven straight through, and his eyes burned, but he had a racing urgency, a need to know. He drove up the hill, following the same directions he had followed that first day. Had it just been months ago? He remembered how he had felt that day and didn't feel much different now. Here he came again with his heart in his hand.

He passed the grocery store where he had first seen Lenore, turned left onto Chestnut Street, and there it was, the huge old house with the sweeping yard, the graceful porch, the red trim. He held his breath, afraid even to look. He pulled up to the curb and cut the engine.

Every light was on, but something else made his heart thump. In every window was one of those electric candles. Glowing and warm. He flung himself out of the truck, opened the gate of the picket fence, and stepped through, not bothering to close it behind him. A dark shape moved in front of the window, and then the front door opened, light and welcome spilling out, and Lenore was running toward him, flinging herself at him, and Daniel wasn't sure which of them was laughing and which was crying. The rain pelted down on them. He held her and was amazed again at how right it felt, like two halves of something finally back together again.

"You came back," she said, and all the fears he had had about her feelings toward him evaporated with those three words.

"I told you I would." The labors had been completed. The long journey was over.

She smiled, and his heart felt too big for his chest.

"I have a question to ask you," she said. "And I want to ask it now, before I lose my nerve." The rain plastered her hair against her cheek. He brushed it away.

"I'm listening," he said.

"Daniel, will you marry me?"

He smiled. There was no tension or fear now as those words came to him. He welcomed them and answered quickly.

"Yes. I will. And the sooner the better, before you change your mind."

She smiled again. He smiled back, both of them foolish in their joy. He lowered his head. She raised hers, her forehead colliding with his chin. He leaned over. They brushed noses, backed up, and tried again. He laughed out loud. So did she. Finally their lips met. He kissed her. It was hesitant, fumbling and awkward, warm and real and sweet. Nothing at all like the movies.

Fifty-eight

$\mathcal{D}$ANIEL CARRIED THE ARMLOAD of wood to the box beside the old stove where Lenore worked on her soup. She was chopping vegetables on the butcher block and adding them to the turkey she had waiting in the stockpot, their wedding day apparently a soup-worthy occasion. They would be married tonight at the church. Simple, with their closest friends in attendance. They would come back here for a potluck wedding supper of soup and the rolls that were rising on the counter, as well as a store-bought cake Mr. Caputo was picking up now. Scott had been ecstatic at the news and said there was no way they should wait for his return. Not that they had offered.

"Would you like a cup of tea?" she asked.

"Coffee's better."

She smiled, poured him a cup, and took it to him. She leaned over him when she set it down. He could smell her shampoo. The light glinted off her hair, and he could see it clearly. It wasn't just plain brown, he realized, and he wondered how he could have missed that fact all these years. Maybe he'd never looked carefully enough or taken the time to really examine it. It wasn't just brown. As it spilled across her shoulder, he could see its true colors. It cascaded down onto her arm, each thick strand sliding off the next to make a rippling wave. There were dark, glossy chestnuts, rich, warm mahoganies, flashes of bright silver, glinting gold against ruddy maple, and copper the color of new pennies. It only looked plain from far away. Up close it was beautiful, a swirling, shimmering sea of color. She raised back up and went back to her soup.

"You know, I've been thinking," he said.

She looked at him, pretending to be suspicious.

"We should have another baby."

Her mouth dropped. He grinned, and after a moment she joined him in a smile but shook her head. "You're crazy."

"Tell me one good reason why not."

"I'm thirty-nine."

"Another one."

She shook her head, but the smile stayed in place.

"Think how much fun it would be," he pressed. "And Scott has always wanted a little brother or sister."

She gave him another look. "Are you serious?"

"Absolutely."

She turned back to the counter and began her chopping again. "Well," she said without looking up, "we'd have to have at least two."

He smiled in triumph. "Oh, at least."

She looked up at him and shook her head again. "You're crazy," she repeated, but her eyes were shining.

"I'll wear you down," he promised. "Like water on a rock."

"We'll see."

She went back to her soup, humming this time, and Daniel took it all in. The worn, yellow carpet, Rudy asleep in the corner, and Lenore— crazy, wonderful Lenore—cooking soup on a wood cookstove. On her wedding day. He gave her a slow smile and leaned his chair back against the wall.

She finished with the onions and celery and moved on to the carrots. She was saving the potatoes for last. She'd always hated to peel potatoes and had always saved them for last. As long as he had known her. Maybe he'd do it for her, but he'd watch her for a minute first.

The mound beside her was growing, and her upper body and arms moved in rhythmic pulses, the only sound the regular, quiet *chat, chat, chat* of the knife against the butcher block and the hiss of the cast-iron kettle on the stove.

The kitchen was warm, and Daniel sat in his chair and watched her, and he wondered how he could have missed it. She was beautiful. She was the most beautiful woman he had ever seen.